THE PALEONTOLOGIST

ALSO BY LUKE DUMAS

A History of Fear

THE
PALEON

TOLOGIST

A NOVEL

LUKE DUMAS

ATRIA PAPERBACK

New York · London · Toronto · Sydney · New Delhi

ATRIA
PAPERBACK

An Imprint of Simon & Schuster, Inc.
1230 Avenue of the Americas
New York, NY 10020

First Atria paperback edition October 2023

ATRIA PAPERBACK and colophon are trademarks of Simon & Schuster, Inc.

For information about special discounts for bulk purchases, please contact Simon & Schuster Special Sales at 1-866-506-1949 or business@simonandschuster.com.

The Simon & Schuster Speakers Bureau can bring authors to your live event. For more information or to book an event, contact the Simon & Schuster Speakers Bureau at 1-866-248-3049 or visit our website at www.simonspeakers.com.

Interior design by Dana Sloan
Illustrations by Armando Sánchez Rodríguez

Manufactured in the United States of America

1 3 5 7 9 10 8 6 4 2

Library of Congress Control Number: 2023026702

ISBN 978-1-6680-1826-2
ISBN 978-1-6680-1828-6 (ebook)

*For anyone who has sought refuge in the prehistoric past
in order to escape their present.*

I thought, too, of the glimpse I had in the light of Lord John's torch of that bloated, warty, blood-slavering muzzle. Even now I was on its hunting-ground. At any instant it might spring upon me from the shadows— this nameless and horrible monster.

—ARTHUR CONAN DOYLE, *The Lost World*

CHAPTER ONE

SOMETHING IS COMING

Sixty-six million years after the asteroid Chicxulub slammed into the Yucatán Peninsula and set in motion the extinction of three quarters of life on Earth, Dr. Simon Nealy turned his gaze toward the heavens, oblivious to the terror hurtling toward him at unfathomable speed. Unlike the last day of the Cretaceous Period, there was no gigantic orb in the sky, its luminous edges racing outward to swallow the horizon. There was nothing at all in the atmosphere to suggest Simon's world was about to change forever.

Steely clouds hung low over Hawthorne Hollow, the flat-bottomed basin sunk into the Appalachian woodland like the imprint of a giant's fist. Rather than a shock wave of superheated ash, an icy wind threaded through the trees encircling the clearing. It carried not the wails of prehistoric creatures set ablaze, but the fragrant rustling of autumn leaves. Their red-and-gold vibrancy might have resembled a world on fire if not for the mist that dulled it; thickest near the ground, it churned around the paleontologist's shins, merging and eddying like opposing flows of silver lava.

But it wasn't the dismal November weather that caused Simon to falter before his new institution of employment. That he owed to the great edifice itself. The craggy facade of red sandstone loomed above him like a desert butte.

Twenty-two years had passed since Simon had looked upon the museum—a blink of an eye in geologic terms—and yet it was all but unrecognizable. Once the crowning jewel of southeast Pennsylvania, the Hawthorne Museum of Natural History had been left to decay in the mire of its flagging prestige like a once mighty *Edmontosaurus* caught in a peat bog.

Set in sprawling lawns scabbed with necrotic patches of brown, the three-story building was a moldering embarrassment to Neo-Romanesque architecture. The gabled roof, pockmarked with missing shingles, buckled like paper that had met with a spill. The windows were opaque with grime, many riven with spidery cracks sealed with duct tape. Weeds twisted up the base like snakes attempting to scale the facade, and the dome that protruded above the north wing resembled a badly infected hernia, raw and blackened where the masonry had fallen away. Even the tarnished clock over the arched entrance was halted in a state of disrepair; the hands pointed motionlessly at fifty minutes past one.

Altogether it put Simon in mind of a great decomposing carcass buzzing with flies. He adjusted the mask protecting his face, sealing the top beneath his glasses to keep the lenses from fogging, as if to hold the stench at bay.

But his qualms with the Hawthorne ran deeper than its clear financial woes; those were to be expected. Even Chicago's illustrious Field Museum, where Simon had been employed for the past six years, was feeling the impact of the ongoing pandemic. His hands jittered at his sides, and his stomach roiled with unease. *What are you doing here?* he thought for the umpteenth time—but deep down, he knew the answer.

Marshaling his courage, he proceeded up the crumbling limestone steps. The oak doors towered above him like the trees they'd been made from, out of proportion with his scrawny five-foot-three frame. He paused before the motto inscribed above the entrance: IN OSSIBUS TERRAE VERITAS INVENIETUR. Simon had never studied Latin, but his familiarity with the conventions of scientific naming gave him a rough sense of its meaning.

In the bones of the Earth shall the truth be found.

He drew himself up and pulled the handle. The door didn't budge. He tried the other one, but it too resisted. Fearing his strength was to blame, he gripped both handles and leveraged all of his 105 pounds against them, but there was nothing for it: the doors were well and truly locked.

With a sigh, Simon rapped on the wood.

"Hello?" he called out.

When after several attempts there was still no answer, he stepped back and spied the windows above for some sign of movement.

"Hello?" he shouted up. "Is anyone there?" How could there not be? He'd been instructed to report to the museum at nine. That was just three minutes from now according to his phone, whose last dwindling bar of service he eyed with consternation.

Returning the device to his pocket, he turned to assess the paved roundabout in front of the museum. The loop circled a bronze statue on a plinth, the likeness of a man Simon didn't recognize. With nowhere to park, Simon had been forced to abandon his aging sedan in the dirt shoulder of the narrow, wooded driveway and hike the remaining quarter mile to the front of the building.

Now, a feeling of unease crawling about his heart, he fought the urge to retrace his steps and flee.

He resumed his place before the door and pounded.

"Hello," he shouted. "Is anyone there?"

The sound of a bolt sliding in the lock cut his question short. A door opened and Simon stumbled back from the head that appeared there.

"Damn, boy," it said, "can't you see we're closed!"

The head was attached to an older man with a dark pitted face, silver curls receding from his forehead in a wobbly semicircle. He stood nearly a foot taller than Simon, who bristled at being addressed as *boy.* For years he had been tormented for his childlike stature. Given the regularity with which he was still mistaken for a preteen in public, it remained a sensitive subject.

"Sorry to disturb you, er, Maurice," he said, noting the name on the embroidered patch on the man's coveralls. His eyes paused on the blue surgical mask hanging uselessly around Maurice's neck. "I'm Simon Nealy."

The man tugged up the mask to just under his nose. "Don't matter what you're called, the museum's closed and *been* closed for months. You blind, or don't you know how to read?" He pointed to a sheet of paper taped to the other door.

CLOSED UNTIL FURTHER NOTICE
BECAUSE OF COVID

"I can," Simon said sniffily. "But I work here. That is to say, today's my first day—"

"Nobody told me about that. Not that anybody tells me anything unless they got trash that needs taking out. Now please, I ain't got time to stand around here all day, not with a whole museum that needs cleaning and just me to do it—"

"Sorry," Simon said, aghast. "Did you say just you?"

"There was three of us at the start of the year. Laid off the other two as soon as we shut down. Thought I was the lucky one. Now *they* sitting at home collecting unemployment plus three hundred dollars a week, and here I am working like a dog to clean a museum that won't never be nothing but nasty. Now if you'll excuse me—"

"Wait," Simon said, fumbling his phone back out of his pocket. "Please, I can prove it. I have an email from my boss, Dr. Roach."

"Who the hell?"

"Harrison Roach?" Simon was beginning to worry he had reported to the wrong Hawthorne Museum altogether. "Vice president of research and collections?"

"You mean Harry. Shit, you're working for Harry, huh? Guess that makes you the new Bert, rest his soul."

"Is that the old paleontologist? Is he—" Simon said, and thought better of it.

"Bit younger than I expected, anyway." Maurice coughed out a wheezy chuckle, which Simon interpreted incorrectly as a dig at his age.

In fairness, it would not be the first. Just a few weeks earlier the local newspaper, the *Wrexham Gazette*, had run an article on Simon's hiring that, even while touting his pedigree, took potshots at his inexperience. "At thirty-one, Dr. Nealy will be the youngest director of paleontology and curator of Dinosauria in the museum's history, a title traditionally reserved for professionals two decades or more into their careers."

This was not untrue per se, but if the museum's leadership hadn't questioned Simon's age, then what business had anyone else?

The position had been posted for a full seven months before Simon decided to apply, and another two before, to his great surprise—for he'd already given up hope of hearing back and decided on the whole it was probably for the best—he received an email inviting him for the first in a series of virtual interviews. Over the course of weeks, Simon had met with HR, Harry, Harry again with a trusted consultant, the executive director on his own, and finally a sampling of the board of directors, before he'd at last been made an offer he couldn't refuse, despite the voice in his head telling him to run for the hills.

"Aright, aright," Maurice said, evidently having been giving Simon a hard time. He grinned, stood back, and waved the younger man in.

As he crossed the threshold, Simon experienced a moment of visceral contradiction: the lure of his new life pulling him in and the warning hand of memory thrusting him back.

He stood in a cavernous hall of marble floors and high vaulted ceilings, ending in a handsome split staircase leading up to a wraparound mezzanine. Even by the tepid light filtering in through the cathedral windows (for the sconces on the walls were either switched off or defective), it was clear that only the gleaming floors had received any of Maurice's attention in months. The unoccupied ticket desk by the entrance supported a nasty pelt of dust and a parasitic gift shop, stocked with dull coffee table books, faded postcards, and floppy, beady-eyed plushes. Even through his mask Simon perceived a dank smell on the air. A spray of black fungus that looked disconcertingly like mold darkened the corners of the room like a colony of spiders.

A shiver rattled through him, unrelated to the frigid temperature of the room. His misgivings about his new position seemed to deepen by the minute.

They released him, however—at least momentarily—as he looked up, gazing through the cloud of dust motes swirling like plankton in the light. His heart sprang into his throat at the sight of three prehistoric skeletons suspended from the ceiling, articulated in overlapping poses of flight. The largest, a *Quetzalcoatlus*, was a middling example of the species' magnitude, its wingspan stretching thirty feet, with an eight-foot-long neck ending in a small skull and a pointed beak like a supersized stork's. The *Pteranodon* was smaller, with a twenty-two-foot wingspan, a shorter neck, and a backward-facing cranial crest like a yard-long spike jutting from the back of its head. The *Ornithocheirus* was slighter still, yet fiercer than any modern bird or flying mammal: sixteen feet from wing tip to wing tip, with semicircular ridges on its snout and the underside of its lower jaw, giving its beak a paddle-like shape, with short pointed teeth protruding at the sides.

Simon had forgotten the pterosaurs; the events of his fateful visit at the age of ten had swallowed up all but his most powerful memories of this place. But in that moment it all came flooding back. The dark shape of them against the lighter gray of the ceiling. The dynamism of their poses. The jaw-dropping awe they inspired in him even now, despite the sickening dread that had been brewing inside of him all morning.

Maurice registered Simon's goofy smile with a smirk of his own. "Guess you really like dinosaurs, huh?"

The question reverberated through the hall in a ghostly echo. *Really like dinosaurs . . . like dinosaurs . . . dinosaurs . . .*

"Technically," Simon said, "these are pterosaurs. You might know them as pterodactyls, a clade of prehistoric flying reptile that lived contemporaneously—"

"Ah, shit." Maurice batted a hand. "See you around, dino boy." He turned and hobbled off.

"Wait—Maurice. You wouldn't happen to know the way to Harry's office?"

"Sure I do, but he ain't there. Nobody's there. They all working from home."

Working from home?

"What would you advise?" Simon called after him.

It startled him how suddenly the custodian halted. An eerie quiet reverberated through the hall, strumming through Simon like a strain of silent music.

Maurice turned his head an inch to the side. "My advice?"

Simon nodded.

"You hear something in the dark, don't go looking for it."

CHAPTER TWO

INSIDE THESE HALLOWED HALLS
FIND DEATH

S imon lingered in the entrance hall, attempting to contact his supervisor in defiance of his phone's remonstrations of No Service. The
best he could manage was to tap out an email requesting clarification
on what he was meant to be doing and where, and hope that if he moved
about the building, he might happen upon a wayward pocket of Wi-Fi
from which to send it.

And so Simon turned his gaze to the dark, deserted rooms off the
entrance hall. The museum's four main exhibition halls were spread
over two floors, three on the ground floor and a larger one above. Over
the nearest set of doors was displayed the name of the first in tarnished
lettering: SAMUEL AND JANE ABERNATHY HALL OF MAN.

A flicker of memory drew Simon toward it, then stalled him. But
this was his home institution now. If he could not face the past, then he
wouldn't last the week.

Passing through the open doors, he entered a wood-paneled shrine
to the origins of humanity, not greatly changed from when he had
visited the hall on a field trip with Mrs. Kramer's fourth-grade class.
Dusty curio cabinets displayed a wide assortment of artifacts, rudimentary tools, and fragments of Paleolithic pottery. A glass case lined with

red velvet contained a broken skull, vertebrae, and several rib bones laid out in the shape of a very small person—"*Homo neanderthalensis* child, c. 38,000 BC," read the label. Along the opposite side of the hall, rough-featured wax hominids mimed their evolving intelligence against a backdrop of artificial ferns and rock, from the chimpanzee-like *Australopithecus afarensis* dangling off a branch, to the slightly less hirsute *Homo habilis* bashing away at a rock to make a spearhead, and finally the rugged *Homo sapiens* at the end of the row, his uncircumcised genitalia hanging heavily beneath a bush of wiry hair.

It was while looking at this figure that nine-year-old Simon, who had always nurtured a special fascination for the male anatomy, had begun to question whether the attraction was more than academic. While his classmates whispered and laughed behind their hands, Simon stood rapt, palms sweating at his sides, a pleasant squeeze of yearning in his lower abdomen.

"Everyone, look!" erupted Jason Boudreaux through a scream of laughter, pointing at Simon's jeans. "Nealy's got a boner! He was staring at the caveman's dick and now he's got a boner!"

Though Mrs. Kramer removed Jason from the hall, she couldn't banish the cruel mockery his observation had elicited. Already Simon's classmates had rushed forth to bury him under a mountain of jeering questions—*Do you have a hard-on? Are you gay? Do you want to marry that caveman?*—while Simon stood before them like a trapped mouse, his eyes darting from one sneering face to another, forearms crossed over his fly.

The humiliation would follow him for years, replacing the hackneyed size-related taunts he'd endured since kindergarten. Now it was his fascination with prehistoric bones that was weaponized against him, often in the most unimaginative ways.

"Hey, *boner* boy," his classmates would say as they passed him in the cafeteria, a junior guide to paleontology lying open before him. "Are you reading about *boners, boner* boy?"

But that all ended the day Simon was withdrawn without warning from his morning math lesson and told to pack up all of his things. Told that his aunt had come to collect him, that he would not return to the school again.

Adjoining the Hall of Man was the Hall of Gems and Minerals, a small polygonal tower room bursting with purple-mouthed geodes of amethyst, swirling cross sections of agate, and icy clusters of quartz. Like the previous rooms, it exuded an air of spoiled grandeur, its antiquated fittings and interpretive materials proudly asserting the Hawthorne's place at a "cutting edge of science" that had long since dulled and rusted over with neglect.

At the back of the entrance hall were the doors to what Simon had known as the planetarium, since rechristened as the Eberhard and Luanne Rutherford Science Theatre. He found them locked, and moved on to the Hall of Insects and Animalia—poorly named in his opinion, for the kingdom Animalia was inclusive of insects and all other arthropods for that matter. The largest exhibition area on the ground floor, it spread across the entire west wing.

He hesitated at the threshold. The hall's taxidermied residents cut monstrous shapes in the dark, shapes that seemed to shift and gnarl the longer he watched them. But it was not the dead-eyed specimens that prevented him from entering. Like the Hall of Man, this room contained memories of the past, these of a darker, more venomous species. Even from where he stood, he could hear them hissing from the shadows.

You're sure? the officer was asking him. *You're positive this is the last place you saw her?*

She was right here, Simon sobbed, *I s-swear.*

Abruptly he retreated from the doors.

He fumbled the phone back out of his pocket. Still no signal.

There was only one hall left to try.

The Hall of Dinosaurs was the most expansive in the museum by far, encompassing most of the second floor. Simon felt like a fraud. Any paleontologist worth his salt would have marched straight upstairs, but he'd been dreading it, knowing what awaited him there. But he needn't have worried; where the staircase split, Simon turned left, and his concerns evaporated in an instant. As his sight line drew level with the floor of the west wing, it was not a memory of shame and panic that greeted him, but the sweeping enormity of a *Brontosaurus excelsus*.

Nearly seventy feet in length, from its long-necked head to the tip of its tapered tail, the sauropod snatched the breath from Simon's lungs. He staggered forward to admire it—a fine adult specimen, about 30 percent complete, with only minor visible defects: a fracture along the left front leg that had been repaired with epoxy, a few broken vertebral spines. Tooth and claw marks along the dorsal ribs suggested it had been attacked by a medium- to large-sized predator or, more likely, scavenged by one. The educational signage stated that its given name was Beth and that its genus name meant *thunder lizard*. "It is unlikely," it read, "that any creature that heard *Brontosaurus* walk would have questioned why."

Rather unexpectedly, Simon found himself fighting back tears. The sight of her—he couldn't help but think of the dinosaur as female, though it was virtually impossible to tell the sex by looking at its bones—had brought him straight back to their earliest encounters.

Growing up, he'd visited the Hawthorne just a handful of times; in his mother's home, there was little money for frivolities that couldn't be drunk, smoked, or snorted, and transportation was a constant battle. But the few times he had, these fossils had been the ultimate escape. Had transported him to another time and place, a lush and wild frontier of strange lands and fantastic creatures, a world apart from the bitter, gnashing one to which he'd been born.

The one from which, he had eventually learned the hard way, he could not escape for long.

Simon's spirits lifted as he gravitated toward the east side of the hall, his frown twitching upward at the sight of the *Triceratops horridus* specimen that had been his boyhood favorite and sparked his love affair with Late Cretaceous ceratopsians.

Built like a thirty-foot ox, the skeleton stood with its massive head lowered to the ground as if to munch on the invisible undergrowth, a rounded frill rising from the back of its skull like a shield of bone. Its natural weaponry protruded from its face: a pair of four-foot brow horns ending in lethal points, and a blunter horn protruding above the nose.

Simon noticed with curiosity that the left brow horn, unlike its brother, was a cast replica. Had the horn not survived the fossilization process, he wondered, or had it been damaged during the excavation? The question fascinated and delighted him. It was unearthing the mysteries contained within every fossil that he loved best about his work.

He continued through the hall at a luxuriant pace. Along the wall, a trio of skulls gazed out in a size-ordered row. There was the dome-headed *Pachycephalosaurus*, its broken ten-inch-thick cranium decorated with a crown of spikes; the duck-billed *Lambeosaurus*, its distinctive pompadour-shaped crest swooping upwards from its skull; and a stunning example of *Triceratops*'s smaller-horned cousin *Chasmosaurus*, with its distinctive V-shaped frill containing gaps in the bone that Simon once described in a paper as "resembling the wings of a butterfly."

Like the *Brontosaurus* and *Triceratops*, these skulls were genuine fossils, which surprised Simon, who knew that most of the prehistoric skeletons on display in museums around the world were cast replicas.

In general Simon approved of the display of replicas. It allowed the original fossils to be held back and stored safely for future research, and, for museums with limited budgets, imitation skeletons could be acquired for a fraction of the cost of real bones. However, as Simon had learned in his interview with four elderly male board members, it was a matter of pride among the museum's directors that the dinosaurs on display at the Hawthorne were, and always had been, "the genuine article," with resin bones like the *Triceratops*'s second horn used only to fill the gaps in the fossil record. In time, this was a policy Simon hoped to modernize.

And not just that. Like the rest of the museum, the Hall of Dinosaurs was badly in need of renovation. The displays were like something out of a period drama, the interpretive copy was woefully outdated, and the poses of the skeletons didn't reflect current scientific knowledge in the least—the *Triceratops* too low-slung, too much bend in the forward limbs; the *Brontosaurus*'s head too elevated and its tail too straight, with none of the bullwhip motion it would have made when the animal lived.

But that's not why you're here, remember? That's not why you've come back.

Brushing the thought aside, Simon pressed on to the southeast quadrant of the hall. It was underutilized, with just a few display cases that could easily have been moved toward the center of the hall to make room for a whole new exhibit. (Somehow he doubted there would be budget for that if the institution couldn't even afford to stay on top of basic repairs.) Among the various fossils contained in the cases was a bulb of bone like a small, stemmed boulder: the club of an *Ankylosaurus* attached to a segment of tail. The armored creature would have wielded the weapon with devastating effect, capable of crushing the bones of its enemies with a single blow. Simon studied the fossil through the glass, exhilarated.

Then something in the glass caught his eye and his smile dropped. Something behind him was moving. He could see its reflection in the case—a hovering mouthful of daggerlike teeth. He spun around and—

Nothing.

But of course. The Hall of Dinosaurs didn't have any carnivores on exhibit.

Eventually Simon's heartbeat returned to normal speed, though he struggled to shake the discomfort of having seen something he couldn't explain.

Once again he fished the phone from his pocket, and this time he was relieved to find he still had no signal. Reasoning that he would have an easier time reaching Harry at home, he descended the stairs and strode quickly toward the exit.

CHAPTER THREE

FIELD OF SCREAMS

Simon's apartment was located on the second floor of a 1930s redbrick walk-up. He'd chosen it for its quiet oak-lined street, proximity to the shops and restaurants of downtown Wrexham, and resplendent hardwood floors. Nearly a week after he'd moved in, they remained entombed under a thick stratum of cardboard boxes, open suitcases, and books.

Simon sat splay-legged, sifting through them, feeling only slightly guilty that he wasn't at work. It wasn't his fault that Harry had "lost track of the weeks" and scheduled a family vacation to the Poconos on Simon's first day. Chuckling at the oversight, Harry had instructed his direct report over the phone to "lay low" until he got back, a request Simon unquestioningly interpreted as an off-the-record order to take the week off.

He continued to unpack, pausing only when Philomena, his seven-year-old domestic longhair, leapt inside the open box before him, her tortoiseshell tail rising like a cobra between the cardboard flaps. "Are you helping me?" he said, Phil thrumming as he scratched behind her ear. "Are you helping?"

Almost as quickly as it had come, Simon's smile faded. His first thought had been to take a photo and send it to Kai with some amusing caption—an impulse he was still working to unlearn. Kai belonged to a bygone era now, a buried specimen he needed to stop unearthing.

Finding he had lost interest in his task, Simon rose to find something to eat. There wasn't much of substance in the kitchen cabinets. Store-brand toaster pastries, cheese puffs, cereal—the foods on which he had been forced to survive as a child and now were practically all his palate would accept. He sniffed a take-out container from the back of the fridge and his head rocked back in horrified retreat.

Reassuring Phil of his swift return, he grabbed his jacket off the hook and went out.

As he set off on foot toward downtown, Simon was struck by the unfamiliarity of his surroundings. Architecturally, the town of Wrexham had hardly changed in two decades, its Colonial brick-and-white charm protected by borough ordinances. But beyond the columns and gabled roofs, a palpable shift had occurred. The vehicles that lined the streets were newer, more luxurious, than he remembered; there was less variation in the faces that passed him on the sidewalk; and nearly all of the shops and diners from his childhood had gone extinct, overtaken by invasive species of upscale bars, art galleries, and vegan restaurants, their working-class grit painted over in the trendy colors of gentrification.

In a sense, Simon preferred it that way. The less that remained from the past, the less there was to remind him of what he had run from.

Until a few months prior, he had never expected to find himself back in his hometown, or any part of Pennsylvania. He had understood that, like the site of a nuclear tragedy, the place was uninhabitable for him now. A zone of exclusion, tainted by the horror he left behind.

Simon had barely known his Aunt Colleen the day he was forced to board a plane to O'Hare. She had only visited Wrexham once and spent much of the weeklong trip bickering with Simon's mother, Joelle. Until he was placed in her care at the age of ten, Colleen was best known to him as the sender of the gifts that arrived in the mail every Christmas and birthday, sometimes the only ones he would receive not from a charity but from an actual person.

Still, he had welcomed the chance to leave his mother's guardianship. He had grown used to her constant ups and downs, but her condition had worsened since it happened, making life with her more unbearable than he'd thought possible. Though he would never want to relive the events that finally drove her over the edge, leaving her was the best thing that ever happened to him.

Unlike her sister, who was small and rawboned with a wild tangle of dark hair, Colleen was voluminous in body and spirit, her florid cheeks and earnest smile framed by salon-dyed locks of vanilla blond. The difference in the sisters' appearance was mirrored in their homes. Colleen's three-bedroom Naperville house was newly built, unfussy but comfortably furnished, and more than double the square footage of the rundown townhouse where Simon had grown up. Knowing her nephew's passion for prehistoric creatures, Colleen had filled his bedroom with dinosaur books, puzzles, and an amateur dig kit. A poster of Rudolph F. Zallinger's famed mural *The Age of Reptiles* hung on the wall, and on his desk, Simon found a letter from his new guardian, a single handwritten page front and back, expressing in no uncertain terms just how loved and wanted he was.

Colleen worked as a nurse at the local hospital but had taken two weeks off, and delayed Simon's return to school, so they could get to know one another. At first he found it strange having her around so much, not passing the day in bed or entertaining strangers, but cooking meals, doing dishes, saying things like "I'm going to the store, want to come?" and, as she delivered a stack of folded laundry to his bedroom, "We'll need to get you some new clothes." She took him to Target, a place Joelle had only ever gone to steal. Simon's eyes bulged as Colleen filled the cart with shirts and jackets and shoes, thinking, *How's she going to fit all that in her purse?*

Before she returned to work and Simon to school, they took an overnight trip to Chicago. Staying in a fancy hotel off the Magnificent Mile, they explored Millennium Park, gorged on deep-dish pizza at Giordano's, and rode the Centennial Wheel at Navy Pier. Simon thought they would head back first thing in the morning, but Colleen had other plans.

"I have a surprise for you," she said as they drove south along State Street. She wouldn't say where they were going, but the gleam in her eye made him nervous. He feared she was taking him to the airport, shipping him back to Wrexham to be placed in the care of a stranger. On some level he'd been expecting it since the moment he landed, that eventually she would find out what he'd done and snatch back the letter, tearing it to pieces before his streaming eyes.

But a few minutes later they were parking, walking, standing on the sidewalk in a stiff autumn wind. The vast building before them had a stately character and was constructed of pale marble, reminding Simon of the White House, or maybe the Capitol Building. He did not immediately recognize the institution, whose name appeared frequently in his paleontology books, but the banners strung between the snowy columns depicted a skeleton he would recognize anywhere.

"We're going to see *SUE*?" Simon exclaimed.

He could not believe it. He had fantasized about this moment since he had first read about the existence of Specimen FMNH PR 2081, aka SUE, the largest and most complete *T. rex* skeleton ever discovered. But that was before the incident at the Hawthorne had changed everything.

As Colleen led him up the sprawling steps of the Field Museum, Simon struggled to articulate the feeling crawling around inside his chest, the one that told him not to enter the museum—*any* museum. That museums were places where bad things happened when he was in them. So Simon said nothing, kept his mouth shut like his mother had taught him. Before he knew it, they were inside, traversing a long room of ivory arches. Colleen gripped his shoulders, steering him through the crowds of Stanley Field Hall. He could feel her excitement vibrating through him, bullying his panic into submission.

Finally the enormous skeleton came into view, brown, lunging, pot-bellied, her smile revealing two rows of teeth like twelve-inch knives. "*Wow*," Colleen gasped behind him. "Look at that!"

Simon tried, but a clanging din of disparate voices was pressing in on him, drowning his thoughts. In his mind he was back at the Haw-thorne—

What does she look like?

Do you remember what she was wearing?

You're sure? You're positive this is the last place you saw her?

Colleen released him as she felt him shaking. "Simon, what's wrong?" She spun him, his face a sick twist of white. "Simon—"

"*She was here,*" he said. "*She was right here, I s-swear.*"

A pallor swept Colleen's wide-eyed face. She took his wrist and pulled him out of the hall, cursing herself under her breath. How could she have been so stupid? He realized they were headed toward the exit, moments from leaving what he had once considered the museum of his dreams. At this realization, a new panic started in Simon. If history had taught him to fear such places, it had also taught him they were the rarest of treats; once he left, he would never return—they wouldn't be able to afford it. A fierce resolution rose in his chest.

"No." He planted his feet and pulled his arm from her grip. She stopped, her head turning to face him.

"Simon—"

"I want to stay. I want to see SUE."

"It's okay, honey. It's okay to be scared."

"I'm not."

And he realized he meant it. Realized what he should've realized hours ago, days, the moment he stepped into the warm crush of her arms in the principal's office, into the enveloping relief and reassurance of her care.

"I know with you," he said, "nothing bad will happen."

A bell chimed as Simon entered Dellucci's Deli on Market Street. With its black-and-white-checkered floors and selection of fine meats behind glass, it was one of the few remaining holdovers from his youth. After glancing at the menu, he stepped up to the counter and recognized the owner. He was older now, grown plump on his own capicola. He took down Simon's order of half a pastrami sub, then seemed to have his own moment of recognition.

"Hey, aren't you that kid—?"

"No," Simon answered, a little too quickly. "Er, I don't think so."

"Yeah, you are. The one whose sister—"

"I'm new to the area."

The shop owner stared. Then he nodded, seeming to understand. He turned and called flatly down the counter, "Half pastrami, extra dressing."

The knot of tension in Simon's chest loosened.

Several minutes later he headed back to the apartment with his sandwich. The wind had picked up, blowing a chill up his back, and he tugged his coat closed over his T-shirt. The garment was old and ratty, faded to pastel after too many washes, the V-neck stretched to a doleful U. The kind of shirt Colleen would have described as "begging to be a dishrag."

Simon bit his cheek, punishing himself for thinking about her again. He'd left Chicago to get away from the memories. Perhaps he should have known better than to think it would ever be enough.

CHAPTER FOUR

THE HATEFUL BONE

Simon would later joke that his first weeks at the Hawthorne were not unlike the Cambrian Period: from the primordial solitude of his first day of work burst a plethora of new and interesting life-forms, each critically important in their way—if not particularly complex.

When it became clear that Harry had not the slightest plan to introduce him to his new coworkers or workspace, Simon set about onboarding himself, studying the staff directory and scheduling introductory meetings with various departments.

Via Zoom, he met first with CFO Dave Henry, a balding man who complained in monotone about the museum's perilous financial state. With no ticket revenue to speak of and memberships down 50 percent, the Hawthorne was hemorrhaging money and cannibalizing its endowment just to keep its head above water.

"But I hear you're gonna help us out with that," Dave said with a listless chuckle.

Simon nodded and smiled, having not the faintest idea what he meant.

Next he met virtually with the chief marketing officer, another David; the kind woman who ran the education department, who held her tablet up to her face, speaking into the webcam as if it were a microphone; and Priya Chandra, the overworked twenty-five-year-old exhibit coordinator. In addition to managing an ever-expanding list of duties including curation, collection management, and exhibit design for the three non-dinosaur halls, Priya was pursuing her MA in museum studies part-time. Simon knew better than to ask whether the Hawthorne was subsidizing her tuition, but was unprepared to learn they were actually docking her pay by two hours a week to account for her online, Tuesday morning Ethics and Professional Standards seminar.

"Ethics and professional standards," he joked. "Why would you need those to do your job?"

She shrugged, nodding. "That was pretty much HR's response."

Determined not to sour to the institution just yet, Simon finished out his meetings and reported to the museum the following day. He was on a mission to locate his office and tour the research facilities, a task he could no longer put off in good conscience.

Following Priya's instructions, he found what he had missed on his previous visit: an elevator skulking in the darkness of the entrance hall. A pair of buttons in an ornate brass escutcheon offered options for up and down. The down button flickered as he pressed it. He waited, assaulted by the cranking of machinery behind the wood-paneled doors, until a louder, high-pitched gnashing replaced it.

Slowly, as if the effort pained them, the doors pried themselves open to reveal a compartment barely large enough for two, a brass *H* emblazoned against the back wall. The only illumination came from the wavering glow of a tarnished candelabra, a strand of cobweb fluttering off its slender arms.

Simon hesitated before stepping inside. Even under his slight weight the compartment shuddered and moaned, doing little to reassure him. This was not helped by the inspection certificate, whose original expiration date had been struck through and a new date penned dubiously in the margins.

Below, a panel of buttons indicated four levels. Simon selected the letter *B*.

A few minutes later, in the gloom of the basement level, Simon found what he guessed to be his office, an old windowless room that appeared to have started life as a storage closet. The frosted-glass door read *Paleontology* in flaking gold leaf, and the walls were lined with stacked boxes. The room seemed somehow more lifeless and disused than the rest. The surfaces were that little bit filthier, the musty air redolent of prolonged neglect. It was like no one had stepped foot in the room for years—but that couldn't be true; this was where his predecessor had worked. The plaque on the desk still bore his name: DR. ALBERT J. MUEL-LER. Bert, Maurice had called him.

Had the old paleontologist died in here? wondered Simon grimly. The thought was an unwelcome one. And yet whatever had separated Mueller from his post, it must have done so quickly enough that he hadn't had time to clear out his stuff; peeking inside the boxes, Simon found them full of Mueller's personal files, letters, and junk.

All too eager to escape the image of his predecessor's corpse laid out on the desk, Simon departed the office and explored the rest of the clammy basement. A network of rusted pipes thunked and rattled overhead. A furry shadow skittered past his feet, causing Simon to recoil into a heavy metal door.

He turned, and spotting the sign above the door, realized he had found Collection Storage, the low-ceilinged warehouse of metal shelves and cabinets housing the museum's modest collection of scientific specimens.

Simon experienced a ripple of discomfort as he entered the room. Glass jars of preserved snakes and salamanders infused the atmosphere with the stench of formaldehyde. Fluorescent lights buzzed from the institutional ceiling tiles overhead.

As he waded down an aisle of metal drawers reaching up to the ceiling, a strange rattling stopped him. He paused, listening. The sound returned, drawing his gaze down to a waist-high drawer. It shook and shook, then went silent.

Simon reached down and opened it, the drawer's high-pitched squeal meeting his own as a large hairy rat leapt out of the opening, hit the floor by his feet, and scuttled away under the cabinetry.

Simon jumped back, his heart hammering. He was about to retreat from the room altogether, until his eyes latched on to the contents of the drawer. Inside, a dozen taxidermied rodents, increasing in size from dormouse to beaver, lay stiff as planks in their aluminum coffin. The second-smallest specimen appeared to be missing.

A drawer lower down, labeled *Cryptodira*, was dedicated to turtles and tortoises, and another, *Strigiformes*, to owls—great horned, short-eared, barn. Cotton filled their empty eyeholes, their beaks wrenched open in a choir of silent screams.

Simon thrust the drawer shut.

As he made to leave the room, he noticed a structure of open metal shelving like scaffolding at the end of the aisle. Curiosity overtook his unease, and he approached.

To anyone but a paleontologist, the contents of the shelves may have resembled little more than a scatter of broken rock, but Simon instantly perceived its value. Like all members of this profession, he had been trained to not only differentiate fossilized bone from regular rock, but look at a specimen like the ones before him and know immediately (1) what part of the body it came from, and (2) which of the seven major dinosaur groups it belonged to—ankylosaur, ceratopsian, ornithopod, pachycephalosaur, sauropod, stegosaur, or theropod—if not the animal's specific genus or species. It was the accepted practice within the field to write each bone's unique specimen number directly on it in ink. However, to each of the specimens before him, a sallow paper label had been tied with twine, bearing what he assumed was Albert Mueller's spidery cursive. To a large, hook-shaped fragment were attached the words:

> *Unidentified hadrosaur pelvis*
> *Hornerstown Formation, NJ*
> *Specimen HMNH 2292*
> *A. Mueller, collector*

The collection was exhilarating but not terribly diverse, comprising mostly small- to medium-sized fragments from Middle Jurassic to Late Cretaceous. Among the largest specimens were a beautiful *Camarasaurus* ulna and a curved four-foot tube of bone that had formed the cranial crest of a *Parasaurolophus*. All herbivores, he was surprised to find. Herbivorous dinosaur fossils were ten times more common than carnivore fossils, and yet it was a rare museum that didn't keep any meat eaters on hand, if only to placate their thrill-seeking visitors.

For more than an hour Simon explored the collection, inspecting each fossil for research potential, keeping a mental tally—for, as Priya had regretfully informed him, the Hawthorne maintained no central collection management system he could easily search, one of several major projects stacking up in his head.

But of all the fossils that grabbed Simon's attention, there was one in particular—or rather, a cast replica of one—that would not let him go. Even as he lay in bed that night, he would still be turning it over in his mind, trying to make it make sense.

He found it in a cabinet of metal drawers reserved specifically for the smallest specimens—claws, teeth, skin impressions. The reproduction was not much to look at. Bedded down in a lidless box lined with foam, it was slender, delicate, three inches long and less than a centimeter wide, gently tapered and broken off at one end. A fragment of tibia from a small theropod. This Simon knew from the presence of a fibular crest, a feature still found in birds today. He didn't bother hazarding a guess at the species; theropods weren't his area. Should he decide he really needed to know, he could consult Dr. Romina Godoy, one of his research partners at the University of Buenos Aires, who specialized in that group.

For now, he was more interested in the label tucked under one corner of the box. The rectangle of paper was just as old and yellow as the others, but strangely, it contained no description, no facts of the specimen's provenance.

Written in Dr. Mueller's old-fashioned scrawl was a string of words so out of place, and so malicious in its tone, it forced a snort of dark surprise from Simon's nostrils.

Banish it to hell—
There will she find her brother

As he departed Collection Storage, moving deeper into the labyrinth of dank hallways that made up the basement level, he puzzled over those hateful words.

What ill will could a paleontologist of all people have for the bone of an animal that had been dead more than sixty-six million years?

At last Simon paused before a pair of double doors. The metal lettering over the entrance read EDWARD DRINKER COPE MEMORIAL RESEARCH LABORATORY. He exhaled, his gut buzzing with anticipation. The doors let out a horrific, almost human scream as he pushed them open and entered the pitch-black room.

He groped at the wall, located a switch. The lights stuttered on.

Simon experienced a great sinking feeling, as of the ground softening up and swallowing.

He hadn't kidded himself that in a contest of research facilities the Hawthorne could ever compete with his previous museum. He'd been reminding himself for weeks that he had been spoiled by the Field's three fossil preparation labs and bioinformatics center, that however low he thought his expectations were, he ought to depress them still further for good measure. And yet no amount of preconditioning could have fully prepared him for this. In addition to being the smallest he had ever visited, the lab before him was the least in keeping with modern tastes and scientific standards. Illuminated by the stark light of a single hanging bulb, it resembled a tiny, overstuffed cave of antiquities. Filthy wooden worktables traced the perimeter of the room, wobbling under heaps of outdated tools, equipment, and half-empty bottles of adhesive and epoxy nearly as old as Simon. The wall-mounted shelves bowed under heavy burdens of books, children's dinosaur figures, and boxes. Glass-fronted cabinetry contained wide drawers of fossil fragments, and a filing cabinet spilled over with decades' worth of handwritten scientific records. Simon staggered back in horror from their undigitized knowledge.

Not looking where he was going, he tripped, fell back, and let out a cry, his backside breaking through the mesh top of a glass case on the floor. He felt something crack under his weight—like a bone laid on a soft, cottony base. He attempted to get up, but he was wedged in deep. He pushed and pushed and finally popped himself free—then stopped in horror as he regarded the case and the crushed skull that lay inside on several layers of cotton padding.

The sight sent a sensation of tiny legs skittering up his arms, of tiny bites in his flesh. Violently he brushed himself off, a scream straining against his voice box.

He knew all too well what this was. Like natural history museums around the world, the Field had maintained several terraria of dermestid beetles, tiny brown flesh eaters used to clean meat from the bones of recently deceased specimens. They were barbarically efficient. After the Field acquired a departed jaguar from the Brookfield Zoo, a few hundred dermestid beetles had reduced the cat to bones in under a week.

But to his surprise, his hands met with no such insects. There was nothing on him.

Confused, he stepped forward and peered over the skull. The beetles that lay in and around it were nothing more than desiccated husks, curled in on themselves with their little legs in the air. Dead, all of them.

He felt relief—followed by a gut punch of secondhand sadness.

Don't, he scolded himself, and thrust the memory of her back down deep.

After several false starts, Simon eventually found his way back to the elevator. He hadn't yet pressed the up button when the doors juddered opened, revealing a tall stooped figure.

"Goodness, Maurice—"

The custodian hobbled out, pushing a mop and a bucket of sloshing gray water.

"Hey there, dino boy. You're back."

"I am. I mean, why wouldn't I be?"

"Wouldn't be the first to go running," Maurice said, squeaking and rattling as he passed. "You got mail, you know."

"Mail?"

"In your box. Admin office. Third floor."

"Right. Well. Better grab it, then."

Simon was all too happy for the excuse to get away.

CHAPTER FIVE

TO WHOM IT MAY CONCERN

The elevator was as slow going up as going down, moving in a fragile, stuttering way, as though being pulled from above by old and sickly hands.

Finally it reached the third floor and the doors screeched open. The gloomy warren of hallways beyond had the wan look of an abandoned office building, an endless stretch of threadbare carpet lined with darkened offices, leading to more hallways and more offices. A few overhead lights were aglow, casting tepid islands of illumination against an ocean of shadow.

Simon stepped out. A succession of oil paintings in ornate frames adorned the walls at odd angles: portraits bearing witness to the museum's legacy of white male leadership, starting with its mustached founder, Augustus Hawthorne—recognizable as the man memorialized in bronze in front of the museum—and concluding with the present-day leader, Craig Rutherford.

Simon considered the latter portrait a failure. It didn't capture Rutherford at all—his goofy midwestern charm, or the doughy smile that made him look like an overgrown, sixty-three-year-old baby. His figure had been altered, made leaner, more powerful. The eyes that stared out of the canvas were wolfish and hard, his white veneers set wide in a carnivorous grin like a taxidermied specimen in the Hall of

Insects and Animalia. The only thing it got right were the wild eyebrows that crouched above his baby blues, grizzled and naturally mustachioed, bristling upward like devil horns.

Simon had met the executive director virtually as part of his weekslong interview process. Rutherford had held the role of executive director for the past four years, emboldened to take the helm after serving back-to-back terms on the board of directors while leading a large telephone sales corporation. The interview had taken place via Zoom, and Simon wasn't obliged to say very much. Rutherford spent most of the meeting talking about himself and relentlessly touting the museum's "prestige," the innovation of its exhibits and educational programs, even its preeminence as a center of research.

This final delusion offended Simon especially. The Hawthorne may once have been the premier research body of the mid-Atlantic, but four decades of diminishing research outputs, falling to zero around the mid-eighties, had reduced the institution to the lowest rung of academic relevance.

Until now.

According to Rutherford, the museum's strategic plan for the next three to five years—ratified by the board just weeks earlier—promised a renewed focus on groundbreaking research, particularly within the paleontology department. Thrilled by the idea of being able to devote himself fully to the part of the job he enjoyed most, Simon had impressed Rutherford with his accomplishments in that area: more than a dozen publications on the ecology and niche partitioning of Cretaceous ceratopsians, research partnerships with institutions in Argentina, Bulgaria, and the UK, and extensive fieldwork in the Lance Formation, where in his twenties he had discovered the skull of a new species of ancient bird later named *Simonopertyx neali* in his honor.

"Well, heck, that's exactly what we need!" Rutherford had said. "A Hawthorneasaurus. Why didn't I think of that before?"

Simon couldn't deny the appeal of the position: directing his own paleontology lab, managing his own fossil collection, helping to restore his hometown museum to its former glory.

But under the leadership of Craig Rutherford?

Simon resisted the temptation to judge the man too harshly based on the scant data of a first impression. Paleontologists had been making that mistake since 1824, when William Buckland described *Megalosaurus* as an amphibious iguana-like quadruped based on a few fragments of fossilized femur, only for later specimens to reveal a bipedal theropod with a mouthful of razor-sharp teeth.

And yet Simon wasn't greatly surprised when Rutherford admitted he was a descendant of Augustus Hawthorne himself and that, with few exceptions, the Hawthorne had "remained in the family" for more than a hundred years. The information seemed to answer for quite a lot, helping to dispel Simon's discomfort that he and the ED may have belonged to the same club of privileged white men appointed to positions of leadership for which they would not otherwise have been considered. True, Simon was young for a director, but if he had benefited from his race, sex, and ability to pass as straight, at least he couldn't claim the advantage of institutionalized nepotism.

He reassured himself that he was not very privileged at all. How could he be when he came from less than nothing? He had earned his place. Had beat the odds. If his luckiest break was being ripped away from his lunatic mother and shipped off to live with a stranger eight hundred miles away, he could sleep easily knowing he was as marginalized as the best of them.

Halfway down the hall Simon found the tiny mailroom Maurice had mentioned, containing two dozen wooden mailboxes mounted on the wall, some of them so full they could scarcely hold another letter. Simon's—or at least the one he assumed to be his, as it still bore Mueller's name—contained a single envelope addressed to him. No return address. The postmark was local to Wrexham.

He tore it open and removed the contents, a single sheet of Hawthorne Museum letterhead. By the supple texture of the paper and the discoloration around the edges, he guessed it was at least a decade old. Even more curious was the message itself: a few words formed from cut-up bits of newspaper taped on to the page.

i WANT yoUR BONeS

Simon stopped. A frosty sensation crackled under his skin. Suddenly he no longer felt safe.

Almost as quickly, the feeling broke and he exhaled an embarrassed laugh. Of course. It was a reference to his profession. Perhaps a joke from one of his colleagues, or someone who'd read about his appointment in the local paper.

That was when he heard the voice.

It drifted to him from its source along a sidelong corridor. He moved toward it and looked around the corner. A spill of illumination across the carpet at the end of the hall told him the lights were on in one of the far offices. Maybe a colleague, one he had not yet met.

As he approached, the voice became clearer. It seemed to belong to a woman. Friendly but forceful with a touch of smarm, it would not have been out of place in the showroom of a Delaware County used-car dealership.

"Well, I hear ya, Frank, but a big-shot editor at the *Philadelphia Inquirer* like yourself—I'm just thinkin' about your tax liability. You can write a check to the Hawthorne or you can write a check to Uncle Sam, but at least we'll put your name on the damn wall."

Simon paused outside the open door and peeked in. A woman sat back in her chair with a wired phone to her ear, her feet on the desk, which was covered with stacks of paper, newspaper clippings, Post-its, and a boxy beige computer monitor that reminded Simon of his elementary school computer lab. Well into her fifties, the woman sported a stiff cloud of dark orange hair and dangly earrings that stretched her earlobes like taffy. Noticing Simon in the doorway, she rolled her eyes, swung her feet off the desk, and knocked a stray newspaper to the floor as she riffled through the mess. A moment later she found the cloth zebra-print mask she was searching for and put it on without a second glance at Simon.

"That's what I like to hear, Frank. We'll keep an eye out for the check. My love to Doris and the girls."

She slammed the phone down. Her eyes narrowed on Simon.

"S-sorry to interrupt. I was just looking for something and I thought I'd stop in. I'm Simon Nealy, the new paleontology director."

She scoffed. "Of course you are."

There was no hint of a smile in her eyes as she pushed out of her chair and extended a hand for him to shake. "Fran Boney, director of development."

He looked down at Fran's hand, his mind flashing with CDC warnings. The hesitation didn't go unnoticed. He grimaced under the fundraiser's punishing grip. Simon knew from the Field Museum that *development* was old-fashioned nonprofit jargon for philanthropy, his least favorite part of the nonprofit sector. It had never sat right with him, soliciting enormous gifts for exhibits and executive salaries when local families were starving right under their noses.

"Boney, huh?" he said. "Did they make you change your name when you started working here?"

"Joke gets funnier every time I hear it." She released his hand and walked back to her desk. "What are ya, fourteen?"

Simon reddened. "Thirty-one."

She sat, rapping the mouse to wake her sleeping monitor. "If you're lookin' for your office, don't ask me. Wouldn't be surprised if they gave ya mine. I've only been here twenty years."

"No need. I've already—"

The phone rang. Fran answered it, turning her back to Simon without so much as a look. "Gina, thanks for gettin' back to me. Been tryin' to reach your client for days. Don't tell me our favorite little cash cow's got the corona."

Realizing no further acknowledgment was forthcoming, Simon retreated from the door.

He remembered the letter in his hand and looked back toward Fran's office. His gaze paused on the front page of the *Wrexham Gazette* lying on the carpet, cut-up and full of holes like a slice of Swiss cheese.

CHAPTER SIX

THANKSGRIEVING

Rain fell outside the apartment, drumming the leaves of the trees, the hoods of the cars, and the pavement in a sad percussive rhythm. It had just gone dark and Simon lay on the couch beneath the window, one hand on his distended belly and the other scrolling through photos of other people's more satisfying holidays.

It had been showering on and off all day, adding soggy weather to a Thanksgiving that hardly needed dampening. With no friends in the area, Simon had spent the day alone but for Philomena, catching up on paleontology podcasts as he dished up his best attempt at dinner for one: microwave turkey, a scoop of instant stuffing, and two ridged circles of canned cranberry sauce. Even the cat had balked.

A bubble reading *New Posts* appeared at the top of Simon's feed. Eagerly he tapped it, but his hope was misplaced. Kai had not posted anything in days.

Simon yearned to know what his ex was doing. No doubt he had spent the day with his family, the apartment rich with the aroma of his mother's glazed duck and sticky-rice stuffing with Chinese sausage. He could hear the Mandarin-infused chatter around the table, the chopsticks clicking as they ate. Kai would have insisted they go around the table and share what they were grateful for, him first. "I'm grateful for my family."

Because, unlike Simon, he still had one.

The pair were PhD students at the University of Chicago when they met at the house party of a mutual friend. Simon, recently returned to the States after completing his master's degree at the University of Bristol in England, was a first year in the paleobiology department. Kai Liu was a year ahead, studying anthropology. It is a curious fact that paleontologists, like A-list actors and musicians, tend to date within their field, but Simon and Kai were a rare exception. Known around campus as "Kai and Si" (and occasionally, to Simon's secret pleasure, "Kaimon"), they were a popular and apparently "cute" couple. People seemed to derive an inexplicable delight from the fact that they were both small statured and slim. More important to Simon was that they balanced each other's personal shortcomings: his proclivity for neurotic over-analysis stabilized by Kai's nurturing reassurance, and Kai's tendency toward lateness, disorganization, and intense emotionality shored up by Simon's natural leaning toward order and reason. Colleen, the first time she met the pair for dinner in Chicago, had called it a match made in heaven.

They moved in together after just a few months, and immediately started building a future together.

Simon was still a student when he took a part-time job as a research associate at the Field Museum, the first of several titles he would hold there. The ink was barely dry on his PhD before he was offered a postdoc position, and not long after that before the assistant curator of vertebrate paleontology role opened up. Simon had no delusions about his chances; with so few jobs on offer nationwide, every paleo grad in the country would be throwing their hat in the ring. He might not have applied at all except for his timely discovery of *Simonopertyx neali* while on a museum-funded expedition to Wyoming. In addition to commanding national headlines, the discovery proved scientifically significant, with many arguing that the specimen's cranial structure settled a longstanding debate regarding the modular evolution of the avian skull. Already fond of Simon and delighted by the positive attention his discovery had brought to the museum, the Field ultimately agreed he was the man for the job, before a further string of significant publications earned Simon a speedy promotion to associate curator, overseeing the museum's extensive collection of Dinosauria and a team of eight.

The Field was beginning to feel like home, not least because Kai had recently joined the staff of the biological anthropology department, specializing in ancient human remains. Neither was in danger of being overpaid, but they loved their work and, Simon had thought, each other. They had a nice apartment in Hyde Park and a car and Philomena, whom they had raised as their surrogate child for more than five years. They took a big vacation every other year, to China or Canada or some other destination of geological interest. They had even talked in vague terms about marriage one day, moving to the suburbs, rescuing a human baby as a pet for Phil.

In so many ways Simon had seen his life laid out before him. A life that made him feel normal, unbroken. A life that one day, if he kept at it, would make him whole again.

But 2020 had other plans.

Rapidly and unalterably his mental health deteriorated, and so his relationship followed. By Easter Kai had moved his stuff out of the apartment, excavating six and a half years of collected memories from the place that no longer felt like home.

Simon moved back in with Colleen, taking Phil, while Kai went to live with his mother in Logan Square. That neither she nor Kai's sisters made contact with Simon after the breakup felt like a betrayal—like a tacit ejection from the family to which, though he was a white boy, a *lǎo měi* as they affectionately called him, Simon had always felt he belonged.

Just when Simon thought life couldn't get any worse, Colleen tested positive for Covid, a diagnosis he only managed to avoid by isolating in his bedroom and wearing a mask nearly twenty-four hours a day. Shortly thereafter Colleen was admitted to the hospital where she had been working on the front lines since the start of the pandemic. They spoke on the phone often, Simon telling her about work and the cat and how he had vacuumed and put fresh sheets on Colleen's bed, how he was getting everything ready for her to come home. He refused to believe that any other outcome was possible. Even when Colleen's doctor pointed out—incessantly, he felt—that her obesity put her at high risk. Even when he could hear in her voice that breathing had become a struggle, and she was put on a ventilator.

Only when the call finally came, not from Colleen but from the doctor, did he finally accept that she might not always be around for him.

That, in fact, she was already gone.

With Colleen's passing, something fractured inside of Simon. Something like a bone—a part of him that, even if it managed to heal, would always bear evidence of its imperfection. A tiny part of him that would always be broken.

As he laid Colleen's ashes to rest in the anxious gray waters off Navy Pier, where once they had eaten funnel cake and ridden the Centennial Wheel and Colleen had admonished him for rocking the gondola, he knew he couldn't stay.

For the second time, he found his surroundings were irrevocably tainted. Everywhere he went he was met with reminders of his loss in one direction or the other. Even his position at the Field, a veritable dream job, had shed much of its luster. Forced to work from home since the start of the pandemic, he had become increasingly disconnected from the parts of the job he enjoyed: working hands-on with the collection, the research facilities, his colleagues. Even if nothing else had changed, the place still would have been ruined by the fact that Kai remained there, and by the memory of going to see SUE with Colleen, the very experience that made him want to work there in the first place. They were like ghosts prowling the halls of the museum. He needed a fresh start—somewhere, if not better, then at least less haunted.

Simon started looking.

As expected, there were barely a handful of open positions in his field across the country. Nevertheless, when he first saw the Hawthorne job on a museum careers board, he initially discounted it. He had sworn he would never return to Pennsylvania, least of all to that accursed museum, the place that had screamed his life into chaos. Not to mention that the Hawthorne was, some would have said, beneath him. Simon was a one-time Marshall Scholar. He held two of the most prestigious degrees in the paleontological sciences and a curatorial title at the Field. With his pedigree, he could have done far better than a small regional museum that had not produced a significant piece of research in decades.

And yet.

As the pandemic dragged on, continuing its slow work of hollowing every joyful molecule out of his body, leaving him with nothing but chronic virus-related anxiety and loneliness, he found his mind returning often to the Hawthorne. He visited the careers board daily, sometimes more than once, to see if the position was still posted. Every day, he found himself a little more open to the prospect, a hair more interested. The opportunity whispered to him, and not just about the promise of escape, or his ability to fast-track his career and make significantly more money.

It didn't make sense, ran counter to every instinct he'd had for the past two decades. But he could feel it deep inside him. *In his bones.* The Hawthorne was where he was meant to be.

It was as if, after all these years, the place was calling him back.

As if *she* was calling him back. If he listened, he could just about hear her.

Come find me.

CHAPTER SEVEN

DR. NEALY'S
UNEXPECTED ASSIGNMENT

Recently cleaned and cleared of the boxes containing his predecessor's old things, Simon's office was finally starting to look like his own. His diplomas, which he put up himself, hung low but proudly on the wall, and his name plaque had replaced Albert Mueller's.

He was just putting out a few items from home—photos of Colleen and Philomena, a scale *Triceratops* skull from the Field Museum gift shop—when a meeting appeared on his virtual calendar. It was titled *Simon & Craig Check-in*. No description was included.

Simon first asked Patricia, the ancient senior executive assistant who had scheduled it. "I do not receive that information," she wrote back. "I was just asked to schedule the meeting but I can ask if you wish although I believe that Craig is out the rest of the day ☹ Should I ask tomorrow???"

Harry, whose presence was also requested, wrote back, "Craig just wants to fill you in on some things."

The appointment's uncertain purpose concerned Simon. Was he in trouble? Did the executive director feel Simon ought to be further along by now, already stuck into the research for which they were paying him so handsomely? If they thought he was going to put the Hawthorne back on the map working in that scabby little hole of a lab, he was afraid they were in for an unwelcome surprise.

Prior to the Thursday meeting, Simon prepared a brief proposal for renovating the lab and outfitting it with the bare essentials: new work-tables and light fixtures, a small suite of air scribes and tools, a shipment of new adhesives and consolidants to replace the more-traditional But-var brand of polyvinyl butyral resin his predecessor clearly favored. It would be a tough sell given the continued closure of the museum and its lengthy list of maintenance needs, but a necessary investment if they wished to reclaim their scientific relevance.

Apparently they did not. Just minutes into the dreaded meeting, Ruth-erford explained all such ambitions had been put on the back burner.

"I'm not sure I understand," Simon said. "I was under the impres-sion that strengthening our research function was one of the board's top priorities. That it was a key component of their three-to-five-year plan."

"Oh that. Yes, well. We do one of those every year."

Heat rose to Simon's cheeks. He feared it would show, but, thanks to his weak Wi-Fi signal, his video had frozen on a more agreeable version of his face.

"Now don't get me wrong," Rutherford continued. "All that research stuff certainly seemed like a good idea at the time—heck, that's why we hired you! But this pandemic's got us running all over the shop. We gotta stay nimble to whatever it throws at us."

"Of course. We'll never survive if we don't. Even so—"

"I wouldn't say that." The ED's tone had shifted, a glint of steel be-neath his hokey exuberance. "The Hawthorne *always* survives."

Harry smirked conspiratorially. Something about it made Simon un-comfortable.

Rutherford chuckled, signifying the return of his good humor. "But even so, we're pivoting our focus. That's where you come in."

He explained that in the five weeks between Simon's accepting the position and his first day of work, the board of directors had abandoned their research lark for a new strategic focus designed to address the mu-seum's perilous financial position.

Though Rutherford hoped to reopen in January, it was no silver bullet; admissions had been in free fall for years, promising little in the way of financial savior. "In order to bounce back, we need something big—a shiny new object to rally our donors around and drive ticket sales and memberships in 2021." A consultant had been engaged to conduct a focus group of community leaders and stakeholders—i.e., Rutherford's friends and the museum's most generous supporters—who collectively decided that what the Hawthorne really needed was a new flagship exhibit in the Hall of Dinosaurs, a large carnivore to draw in crowds.

"Preferably a *T. rex*."

Simon's stomach dropped. Although they were outside his area of expertise, he knew that genuine *rex* specimens were exceedingly rare and unaffordable to all but the best-heeled institutions. Just weeks before, the skeleton named Stan had sold at Christie's New York for a record-breaking $31.8 million.

"Don't worry, I'm not gonna ask you to find me a *T. rex*," Rutherford said. "Luckily for you, we've already got one."

"Pardon?"

"Or one of his cousins. One of the big meat eaters with the teeth and the little arms, what d'you call 'em?"

"I think you mean theropod, but they're not all—" Simon faltered. "Sorry, I'm confused."

"Dang it, Harry, what's his name again?"

The VP, who had found better entertainment on his phone, sat up in his chair, the smile dropping off his face. "Say again? You broke up."

"Mueller's skeleton, what's his name?"

"Oh, I know this. Shoot. What's it called? It's on the tip of my tongue."

"Theo, isn't it?"

"Theo, right. I thought it might be."

"Do you know the species?" Simon said.

"We were gonna ask you."

"But when—? Where—?"

The video froze. Simon clicked around pointlessly, impatient to get them back.

"—him for years," Rutherford was saying as the video resumed.

"Sorry, were you saying you've had him for years?"

"He was Albert Mueller's pet project—that's the kook who ran the paleontology department before you. Never met the man personally, but I hear he was—well, I'm sure you've worked with plenty of nutty scientists in your day."

"From what I hear, the guy had a screw loose for years," Harry said, appearing to have at last found a topic that interested him. "Spent all his time chipping away at it in the lab. Getting it ready to go up in the Hall of Dinosaurs. It was all planned out."

"What happened?"

"Apparently he started to lose it. Started talking to himself, screaming at things that no one else could see. Seemed to think the place was haunted. Eventually the janitor caught him trying to throw himself out of a window up on the third floor and that was it, they had to cut him loose. He was a liability."

Rutherford cleared his throat.

"He retired, I mean," Harry said.

An abrupt forced retirement. That explained why Mueller hadn't had time to sort through his things.

"But what about the exhibit? Didn't the museum want to finish it?"

Rutherford cut across Harry, who had opened his mouth to answer. "They did, of course. But the museum was going through a rough patch. Budget was tight. They decided not to refill the position right away, and plans for the exhibit were put on hold."

"For a while, it seems."

"Just these last fifteen years or so."

Laughter burst like a bird from Simon's mouth and fluttered away. But the look on Rutherford's face told him he was only half kidding.

"So," said Simon, struggling to make sense of it all. "Why refill the position now? With the museum's finances being what they are—"

"Finances, shminances. You have to spend money to make money. That's something we used to say in the for-profit world."

"Right. But research isn't exactly revenue generating."

Rutherford sighed, appearing to be losing patience with this line of questioning, which included far fewer occurrences of the word *yes* than he was accustomed to. "Like I said, it's what the board thought we needed at the time."

"At the time, two months ago?"

"Things move quick around here," Harry said.

Simon was starting to feel uneasy. The more he heard, the more tenuous his situation appeared. From what he could tell, he'd been hired on a whim, and on a whim the museum had disbanded any need for him. They were going to fire him. He'd left one of the top museums in the world to come here and they were going to fire him.

"I know what you're thinking," Rutherford said. "But you can't get rid of us that easily. Now that we've got you, we might as well use you."

"Use me how?" said Simon warily.

"We got a project for you. You're gonna like this, I promise. We want you to finish what Mueller started."

"You mean—?"

"The museum's crying out for a new exhibit," Rutherford said. "It's high time we bring Theo back to life."

CHAPTER EIGHT

BORED OF DIRECTORS

Simon closed his laptop at the end of the meeting and slammed his fist on the desk.

He knew he ought not to complain. As a boy he could have imagined few things more thrilling than overseeing the construction of a major dinosaur exhibit. Even as an adult it was an exciting prospect—but he knew all too well what it would cost him.

In the natural history museum of the twenty-first century, the curator role was focused on the production and publication of research. The opportunity to direct his own studies, and avail himself of the Hawthorne's ceratopsian specimens in furtherance of them, had been the primary reasons he had taken the role (or at least, those most easily explained to others). But if Theo was anything like Rutherford described, the undertaking would change everything. A complete carnivore skeleton could comprise as many as four hundred bones, each one needing to be painstakingly separated from the matrix, cleaned with specialist tools, repaired, and sealed, before being documented, cataloged, studied, digitally scanned—and only then could work begin on the exhibit itself.

Depending on the extent of Mueller's work on the specimen, the preparation process was likely to last several months. After the Field acquired SUE at auction in 1997, it had taken a team of twelve highly skilled preparators two years and more than thirty thousand hours to ready her bones for mounting. Simon had no such resources at his disposal. A paleontology department of one, he would bear the full burden of the project—the largest the Hawthorne had undertaken in more than three decades.

That it was being asked of him, with no additional support offered, intensified Simon's doubts about the museum's leadership. In his experience, boards of directors were iffy to begin with. Composed largely of corporate executives and social elites with no real nonprofit experience except as visitors or donors, they could at times be wonderfully supportive, deferring amiably to the staff's vision and expertise while offering helpful connections and heaps of money. More often, they were an unremitting disaster—uninformed in their assumptions, mercurial in their moods, and colossal in their egos.

It appeared Simon was stuck with the latter kind. Even worse, Rutherford was not even trying to steer the ship. Judging by their recent meeting, he had all but removed his hands from the wheel, abandoning its course to the changeable winds of board input.

Then again, they were not necessarily wrong. A new carnivore exhibit *would* be a financial boon to the museum. A flourishing Hawthorne would have ample resources to invest in Simon's research, perhaps even update the lab.

He thought too of the equity he would build with the leadership by guiding the project to success—by helping to lead the Hawthorne out of its perilous present and into a shining new era of hope and prosperity.

Finally, he thought of a child—a boy, perhaps one who looked a lot like a school-aged Simon—and the expression that would appear on his face as he stood looking up at the twelve-foot-tall *T. rex* towering over the Hall of Dinosaurs. Or was Theo one of *T. rex*'s cousins such as *Albertosaurus*? Perhaps *Yangchuanosaurus*, if the fossils had been found in China. Or *Carcharodontosaurus*, if in Africa. Simon's head swam with the possibilities of what Theo might be, of what paleontological discoveries lay waiting in his fossils—and most of all, what magic his exhibit might bring to the life of a child in desperate need of it.

Perhaps it would not be so bad after all.

CHAPTER NINE

SKELETONS IN THE CLOSET

Simon expected that the bones of a nearly forty-foot-long dinosaur would be easy to find in a small museum, but, like most of his recent assumptions, this was far from the reality.

The theropod was not in Collection Storage, and the wider network of basement corridors proved equally fruitless. He found closets packed with chairs and tables, old decor, and forgotten event banners. A break room with a few stitches of furniture and a whiny avocado-green refrigerator. A scientific library of leather-bound tomes and journals, each encased in a slipcover of dust. Nothing even resembling a *T. rex*.

He halted his search when there came a sound from the depths of the basement. Simon felt it more than heard it, a low burr like a deep rumbling breath. It reminded him of a crocodile's bellow, thought by some to be the closest relative of what many dinosaurs had sounded like. Then a thin sound, like a nail being dragged across glass. *Screeeeap.* Likely something mechanical, Simon thought reasonably. The groaning of an overworked boiler, or a heater straining against the early December chill.

He was more immediately intrigued by what he heard next: the squealing of the research lab doors. Someone had just gone in or come out—but who?

A moment later, he pushed open the doors of the lab and held them ajar to let light into the dark room. No one was there, at least that he could see. But still something didn't feel right.

"Hello?" he called out.

No answer.

He flipped the switch on the wall and the bare lightbulb flickered on.

Slowly Simon scanned the room. His eyes lingered on the wall of wooden shelves stuffed with geological specimens, reference manuals, composition books, and boxes, many visibly overflowing with papers. Wondering if their contents might point him in the direction of Theo's remains, Simon crossed to the shelving unit and started pulling things down. He was digging through a box on the floor filled with invoices and receipts when a toffee-colored cockroach skittered up his arm.

He yelped and flailed back, knocking his head painfully against the edge of a wooden shelf. It jolted him from his horror and he massaged the back of his skull, grimacing at the sight of the roach racing across the floor and under a table.

As he stepped away from the wall, a thin stretched note sounded behind him.

He looked around, wrinkles of surprise etching his forehead. His collision appeared to have disturbed the wall of shelves, caused it to swing forward on one side like a door.

Simon stared. Gently he pulled the wall toward him, and a wedge of darkness opened behind it, revealing the entrance to a hidden room.

Simon put his mask on. The air that wafted from the opening was dank and mildewy, moister than in the rest of the lab. He could hear a faint *drip-drip* of water, though he couldn't see beyond a foot or two.

Cautiously he stepped inside and noticed the outline of a cord hanging from the ceiling. He pulled it and there was a meteoric flash; the overhead light had exploded, offering a momentary glimpse of a narrow, rectangular, and extremely cluttered room, like the attic of an archaeologist with a hoarding problem.

Simon took out his phone, activated the flashlight, and used it to take a closer look.

The room's arcane contents could have filled a small exhibit hall. Cuneiform tablets, ancient animal statues, stelae inscribed with hieroglyphics. A wraithlike shape that turned out to be a sarcophagus under a sheet. Containers stacked to the ceiling with handwritten labels that had been furiously blacked out, as if to conceal the identity of the items within. An air of forgotten confidentiality hung about the place and intensified Simon's curiosity.

At the back of the room, he found a few large splintery crates and, above them, several rows of open shelves bolted into the wall. Their contents varied widely in shape and size, some large and bundled loosely in sheets and blankets, others smaller, boxed, and wet.

Wet?

The drip was coming from a leaky pipe overhead, splashing down onto the topmost shelves. Simon's stomach plummeted—all the more when he read by the light of his phone the label attached to the long sodden bundle before him.

The handwriting was unfamiliar, likely not Albert Mueller's.

Dinosaur-leg bone???

Simon cursed. Even without a hygrometer at hand, he had no doubt the relative humidity of the room was well above the recommended 45 to 55 percent—a recipe for irreversible damage. If that drip had gotten into the bones . . . Not to mention that if the museum was found to have been storing specimens without proper moisture control, it could lose its accreditation.

Don't worry about that now, Simon thought. All that mattered was getting these fossils out—quickly.

He secured his hands under the bone, the wrappings cold and fetid with damp. He lifted it carefully, but he was too late—months, maybe years too late. Though he couldn't see it, he could feel it through the blankets: the waterlogged bone crumbling to dust in his hands.

꧁

It took Simon and Maurice more than an hour to dig out the surviving fossils. Simon was despondent at the loss of the leg bone, for which he blamed himself. And yet it was clear that whoever had stored the fossils had not a clue what they were doing. He tried not to imagine what the rest of the skeleton would look like once he got it out of its wrappings.

In a compassionate but misguided attempt to distract him from his pain, Maurice refused to stop talking, regaling an uninterested Simon with endless scraps of institutional history collected over seventeen years of employment.

Much of it Simon already knew from the dubious "About Us" page of the museum's website.

Nationally recognized as a leader in scientific research and education, the Hawthorne Museum of Natural History was founded in 1897 by industrialist Augustus Hawthorne, whose vision for a world-class exhibition of natural antiquities was matched only by his sky-is-the-limit approach to philanthropy.

Drawing upon the expertise gained from his extensive travels, he developed a revolutionary plan to build and open a not-for-profit museum dedicated to exhibiting his personal collection of fossils and scientific specimens. With Hawthorne's generous financial backing, construction of the 40,000-sq.-ft. building began in 1895, on a twenty-acre hollow donated by the founder in memory of his late father, who had gifted the land to Augustus for his thirteenth birthday.

Nearly 125 years later, the Hawthorne carries on its founder's legacy of altruism, prestige, and scientific curiosity through the responsible acquisition and conservation of a diverse collection of specimens and artifacts. Guided by this noble mission, the Hawthorne welcomes thousands of visitors a year, including hundreds of students from schools across the state, who leave having made in its hallowed halls memories that will stay with them forever.

What Simon hadn't learned from the website was that when the museum opened, before it was renovated to create the research lab in the 1950s, the basement room had served as the founder's private lounge, a place where he could relax and sleep over when he was working late. At least, Maurice said, that was the official story.

"What do you mean, the official story?" Simon grunted, helping him transport a crate into the safety of the lab.

The job done, Maurice sighed, breathing heavily.

"On the DL?" he said.

Simon nodded.

"People say that August was a bad dude."

"Bad how?"

"Had a thing for little girls. He used to bring 'em down here, give 'em candy, toys to play with. When he built the place he had this little room added on for I don't know what. A room nobody knew about but him and the folks who built it. Sounds more like a dungeon than a den if you ask me."

Simon felt nauseous.

"Lucky I found it," Maurice said. "Or I don't know, maybe unlucky."

"*You* found it?"

"About a decade ago. I was on maintenance duty. Got a work order to fix a broken shelf in the lab, and when I pulled it out the whole wall opened up."

"What was in there?" Simon said.

"Nothing but mold and spiders. But once the ED found out, he loaded it up with all the shit he didn't want nobody seeing. *Including* Bert's old dino."

So the skeleton *was* Theo.

"But why wouldn't they want anyone to see it?"

"Same reason nobody came looking for it all these years."

Simon shook his head, not understanding.

"People say there was something about that skeleton that done fucked up Bert in the head. That there was evil in them bones."

The continued *drip-drip* intruded upon the silence.

"Right," Simon said. "Well, we should probably finish up. It's already after five."

By the time they finished, Theo's fossils covered every surface of the lab. The room was barely navigable, and Simon, a wheezing jelly-legged mess, but it was done. "Thanks, Maurice." He shook the custodian's calloused hand before remembering it was forbidden. "Couldn't have done this without you."

Simon checked his phone. "Goodness, look at the time. It's nearly seven."

"Shit, better get out of here."

"Think I'll stay a little longer. But you go ahead."

Maurice looked a little uneasy, but nodded. "If you say so, dino boy. Have a good night now."

"You too, Maurice."

Maurice departed at his usual hobbling pace.

Now that he was alone, the full impact of Simon's disastrous discovery washed over him. He let out a despairing sigh, his heart heavy, and set about loading bones onto the table at the center of the room.

Under the flickering light of the lab, he assessed the damage. The fossils were a mixture of prepared and unprepared segments. The ones secured in crates were mostly undamaged and largely still coated in the earth with which they had been excavated, which in the paleontological world was known as matrix. Many of the others were irretrievable, reduced to silt by water and moisture. The leg bone, as expected, was beyond repair: a sliding pile of permineralized dust, like a toppled sandcastle in the shape of a femur. He wanted to weep.

But its twin was not so bad off. Resembling a knobby club hewn from dark wood, the thigh bone was some two and a half feet long, thick as a baseball bat, and pitted with tooth marks Simon could not immediately identify. Presumably unlike its brother, it had already been prepared and sealed when it went into storage, protecting it from an incursion of moisture.

But Simon couldn't rejoice yet. Just as he knew innately he was looking at the femur of a theropod, he knew, from its stunted proportions, that this was no *T. rex*. The shape of the femoral cross section, more oval than round, suggested Theo was fully grown at the time of his death. It was more probable he had been a medium-sized theropod, at most six or seven feet tall at the hip. *Ceratosaurus? Neovenator?* The possibilities added a spice of excitement to Simon's dread. Whatever it was, it clearly wasn't the mega predator the board had demanded. Rutherford was going to rage when he found out.

He pressed on, taking little notice of the time. It had been one of Kai's most frequent complaints that once he set his mind to his work, Simon could hardly separate the two again. At the Field it hadn't been uncommon for him to be the last to leave the building, waking Kai as he stumbled into the apartment well after midnight. Even now, he scarcely acknowledged the grumble of his stomach as the clock hands inched toward double digits. He barely registered the rattle of his bones as a breathless chill crept into the basement. Even as the lab took on a waxy, oversaturated quality, he didn't once consider calling it a night.

He opened yet another crate, the contents of which were not coated in matrix, but clean and protected by foam batting. First he found a short cylindrical bone—clearly a vertebra but not theropod. It was far too small, the shape all wrong, the color like that of decaying teeth.

As he reached into the box again, the light began to strobe overhead, and the sound from before was back. *Screeeeap.* Simon dug out a more delicate bone, what appeared to be a radius from a very small forearm. This wasn't right either—not Theo's, at least.

The sound was getting louder now. Pushing closer, attended by a deeper, heavier sound. *Screeeeap*—THUMP. *Screeeeap*—THUMP.

Fighting back the discomfort rising in his chest, Simon stood on his toes, leaned over the box, and stopped at the sight of the yellow dome peeking out from under the batting. A bone, he knew instantly, that didn't belong to any prehistoric creature.

His mouth filled with saliva. He repressed the surge of vomit spiking up his throat; the skull was not just human, but a child's. Only as he staggered back did he notice the words penned on the side of the crate in Mueller's spidery writing, flashing under the strobing lights.

M. Jenks, 1993–1999

SCREEEEAP—THUMP! *SCREEEEAP*—THUMP!

Simon screamed and experienced a sudden feeling of falling—

Then he jolted up, lifting his head. Blinked. Though his vision was bleary, he saw the room had returned to its normal state. The lights had steadied, the commotion ceased. He sat before a table covered with bones. *Dinosaur* bones.

He must have dozed off. His phone's screen told him it was nearly midnight.

His joints crackled as he stood, deciding to leave Theo's remains for the morning.

As Simon drifted toward the exit, a sick discomfort clung to him. He cast a last look over the bones, reassuring himself they weren't hers.

CHAPTER TEN

A FAR-OFF LIGHT IN THE DEEP EXPANSE OF BLACK

In the town of Wrexham there was a place where the sun didn't reach. A place of expansive long-armed trees, for the soil was rich with the bodies that nourished it. A grassy place where squirrels loped, sparrows sang, and butterflies batted their wings at the grayness of the sky. From the lawns of this place sprouted hundreds of weather-beaten stones, engraved with words of heartbreak and remembrance.

Among them was hers. Modest, rounded at the top. It bore the date of her birth—only her birth.

In the earth beneath the stone, rabbits burrowed and ants inscribed tunnels and an infinity of microorganisms multiplied. Perhaps deeper down, the fossils of ancient wildlife slept, waiting to be woken by the dawn of discovery.

What wasn't present beneath the stone was the little girl whose name it bore. The soil languished and the earthworms moaned, deprived of their promised sustenance. It was this that maddened Simon most of all, for nothing would have delighted his sister more than to feed them—for her life force to pulse through the veins of the earth as once it had pulsed through him, unburdening him with her boundless wonder and confidence, her perfect hiccupping laugh.

Without her the ground beneath him felt charred and lifeless, like the site of a catastrophic collision. A crater formed by the impact of her disappearance. No survivors but the questions that echoed back at him still.

Where is she?

Who took her from me?

Is she really gone, or is she still out there, waiting to be found?

Morgan was Simon's half sister, a distinction of no significance to them but that their mother, Joelle, seemed to relish. It gave her a second absent partner to decry, another missing child-support check to blame for the lack of food in the fridge after she walked out on her third minimum-wage job in a year.

Behind her scabby skin and sunken expression, Joelle was the spit of Simon—small, reedy, dark hair and eyes. Simon couldn't say what traits he'd inherited from his father, for Marcus Nealy had died in jail when his son was only a toddler, and any remaining photos of him Joelle had burned, without thought as to whether Simon might want them.

As a mother, Joelle was selfish, mean, and listless. She hung around the house like a slumbering viper, passing the day in bed or guzzling cheap, off-brand vodka before an endless stream of Maury Povich and Montel Williams, lashing out at the slightest disturbance. On a good day, she would tell her kids to shut up, get out, fuck off; on a bad one, threaten to hand them over to the government, blame them for her wanting to die.

When she was in one of her jealous moods, the kind that made her resent her children's bond, she might use it as a wedge to be driven between them. "Fuckin' idiots," she would slur, poured over the couch as Simon helped Morgan with homework at the coffee table. "No' even really brother and sister. I'm your only real family. You sh' be asking me for help, not him." Yet the children knew that to ask their mother for anything would only make her curse and gripe and speak of life like a cosmic attack on her comfort.

Half blooded or not, they were each other's family.

Their everything.

Simon's earliest memories were scattered across homes—he and his mother seemed to move apartments every few months—but that changed after his grandmother died and left Joelle the two-story townhouse on the edge of town that would become their long-term residence.

The house was outdated but quaint and tidy, at least before the squalor set in. Before the siding warped, and the paint began to flake from the window frames, and the fence lining the covered porch sneered at the street with its broken-tooth smile.

Soon the inside of the house was as uncared for as the boy who lived there. The rooms were chaotic with mess—fast food bags and wine bottles piled on the surfaces, trash overflowing. Much of the furniture had been rescued from a curb or back alley. The place reeked of Joelle's self-rolled cigarettes; it saturated the walls, the furniture, Simon's clothes. He never heard the end of it from his classmates, who plugged their noses and refused to sit next to him. And yet, because of his mother's constant carping, he believed his inability to make friends went deeper than that. He was too small for a boy, an "ant." He was stupid. He would never go to college or get a good job, certainly not as a paleontologist.

"By the time you grow up," she said, "all the bones will be dug up already. There'll be nothin' left to find."

For years Simon accepted this as fact, and it devastated him.

He was four when his sister was born and a crib was carted into his bedroom. Morgan's dad—a gawky, freckle-armed man who lived with them for nearly a year, longer than any of the others—had refused to share a bedroom with his newborn daughter. "I can't sleep with that fuckin' baby cryin' in my ear all night!" By the time he left a few months later, disappearing one night after an ugly fight with Joelle that ended in the police being called, Simon was already adept at soothing his infant sister through the bars of her crib. Often he bewitched her into a distracted giggle with the help of Lucy the Ladybug, her favorite soft toy, and the song he attached to her bouncing jig.

> *"The ladybug gives you hugs / She does a twirl for her favorite girl /*
> *She says, 'Morgan, please don't cry / or I will have to go bye-bye.'"*

Seemingly from birth, Morgan adored all things creepy and crawly, from the cartoony, big-eyed plush toys that lined her top bunk to the chipped butterfly clips she wore like jewelry in her reddish-brown hair. If she wasn't engaging a family of rubber tarantulas in an elaborate fantasy or reading aloud from her *Bug's Life* storybook, Simon could trust she was probably somewhere coaxing a centipede onto her finger.

Morgan was never afraid to get her hands dirty. Behind the house was only a tiny paved patio, but out front was a small rectangle of untended soil, the remnants of an abandoned landscaping job. In the summers Morgan would spend all day out there, digging up earthworms and roly-polies with her toy spade, collecting them in jars for observation and releasing them back again in time for supper. Often she sang, a riff on the song Simon had invented to soothe her.

> *"Digging for bugs to give them hugs / Under the dirt is where they live /*
> *or in the grass, or in the trees / Don't hurt bugs, pretty please."*

The sound of it never failed to bully a smile out of Simon. It was not just love he felt for his sister but admiration. Morgan possessed so much that he lacked. The kind of personality that spread its happiness to everyone it touched, a verve for life undiminished by the circumstances laid against it. A spirit of intrepid wonder he envied in her, even as it discomfited him.

By the age of nine Simon knew enough of the world to understand it was full of bad people, people who would take advantage of a child so unbridled and trusting. Sometimes when he heard his sister singing he would stand at his bedroom window, watching over her protectively. Hurrying down to join her at the first sign of anyone approaching.

"Find any dinosaur bones?" he once asked, crouching beside her on the sidewalk. His chest tightened as the passerby drew near, then relaxed again as he walked by without stopping.

"No, but hmmmm," she answered, eyes to the sky, tapping the plastic spade against her cheek. "I think there are some, but you have to dig a really, really, *really* far way down. Like a hundred million miles!"

"Like to China?"

She laughed, a long, high-pitched chirrup. It had a restorative effect, bringing a bit of color back to Simon's face.

He wished he could still laugh like that.

More important was that his sister never stopped.

Simon looked up, his eyes red and stinging. An adult family without masks had entered the cemetery, laden with grocery-store flowers and forced solemnity. Ashamed of not having thought to bring anything himself, he lowered his gaze back to the headstone, his unwanted gift from the community.

In Cherished Memory of
MORGAN ANN JENKS
Born June 2, 1993

He had been grateful at first for the town's eagerness to get involved—the missing-child posters they put up around town, the volunteer search parties, the campaign to raise money for the family. That was how he and his mother would be known going forward: *the family*. Less people than anonymous figureheads of sorrow. Holes to be filled with pity and cash.

More than four thousand dollars was raised for their benefit. Joelle spent every penny on drugs and alcohol. This went mostly unnoticed except by Simon, until his mother showed up incoherent and slobbering at the candlelight vigil held in Morgan's honor, making a scene that was the talk of the town for weeks. After that no more checks were delivered to the house. The remaining funds were placed in a trust for Simon's college education—all but a small amount reserved for the memorial. Colleen was against it, but her protests fell on deaf ears. This was a community matter now, even more so now that "the family" had left the area. The community must be given a chance to heal.

The service was held at the cemetery. Despite her opposition, Colleen was prepared to fly herself and Simon back so they could attend. But he didn't want to go either, for the same reason he hadn't wanted the search parties to give up looking or the posters left to wither on their telephone poles. *She could still be out there. She could still be out there, waiting to be found.* He couldn't bear the thought of strangers mourning his sister when she could be crying out for them at that very moment, her voice buried under the din of their empty grief.

Even now, as Simon stood empty-handed before the stone, tears scorching his cheeks with hatred and blame, he wondered if she was still calling out to him.

If she was, then at least now he was in the right place.

At least now, Simon was listening.

CHAPTER ELEVEN

CREATURE COMFORTS

Simon couldn't wait until Monday to continue his examination of Theo's fossils. He went into the museum Sunday morning and set about opening the rest of the crates. Pulling back the protective blankets heaped inside the largest, heaviest one, he experienced a jolt of surprise, then a euphoric rush of recognition.

Lying in a cutout in the foam base, still largely encased in matrix, was what he knew without doubt was the skull of a *Ceratosaurus*. Slightly squarer in proportion than its contemporaries', the skull measured twenty-four inches long, sixteen inches wide from the angular bone (forming the back of the lower jaw) to the semicircular ridge in front of each eye. Simon observed five openings from snout to brain, and a deep-set jaw to support its proportionately large teeth, only a handful of which were present on the exposed side.

But none of this was why Simon was so certain of Theo's genus. Rather, it was the feature for which *Ceratosaurus* was best known: the rough, ridge-like horn that rose like a rocky outcrop behind the nostrils. The protrusion was clearly present on Theo, though slightly chipped at the front, giving it the intimidating appearance of having been intentionally sharpened.

Simon reached out to his friend and colleague Dr. Romina Godoy. A large, slightly masculine woman with rectangular black glasses, she confirmed via a stuttering video chat that Theo was a member of his genus's type species, *Ceratosaurus nasicornis*—roughly translated to "nose-horned lizard."

"Extraordinary," she said, leaning closer to her screen. "Simon, do you understand—looking at? Depending what you find in the matrix, this—among the most complete *Ceratosaurus* skulls in existence."

"You're joking."

"The lacrimal ridge is just—and look at that orbital fenestra, almost a perfect triangle. Tell me the rest of the skeleton is this—and I'll jump on a plane right now."

"Don't book your ticket just yet," Simon said.

He told her about the suboptimal storage conditions and the damage to several key bones.

Romina was apoplectic.

"Who did that?" she exclaimed. "What idiot would store fossils in a leaky closet? They ought to be banished from the SVP and flung out into space on a plank of shit!"

But Simon was not convinced the person responsible had been a member of the Society of Vertebrate Paleontology. Based on what Maurice had told him, he gathered that Mueller was long gone when the bones were moved into storage. With no paleontologists left on staff, it may well have been an intern or volunteer.

Whoever was responsible, they hadn't made things easy for Simon. Nowhere among the fossils had he found a speck of documentation as to where they had been discovered, when, or by whom. No records of their accession either, the process by which an institution establishes legal title and ownership over the fossils. The specimen numbers attached to some fossils suggested they had been individually cataloged, but after hours spent poring through paper files and journals in the lab, he had not found a single mention of the *Ceratosaurus*.

Not knowing where else to turn he called Harry, who as usual had not a clue to offer.

"Was there nothing in the Cave?"

"In the what?" Simon said. A low bubbling on the other end of the line sounded suspiciously like a hot tub.

"The Cave. The museum archives. It's where they keep all the historical records."

Even before accepting the curator position, Simon had harbored doubts about Harry's qualifications. If Simon was young for a director, then Harry, a VP at forty, was no less so. His spare LinkedIn profile showed that he'd held his current role for two years and attended Cornell. No dates or degrees were listed, but, given his elevated title, Simon had made the charitable assumption that Harry at least had a PhD and several unlisted years' experience in collections management.

His confidence in that was beginning to wane. Visiting the profile again, Simon noticed for the first time the decade-old recommendation at the bottom of the page, written by none other than Craig Rutherford.

"I've been acquainted with this fine young man since move-in day at Cornell University, where my eldest son was lucky enough to be his roommate . . ."

Suddenly, it all made sense: Harry was a friend of the family. A good old-fashioned nepotism hire.

Still he followed Harry's advice. The following day he went looking for Maurice, and finding him cleaning a ground-floor restroom, asked to be let into the archives when it was convenient.

At the mention of the room, the custodian halted his vigorous scouring.

"Archives?" he said, looking uneasy. "Ima have to run that one up the chain, dino boy."

Simon's ego twinged.

"I have Harry's permission. He's the one who told me to—"

"Then Harry ought to know you need a signed authorization form before I let you in."

"A form?"

"Last person who got caught down there without permission got thrown out on they ass. That Rutherford's real touchy about who knows what around here."

And so Simon returned to Harry, who bounced him to Priya, who sent him a copy of the required form. He completed it at once, providing a thorough justification for needing to enter the archives and a description of the specific records he required. It was left up to Harry to get Rutherford's signature.

Simon had no doubt he would be waiting for some time.

Philomena was yowling hungrily when Simon walked through the door. "All right, Phil, hush," he said, scooping her into his arms and delivering her to the kitchen counter.

Not where I'm cooking, he imagined Kai complaining.

He opened a can for the cat and ordered a pizza, which he ate in front of the TV, streaming *Jurassic Park*. He'd seen it enough times that he could all but recite it from memory, less watching the film than allowing it to envelop him in its familiar hug.

He remembered watching it as a kid, the black-and-red paper slipcase of his prized VHS worn loose from near-constant use. Unlike his classmates, Simon had never outgrown his fascination for prehistoric creatures. In fact, the more his home life deteriorated, the more he found himself drawn to them. Unfortunately, he hadn't been back to the Hawthorne since his field trip with Mrs. Kramer's class. He was desperate for a return visit, but it seemed unlikely they would ever be able to afford it. At least, so his mother claimed, while spending their welfare checks on booze and rolling papers.

And so he returned, time and again, to *Jurassic Park*, soothed but not quite satisfied. Even as his spirits soared on John Williams's triumphant score, his heart ached to step into the world of Isla Nublar. A world in which dinosaurs existed not as images on a screen but as living, breathing animals. A world where staying alive meant outrunning a *T. rex* on the back of a Jeep or outsmarting a *Velociraptor* with a clever bit of code, not learning to dig dinner out of a cereal box, or steer clear of the strange men his mother entertained upstairs when she had no other options.

There was one memory related to the movie that Simon returned to more than any other. July 13, 1999: Simon sat watching from the living room couch. Morgan came in, stopping as she skipped past the TV. It was early in the film, Drs. Alan Grant and Ellie Sattler joking about Alan's dislike of children at a dig site in the Montana badlands. Morgan stood watching for a minute or two, then almost automatically backed up to the couch and sat beside Simon. Thirty minutes later, she was still there. Simon's enjoyment of the movie was heightened tenfold by his sister's. Through her *ew*'s and laughs, he felt like he was watching it for the first time. The way she turned away from the scary parts, gripping his shirt-sleeve, made him feel strong and important, like he was keeping her safe.

Eventually their mother came through the front door. She looked tired, bags of purple sagging under her eyes, a neon vest over her clothes. She was halfway through a week of community service, punishment for being caught with marijuana after a cop pulled her over for missing tags. The car was impounded, but at least Joelle had been clean since the arrest.

"You ate already?" she said, spotting the open box of Cinnamon Toast Crunch on the coffee table. Simon noticed the Little Caesar's box in her hand. Joelle tossed it angrily onto the floor.

"Pizza!" Morgan exclaimed.

She clambered off the couch and crouched down on the floor to open it. Simon paused the movie before joining her, breathing in the salty steam rising from the open box. They thanked their mother, lifting slices to their mouths.

Joelle's lip twitched, appeased.

"Got you somethin' else."

She waved something in the air, white and flimsy, and left it on the end table under the lamp with the broken shade.

"You can go tomorrow, while I'm workin'."

Simon wiped his hands on his clothes as he stood, his eyes on the gift. They were tickets of some kind.

Joelle lingered, watching him as he read the words printed upon them.

Hawthorne Museum of Natural History
Admit One, Child, $13.50
Expires 07/14/1999

"The *museum*? We get to go to the museum?" Simon exclaimed.

Joelle smiled and he threw his arms around her. It was like hugging a bag of bones. Simon couldn't suppress the emotion surging through him, emotion he hadn't realized he was still capable of feeling. He sobbed, wetting the thin ribbed cotton of her top with his tears.

"Don't be a baby," Joelle said.

But he felt her hand soft against his back, and her chin, resting gently on his head.

"Why are we hugging?" Morgan said, not waiting for an answer before she wrapped her arms around them both.

At last Simon pulled back, wiping his eyes.

"Why are you crying?" Morgan said, crestfallen.

"I'm just excited. We're going to the museum tomorrow. You wanna go to the museum? They have a whole Hall of Bugs and Insects!"

"*Bugs and Insects?*" Morgan let out a garbled scream, her excitement instant and irrepressible.

She danced around the room.

Joelle was halfway to the stairs when she turned and caught Simon's eye. "You'll look after her, won't ya?"

His smile faded; she had no right saying that. Not her.

"I always do, don't I?"

CHAPTER TWELVE

THE UNEARTHING

In the end it took two weeks, half a dozen voicemail and email reminders to Harry, and—to Simon's eye-rolling contempt—the signing of a nondisclosure agreement, before Rutherford consented to allowing Simon onetime access to the Cave.

"It all seems a bit much, don't you think?" Simon said as Maurice walked a step ahead of him, leading him to the entrance of the archives with the signed form tucked in his back pocket.

"I just do what they tell me, dino boy."

If Simon was honest, the nickname was beginning to grow on him.

Simon didn't know where he was expecting to be led, but he was surprised when Maurice opened the door of the basement library. Simon's mask was weak protection against the musty odor of the leather-bound books and journals slouching along the sagging shelves. He followed Maurice across a squishy carpet past a table, chairs, and a separate seating area to the back of the room. A plaque, much newer than the door it was affixed to, read RESTRICTED.

Maurice dug out a key ring and selected a stubby brass skeleton key with an *H* in the bow. It turned in the lock with a deep click, and the door yawned open onto a dark shaft of stairs leading down.

"Lock it up when you're done," he said.

"You're not coming?"

"You'll be aright."

Despite Simon's obvious dismay, Maurice clapped him on the shoulder and hobbled off.

Simon experienced a chill not just internal, but atmospheric, as he eased down the narrow, twisting stair; the temperature seemed to drop with each step toward the subbasement level, as if he were wading into a dark and frigid lake.

Using his phone, he found a switch at the bottom of the stairs. A buzzing light flickered to life and Simon flinched, as much at the sight of the room as the aggressive illumination.

He understood now why they called it the Cave. The archives combined the clerical mundanity of an office supply closet with the clammy desolation of a subterranean grotto. He found himself in a warren of low-ceilinged, earthen-walled rooms furnished with a disordered jumble of filing cabinets. Ranging from short and wide to tall and broken, each exploded with paper files too numerous to contain.

Simon wasn't sure where to start. If any system of organization was present, he couldn't parse it. From one row to the next, he found documents related to the acquisition of several taxidermied warthogs, designs for an abandoned "Savages of the Schuylkill" Native American exhibit, and decades' worth of press clippings, not all of them favorable. One *Philadelphia Inquirer* feature from the 1990s alleged that the museum's collection of human remains and cultural artifacts had been largely procured through "an unsavory combination of guile and grave robbing," followed by a volley of blistering editorials calling for the Hawthorne to repatriate the stolen treasures. In the articles' photos and accusations, Simon recognized several of the artifacts he had seen squirreled away in the hidden room off the lab.

As he riffled through an exhaustive register of the museum's Peruvian hematite collection, he happened to notice a cluster of red-brown crystal on top of the cabinet. Its proximity to the archives' geological records made him wonder if it hadn't been left there as a marker. Then in the next room he noticed an old *Brachiosaurus* figurine—brownish-green and grotesquely inaccurate, with bulging eyes and sharpened teeth— perched lopsidedly on top of a tall cabinet, and he thought, *Could it be?*

He stepped toward the cabinet, pulled open the nearest drawer, and was delighted to discover within it an extensive inventory of vertebrate fossils, albeit disorganized and committed to random scraps of paper and notebooks, many in the spidery cursive of his predecessor. The whole cabinet's worth would have to be digitized and backed up to the cloud—a project for another day. Or decade.

Though the Hawthorne's fossil collection was small by most standards, it was still several thousand specimens strong. Each record contained its own file folder of background documentation—photographs, field maps, early drafts of unpublished research. Looking through it all would take him ages, not least because he kept getting lost in what he was reading. Two hours had passed in the blink of an eye before he happened upon a folder labeled *1997-4589.* Simon recognized the notation as the year of Theo's excavation followed by his personal specimen number. Inside was a slim clothbound notebook detailing every piece of the skeleton that had been found, each bone assigned a unique suffix. More than 120 had been cataloged and roughly sketched, about two-thirds of which, Simon estimated, survived to that day.

Along with the notebook he found reams of additional material, including several photographs from the dig site. Their subject was a small balding man, late fifties or so. With a dorky kindness and quirky intelligence common to the profession, he was depicted conferring with his team, crouching in the dirt before an audience of young fossil hunters, smiling at the camera from under a floppy hat, his nose plastered white with zinc oxide. Handwritten on the back of the final photo was *Dr. Mueller at Dulzura, July '97.*

Simon lowered the photo and paused, furrowing his brow.

He reached inside and pulled out the final item in the folder: a thick bundle of papers, a hundred pages or so. They were yellowed with age, curled at the edges, tied together with a crisscross of twine. He turned it over to read the words inked upon the title page.

The Research Diaries of Dr. Albert Mueller
pertaining to Specimen H MNH 4589
(aka Theo)

Simon released the manuscript from its binding and flipped through the opening pages. Adrenaline flooded his body, dampening the tremor of unease nudging up toward his consciousness. This was not just a few preparators' notes. The manuscript appeared to contain far more—an exhaustive narrative of Theo's excavation and preparation, even a few accompanying sketches. How many shortcuts Simon might glean. How many pitfalls he might avoid.

And yet a thought niggled at the back of his mind, a thought that spoke in Harry's sneering voice.

From what I hear, the guy had a screw loose for years.

He had made it sound like Mueller was unhinged, a full-bore loon— at least toward the end. Maurice had given a similar impression. *There was something about that skeleton that done fucked up Bert in the head.* Could Simon trust anything Mueller had written? Or had reports of his insanity been exaggerated? Though he'd never met the man himself, Simon couldn't rule out the possibility that Mueller had merely been an eccentric scientist, one whose natural oddness, perhaps grown pronounced with age, had been misinterpreted as something more sinister.

It was curiosity now as much as opportunity that compelled Simon to start reading. He'd just flipped back to the opening page when a gut-quaking rumble echoed through the Cave.

That dang generator again, he thought, though less confidently than he had the first time he heard it.

In any case, he felt he'd been down in the cold long enough. He collected every Theo-related note and scrap, and, with the folder tucked under his arm, departed in victorious spirits.

From the Research Diaries
of Dr. Albert Mueller

August 13, 1997

When in the spring of this year Mr. Eustace
Abernathy, executive director of the Hawthorne
Museum of Natural History, informed me that I
would soon depart the comforts of my curatorial
abode for the arid climes of western Colorado,
I could never have predicted that I would soon
be staring down the jaws of the most significant
discovery in the museum's history. Though the
dinosaur in question is still en route to the
museum, it has already been heralded as the
future star attraction of the Hall of Dinosaurs
and the Hawthorne altogether—a claim I would
respectfully debate, being rather partial to our
long-necked girl myself.

Personal biases aside, specimen HMNH 4589
represents a magnificent addition to the
Hawthorne's fossil collection, abounding with
the promise of scientific knowledge, inspiration,
and a much-needed boost to the museum's ticket
sales. To what degree, we can only hope to
learn sooner rather than later as we undertake
the monumental task of bringing this ancient
predator back to life.

In recognition of the significance of this
discovery, I will endeavor to maintain in these
diaries a running chronicle of the preparation,

study, and exhibition of the specimen for
scientific posterity. (And should my superiors
cast a glance over these scribblings and wish to
publish them for sale in the museum gift shop,
well, that would not be so bad either.)

But before we begin, please indulge me in a few
brief words about myself and how our prehistoric
friend came into my grateful possession.

My name is Dr. Albert J. Mueller. For nearly
twenty-five years I have had the privilege of
serving as paleontology director and chief
dinosaur curator for the Hawthorne Museum in
Wrexham, Pennsylvania.

Originally from Massachusetts, I was first
introduced to the Hawthorne in my late twenties
after graduating from Harvard University, where
I had studied under esteemed sauropod expert
Wallace Fortescue (1903—1981). Dr. Fortescue was
well known in the paleontological field for his
staunch traditionalism and rigorous instruction.
It would be a lie to say I was fond of the man,
but he shaped me in ways I cannot deny and have
since, on some level, come to value. For one,
it was under his influence that I cultivated
a passion for Sauropoda, that clade of long-
necked, lizard-hipped saurischians that crushed
the landscape beneath their titanic heft and
even toppled trees with ease.

For a year after I received my PhD, I stayed
on at Harvard as an instructional postdoc, but
I quickly grew tired of the politics within

the department, which Dr. Fortescue ruled with
an iron fist. In search of greener pastures, I
accepted a role as a lecturer in undergraduate
geology at Swarthmore College, some twenty
miles outside of Philadelphia. The college had
very little to aid my research, but, through
a partnership between the institutions, I was
able to avail myself of the Hawthorne's handsome
fossil collection—most notably Beth, our resident
Brontosaurus, which has stood proudly in the Hall
of Dinosaurs since the museum's opening day.

Around this time I formed a strong working
relationship with the then deputy director,
Dr. Glennon Shiel, who oversaw the Hawthorne's
operational departments and research partnerships.
Glennon would go on to become the first and, to
this day, only executive director in the museum's
history to hold a doctorate. His tenure as
chief executive was sadly short-lived, but he
accomplished much in those brief years, including
a comprehensive restructuring of the institution's
research function. With that came the creation of
a new curatorial position for the museum: my own.

The day I learned this, I was working in
the lab, studying the mineral composition of a
fossilized eggshell from a *Camarasaurus grandis*,
when Glennon called me into his office. What I
thought was an informal meeting turned out to
be—on paper at least—a very formal interview. He
offered me the job on the spot, I accepted, and
the rest, as they say, is prehistoric history.

In the interest of brevity and your no doubt
flagging attention, allow me to jump forward

in time. Before I knew it, the year was 1993.
The preceding decades had brought challenges
for myself and the museum. The Hawthorne was
struggling financially and had been for some time.
In the 1970s into the early '80s, the museum had
maintained its reputation as a research leader by
undertaking annual fossil-finding expeditions to
the far-flung West, each dig resulting in exciting
new finds and published papers. But as the museum's
ticket revenue steadily declined, the expeditions
that had once been a regular occurrence were
slashed from the budget, providing little new
material to fuel my research. I advocated fiercely
for the reinstatement of annual field trips,
arguing that new publications would keep our
name in the headlines and improve attendance.
Unfortunately, the leadership of the day took a
firm line. If I wanted a dig, they told me, I would
have to find a way to pay for it.

My lucky break came a few years later. Garfield
Mitchell, who had served as executive director
of the Hawthorne from 1980 to '89 (and would
later return to the role in 1998 until his death
two years later), had mailed to the institution,
with no advance warning or later explanation, a
significant donation earmarked for the paleontology
program. This was especially surprising because
Mitchell had never taken a particular interest in
paleontology during his tenure. Suffice it to say,
rather the opposite was true. Still, I wasted no
time in cashing the check.

In July of this year, with Mitchell's funding,
I led a team composed largely of volunteers and

students to the remote Dulzura Mesa Canyon. Located thirty miles outside the small town of Dulzura, Colorado, the canyon formed an important section of the Morrison Formation, a sequence of sedimentary rock stretching from New Mexico to Montana. Some of the world's finest and most iconic Jurassic species have been found there, among them the meat-eating *Allosaurus*, the plate-backed *Stegosaurus*, and, once thought to be the longest dinosaur in existence, the whip-tailed *Diplodocus*. But my sights were set on something even more extraordinary.

In the early 1970s, remains of a new sauropod genus were found at the nearby Dry Mesa Quarry, a dinosaur even larger than *Diplodocus*. Aptly named *Supersaurus*, this colossal sauropod is thought to have reached 140 feet long and 55 feet tall, with one of the longest known necks ever discovered (my humble sketch hardly does it justice).

Though its magnitude was without question,
very little was known about the sauropod. Only
a handful of its bones had ever been discovered,
washed up in a bone bed with dozens of other
species, likely as a result of prehistoric
flash flooding. I hoped we might fare better at
the Dulzura site, whose favorable depositional
conditions had produced several near complete
specimens and invited hopes of finding an intact
skeleton.

The canyon provided a demanding but beautiful
dig site, the rugged desert landscape entangled
with scrub and gnarled trees, offering sweeping
views to the flat-topped mesas across the wide
canyon. The heat was blistering, the terrain
unforgiving. Our initial prospecting turned
up little more than a few bits and pieces of
Dryosaurus and a set of colossal footprints that
I hoped, but doubted, belonged to *Supersaurus*.
I admit I was disappointed—and getting concerned.
Our intrepid paleontology students were more
resilient, insisting we leave the trail behind
and trek out into unknown territory. Eventually
I had no choice but to yield to their demands.

It was the best decision I have ever made.

About a mile off the trail, we discovered
a rugged gem of Upper Jurassic sandstone. The
low-lying cliff looked practically untouched,
with a leafless tree growing diagonally out of
the rock like a great twisted hand beckoning us
forth. Beneath the roots of the tree, a lateral
accumulation of fluvial deposits burst with the
ephemera of prehistoric life. Fossils jutted

from the rock everywhere we looked. The lower jaw of an *Allosaurus*. A piece of the carapace of an ancient turtle. Then I heard someone shout.

"Dr. Mueller! Dr. Mueller, we've found something!"

And so they had. A theropod, a member of the suborder of bipedal carnivores characterized by their hollow thin-walled bones and small forelimbs. This much was clear from the skeleton weathering out of the rock, contorted in the death pose characteristic of its clade: the skull looped back toward a jumble of pelvic and leg bones, the tail flung up in an elegant curve, jaws parted in an upside-down scream. It took six of us more than a week to dig through twelve feet of overlying rock and carve the skeleton out of the ground in large chunks. We wrapped the pieces in burlap and slathered them with plaster, a coating that when dry would form hardened jackets in which they could be safely transported more than two thousand miles back to the museum.

The final night of our expedition—from what I can recall, for my memories of that night are patchy—we commandeered a bar in Dulzura and celebrated over several pitchers of cold beer. A few members of our group got tattoos commemorating the find, and—I have recently learned—two of our cohort even conceived a baby in the throes of that jubilant night. (I have already suggested to the happy couple that if the child is a boy, it is only right they name him Albert.)

But thrilling as the discovery was for all involved, the most exciting discoveries—and greatest challenges—lie ahead. For the real work of the paleontologist is not digging fossils out of the ground, but unearthing the secrets that lay buried within them.

It is not unlike detective work, in fact. Through the study of HMNH 4589's remains, I shall seek to build a picture of its death—and more important, its life—from the minutest and hardest-to-spot of clues.

I have no doubt that we shall succeed.

Death, I find, always leaves traces.

CHAPTER THIRTEEN

DIGGING DEEPER

Partly due to his personal upheaval and partly the constraints of the pandemic, Simon had taken to seeing an online therapist. He was still living in Chicago when he connected with Amira Khatoun through a web-based counseling service. Initially skeptical of therapy, he was surprised by how much he looked forward to their sessions, how unburdening it felt just to speak and be heard. Amira was, if nothing else, an able listener, professional, and naturally compassionate. "Simon, hello," she began on their Thursday evening Zoom call, her faint Beirut accent lending an air of elegance to the greeting. "Can you hear me?"

"I can, hi. How are things in Texas?"

"Dark and stormy," she said expressively. "And with you?"

He sighed. "Same."

Six weeks had passed since Simon joined the Hawthorne, and hardly anything was as he had expected. Far from the shining edifice of his childhood memories, the museum was a crumbling ruin on every level.

As anticipated, Rutherford had been irate to learn that Theo was in fact not a *T. rex* but one of its smaller cousins. It seemed he had been banking on the dinosaur to pull the museum out of its downward spiral and was desperate to salvage the situation at any cost.

"Maybe we say it's a baby *rex*. Yeah, that's it. Visitors would love it. It's not like the board will know the difference."

Seeming to sense Simon's contempt, Rutherford had huffed out a hard laugh. "Come on. I'm joking."

Unable to afford a new specimen, and unwilling to lower themselves to a cast replica, the Hawthorne would have to make do with what it had. Rutherford insisted the project move forward, and quickly.

"It sounds like you're under a lot of pressure," Amira said. "But that manuscript you found. That should help."

He admitted finding Mueller's research diaries had been a stroke of luck. Simon had not yet read beyond the first few entries, but Mueller *seemed* sane enough. Peculiar, perhaps—a bit old-fashioned in his prose, and unusually committed to pen and paper despite almost certainly having had access to a computer. More troubling were the evident similarities between the paleontologists—both men being physically small, Ivy League educated, hired in the role of paleontology director at a young age. He couldn't help but identify with Dr. Mueller, which would have been fine, except for the ominous scuttlebutt still scratching at the back of his mind. If it proved true that Mueller had gone wacko, what did that say about Simon? None too eager to discover more similarities between them, he was in no rush to get through the manuscript.

In any case, he had plenty else to keep him busy. Simon had spent the last several weeks completing a thorough assessment of Theo's skeleton and determining the amount of preparation work left to be completed. As he explained to Harry during their recent check-in, he would require additional staff to finish the job, two part-time preparators at the very least.

Harry had rejected the proposal out of hand. "Sorry, but there's no budget for that. You can handle it on your own, right? You've done it before?"

"Well, no, actually."

"Sorry? Think you broke up for a second. It sounded like you said—"

"No," Simon repeated. "I did."

There was silence on the line.

"Thaaaaaat's not good, Simon. When we offered you the curator job, we kinda thought you were an experienced paleontolo-whatever—"

Simon bit back a sudden surge of indignation. "I am," he said. "A paleonto*logist*. An expert in the study of prehistoric fossils, scientific research. As I'm sure you know, fossil preparation is a completely different profession, a specialized skill that people train for. At the Field, we had a whole team of preparators. Even if I knew what I was doing, it would take me at least a year to get the bones in order."

"A year. That's not too bad."

"That's just preparation. Then there's exhibit design, construction of a custom armature, installation. Altogether we could be looking at two years easily. Maybe three."

Three years. Just saying it aloud made Simon feel sick.

"Look, I wish I could help, but I don't think we can swing more staff this year. You're just gonna need to dive in headfirst. We're a nonprofit. It's all hands on deck."

Simon bridled. *Nonprofit?* What exactly did Harry know about working at a nonprofit? He had less experience in the sector than Simon. It was like Rutherford said: one had to invest to turn a profit. The institution's tax status be damned, this was not what Simon had come here for.

No, spoke a voice in his head, *you came here to find your sister. And you're not doing that, either.*

"That sounds very frustrating," Amira said, bringing him back to the session.

Simon massaged his eyes, nodded. He felt worn down, exhausted. At least he had the upcoming winter holidays to look forward to; the Hawthorne had announced that "as a holiday treat" they were giving staff the week between Christmas and New Year off, unpaid.

Amira frowned.

"May I ask, have you been sleeping?"

Simon gave a feeble laugh. "Not really."

"What's keeping you awake?"

He shook his head.

But by the look on her face, Amira knew already.

"It's the nightmares again, isn't it?"

~∽∘

The dreams that had destroyed Simon's relationship had unfortunately plagued him long before he and Kai ever met. It all started when he was in college, sharing a dorm with an intensely studious econ major who barely endured a couple of months before begging Student Housing to find someplace else for him, with a roommate who didn't wake up screaming in the middle of the night three times a week.

Rarely would Simon be able to recall the specific events of his dream, but nor could he sponge its subject from his mind. The cloaked half-human creature that pursued him in slow, lumbering steps. The long mouth of knifelike teeth dripping blood from the shadows of its hood. The meaty stench of its rattling breath as its scaly hand, ending in twelve-inch claws, dragged a sack of bones behind it. Though the creature never spoke, Simon knew innately the bones were Morgan's—and soon the burlap sack would jangle with his skeleton too.

"Forgive me," Amira said. "You had a name for it, this creature. Remind me."

The words rose, crawling and cadaverous, from the depths of his psyche in which he had attempted to bury them.

"The Bone Man."

For as long as they lived together, Kai had entreated Simon in vain to seek treatment for the night terrors. Simon insisted he couldn't afford it, that his measly student health insurance wouldn't cover it. But when he started working full time he could no longer deny that cost had very little to do with it. The real problem was that a therapist would want to go prospecting in his past, dig up secrets he had told no one but his partner. Not to mention that to seek out care was, in Simon's view, to admit that he was psychologically unwell. He had managed for nearly twenty years not to become his mother. He was not about to start now.

Then the pandemic arrived, adding pressure to the cracks already beginning to form in the relationship. Simon's dreams intensified, became more frequent. Many a night they jerked him awake, forcing a half-formed scream from his mouth, then submerged him under a wave of molten guilt so powerful he could not even get out of bed the next morning.

But the more emphatically Kai urged Simon to seek treatment, the more he dug in his heels, reminding Kai that lots of people were experiencing Covid dreams, that it was perfectly normal. When that didn't work, he claimed Kai was being selfish, unsupportive, that his refusal to accept this about Simon demonstrated a lack of unconditional love.

Wounded, Kai backed down. Then one night in April 2020, Simon had a nightmare so bad his whole body thrashed upon the mattress. Kai leapt out of bed and staggered back in bleary fear. He shouted at Simon, crying as he failed to wake him; Simon was in too deep, his senses lost down a black well of terror. As Kai attempted to grab his swinging wrists, Simon's leg kicked out and thrust Kai back. It was his shout of pain that finally, violently, yanked Simon awake. He turned on the light to find Kai on the floor, clutching his right hand, the pinky bent back at a gut-churning angle.

Kai crumpled, a low sob racking his core.

"I can't do this anymore! I can't do it!"

"I'm sorry," said Simon frantically, sliding off the bed, but Kai refused his help standing or even getting dressed. He ordered a Lyft to drive him to the hospital.

Simon stood by, impotent and afraid, as Kai pulled a coat over his shoulders one-handed. "We'll talk when I get back." Kai wasn't crying anymore. His voice had changed, a hard line.

"Kai, I'm sorry. You know I'd never—"

"I'm moving out," Kai said. "This weekend. I'm done."

The words hit with sudden and devastating impact, forcing the air from Simon's lungs.

"I'm sorry, Si. I love you. I just can't do it anymore."

"Simon? Did I cut out?"

Amira's voice brought him back to their session once again.

"Sorry. I—I'm not sure. What were you saying?"

"You said you were having nightmares of the Bone Man again. I asked when you wake, what do you feel?"

"Right," he said, though he couldn't remember having heard the question. He thought for a moment. "Guilt?"

"Guilt. Really. Why is that?"

An image of Morgan flashed across Simon's mind: laughing in the patch of soil outside their house, himself crouched protectively beside her.

"Because I should've been there. I should've saved her from him."

Amira regarded him, her expression as soft as her voice. "You must forgive yourself, Simon."

He nodded, but it was a lie. Simon would never forgive himself, not until he had completed the job Morgan had called him back to do—whatever that was. Find the truth of what happened to her? Untangle the mystery of her past like he did the skeletons in his care?

But how can I, he thought, *when they never even found her bones?*

CHAPTER FOURTEEN

FEAST FOR A SCAVENGER

Simon waited on hold for several moments before a voice came on the line. "Criminal Investigations Division." It was sonorous and male. A touch exasperated too, as if Simon's call had interrupted an activity requiring concentrated thought. "Detective Officer Lawrence Williams speaking."

"Good morning, Officer Williams. This is Simon Nealy from the Hawthorne Museum of Natural History."

"How can I help you, Mr. Nealy?" There was commotion in the background. A busy day at the precinct. Simon could hear someone speaking at Williams. "There a problem at the museum? Perhaps one of my colleagues in the Patrol Division could—"

"No. Nothing like that."

Williams waited.

"I'm not calling on the museum's behalf. Actually, I'm calling—" Simon spoke over the rising din. "I'm calling with regard to a missing persons case."

"Missing person?" He had Williams's attention now. "Who would that be?"

"The name is Morgan Jenks."

"Jenks? Let's see. Jenks."

"You might not—it's an old case. From the nineties."

The ambient noise of the precinct filled the silence. "You're talking about the little girl who disappeared from the Hawthorne?"

"You know her."

"Of course. Biggest news story this town has seen since LaDarius Turner."

Simon had not heard that name in years. Every child raised in Wrexham knew about LaDarius Turner—whether as a villain or victim depended largely on the child's ethnicity. A member of the Wrexham police force in the early nineties, Turner had been off duty and walking through the park at night when he came across an unprovoked attack of a man in a wheelchair by a homeless person who would later be diagnosed with schizophrenia. Turner tackled the perpetrator and was holding him on the ground when police arrived. Though the attacker was reported as white, a fellow police officer, mistaking Turner for the attacker, shot Turner on sight. He was pronounced dead at the hospital.

Someone was speaking to Williams again. The line went silent and Simon imagined the detective palming the speaker to get rid of them. Williams's voice returned a second later. "Sorry. What exactly is your interest in this case, Mr. Nealy?"

Simon rose and closed the office door, stretching the wired phone cord across his desk. He didn't want to be overheard, especially here.

"Morgan's my sister. Was. My half sister."

"I see."

"I was hoping I might be able to come in to the station and speak with someone." He sat. "Learn more about the investigation. I was just a kid when it happened—"

"Wish I could help. Really, I do. We're not allowing visits to the station right now. Half the force is out with Covid. Commander wants to limit exposure where we can."

"Perhaps a virtual meeting, then."

"Virtual?" The Zoom fatigue was audible in the detective's voice. "I'd prefer in-person, especially for something like this. If you could just wait until things die down—"

"Twenty-one years."

"Sorry?"

"Twenty-one years. That's how long I've been—" Simon broke off. "Sorry. That's got nothing to do with you. I just—"

"I get it." Williams sighed. "Look, how about we meet tonight? Off the record. Market Street Diner, eight o'clock."

"Thank you!" Simon said. "That would be—thank you. I'll see you then."

The restaurant was quaint and aging, the benches upholstered with cracked brown leather, walls strung with plastic-pine garland and red bows for Christmas a few days away. Simon arrived at ten to eight, and the host seated him at a booth by the window, between tables blocked off with signs reading CLOSED FOR SOCIAL DISTANCING. Chester County had been in the green phase of reopening since June, allowing indoor dining at 50 percent capacity. At this hour, the diner was nowhere near that limit.

A few minutes later a large Black man entered the restaurant. He was well dressed, a leather satchel slung over the shoulder of his Banana Republic trench. He looked around and spotted Simon, who smiled under his mask.

"Officer Williams?"

He approached, nodding. "Mr. Nealy." Williams removed his coat and flung it over the back of the seat. Simon smoothed out the wrinkles of his faded button-down self-consciously. To his relief, the detective didn't make an attempt to shake his hand. The bench made a flat noise under him as he sat.

"Thanks again for meeting me," Simon said. "Sounds like things are pretty busy at the minute."

Williams paused as he unlooped the mask from behind his ear. "You mind?"

Simon shook his head, and removed his too to be polite. "Anyway. I know it's probably pointless, rehashing a case this old—"

"Just don't want to get your hopes up, is all. After two decades with no new evidence—unless you've got something to share?"

"No. No, I don't think so. I'm just here—" Simon faltered. *Why am I here?* he thought. "I'm just here to get clarity."

Williams nodded, holding Simon's gaze. "You said you were pretty young when it happened?"

"Ten."

"Sounds about right. I was fifteen." Williams reclined against the back of the bench. "Still remember the night I found out. I was having dinner at a friend's house. Cute little white girl comes on the news, and a headline saying she disappeared at the Hawthorne. There one minute, gone the next." He sat forward again, wagged his head uneasily. "My sister Kiara was the same age. Six, right?" Simon nodded. "Went straight home. Just needed to make sure she was okay."

Simon dropped his gaze, feeling bruised. Bing Crosby's voice crooned from a speaker mounted on the wall.

"Okay if I order something?" Williams said, reaching for a menu behind the condiment caddy. "I'm starving."

"Go ahead."

Williams ordered a burger.

"Just a coffee for me," Simon told the waitress. As she left, Williams opened his satchel and removed a folder.

"I was able to pull some of your sister's case files. Can't show you everything, but I made copies of what I could."

Simon accepted the folder, his intestines knotting.

Inside was a handful of documents, starting with the missing persons report, which had been filled in by hand. Name: *Morgan Ann Jenks.* Sex: *Female.* Race. Date of birth. Height. Weight. In many of the fields the reporting officer had written *Unk.*—shorthand for *unknown,* Williams explained—and Simon wondered if his mother had even been present when it was filled in. She must have been—her lazy scrawl of a signature was present at the bottom, and yet the form was barely half complete. Social Security number: *Unk.* Last wearing: *Unk.* Eye color: *Unk.*

A hot pressure collected in Simon's chest. What kind of parent didn't know their own daughter's eye color?

Even worse, what kind of *mother*?

It was no wonder the police had never found her. How could they, when they didn't even know she had honey-green eyes and freckled cheeks, that her fingernails were brown with dirt from digging for bugs earlier that morning. That when they boarded the 73 bus around 9 a.m., she was wearing her favorite white stretch pants patterned in ladybugs, faded from too many washes. Why had Joelle been asked these questions and not Simon? Would it have made a difference if he had?

In a box farther down, labeled MISC. INFORMATION, the officer had penned a short narrative, and here at least Simon's testimony was present.

Missing person was with half brother, Simon Nealy, at Hawthorne Museum when she disappeared Wed. morning. Only parent, Joelle Viccio, claims she was busy doing community service (tbc). Nealy says Jenks would not leave hall of insects. Says he left her there around 10:45, went upstairs to hall of dinosaurs, and when he came back to get her around 11:15 she was gone. Searched the museum for approx. 1 hr on own before approaching museum staff for help.

Simon took a swig of coffee. A lump had risen in his throat at the memory of his younger self, barely holding it together as he hastened from hall to hall, searching the nooks and crannies behind every exhibit, shouting into ladies' bathrooms, dampening his rising panic with thoughts of, *She's in the next room, the next one, please be there,* please.

It softened his anger toward Joelle. How could he blame her when the truth of the matter was right in front of him, inscribed in fading policeman scratch: Morgan had been his responsibility that day.

And he had lost her.

Williams's food arrived. Simon continued to review the files as the detective ate. Following the report was his witness statement. "I can only show you yours," Williams explained through a mouthful of cheeseburger. "But we've got dozens. Looks like police interviewed just about everyone in the museum that day—staff, volunteers, visitors. One lady reported seeing a little girl leaving the Hall of Insects around 11 a.m. with a kid."

"A kid?"

"Boy. Caucasian. Brown hair."

"That sounds . . ." Simon said.

"Like you?" Williams wiped his hands on a napkin. Seeming to sense Simon's discomfort, he added, "The lady was pushing eighty. The investigators figured she must've been confused, saw you walking around with Morgan and mixed up the time."

"Right," Simon said. "That makes sense, I guess. So they didn't find anyone?"

"Whoever he was, I doubt he hung around. More likely he coaxed your sister outside and took off with her."

"Took off with her?" The closest parking area would have been a quarter mile away. Surely someone would have seen if the abductor had carried a screaming child away on foot.

"Gilpert seemed to think the perp had a vehicle waiting out front," Williams said.

"Who, sorry?"

"Glen Gilpert. Investigating officer on your sister's case. Older guy, but a decent detective from what I hear. Passed away a few years ago."

"And what kind of vehicle—"

"A van. A volunteer called in to the station later. Said they remembered seeing an unmarked white van idling in the loop. Gilpert looked into it, but no one could say why it had been there—there were no deliveries, no service calls on record. He was pretty sure the van driver helped the perp make a quick getaway."

"An accomplice."

The thought pummeled Simon. In two decades, he had scarcely considered that Morgan's abduction could have been a two-man job. It felt too grand, too orchestrated, a crime better suited to the kidnap of an heiress or a CEO's daughter. Their family could barely afford groceries, let alone ransom. Not that anyone had demanded one.

Williams dragged his fries through a smear of ketchup and explained about the search parties. "Whole community got involved. You probably remember. Combed almost a hundred acres of woodland around Hawthorne Hollow. Covered half of Chester County, far as I can tell."

Nothing had been found. Not a body. Not a scrap of clothing. Not even a strand of her reddish-brown hair.

Williams leaned back, chewing. "It was like she never existed at all." After a moment, he seemed to think better of the statement. "Sorry. Of course she did. She was your sister—"

"Death always leaves traces."

The words came low and unbidden from Simon, as if escaped from some pocket of hidden memory. He looked up when Williams spoke, brow furrowed uncomfortably.

"Come again?"

"Er, 'Death always leaves traces.' It's—just something we say in my profession."

This wasn't quite true. The words were fresh in Simon's mind, but where had he read them?

"Can I keep this?" he said, closing the folder.

"All yours." Williams signaled to the server for their check. "Sorry I couldn't get you more. Feel free to reach out with any questions. I'll answer what I can."

The check came, and Simon took it. "On me."

"Hey, thanks a lot."

Simon reached for his wallet and Williams exhaled, shook his head. "Can't imagine what it's been like for you. Missing her all these years. Kiara, she's like a piece of me. Guess you must feel the same way about Morgan."

Simon stood.

"In my field, a partial skeleton can still be considered complete," he said.

"That right?"

Simon smiled sadly as the detective squeezed out of the booth.

"I don't believe it myself."

CHAPTER FIFTEEN

CLOSE CALL

B ack at the apartment, Simon brooded over his collection of Schleich dinosaur figures—the expensive, authentically detailed kind he could never afford but always longed for as a kid—rearranging them on top of the low bookshelf in his bedroom. His mood had deteriorated since leaving the diner, his mind set upon the details of the case like a *Coelophysis* ravaging a septic carcass. Why had he gone to the police at all? What had he accomplished but to remind himself that however much he grieved Morgan's disappearance, it was his own fault that she was missing or dead?

He couldn't extricate himself from the memory of July 14. They had arrived at the museum with every intention of making the visit last all day. After handing over their tickets, they started in the Hall of Insects and Animalia. Morgan planted herself before the cases of pinned beetles and butterflies, their wings spread like petals of iridescent flowers. Simon's impatience to get upstairs was tempered by his sister's obvious delight. "Dung beetles! They eat poop!" she exclaimed. Simon circled the hall and rejoined her twenty minutes later, but still she refused to move on.

Why would she? Simon thought now. It had been her first time at the Hawthorne since she was an infant. What rush had there been but Simon's own impatience?

"Come on, we've been here *forever*. I want to see the *dinosaurs!*"

She was too deep in thrall. He couldn't dislodge her.

"Fine, then," he said eventually. "Stay here. I'll come back for you."
But he didn't. Not in time, at least.

But surely the fault wasn't his alone. He was only a kid himself. If
Morgan was anyone's responsibility, she was Joelle's—Joelle, who ought
to have been at the museum with them, instead of serving her second
misdemeanor sentence in a year, pawning her parental responsibility off
on Simon like she had practically done since the day her daughter was
born. *Watch your sister. Feed your sister. Put some clothes on your sister.* Why
should he blame himself for leaving Morgan, when their mother hadn't
been truly present for years?

Now that the thought occurred, Simon needed it reinforced at once,
in case it should sidle away. There was only one person to call. Surely
this one time would be okay. Kai could hardly blame Simon after what
he'd just been through.

He opted for a video call; he needed to see Kai's expression, make
sure he wasn't just telling Simon what he wanted to hear. As it rang,
his own face appeared on-screen, unforgivingly rendered. He looked
appalling, washed out, eyes sunken from sleeplessness. A bolt of panic
ran through him. He didn't wish to be seen like this, least of all by his
ex, and ended the call just in time.

A moment later his phone pinged with a text.

Did you try calling?

Simon unlocked it to respond, closed it again. *Better not.* He shouldn't
have called in the first place. It scared him, how potent the impulse remained all these months later.

Death always leaves traces, he thought. *Apparently even the death of a
relationship.*

Back at the diner, Simon had struggled to remember where he'd
read those words before, but as they echoed through his mind a second time, the answer came to him. Mueller's diaries. Simon crossed the
room and dug the manuscript out of the bottom shelf of his nightstand.
He had brought it home a few nights before as bedtime reading.

Settling himself on the edge of the mattress, he turned to the beginning of the next unread entry, smiling at the opening lines.

From the Research Diaries
of Dr. Albert Mueller

December 27, 1997

What a year it has been! From great blocks of
earth wrapped in paper and hardened plaster, a
dinosaur has begun to emerge like a phoenix from
the ashes of the Mesozoic.

In just a few short months since HMNH 4589,
aka Theo, arrived at the museum, my team
has made awe-inspiring strides toward his
resurrection.

Thomas Cord, my bright-eyed paleontology
specialist, has assembled a crack team of
preparators from some of the best institutions
the country over. Just enter the Edward Drinker
Cope Memorial Research Laboratory and you shall
find the place full of them, huddled around
tables, jockeying for position at the dissecting
microscope, bartering for the last bottle of
Butvar B-98. Darla Beets, our new addition from
the Smithsonian, once wisecracked that it should
be called the Can't Cope Memorial Laboratory,
and we've hardly called it anything else since!

Using an array of specialized hand tools—from
the biggest rock hammers to pin vises securing
needles half a millimeter wide—our preparators
are busy removing the matrix from Theo's fossils
with painstaking precision, every bash and
scrape calculated to shed dead earth while

preserving the integrity of the fragile fossil beneath.

It is thrilling to imagine the passage of time represented in each layer we remove—each inch of matrix the accumulated sediment of a million years, a millennium contained in a single speck of dirt. It makes one marvel at the magnitude of geological time. Much is said of our own insignificance within it, but more often I am struck by the loving devotion of our planet's note taking. The diligent if messy process by which it preserves each bygone era, as if in a diary of sediment and rock.

In death there is much that is lost, but never too little to be found.

I say, there is always hope of finding.

But I digress! Thanks to the team's good work, enough of the skeleton has now been revealed that we are learning more about the specimen by the day. Almost from the moment of discovery, we knew Theo was a theropod of moderate size, but even with the skull still encased in its field jacket we have identified him as an adult *Ceratosaurus nasicornis*. We can be certain of this due to the presence of osteoderms above the neural spines of several vertebrae, not to mention the four-fingered hand, which sets *Ceratosaurus* apart from many more-derived theropods.

Theo represents the first carnivore skeleton in the Hawthorne's collection and among the most complete—we are estimating around 60 percent. Once fully prepared, he will likely attract the

attention of researchers from around the world
and perhaps even expand our collective knowledge
about this fascinating species, of which only a
handful of specimens have yet been found.

What we know is that *Ceratosaurus* lived in
the late Jurassic between 145 and 161 million
years ago in western North America, specifically
Colorado and Wyoming. This bipedal carnivore is
typically identified by its prominent nasal horn,
but *Ceratosaurus* also had rounded horns in front
of its eyes and a row of bony osteoderms running
along its neck, tail, and back, resembling the
scutes on the back of a modern crocodilian.

A fully grown adult like Theo would have
measured around 20 feet long, 6.5 feet tall,
and weighed more than a ton, making it a light
yet formidable predator. It had a deep jaw of

curved bladelike teeth and powerful legs adapted
for running in open terrain, capable of taking
down herbivores such as *Camptosaurus*, *Othnielia*,
and even young or vulnerable stegosaurs and
sauropods.

According to the available research,
Ceratosaurus is likely to have preferred
solitude to the company of others. Nevertheless,
it faced stiff—and potentially lethal—
competition from the larger theropod genera that
shared its habitat, animals such as *Allosaurus*,
Torvosaurus, and even *Saurophaganax* (NB, many
paleontologists debate whether the latter
represents a genus unto itself or was merely an
oversized species of *Allosaurus*).

Due to its middling size, *Ceratosaurus* may
too have been threatened by large herbivores,
and this appears to have been the case with
Theo. Early assessments of the skeleton suggest
he may have died in a fight with the plate-backed
plant eater *Stegosaurus*; the exposed portion of
Theo's right femur shows a deep puncture wound
matching the shape of *Stegosaurus*'s lethal tail
spikes, which measured up to three feet long.
Given the lack of any visible abscess, it is
possible the wound had not yet healed when Theo
died.

Such is the nature of paleontology that every
discovery breeds only more questions. We know
Theo quarreled with a *Stegosaurus*, but why? At
thirty feet long and eleven thousand pounds—five
times heavier than Theo himself—a full-grown
Stegosaurus would have been an intimidating

matchup for even the bravest of his kind. I am
left wondering, what force of need or foolish
miscalculation compelled our subject to pick
this fight? Had the herbivore in question been
sick or injured, presenting as an easy kill? Had
Theo gone after a vulnerable youngster and found
itself staring down the tail end of its mother's
wrath? Or had the carnivore been so mad with
hunger, he was willing to risk it all for the
taste of blood?

A mystery lurks in the bowels of this museum.
Let us hope we solve it soon, or I fear it may
drive me, perhaps literally, to insanity!

CHAPTER SIXTEEN

THE HALL OF LOUD SHADOWS

Late one evening in the doldrums of January, Simon found himself skulking around the museum basement. He should have been home resting; he was battling a bug that, after negative PCR, rapid, and at-home tests, he was beginning to accept was probably not Covid.

Still, after being out for the winter holidays and then his illness, he was desperate to get his hands dirty in the lab. It was all he had thought about since reading Mueller's account of the spike-shaped wound in Theo's leg bone. Tragically, as he learned while inspecting the surviving bones, the femur in question had been the same one lost to water damage, so he couldn't see it for himself—but plenty more insights lay waiting in the fossils Earl was helping him prepare.

Forbidden from hiring additional staff, Simon had set out to recruit two part-time volunteers to assist with preparation. He had hoped to attract graduate students with the promise of on-the-job experience and course credit. Instead he landed Earl, a generously proportioned retiree with a ponytail, a passion for the prehistoric, and a penchant for off-color jokes. "See that one there, how it's all compacted?" he said one day while showing Simon his personal collection of coprolite (fossilized dung). "That's how you can tell the dinosaur that left it was homosexual."

Despite himself, Simon had laughed. Earl didn't have a malicious bone in his body, and having briefly worked as a preparator on Albert

Mueller's team, had a skill set Simon desperately needed. If Simon was being honest, there was quite a lot he was willing to endure in exchange for Earl's help.

Contributing twenty-five hours a week, he was working on extract-ing a segment of caudal vertebrae—the bones of Theo's tail—from a block of matrix. Mueller's team had begun but never completed the proj-ect, and it was still ongoing when Simon pulled a seat up to the table, sniffling back his cold. As he examined the half-exposed fossils under the flickering lights of the lab, he noted that Theo's tail had almost cer-tainly been shattered at some point. The bones hadn't fused back to-gether, suggesting it had happened shortly before he died.

A sudden bellow from above, like a distorted foghorn, startled Simon and jerked his gaze toward the ceiling. This was followed by the sound of glass breaking, and something heavy crashing to the floor.

Simon's first thought was of an intruder, perhaps attempting to steal collection materials, and he considered dialing 911. But what if it was something more innocent—say, an accident by a member of staff? He would look foolish having summoned the police. Officer Williams might hear about it and decide Simon was too much trouble to keep helping.

Resigned to having a look for himself, he took the stairs up to the entrance hall.

His heart was vigorously pumping as he opened the door at the top of the stairwell. It was hardly the first time he had visited the hall at night, but to linger in the darkness was a different experience altogether. For one thing, it was surprisingly humid. He was reminded of the trip to Walt Disney World he and Kai had taken a few summers before, the dense, body-melting heat like the vapor of a scalding shower. Already his shirt was sticking to his body, his glasses fogging even though he wasn't wearing a mask. His head felt light and sloshy, as if from an excess of oxy-gen in the atmosphere, like a door opened onto an alien world.

He stumbled across the hall and passed through the silver light pour-ing in through the high windows, his shadow stretched like a funhouse silhouette across the marble floor. His legs wobbled beneath him, an effect of the light-headedness. He flinched at the swirl of winged shadows above.

The pterosaurs, he reminded himself with relief. *It's only the—*

"BWHAAAAAAAGGGHH!"

The sound shook through him and made the hairs on his arms stand up—a deep, thunderous blast of animal sound, both bovine and like nothing he had encountered before. It was coming from inside the Hall of Insects and Animalia.

Simon hesitated, gripped by an icy, crawling feeling. His head swam with a vision of the past.

"*Come on,*" Morgan was saying, racing away from him. "*I wanna see the ladybugs and butterflies and—*"

He reached out for her, his hand clasping empty air.

A crashing sound drew his eyes to the entrance of the animal hall. He forced himself forward, approaching the double doors in slow inching steps.

The air was even sweatier inside, a sauna of musty and chemical stench. A zoo of preserved corpses in life-size dioramas lined the walls. The first of them was a tableau of native fauna: a black bear rearing up against its painted forest backdrop, a pack of gray wolves disemboweling a deer, a fox slinking voyeuristically in the shadows, hungry for scraps. Each stared out with the same orbs of black glass, eyes that seemed to track Simon as he circled the room.

He intended to keep to the perimeter, away from the cluster of glass cases at the center of the hall, until he noticed the glimmer of broken shards across the floor a few yards away. A heavy-bottomed wooden case lay toppled on its side.

Simon hurried over. The side of the case contained a deep gash, as if from a sharp object rammed in and dragged upward. The glass top had shattered open on impact, disgorging its inert winged specimens across the carpet, as delicate and fragile as scraps of tissue paper. Each species was assigned a number on the legend clinging to the corner of the display: *7. Blue morpho butterfly. 23. Predaceous diving beetle. 41. Iridescent snake-tailed dragonfly.*

"Why don't they move?" Morgan had said, standing on tiptoe before the case.

"They're dead," Simon had explained.

"Dead? Whyyy?"

"Everything dies. That's life."

A sound like a low snort from the back of the hall jerked Simon's head around. His eyes traced a scene from the African savanna. The dark outline of the animal posed there was so big it could only be an elephant. But there was something not right in its proportions, or at least in the parts he could see. The legs were too stocky. The body overlong. The tail not thin and dangly, but thick, muscular, sweeping away from the backside in a gentle U. Was it just Simon or did the appendage seem to be swaying?

As he peered through the darkness, a foul and unaccountable smell struck him full in the face—a deep, earthy, pestilent funk, like a cross between manure and decaying flesh.

Simon froze.

The figure had moved. Impossibly but unmistakably. Repositioned its feet with a heavy drum.

Its head, deep in shadow, appeared to tear a mouthful of artificial grass from the diorama floor.

This was no taxidermied mammal, Simon thought. No *mammal* at all. As it reared its head into the light, revealing a round bony frill riven with festering wounds, a circular gouge mark disgorging a torrent of blood, Simon knew instantly what this was. Even a child would have known. But that wasn't possible. It *simply couldn't be.*

An involuntary sound escaped his mouth. The animal swung its gigantic horned head around in apparent surprise. The floor shook beneath Simon as it wheeled its thirty-foot heft to face him, trampling the architecture of the diorama to pieces beneath its feet. A trumpeting bellow of fear—of warning—flew from its beaked mouth:

"BWAAAAAAARRGGGHH!"

The cry echoed through the hall like a ghost. Then the animal began to charge.

Simon stumbled back and sprinted toward the open doors of the hall, fueled by the soundtrack of destruction racing toward him. *CRASH! thump. CRASH! thump.* The animal's battering ram of a head was barreling through one display case after another, each impact blasting a cloud of broken glass at Simon's back. Looking behind him, he caught sight of one of the long brow horns, broken off at the base but still attached, flapping around the animal's bloodied face as it galloped.

Simon ground his muscles into a higher gear and hurtled through the wide opening, slammed the doors shut behind him, and took off toward the main exit of the museum.

But the great collision he was expecting—of head meeting wood and doors sent flying in a shower of splinters—never came.

He faltered. Though he ought to keep running, a terrible confusion held him back. The hall was as still and silent as a church. The temperature was dropping by the second.

It was as if the whole thing had never happened, the figment of a dark and disturbed imagination.

CHAPTER SEVENTEEN

THE SCIENCE OF DENIAL

Simon didn't sleep. He lay in bed, eyes to the ceiling and one hand idly stroking Phil for comfort. He could not reconcile what he had experienced with what he knew without question to be true. Non-avian dinosaurs had gone extinct sixty-six million years ago. They existed now only as fossilized bones, or replicas of bones, in museums just like the Hawthorne all over the world.

And yet he had seen it with his eyes. Had felt it. The ground shaking beneath his feet. The vibrations its trumpeting call sent through his body like breaking thunder. He had seen something in the museum. Something unexplainable.

Or had it all been in his head?

He wouldn't be the first in his family to see things they couldn't explain.

Simon remained in a state of agitated half consciousness most of the night and overslept the following morning. By the time he logged in remotely from his personal computer around ten, an email was already waiting in his inbox.

Sent: Thurs 1/7/2021 9:43 a.m.
From: Craig Rutherford
To: Senior Staff
Subject: CONFIDENTIAL: Break-in Last Night

Dear Senior Team,

At approximately 9:15 this morning, a member of custodial staff reported finding significant damage to the Hall of Insects and Animals consistent with a break-in. Although nothing appears to have been taken, numerous antique display cases have been destroyed and dozens of specimens damaged. I'm told that police are currently at the scene and they are confident this is the work of the same rogue trespasser who has been wreaking havoc on many local businesses. Similar disturbances were reported at Quick-E Liquor last month and Wrexham Record Shop in October.

If you or your teams were working at the museum last night and saw or heard anything suspicious, please come forward immediately. Your assistance is urgently needed to help us find the individual responsible.

In the meantime, this matter is to be treated as highly confidential. Direct all media inquiries to Dave Simpson. All messaging on this must go through Marketing.

Craig Rutherford
Executive Director

Never had Simon experienced so many reversals of fear and relief in the course of a single email. Initially terrified that the alleged damage bore evidence to his unthinkable encounter, he was reassured in the knowledge that it might have been something as mundane as a break-in, then disturbed again, for if that was true it meant that he *hadn't* seen a *Triceratops* in the Hall of Insects and Animalia—that in fact he was experiencing hallucinations such as he had dreaded for years.

But perhaps it was not as bad as all that. Perhaps there was a more rational explanation.

When he had seen the ceratopsian skeleton his first day of work, Simon had noticed its left brow horn was not like the right, a cast replica rather than a genuine fossil. Similarly, the dinosaur he had imagined the previous night—for already he was beginning to disavow his credibility as a witness—had sported a broken horn on the same side. An uncanny coincidence, or could Simon, haunted by the memory of abandoning Morgan for his favorite dinosaur, dreamt he'd been chased by the source of his guilt? A nightmare that had felt all too real.

It was no more ludicrous than the alternative.

But then, how had Simon gotten home? He couldn't remember leaving the museum except for in his dream. And what of the strange noises he had heard from the basement? Had he imagined them too?

Despite his conviction that none of it had been real, he nevertheless declined to go in to the museum that day.

He was not well, after all. Probably Covid.

The responsible thing to do was stay home.

CHAPTER EIGHTEEN

THE PHILANTHROPIST

A few weeks on, Simon had all but managed to put the incident in the Hall of Insects and Animalia behind him. To ensure he wasn't bothered by any more strange dreams, he had raided his bathroom cabinet and found half a bottle of nighttime cough medicine left over from his recent cold. Two ounces, maybe three, and within minutes he felt his senses being drawn down into a syrupy blackness. Not even the Bone Man could penetrate such a dense repose. He went on to pick up two more bottles at the grocery store, and another couple at the drugstore around the corner, drugging himself nightly into restful oblivion. His eventual return to the museum was reassuringly uneventful.

One morning in early February Simon was answering emails when Fran Boney, the museum's long-serving development director, burst unceremoniously into his office.

"There you are! I thought I told you to meet me upstairs at nine thirty."

Simon eyed the time in the corner of the screen. "It's only quarter past—"

"Never mind. Move your keister. I'm parked in the loop."

As Fran's orange-haired head departed, Simon sat pressing his lips together, gathering his calm.

His first impression of Fran as a brash, foulmouthed egotist had

proved to be an unfortunate understatement. Hardly a day went by
when he wasn't copied on a flurry of frantic emails to the senior staff List-
serv bearing a red high-importance flag and an all-caps subject line to the
effect of "I AM MEETING WITH AN IMPORTANT DONOR TODAY AND I NEED YOU
ALL TO KNOW ABOUT IT." She had endless feedback to share on the other
teams' outputs, insisted on being looped in on projects she had little to do
with, and delivered her updates at the weekly senior staff meeting with
the grandiosity of a royal cavalcade. The way she told it, she was working no less than eighty hours per week and single-handedly keeping the
museum afloat. To the amusement of her colleagues, she more than once
attempted to coin the phrase "in the orange" to describe an imaginary
financial state in which the museum had been about to flatline before
being rescued by her heroic fundraising efforts. All the while, she failed
to realize the finance team had coined several of their own Franisms,
including a new nickname for the fundraiser: Pennywise the Clown.

Simon didn't participate in the name-calling, but nor did he actively
discourage it. He had little sympathy for Fran and her constant demands,
one in particular, which he had been actively avoiding for months.

Despite the worsening pandemic, she had been eager to get Simon
in a room with Evilyn Mitchell almost since he arrived at the museum.
Seventy-four-year-old Evilyn was the widow of former executive director Garfield Mitchell and the Hawthorne's most generous living donor,
a fact Fran wielded like a golden sword. She seemed to think Mitchell's
philanthropy obliged the museum to grant her every request, including
to meet the new paleontology curator.

"What if one of us gives her Covid?" Simon had objected. "She could
die."

"You think I'd let that happen? We're not even in her fuckin' will yet."

But for weeks Simon had been running out of excuses. Evilyn had
received her second dose of Pfizer, and Harry was pressuring him to
bow to Fran's demands; the museum's reopening had been delayed, and
donations like Mitchell's were their only lifeline. With it being too cold
and dreary to meet outside, Simon had finally conceded to a brief, so-
cially distanced home visit.

The morning of, Fran insisted they ride together. She rolled her eyes as Simon climbed into the backseat of her alien-green Kia Soul, and hit the gas.

As they rocketed south down the 422 toward Devon, Fran refused to keep her eyes on the road, briefing Simon on the Mitchells over her shoulder as if she were delivering highly classified intel.

"Back in the seventies, Garfield Mitchell was one of the richest men in the county. Chairman and CEO of Mitchell Gemological Enterprises, one of the world's biggest suppliers of gems and minerals for the commercial jewelry trade. He ended up joinin' the museum board, and after he sold his business for eighty mill in '79, he was tapped to fill the shoes of the out-going ED—it was a bit of a revolvin' door in those days. Served for nine years—people loved him, said he was the best leader we've had—before he and Evilyn's teenage son got killed. Charles. I don't know all the de-tails, but God, I could fuckin' murder whoever did it. *Anyone* who would hurt a child—" The thought alone turned her voice to an animal growl.

"Anyway," she went on. "Garf stepped down so they could grieve properly. Took them years to sort themselves out. But don't mention it to Mrs. Mitchell. In fact, don't mention the kid at all."

Garfield would later return to the ED position, but not before he and his wife had personally contributed more than $5 million to the museum, including $3 million to name the Hall of Gems of Minerals and just over $1 million for various updates and gemological acquisi-tions. The outlier among their giving, she explained, was their substan-tial contribution to the paleontology department, which helped fund Mueller's dig at Dulzura Mesa. Simon recalled Mueller mentioning it in his diaries. In recognition of their support, the Mitchells were later granted the opportunity to name the specimen Mueller had brought back. Evilyn insisted, to the puzzlement of many, that it be called Theo.

"That was a couple of years before I started. I don't get it. They were gem-and-mineral people, and from what I hear, Garf didn't think much of Mueller."

"She must have *some* interest in paleontology," Simon said from the backseat. "You said she asked to meet me specifically."

"She did." Fran caught his eye in the rearview mirror. "Hell if I know why."

They pulled off the highway onto a two-lane road through dense forest. Devon, of the Main Line township of Easttown, met Simon's every expectation of a millionaire's suburb. A stone's throw from the country club and golf course, a parade of stone manors and white colonial houses ranged from large to embarrassingly huge, sitting back on frosted lawns of mature leafless trees beside four-car garages likely filled to capacity.

Simon was used to being trotted out to such houses by the Field's so-called "major gift officers," made to woo and entertain their deep-pocketed prospects. For him, it was a performance of restraint. He must not look too out of place. Must not stare. Must not make assumptions about the people who lived there. He must not think about how his childhood home could have fit into the smallest of their grand living rooms, or how a check with half as many zeroes as the one the museum would take away from the visit could have changed his family's life forever—even saved it.

He expected this visit would be much the same, which was perhaps part of the reason he'd been so reluctant to attend. And so he was surprised when Fran hit the brake and they turned into a gated community, not of mansions, but contemporary white (albeit luxury) condominium units.

"Welcome to Arbordeau," said the attractive male attendant as Fran stopped at the security booth. She leaned out the open window.

"We're here to see Evilyn Mitchell. Unit twenty-four."

"Gotcha." The attendant looked across at Simon and nodded. Simon returned a squirmy smile.

The traffic arm came up and Fran gunned it over the speed bump with great violence.

Mrs. Mitchell's unit was at the top of a three-story building that overlooked a manicured lawn. Fran looked back at Simon as they traversed the third-floor hallway. "D'you have to walk like that?"

"Like what?"

"Like ya got a dinosaur bone up your ass."

Simon scowled. They paused at last before Mrs. Mitchell's unit. A brown coir welcome mat read GOT SEED? Fran knocked.

"You're not afraid of birds, are ya?"

"Why—"

Before Simon could finish his question, the door swung open and a pair of flapping wings filled the doorway, attended by a grating screech. The bird was huge and indigo blue from head to tail, except for a splash of yellow around the eye and behind the beak, both of which were black and dangerously sharp.

"Oh, cut it out, Arthur," said a voice, and now Simon noticed the woman on whose shoulder the macaw was perched. She was about Simon's height and unmasked, with a short bob of gray hair. Her appearance said nothing of her purported wealth. She wore a cheap São Paulo tourist tee, too bright against her fair skin, and the scabbed-over cuts on her twig-like arms gave evidence to the sharpness of Arthur's talons. Despite the oversized sunglasses covering her eyes, Simon could tell the donor was regarding him and Fran with suspicion.

"What do you want?"

"Mrs. Mitchell, it's Fran Boney!" said Fran, transforming instantly into a person Simon had never met before. "From the Hawthorne . . . The young man on the phone said we could come and visit you today?"

"Oh, right. The development woman." Mrs. Mitchell shushed the bird, which was squawking again. "Ignore him, he's just jet-lagged. Come in."

"You sure? We can come back another time," Fran said, already following Mrs. Mitchell inside and peering around with great interest, no doubt appraising the unit's value.

Simon entered next. The condo was stiflingly hot, and already he didn't know where to look. Like the pong of bird smell seeping in through his mask, it was overwhelming in a not totally unpleasant way. Though it had to be more than two thousand square feet, it felt smaller due to the abundance of possessions crammed in everywhere, the eclectic accumulation of a lifetime of travel and limitless means. Beyond the life-size wood-carved Iroquois man that guarded the foyer, a hallway of terra-cotta walls peeked out behind a crowded exhibition of African masks, prints, paintings, cuckoo clocks, and floating shelves loaded with knickknacks. Framed photos, swaying hula girls, a wand from the Wizarding World of Harry Potter. Beside the Nepalese lion statue, a luxuriant sideboard of antique mahogany supported a small collection of well-loved books. Simon bent his head to read the spine of a clothbound volume entitled *Advanced Guide to Applied Metaphysics.*

Fran's voice carried down the hall. "*Love* what you've done with the place!"

Mrs. Mitchell's response was unintelligible but sounded bored.

Simon joined them in the large, bright parlor. The rare and exotic occupants of half a dozen cages twittered and belted from the edges of the room, adding a touch of chaos to the elegance of fine fabrics and parquet floors. Tall windows deluged the parlor with natural light and stunning views; the woods behind the complex, dappled with snow, seemed to run on for miles.

As Simon entered, Mrs. Mitchell was transferring Arthur into a flight cage and answering a question about their recent travels.

"Brazil!" Fran said. "*That* must be nice this time of year. And Arthur came with, huh? Lucky parrot."

Arthur screeched, affronted.

Mrs. Mitchell latched the cage against Fran's repartee. "It was a pilgrimage. Back to the land of Arthur's ancestors. He's been feeling disconnected from his roots."

"No kiddin'," Fran said.

"He's a hyacinth, isn't he?" Simon said. "A hyacinth macaw? Brookfield Zoo had one just like him."

As if only now registering Simon's presence, Mrs. Mitchell turned and regarded him.

"Evilyn, this is Simon—sorry, *Dr.* Simon Nealy," Fran said, as if indulging him in a ridiculous personal delusion. "Our new curator of paleontology. Don't let the baby face fool you; he's smart as a whip. Just don't offer him anything stronger than coffee, 'cause I don't think he's old enough to drink it."

"Coffee would be great, thank you, Pam," said Mrs. Mitchell.

Fran stared, momentarily lost for words. The sight of her attempting to work out whether she was "Pam" brought a smirk to Simon's lips. He dropped it as Mrs. Mitchell addressed him.

"Coffee, Dr. Nealy?"

"I—well, I mean—if you're making some."

"Right." Fran managed a smile. "No problem. Let me find your assistant. Dan, was it?"

"Quit. Moved back to Maine. With everything going on in the world he wanted to be closer to family." She didn't look at Fran as she added, "Kitchen's down the hall to the right."

"Sure. Happy to help."

As Fran left the room her eyes lingered on Simon, as if accusing him of orchestrating her dismissal in advance.

Once they were alone Mrs. Mitchell motioned to the seating area before an unlit fireplace.

"Please sit."

Simon moved to one of the matching armchairs. He was strangely endeared to find the upholstery stained and birdseed accumulated in the piping around the cushion. As he sat, Mrs. Mitchell paused to open a cage and pushed her sunglasses up into her hair.

"Come on. Come say hi."

She settled herself on the couch opposite Simon a moment later, a sun conure perched on her shoulder and a second crawling up her arm. Her eyes, now that he could see them, were arctic blue, the whites spotted with freckles, like a dirt-spattered glacier. She looked much older this way, but kinder too.

"So." She pulled a bag of millet spray from between two cushions, sending the room into a frenzy. "You're the new paleontologist."

"I am."

"How's my Theo?"

"Oh—he's good. More or less." Simon squirmed, unsure whether Fran would approve of his mentioning the damage to the skeleton, or the leadership's refusal to fund its preparation. Reaching for something positive to say, he said, "We recently brought on a second volunteer preparator. Carol—she's wonderful. Used to work at the Academy of Natural Sciences. That makes two now. I really couldn't do it without her and Earl. The caudal vertebrae are nearly finished. We've made a start on the ribs, and I've been working on the scapula myself as I have time. I've been busy interviewing potential contractors to design Theo's exhibit. Hoping to make a start on construction by the end of the year." He faltered. "You must be eager to see him finished after all this time."

"We are, yes."

Simon noted the plural with mute interest.

Inclining her head toward the birds in her lap as they nibbled the millet seed off separate sprays, Mrs. Mitchell stroked their backs with a bent finger, nurturing, motherly, focused on their nourishment. A surprising pain bled deep inside of Simon, like the opening of a wound he thought had already scarred over.

"You miss her, don't you?" Mrs. Mitchell said.

"Sorry?" Simon shifted in his seat. How had she known he was thinking of his mother?

But she hadn't meant Joelle at all.

"Your sister," she said. "That's why you came back, isn't it? Because she's been calling to you?"

Suddenly Simon's mouth felt very dry. "I—I don't—"

"You don't want to talk about her. I shouldn't have mentioned—"

"It's fine." He swallowed. "I just—how—"

"How did I know?" Her tone was airy, mundane; her gaze traced the paneling on the ceiling, or something in the atmosphere that Simon couldn't see. "I can hear her. . . . I can hear all sorts of things . . . spirits, vibrations." At last she drifted back, her eyes sparkling with gentle compassion. "She loves you. Morgan. More than anything."

Simon could barely draw breath around the lump in his throat.

"Gorgeous kitchen!" Fran returned with a tray of coffee, lowering it so Mrs. Mitchell could take a mug. "Love the barracudas on the wall. Are they real? Wasn't sure how you take it so I brought milk and sugar—"

"No," said Mrs. Mitchell after a sip. She shook her head, wincing, and pushed the mug back on the tray. "Decaf please, Pat. Didn't I say? There's some at the back of the cupboard." Mrs. Mitchell shooed her with a wave of her hand.

Fran's fists whitened on the tray. "Right." She stormed back toward the kitchen.

This time, Simon was tempted to run after her, insist he be the one to get it. He didn't want to be left alone with this woman anymore, didn't want to hear mention of Morgan, especially her spirit, which implied the deterioration of her physical body. Simon was about to excuse himself for the bathroom when Mrs. Mitchell slumped sideways, her elbow propped on the arm of the couch to support her wayward head. A tear striped her cheek.

"*Stop it,*" she was murmuring. "*Stop it!*" Gently rapping her head with a loose fist.

Simon rose. "Mrs. Mitchell, what's wrong?" She held her hand out to stop him, wagged her head, eyes shut.

"Evie, please," she mumbled.

"Evie." He sat, but remained on the edge of his seat. "Is everything okay?"

"Fine, fine . . . Just Theo nagging at me again." She exhaled, returning to herself by degrees.

"It's gotten worse these last few years," she said. "Not so bad when I travel, but here . . ."

Simon was incredulous. "Theo . . . the dinosaur?"

Evie's eyelids fluttered open in surprise. A laugh. "No. Sorry." She waved a hand. "I meant my son."

"But—" Simon broke off. Fran had told him not to mention it.

"Charles Theophilus. Theo, I called him."

Simon settled back in his seat.

"We lost him," Evie drawled. "Years ago now. He was fourteen." Again her tone was uncomfortably matter-of-fact, as if she were describing the sale of the family car. "He was at boarding school in New Hampshire. Went with some friends to the movies. A man stood up in the middle of the theater, a maniac with a gun."

Simon felt as if he'd been punched, the air vacuum-sucked from his lungs.

"I—I'm so sorry."

He almost added, *I can't imagine what that's like*, but realized it wasn't exactly true.

A reluctant smile broke Evie's sorrow. "He would have loved to meet you. Dinosaurs, paleontology, they were his passion. Just adored them. The skeletons in the Hall of Dinosaurs were more than just bones to him. They were a whole world. A world he never wanted to leave."

"And now there's going to be a skeleton named after him." Simon paused, clamping down on the emotion piping up his throat. "What a lovely way to honor him."

"Yes . . . I thought so," Evie said lightly. "But now all he does is nag, nag, nag. 'I've been waiting *years*,' he says." She gave a little laugh. "He's not wrong."

"I'm sorry it's taken so long."

Evie exhaled and regarded the conures, which had migrated to a freestanding perch by the window. She returned them to their cage.

"How many birds do you have?"

She did a mental tally. "Twenty-three, I think?"

"Quite a flock."

"We've been collecting them since Theo crossed over. He's the one who put the idea in my head. I wasn't sure at first. Now I don't know what I'd do without them."

"Fitting that Theo should be drawn to birds."

Evie resumed her seat on the couch. "Why's that?"

"Well," Simon said, "technically, birds are dinosaurs."

Evie's eyes held on him. Fresh tears dribbled down her cheeks.

Simon found himself struggling to hold back his own, a deep well of sadness pushing up inside him, threatening to overspill his well-worn barriers. A channel that ran deeper than just Evie's loss, all the way down to the ocean of his own. Their eyes joined, holding each other, and in the brackish intermingling of their grief he felt a profound connection with her. A mutual understanding of what it was to have lost suddenly, senselessly. To be set adrift in a moment of violent taking, and the deep tiredness that settled in the body in its never-ending struggle to return to solid earth.

"You will finish the skeleton, won't you?" she said.

"I promise."

She smiled appreciatively.

"Just mind the spirits, won't you? Don't want you going the same way as Mueller."

A cockatoo screeched, as if at the mention of the name. "Pardon?"

"Albert Mueller. He went loopy working on that skeleton."

"You said something about spirits."

"Yes. The spirits that haunt the museum."

Simon felt as if he had been doused with cold water. He opened his mouth, but Fran's voice cut across him as she reentered with the tray.

"Did you say 'haunt the museum'? You're not talkin' about Maurice, are ya?" She laughed.

The next time Simon looked at Evie, she was wearing her sunglasses again.

Despite her obvious apathy for the woman, Evie humored Fran for a few minutes, listening to her updates on the goings-on at the museum and even expressing interest in supporting the cost of Theo's exhibit.

Fran promised to put something together for her to look at.

Finally Evie announced, "Well, that's enough for today." They said their goodbyes and she escorted them to the door. Fran entreated her to stop by the museum soon.

"We can introduce you to Theo," Simon said.

Evie agreed. "Yes, yes, that's fine."

Simon smiled as they stepped out into the hall. "It was a pleasure meeting you, Evie." He sensed Fran's eyes on him the second he uttered the nickname.

"And you," Evie said through the narrowing gap in the door. She lowered her voice. "Say hi to Morgan if you see her." A wink, and the door slammed shut.

CHAPTER NINETEEN

VIGIL AND VIGILANCE

S imon was barely listening as Fran drove them back to the Hawthorne. After twenty minutes on the road, she hadn't yet tired of accusing him of intentionally usurping Evilyn Mitchell's attention.

"Evie," she muttered. "Been workin' her for years and *you* get the nickname treatment. God knows why. Probably put her half to sleep with your little dino facts. Good thing I was there to pull it back at the end. Old girl's primed and ready for a six-figure ask, I can smell it on her."

For a professional whose success hinged on ingratiating herself with and interpreting the motivations of the rich, it was alarming how oblivious Fran was to Evie's apathy toward her. Still, Simon didn't bother defending himself. He didn't care what he called Evie, or how much she gave, or who got to claim credit for the gift. He had more important things to think about.

I can hear all sorts of things . . . The spirits that haunt the museum.

Did Evie really think she could speak to the dead? The idea was ridiculous—and yet Simon couldn't help recalling what she had said about Morgan. Even if she knew about his sister, how could she have guessed it was she who had called him back to the museum? He thought too, uncomfortably, of the dinosaur in the Hall of Insects and Animalia. What if it hadn't been a dream? What if—

What? he thought. *The Hawthorne is haunted by the ghost of an angry Triceratops?*

He shook his head. Dinosaur ghosts. He was beginning to sound as crazy as Mueller.

Before long, the dreariness of February passed into the wet volatility of March, with stretches of blistering cold followed by spells of relative warmth that thawed the snow-covered grounds to a marsh of frigid brown puddles.

With Evie's sadness fresh in his mind, Simon couldn't stop thinking about his own bereaved mother. He hadn't seen Joelle since the night before he was pulled out of class and told that his mother wasn't well, that he was going to live with his Aunt Colleen.

The first part Simon had known already, for months. Though she'd never been all there even at the best of times, Joelle had taken a turn for the worse after Morgan disappeared. The money the community raised for their benefit afforded her mind-melting quantities of drugs and alcohol, and though they calmed the storm raging inside her head, they could not wipe it out completely. It churned behind her deadened eyes and spoke through her in intermittent gusts of droning breath even as she lay strung out on the couch.

"He lost her he did it it's his fault she's missing, left her there all alone and now she's gone, dead, his fault his fault—"

There was no bargaining with it, no escaping its excoriating influence. It wore Simon down. After a while he started to believe it himself, and feared he would be held accountable. The sight of Joelle passed out at the kitchen table became a welcome one, for if she couldn't leave the house, then she could tell no one what he had done. He was safe for a little while longer.

One month to the day after Morgan vanished, a candlelight vigil was held in her honor at Hawthorne Hollow. Simon wanted to go more than anything. All these weeks he had felt so alone in his grief, exiled to that house where nothing mattered but Joelle's sickness and the vices that held it at bay. He longed to be with people who cared about Morgan, not just themselves. He sensed too that his sister could somehow tell if he was there, and he needed her to know he hadn't forgotten her. That he hadn't stopped—would never stop—being sorry.

To his horror, Joelle was determined to go too. This terrified him. What would she be like? What might people hear her say? He couldn't risk it, and so did everything in his power to keep her home. For two days leading up to the vigil, he scoured the house collecting spare bits of her paraphernalia—loose pills of various shapes and colors, a line of white powder on the coffee table—and funneled them into a half-empty red wine bottle on her nightstand as she slept. He hoped the concoction would knock her out cold, but he had underestimated her tolerance. She rose the afternoon of the vigil, staggering, droopy-eyed, telling him it was time to head out.

It was a warm, humid August night. With the last scraps of donated money they took a cab to the hollow, and the driver parked in the museum's front loop. He seemed to take pity on Simon, helping him pull Joelle out of the car and get her on her feet.

Simon put his arm around his mother's waist to keep her from falling, and led her—Joelle stumbling, head lolling, dribbling unintelligible words down her chest—around the side of the building. At five feet tall and ninety pounds, she was just small enough for Simon to maneuver.

More than a hundred people were gathered on the lawn, holding lit candles in paper disks. Simon hadn't expected so many. He stopped with his mother at the back, in the shadow of the museum, where they were less likely to be noticed. A woman Simon didn't know was speaking at the podium. She introduced a police officer, the silver-haired man who had responded to the call that day at the Hawthorne.

As the officer spoke, Simon accepted a candle from a volunteer, a woman whose eyes kept darting to Joelle as she lit it for Simon. He looked across and saw, with horror, a rope of drool dangling from his mother's cracked lower lip, her eyes like pinwheels. The volunteer moved on without comment, but people were starting to stare, to whisper. A frizzy-haired mother started toward them, but the young girl holding her hand—presumably her daughter—pulled her back. Sweat dripped down Simon's temple. He was realizing this was a bad idea.

Then without warning, a short, sharp scream burst from Joelle's mouth. More heads snapped around and the officer stopped midsentence. They stared, Joelle's chin slumped against her chest as if she hadn't uttered a sound. Still the whispers intensified. *"Is that them? Is that the family?"*

Simon decided it was time to go, but holding a lit candle, he struggled to move her.

"Aargh! Aargh! Aargh!" Joelle screamed. This time her cries were frantic, her eyes darting up toward the building. The frightened crowd stood back.

"Stop it," Simon pleaded.

She thrust him away and staggered back from the building, unsteady on her feet. *"There!"* she screamed, pointing at a high window. *"There! It's the one! The—!"* She tripped and fell back on the grass, eliciting gasps.

The frizzy-haired woman darted forward and knelt down, attempting to hold Joelle's arms as she kicked and fought. "Ma'am, just calm down. You're all right."

"It's here," Joelle gasped. *"The one that took her—"* A radiant terror shone taut across her face. *"The one that took my baby!"*

What she saw that night, Simon had never been sure. His mother was admitted to the hospital and received a psychological evaluation. Simon overheard the doctor telling police that her hallucination was narcotic in nature, fueled by the cocktail of drugs and alcohol in her system. He also heard that arrangements were being made to place him in temporary care—a thought that both relieved and terrified him—but before anyone could retrieve him, his mother was up and staggering around, yanking an IV out of her arm and wrenching him toward the exit.

The visions, whatever they were, only got worse from then on. One evening he was doing homework in his bedroom when he heard a commotion downstairs, crashing furniture and breaking glass. Hesitantly, he entered the kitchen to find the table overturned, a chair thrown clear. His mother was scrabbling back against the counter, her hands digging a dirty plate out of the sink.

"*What's happening?*" he shouted, then ducked. *Crash!* The plate exploded against the wall behind him.

"*Stay back!*" she screamed. Her outcry was directed not at Simon but at the indentation in the wall behind him, where her invisible attacker must have stood. She reached for another dish. "*I said stay fuckin' back!*"

"*Mom, stop—*" A bowl flew past his head. *Crash!*

With a surge of adrenaline, he rushed forward to restrain her, but it was she who grabbed him, suddenly overcome with fury. "*You did this,*" she said as she shook him, her face volcanic. "*You brought it here, didn't you? From the museum! I ought to let it kill you! I ought to let it tear you up!*"

Then her eyes looked past him, a scream flew clear, and she thrust Simon forward.

He lost his footing, collided with the edge of the countertop, and collapsed onto the geometric linoleum. It spun beneath him, kaleidoscopic. His head felt hot and wet to the touch. When he pulled them away, his fingers were covered in blood.

She had pushed him. Offered him up. Sacrificed her son to the waiting jaws of whatever monster her mind had conjured up.

Simon experienced a frisson of clarity, a realization that all this time he had been holding on to something—a protective instinct, a flickering hope that eventually this period of darkness would break—and now, finally, he had let it go.

He could not—would not—protect her any longer.

In truth, he didn't have much choice in the matter. He arrived at school the next morning with a bloody welt on the back of his head, stuttering out an unconvincing story of having fallen down the stairs. His fifth-grade teacher, Ms. Sanchez, had been waiting for something like this, undeniable proof of Simon's mistreatment to accompany her stockpile of vague misgivings. A report was made, and Child Protective Services filed an order of protection that same week. With no father or grandparents in the picture, a search began for Simon's closest kin. Apparently Morgan's disappearance had hardly made a blip in the national headlines; only when she received a call from CPS did Colleen learn that her niece had been missing for weeks.

When Simon found her waiting for him in the school office a few days later, he felt a notch of resistance in his chest. He didn't want to go with her, this fat, blond smiling woman he had met only once or twice in his life. Things were fine the way they were. He could take care of himself, like he always had.

But it was not in Simon's nature to argue. The police officer escorted them back to the house so Simon could pack some belongings. They arrived to find Joelle had already gone. Fled into obscurity to avoid a third strike.

Of everything, it was this final act of cruelty that hurt Simon most. He hadn't expected a dramatic farewell. He hadn't expected her to cry and beg, having to be restrained by police as she fought to keep hold of her son. But that she went without saying goodbye, after Morgan had been ripped away from him just as suddenly, made him never want to see her again.

He promised he wouldn't.

And for twenty-one years, he had kept that promise. Colleen, naturally, had been more compassionate. She followed her sister's movements over the years, had even flown out to Pennsylvania a couple of times to help her out of tight spots. She'd given Joelle thousands, maybe tens of thousands, done everything she could, short of bringing her back to Naperville, which after all was Simon's home now—Colleen was adamant her nephew should never again suffer because of his mother's poor choices.

In any case, it was because of his aunt that Simon knew Joelle had been locked up in a state psychiatric hospital in Allentown for the past five years, ever since attacking a man living in the same supportive housing building. Simon refused to visit—until now.

Since the morning he had spent with Evie Mitchell, he could hardly stop thinking of his mother or unlatch the weight of guilt tugging downwards on his heart. For all her failures as a mother, Joelle, like Evie, had suffered one of the worst possible torments for a parent: she had lost her child. However devastating Morgan's disappearance was for him, Simon appreciated he could never fully understand what it had been like for his mother.

It was an interesting coincidence that Joelle and Evie had both started hearing voices after losing children. Perhaps the difference was Joelle had never had access to the care and counseling Evie had. Had never had the one-percenter privilege of being viewed as kooky and eccentric rather than a danger to society.

If she had, Simon thought, who knew where she would have been? Who knew what kind of mother she might have become?

CHAPTER TWENTY

VISITORS WELCOME

The Lehigh State Psychiatric Annex was a small government-run compound nestled in the foothills outside of Allentown some fifty miles north of Wrexham. The boxlike brick-and-concrete buildings gave it the look of a derelict high school crossed with a prison. Established in 1919 as an overflow facility for the later-decommissioned Allentown State Hospital, the Annex persisted in dedicated service to the state as a catch-all for patients with nowhere else to go, a junk drawer for the odds and ends of the psychiatric care system.

Simon called ahead before making the hour-long drive, half hoping he would be told not to bother. "No, vaccinations aren't required," said the woman who answered the phone. "Weekend visiting hours are ten to six, and we'll administer a health assessment when you get here." It was as if they were actively welcoming exposure to the virus, perhaps hoping to free up bed space.

It was around 10:30 a.m. when Simon parked in the lot and entered the cramped and deserted lobby strung with shamrocks and swags of green crepe paper. Except for the holiday decor, the room was gray, institutional, and smelled like a bedpan. The counter was separated from the room by a Plexiglas barrier, but the chair behind it was empty. A framed certificate on the wall bore the seal and signature of the governor. Beneath a clip art graphic of a rising sun, it read *Giving Hope and Transforming Lives for 100 Years.*

"Can I help you?" said a voice.

Simon turned. A woman with high-gloss hair and magenta scrubs took a seat behind the counter. The chair made an effortful noise beneath her.

"I'm here to visit my mother—"

"Does the doctor know you're coming?"

"I don't think so. I called ahead, but no one said—"

"Patient number?"

"I—I don't know."

"Don't worry, honey. Gonna need you to sign in and answer a questionnaire." The receptionist slid a clipboard through a gap in the Plexiglas. On the sign-in sheet Simon wrote his name, his mother's, the time of his arrival, and left the rest blank, then answered no to two questions on a slip of paper. The receptionist took the clipboard, turned it around, and lifted a phone from its cradle.

"Carl, I got a visitor for Joelle Viccio." She typed something into the computer. "Ward three.

"You can have a seat," she added to Simon.

After a few minutes, a man in scrubs entered and looked around the room. "For Joelle?" Simon stood, and the man greeted him with a smile. He was tall and had a sunny, boyish demeanor in contrast to his surroundings. "I can take you back."

They passed without event through a security checkpoint and down a long tiled hallway lined with doors. "Your mom's a lucky lady," Carl said after asking Simon about his drive and where he had traveled from. "Our patients don't get many visitors."

"Since Covid?"

"No, just in general."

Simon could understand why. An open door revealed a small dormitory containing four wan patients, one of them muttering into the wall. In another, a woman thrashed on a twin-sized bed, screaming into a pillow she held down over her face as if being smothered by an invisible attacker. A cafeteria served up a strong whiff of industrial food product that took Simon back to free school lunches.

"The common room," Carl said, pausing in an open doorway.

The dreary dayroom was glutted with patients, from hollow-eyed twentysomethings to elders in wheelchairs, all dressed in the same palette of faded blue and dingy white. Old men played chess. A girl, barely eighteen, carved violent circles into her sketch pad with a pen. Most of the others sat silently in front of the TV, reactionless to it, their expressions devoid of thought. They reminded Simon of fossils, the surviving imprints of the people they used to be, their organic material depleted and replaced over time by something inert, brittle, liable to break if not carefully handled.

At last they came to a solid-looking door marked VISITING ROOM. "Your mom *should* be in here already," Carl said, reaching for the handle. "Ah, there she is!"

He stood back and held the door open. Simon entered, his heart pounding.

The room was smaller, square, painted a cloying shade of seafoam green. A second aide was already inside, but Simon's eyes went straight to the chairs facing each other from a distance of six feet. Slouched in the chair facing Simon was a woman whom, despite her mask, he immediately recognized.

Joelle had never looked more like a plant in need of watering—weak, undernourished, crackling at the edges, closer to Evie's age than like a woman in her early fifties. Her hair, once long and dark, was as short and gray as she was. Her clavicle protruded below her neck like a root pushing out of the ground. The eyes that slanted down to the floor buzzed with inner chaos.

"How are we this morning, Joelle?" Carl said, his voice like a ringing bell. "Excited to see your son?" She barely twitched. Carl turned to Simon, indicated the chair. "You're welcome to sit. We just ask that you social distance, no physical contact. We'll be here if you need anything." He stepped back against the wall.

Simon nodded his thanks and regarded his mother anxiously. Were it not for the pressure of the aides' presence, he might have stood there much longer. He edged forward and sat. Still his mother didn't look up.

"Hello," Simon said at last, reaching for Carl's bright tenor. "M-mom? It's me. Your son, Simon. Do you remember?"

"Simon," she muttered under her breath.

"That's—that's right." He thought he'd seen something cross her eyes, a flash of recognition. "I'm sorry it's been such a long time."

"She took him. Never brought him back."

Was that resentment in her voice? Had she missed him, even? Simon didn't want tenderness from her, not now.

"That's right," he said. "I went to live with Colleen. Your sister. Because you were sick."

She snorted, dismissive.

"We lost Colleen last year. Did you know that?"

"Lost." She muttered it abstractly. He wasn't sure she understood his meaning.

"Colleen passed away. She died. Did you know?"

Her head rattled—whether an answer or a physiological reaction to the news, he wasn't sure.

"I'm sorry," Simon said. "She was very sick."

"Lost."

"Yes. It's sad."

"He lost her. Lost them both."

"W-what? No—"

"Lost Morgan, at the museum, his fault. He left her, abandoned her—"

"I didn't lose her," Simon shot back with an embarrassed glance at Carl. The aide was on high alert, ready to jump forward at a moment's notice. "She was abducted. You know that. She was taken from the museum."

"Taken because of him!" She lurched forward, and the aides rushed forth to hold her in her seat. "He left her! Left her to look at his precious bones—"

"Stop it."

"Stupid, selfish little ant! Never loved her! It's his fault, *his fault!*"

Simon's eyes prickled with tears of hate. He wanted to fly at her, scream: *She* was the one who'd abandoned them. *She* was the one who'd chosen a lifetime of addiction and depression over their care. She was worse than a bad parent. She was a *bad mother*. He couldn't think of anything lower.

As if hearing his thoughts, Joelle lunged out of her seat, arms outstretched with malignant intent. Spit arced from her lips as she strained against them. Had the aides not been there to restrain her, there was no telling what she would have done.

"You hear that?" she snapped at Simon, her rage yielding to a spasming smile. "It's them—the ones that took her."

Simon was on his feet now, retreating toward the door. Carl wrestled her back into the chair while the other aide radioed for help.

"Evil," Joelle spat under her breath. "Nasty lizards."

Simon stopped, turned to face her. "What did you say?"

"Gonna have to ask you to leave," Carl grunted cheerily, but Simon was focused on his mother.

"They've been waiting for you to come back," she shouted. "They're going to get you, going to tear you to pieces and *eat* you! They're hungry for you—they're always hungry. *Evil, nasty, terrible lizards!*"

CHAPTER TWENTY-ONE

THE ANXIOUS HOUR

He attempted to fend off the impulse, but that evening Simon's forti-
tude finally broke and he picked up the phone.

A voice at the back of his head told him it was a bad idea, but a sec-
ondary voice drowned it out, having grown progressively louder since
he left the Annex. It told him that Morgan disappeared because of him,
that he, not his mother, was to blame. It was hardly a new thought—
indeed, it was oppressively familiar—but it had to be addressed each
time it came, beaten into submission by repeated reassurance. He selected the number and the call connected; it was ringing. Kai would
help. He always knew the words to make it go away.

Suddenly Kai's face appeared on-screen and Simon experienced a
warm feeling in his stomach, softening the clanging in his mind.

"Is everything okay?" Kai said, concerned. He had always been the
worrier between them.

"Everything's fine. Er—hi. How are you?"

Kai was walking as he talked. Simon didn't recognize the background. "I'm okay."

"Are you home?"

"Simon, why are you—?" He paused, catching his tone. "What's
happened? You seem upset."

"I just wanted to hear your voice. See how you are." The lie was necessary. Kai must not sense Simon's agenda.

Kai pulled out a chair and sat. Simon spied the open-plan living room in the background, a painful peek into his ex-partner's new life. "Things are okay," he said, and sighed. "Mom tested positive and I haven't been able to see her. It's so hard not to go over there."

Simon nodded. He tried to look like he understood—he *did* understand—but the longer Kai talked the less Simon heard, the voice in his head building little by little, shouting louder and louder until all he could hear was, *It's your fault. Your fault she's dead—*

"I saw my mom today," Simon cut in.

Kai stared. "What?"

"I went to visit her at the hospital. It felt wrong not seeing her when she's so close by."

Kai shifted his phone to the other hand; Simon had his attention. "How was she?"

"She still blames me."

"I'm sure she doesn't. She's not well, right?"

These weren't the words Simon wanted to hear. The voice in his head persisted.

"She said it was my fault for leaving Morgan."

"That's awful," Kai said.

"I don't know," Simon tried. "Maybe she's right."

There was a slight edge to Kai's voice now. "Don't do that, Simon."

"Why? Maybe it is my fault. If I hadn't abandoned her, she wouldn't have been—"

"Simon, I can't do this with you right now."

The words pricked like a needle.

"Do what? I'm just telling you what happened."

"I understand you're going through a lot right now, but I didn't ask for this. I need you to respect my boundaries."

This was not the Kai Simon knew, the Kai he had fallen in love with. "I'm not allowed to call you anymore? So what, you never want to talk to me again?"

"That's not it, Si. You know I'm here for you. But not for this. Not for—"

"For what?" Simon shot back. Kai's nostrils flared.

"Look, you can't keep making these fucking self-destructive choices and then leaning on me to pick up the pieces."

"What are you—"

"I begged you for years to see a therapist and you wouldn't, and every time you had a nightmare about Morgan, I was the one holding you while you wept. I did everything for you, cooked and cleaned and took care of Phil, while you couldn't get out of bed. That's literally why we broke up, don't you remember? Our whole relationship became me comforting you, reassuring you. I couldn't take it anymore, not if you weren't going to make any effort to get better. And now you've moved back to the one place you could be sure would make it even worse. You're even spending time with the woman who tormented you about it and made you believe it was your fault. Well, I'm sorry, Simon—really, I'm so sorry for your loss—but I can't keep shouldering the emotional burden of this for you. I need to move on. And you need to see a shrink."

"I am," said Simon defensively. "I have been since September."

"Great. And what did they have to say about this?"

Simon faltered. The truth was he hadn't spoken with Amira in weeks, not since the incident in the Hall of Insects and Animalia. Deep down, he was afraid of what she might make of it.

A door opened in the background of the call; someone was coming in. "Traffic was a nightmare," said a voice. Simon glimpsed a masked Asian American man carrying bags of takeout before Kai angled the phone down toward the table.

"I'm on a call," he murmured. "Almost done."

Kai reappeared on-screen; the stranger was no longer in view but could be heard opening bags in the background. "Sorry."

Still resentful, Simon took the opportunity to shame him. "We're still in a pandemic. You shouldn't be having visitors."

"Like you didn't visit your mom today."

"That's different."

"Yeah right. Anyway, he's not a visitor. He lives here."

His expression softened at the apparent shock on Simon's face.

"Look, I have to go. Take care of yourself, okay—?"

Simon ended the call.

The momentary buzz of satisfaction faded to profound and empty sadness.

He couldn't deal with this, not after everything he'd been through that morning. He just needed something to take the edge off, something to help him sleep.

Retreating to the bedroom, he removed the cap and downed two large gulps of cough syrup straight from the bottle. The taste, once unpleasant, was a treat to him now. His nerves were already beginning to settle.

Undressed, he climbed into bed, tweaking his legs to avoid disturbing Phil, who lay curled up at the end of the mattress. It would be a few minutes before the medicine took full effect. As he waited, he grabbed Mueller's diaries out of the bottom of the nightstand and turned to where he had left off.

From the Research Diaries
of Dr. Albert Mueller

June 19, 1998

Thanks to the stalwart efforts of the team,
Theo's preparation continues at a steady clip
heading into summer—we are learning more about
this fascinating creature by the day.

You might recall from my entry of December last
year that marks were discovered on Theo's femur
suggesting a grievous injury by a *Stegosaurus*. In
light of that find, I directed the team to focus on
those bones most likely to contain further battle
scars, specifically the legs, arms, tail, and ribs.
On several of these bones we have discovered small
bite marks seemingly unrelated to the encounter.
They are curiously shaped, conical and slightly
curved, not unlike that of a modern crocodile.
Probably left by a scavenger after Theo died,
though I have yet to find one with the right dental
profile. In addition, the ribs show extensive
breakage, possibly sustained in battle or while
hunting. Given the presence of fish bone in the
surrounding matrix, we believe Theo likely met his
end along a river or floodplain, enabling a speedy
burial by marine deposits that kept his skeleton
so well preserved.

But our most exciting discovery was found in
the vertebrae—the fourth cervical vert, to be
exact, along the back of Theo's neck. Embedded

in the bone, we were delighted to find a broken-off tooth! What is more, given the size, serrated texture, and D-shaped cross section, I am quite certain it was left by a fully grown *Allosaurus*.

Surely even the most casual of dinosaur enthusiasts has heard of *Allosaurus*. At up to ten feet longer and a ton heavier than *Ceratosaurus*, this iconic apex predator of the Morrison Formation is distinguished by its disproportionately large skull, the horns above its eyes, and its ability to open its mouth extremely wide and wield its upper jaw like a meat cleaver, repeatedly hacking down into the flesh of its prey in order to bleed them into limp surrender. Needless to say, *Allosaurus* would have made easy work of Theo.

But did he? As the former director of the Harvard Museum of Comparative Zoology, Alfred

Romer, once said, "In vertebrate paleontology, increasing knowledge leads to triumphant loss of clarity." So it is with our friend Theo. From what we know so far, he seems to have welcomed an exceptional level of violence and injury throughout his life, far more than your average medium-sized theropod. Again I find myself wondering why. Was Theo simply more pugnacious or risk-taking than most of his kind, or is there more to his story than meets the eye?

As this mystery bedevils and confuses me still, a new one presents itself for examination.

Inside the block of earth in which dozens of Theo's bones were interred, one has been found that does not fit with the rest. It is certainly dinosaurian, likely a fragment of tibia or fibula, but at three inches in length it is far too small to have been Theo's. While it is not uncommon for multiple species to be found together in the same bone bed, it is curious that Theo's skeleton is so well preserved when only a single fragment of the smaller animal has survived. I sense this fossil too is harboring secrets.

If only it would tell me its story, I could begin to build a picture of what happened that day in the Late Jurassic, when Theo's brutal life came to an abrupt and permanent end.

I feel duty bound to uncover the truth. You could say I am not unlike a gumshoe in a pulp fiction novel, a detective on the edge of a grim discovery. My investigative instincts have led me here and whisper that I am close, one revelation from unraveling the bloodiest of murders.

CHAPTER TWENTY-TWO

THUNDERSTRUCK

As he rode the elevator up, enrollment forms in hand, Simon regretted not having reviewed the benefits package before accepting the job. Only now that he'd surpassed his hundredth day of employment was he eligible to pay obscenely for a high-deductible health plan and barely there dental insurance. During his virtual benefits meeting with Mercedes, the HR manager, who worked from home four days a week, he had learned that the Hawthorne had discontinued its pension program in the early days of Covid, but was "excited" to offer in its place a dollar-for-dollar match on retirement contributions up to five hundred dollars a year.

"Oh, good," Simon joked. "As long as I don't live more than a few months post retirement, I should have nothing to worry about."

Mercedes didn't return his smile.

"Well, we are a nonprofit, Dr. Nealy."

"Of course," he said. "I know that."

"After being closed almost a year, I think it's wonderful the museum is offering anything."

"Right. Sure. I was just being facetious."

Still, he couldn't help thinking about all the things the museum *was* spending money on: Theo's seven-figure exhibit, for example, and eighty thousand dollars a year for a museum operations consultant to, as Harry put it, "make sure I don't burn the place down."

The elevator doors gnashed open onto a dark and deserted third floor. Not bothering with the lights, Simon made his way by the sleepy dregs of twilight dribbling in through the windows and left his forms on Mercedes's desk. On his way back he stuck his head in the mailroom and found a letter in his box.

His mood soured as he withdrew it. There was a blank space where the return address should have been. Presumably another joke. He slid a finger under the back flap and tore it open, guessing correctly it would contain a message on old Hawthorne letterhead, again formed of cut-out scraps of newsprint.

> YOUR SISTERS boNES WERE a
> DREAM LILY WHITE
> BROKE aS EaSY aS
> BUTTERFLY WINGS
> WILL YOURS?

The words drove a spear of cold shock through Simon's chest. He read them again, to be sure he got them right.

Your sister's bones were a dream. But Morgan's skeleton had never been found. If the author had knowledge of her bones, that had to mean—

No. It was a joke, a sick joke. The work of a vile prankster, who derived pleasure from mocking the death of a child.

Disappearance, Simon corrected himself. *The* disappearance *of a child.*

But what about the other part? *Broke as easy as butterfly wings.* A coincidence, or a knowing reference to her obsession with insects? Whoever sent this had known her—and, somehow, that Simon was her brother.

He looked for a postmark, finding not even a stamp. The letter had been hand delivered, no telling when. For all he knew, whoever left it could still be in the building.

At this realization, Simon's heartbeat quickened to a frantic stutter, like the footsteps of a person starting to fear they were being followed. His gaze swept the corridor. It was almost completely dark now, the shadows impenetrable.

Through the grimy mullioned window he peered down onto the grounds. The lawns were uncut and choked with weeds, grown fat on two weeks of near-constant rain. Beneath the window a fox skulked around a rabbit hole, dipping its nose inside for an exploratory sniff. Otherwise the lawn was empty.

No—a man. He was standing on the grounds, staring up at the museum.

Without thinking, Simon retreated from the window and hurried down the hall. He burst through the emergency exit and his feet tumbled down the stairs.

Thoughts streaked across his mind like flashes in the dark. *It's him. The man who left the letter. But who?* Simon needed to confront him. Needed to know who he was and why he had written it. Needed to know it was all a lie.

He exploded into the entrance hall, the door slamming back against the wall; the echo shot up toward the vaulted ceiling like a flock of startled *Dimorphodon*. He strode toward the entrance doors and stopped.

Fog bloomed across the lenses of his glasses. He could barely see. The room was swelteringly hot, the air thick as primordial ooze.

Screeeeeap—THUMP.

Simon turned slowly toward the sound, tucking his folded glasses into his pocket. His vision was poor in the dark, like peering through a film of black mist. Still he could make out a tall shape, bipedal, but not like a person. *Nothing* like a person.

Simon's head wheeled and sloshed, dizzied by the overoxygenated air. He stepped back as the animal emerged from the shadows— or rather, limped. It seemed to drag an appendage behind it, its sharp claws scraping the marble floor with every step. *Screeeeap*—THUMP. *Screeeeap*—THUMP. A meaty, rotten stench permeated the air as it advanced. Simon felt its growl in his abdomen, a vicious rumble. The outline of its body drew back like a coiled spring, preparing to lunge when—

BOOM.

The floor quaked beneath Simon's feet, startling the creature. It cried out and sprinted away into the darkness.

BOOM.

Simon stumbled, destabilized, and wheeled around. The shock of what he saw knocked him literally off his feet. He fell back on the floor, mouth agape as his eyes traveled up, up a moving wall of wan scaly skin soaring into the darkness, twenty, thirty feet high.

BOOM.

Blood crusted down the elephantine body in a blackish-red sheet, a festering diagonal slash exposing a gargantuan rib cage.

BOOM.

The animal seemed to take no notice of Simon as it plodded across the hall, shaking the ground with every step of its round, clawed feet.

With a final *BOOM*, the *Brontosaurus* could go no further. It raised its long-necked head toward the heavens and loosed a wail like a dirge of tubas—a ragged, plaintive cry that echoed through the hall and across the hollow, as Simon burst through the doors of the museum and fled.

CHAPTER TWENTY-THREE

SPEAK OF THE DEVILS

The next morning Simon called Officer Williams and informed him of the threatening letter he'd found in his mailbox. "'Broke as easy as butterfly wings,'" Williams repeated. "That's fucked up." He asked if Simon wanted to file a report.

"You think I should?"

"Up to you. Either way, I wouldn't mind taking a look at that letter."

"I'll drop it by the station."

"You do that. And keep your eyes open, Mr. Nealy. You see anything weird, you let me know."

Momentarily forgetting the stranger he'd spotted out in the hollow the previous night, Simon agreed to be in touch if anything else came up.

He ended the call and got up to shower. It took a few minutes for the water to warm. Gradually steam filled the bathroom, but he remained in place, lost in the swelter of the entrance hall. It had been the purpose of the call to put off addressing what was really bothering him, and now he had no distraction.

He'd seen something the previous night, and this time he couldn't write it off as a dream. He had seen it with his own eyes, felt the thunder of its footfalls through every inch of his body. The living incarnation of a long-dead animal. Not just any animal, but the *Brontosaurus* on display in the Hall of Dinosaurs. He'd known it the moment he laid eyes on it, the exposed rib cage scored with the same marks as the mounted skeleton, as if its spirit, like that of the *Triceratops*, had been reanimated in the same form in which it had died.

So Simon *was* seeing things.

Just like his mother.

No doubt this was how it started. Perhaps one day he would end up just like her, withering to dust in a state psychiatric facility, warning anyone who would listen about the "terrible lizards" that haunted the Hawthorne.

Simon thought back to the night of the candlelight vigil, when his mother claimed to have spotted a monster in the windows of the museum. Was it a coincidence? Simon had assumed, like everyone else, she was hallucinating from the drugs running rampant through her system. But what if the doctors were wrong? Could it be that she'd seen something that night no one else had? Was it possible the "terrible lizards" that still plagued her grief-addled mind were actually the spirits of prehistoric animals she simply lacked the vocabulary to name?

Hope burgeoned in Simon's chest—but of a strange, disturbed kind. If he wasn't the only person who saw the spirits, they couldn't be a figment of his imagination; he was not going crazy. Yet how could he even entertain the thought? *Dinosaur spirits loose in the Hawthorne?* It was too silly, too unbelievable, too at odds with everything he knew scientifically to be true. And hardly a comforting notion if it was.

As he worked from home the rest of the week, eager to keep his distance from the museum, Simon thought often of Evie and the spirits she claimed resided under the Hawthorne's crumbling roof. He was tempted to pay her a return visit, but he could only imagine how Fran would react if she learned they'd spoken without her, especially about something as unlikely to inspire philanthropic support as the museum's potential ghost infestation.

He decided the specters were enough to be getting on with; he didn't need an evil clown chasing after him too.

Simon was obliged to return to the museum sooner than he'd hoped in order to help Earl move Theo's skull block out of Collection Storage and into the lab. The bones were only partially exposed, one side of the skull and jaw pushing out of the matrix. It weighed more than a hundred pounds and required both of them and Maurice to get it safely onto the dolly, into the lab, and up on the worktable for preparation.

"How long do you think it'll take you?" Simon said, panting.

Earl surveyed the specimen like a mechanic working up a quote. "It's a pretty big job. Matrix is soft, but there's a good amount of damage along the maxilla. I'll have to take it slow. Maybe two months?"

A rumble echoed down the corridor; Simon's head snapped around.

"Something the matter?" Earl said. He appeared not to have registered the sound himself, but a strange look had come over Maurice.

"I'll let you two get back to work," the custodian said. "Gimme a holler if you need me." He disappeared into the hallway with his dolly. Simon gazed after him.

A moment later he found Maurice on the other side of the basement, wrestling the dolly back into a storage closet.

"Hey, dino boy. Need something?"

"I have a question for you," Simon said.

"Maybe I got an answer."

"It's just, I've been thinking about something you mentioned my first day on the job."

Maurice nodded, smirking, like he'd been waiting for this. "You hear something in the dark, don't go looking for it."

"That's right." Simon noticed a spare set of keys, identical to Maurice's, dangling from a nail in the wall. "I just—"

"You hear a lot of things around this old place. Some of us do, anyway."

"Some?"

Maurice backed up into the corridor and closed the door behind him. "You gotta be a special kind. Gifted, I mean. What I can tell, God only chooses a few in a hundred."

Simon felt uneasy. "And what do you hear, Maurice?"

"You gonna make me say it? Make me look like a loon and get

my Black ass thrown out on the street? Hell, maybe I should. Nice government-paid vacation for Maurice."

"So you've seen them too. The—" There was no point being coy about it, Simon thought. "The ghosts."

"Now, I don't believe in no ghosts. Once you're gone, you're gone. I trust the Bible on that. This place?" Maurice's red-rimmed eyes traced the rusted pipes along the low ceiling. "This place has got demons."

Simon let out an involuntary chortle.

"Go on. Yuck it up. But don't say I didn't warn you." Maurice stepped past him, shaking his head.

"Wait, sorry. I just wasn't expecting—demons, really."

Is it any more far-fetched than prehistoric spirits?

"That's what I believe," Maurice said. "Ever since—ah, ain't worth losing my job over. This place don't like being talked about, I tell you that."

"Please," Simon said.

Maurice hesitated, a conflict brewing on his face.

"Well, if you won't say nothing."

"You have my word."

He sighed. "We better do this in your office."

Simon agreed. A moment later they settled themselves on either side of his desk. Maurice sat slouched forward in the chair, forearms resting on his thighs.

"Aright. Story goes, a few fellas died here back in ninety-seven, maybe ninety-eight. Up in the dino hall, as a matter of fact."

"I've never heard that."

"It wasn't in the papers. It was all hushed up. My cousin Cordell was here when it happened. He was a good dude, Cordell, but he got caught up in some bad shit. Made friends with the wrong white dudes. Thought he was joining a social club—next thing he knows, he rolling with a bunch of occultists. You know, devil worshippers." Maurice sat back, knees spread. "They were into some sick shit. Demonic rites, animal sacrifice. Apparently they were trying to raise a demon."

"Goodness," Simon said.

"No luck. Decided to branch out, try someplace new. They had this book of spells that told 'em the best places was churches, cemeteries, places full of death. Well, Cordell, he was a custodian here back then. Told his boys they ought to try the museum, and one night they did. Cordell told me you wouldn't recognize the hall of dinos that night— dozen dudes in robes, candles burning a circle around one of them five-point stars on the floor."

"A pentagram."

"That's the one. Anyway, they start the rituals. Chanting spells, cutting the heads off chickens. Then the candles blow out. Ground starts shaking underneath 'em, like an earthquake or something. Like they ain't raised one demon but a whole motherfucking stampede. Apparently they did the ritual wrong—demons came up angry and tore their asses up. They took off running, but they were too slow. Of eight that went in, only Cordell made it out in one piece. Stepped over his friend with a hole in his chest the size of a coffee can. Another one looked like he'd been smooching a wrecking ball. Hawthorne was closed for a week, the longest it ever was before Covid. They couldn't stop finding parts of 'em around the museum."

A hole in his chest the size of a coffee can. It sounded like a wound from a *Triceratops*'s brow horn. And at the words *smooching a wrecking ball,* Simon couldn't help but think of the *Pachycephalosaurus* skull on display in the Hall of Dinosaurs, with its ten-inch-thick skull that some speculated had been used for bone-crushing headbutting.

"But did he *see* any of these—these demons?" Simon said.

"Just one of 'em. Big motherfucker. Stuck to the shadows. All Cordell saw was its eyes. Said they were pink as gumballs. Nasty though. Evil. Eyes that want to rip your soul out of your throat. Cordell was half convinced it was Satan himself."

If the "demons" were prehistoric spirits like Simon suspected they were, then this one sounded like a theropod. *The limping animal from the entrance hall?* He hadn't noticed its eyes.

"Maurice, would it be possible to speak to Cordell? Would you connect us?"

"He's dead. Been dead fifteen years. But don't worry, he found Jesus in the end. Baptized in the church and Christ whispered all kinds of love and mercy in his ear. He was a good dude, Cordell, just got mixed up in the wrong thing. Well, that's all I got." Maurice rose from his seat.

"Just one more question," Simon said. "A personal one, if you don't mind."

"Ain't got nothing to hide." Maurice sat back down.

"It's just, if you believe the museum holds demonic spirits, then why—"

"Why work here?" Maurice shrugged. "Needed a job. Cordell said it was aright, as long you leave before dark."

"But you've been here, what, seventeen years? You could work anywhere. And yet you stay."

Perhaps a similar question could be asked of Simon. Joining the Hawthorne had brought him nothing but frustration, painful memories, and now visions he couldn't explain, and yet he was more committed than ever.

"The way I see it," Maurice said, "God blessed me with a gift and put me here to use it. Just because I don't know how yet, doesn't mean I shouldn't try."

For a person who didn't consider himself spiritual in the least, Simon was surprised to find he understood exactly.

CHAPTER TWENTY-FOUR

THE NESTING GROUNDS

It was a dull cold morning. A harsh wind nipped at Simon's unmasked face as the sun, lethargic behind its blanket of pewter cloud, cast a drab light over the street.

Other than the sidewalk, cracked and uneven like a tectonic disaster, Simon barely recognized it as the block where he had grown up. These days Granton Avenue was almost indistinguishable from the dozen other handsome, blandly aspirational streets leading away from the trendy drag of 4th Street and downtown. Once a mishmash of tumbledown textures and faded color, the townhouses before him were an unbroken line of gray and ivory modernity, new windows and doors outlined in crisp white. Their quaint covered porches, furnished with cozy love seats and benches, invited cups of predawn coffee before a hectic commute into the city. A dog barked in one of the windows, wrenching from the darkness of Simon's mind a memory of a brown pit bull named Bruiser that once had lived in the house at the end of the block.

Amira had all but insisted on Simon's coming here. During his first session in nearly two months, he'd found himself overcome with pent-up stress and anxiety and divulged that he'd been experiencing visions of prehistoric ghosts, heavily implying, however, that the apparitions had appeared only in his dreams.

Amira was little reassured, theorizing that these newest "nightmares" were yet another manifestation of Simon's guilt.

"I think it may be time to stop hiding," she said. "To confront your past head-on."

Had he not done that already? he asked.

"You work at the museum where your sister disappeared, that's true. But where she really went missing was from your home. If you feel ready, it might help you to go back and visit your old house. Allow yourself to feel the loss of her, and process those feelings."

It was not until he was there that Simon understood what she meant. As he regarded the planter in front of the house—now an exuberance of green against the dreary light of early April—he felt his sister's loss from the street, from the world, more keenly than he had in years.

He shouldn't have come here. He couldn't do this. He wasn't ready.

He turned to leave, and as he started toward his car, noticed a pudgy man unloading groceries from a hatchback across the street. The trunk door slammed shut and Simon walked on, pausing only as he heard a crash and a curse.

Half concealed behind the vehicle, the man was laid out flat on the sidewalk, his groceries sprawled before him. Horrified, Simon hurried across the street, stopping to grab a cantaloupe that had rolled out across the pavement.

"You okay?" he said, breaking his usual adherence to social distancing to approach the fallen man. He looked about sixty with overgrown silver hair, his clothes—now torn—colorful and Bohemian. He stirred, a pale bloodied chin visible beneath his home-sewn mask.

"Fine, fine. Just careless," the man said. "Third time I've done that this year."

He had a faint accent Simon couldn't place. British? Kiwi? Regional variations were a weakness of his.

"Here, let's get you up."

The man took Simon's hand, almost pulling him to the ground as he clambered to his feet. He glanced at Simon, instantly blushed, then did a double take, a question swirling in the grayish-blue irises that hadn't been there a moment before.

"Let me help you with these," Simon said, hastily bending down to repack the man's bags—anything to stop him figuring out how he knew Simon's face.

"What's your name, son?"

Pausing, Simon reached for the first one that came to him. "Er—Theo."

"Can't thank you enough, Theo. Truly."

Simon swatted away his guilt like a gnat. The lie was necessary; he couldn't bear having to talk about Morgan, especially here.

The man introduced himself. Simon questioned whether he had heard the name correctly.

"Santa?"

The man laughed. "Santa, no. Though I look more like him every day." He massaged his stubble through his mask good-humoredly. "Zander. A strange name, I know."

"Not at all."

Zander's eyes twinkled, lingering a moment too long on Simon's body before he averted them, blushing.

"Er—just up here."

Surprised and a tad amused, Simon followed Zander with the bags toward a brick townhouse. It had no porch, just a few steps up to the door, and stood out in comparison to the rest of the street for being slightly shabby and dated in its ornamentation. A chintzy metal plant stand beside the steps spilled over with flowerpots in every color. The ceramic wind chimes, shaped like graduated toadstools, tested the boundaries of what one could fairly call kitsch. Zander unlocked the door and limped inside.

"Come in, please."

Simon crossed the threshold and was hit with the strange earthy smell of the room. It conjured a vision of fieldwork, a part of the job Simon secretly disliked. Truth be told, he fancied himself more of an indoor paleontologist. "I'll grab those," Zander said, taking the bags out of Simon's hands and disappearing into the kitchen.

Simon surveyed his surroundings. The main living space was cluttered, small, and had been repurposed as a home ceramics studio. A motorized pottery wheel sat on a low three-legged table, positioned under the window to make use of the natural light. The floorboards were splattered with clay and dried slip, and, against the far wall, a flimsy shelving unit displayed creations in various forms of readiness—a quartet of freshly thrown bowls ready for the kiln, an unglazed dinnerware set in need of decoration. Simon observed a marbled vase with ornate stamped detail that wouldn't have looked out of place in the salesroom of a luxury home furnishings boutique.

"You're a potter," he said as Zander returned to the room.

"Been at it nearly twenty-five years. Got two booths at the Chadds Ford Antiques Mall. Stop by if you're ever passing through. Take ten percent off any item."

"That's very kind," Simon said.

"Please, would you stay for a cup of tea? It's the least I can do to thank you."

Simon sensed, from the redness of Zander's furry ears, that there might be more than gratitude behind the request. He was sympathetic. The potter clearly lived alone, nothing but his ceramics for company. Evie had her birds. No doubt for Simon it would one day be bones.

Were it not for the pandemic he might have taken pity on the man.

"Maybe another time."

"Yes. When things calm down. Right you are. I'll give you my card to take with you."

Zander patted his pockets, disappeared inside the kitchen again, and returned with a watercolor business card, tacky and outdated. *Zander Steyn—Ceramic Artist*. It contained his street address, phone, and fax.

"Call me anytime. And thank you, Theo, again." Zander touched Simon's arm, then withdrew his hand self-consciously. "Thank you."

From the Research Diaries
of Dr. Albert Mueller

July 10, 1999

I had intended these diaries to pertain only to
Theo's preparation and study—which continues
apace; more on that later—but I feel I must
unburden myself of this revelation or I shall
burst. I have made a discovery of unparalleled
importance with regard to the paleontological
history of the Appalachian region and southeast
Pennsylvania in specific. I shall of course
publish my findings in due course, but this entry
shall stand as a testament to this momentous,
even historic, occasion.

It all started in the fall of '96, when a
student from the University of Pennsylvania,
Isabela Velasco, contacted the Hawthorne
regarding her doctoral research. Typically
researchers visit the museum to study specimens
from our collection, but this young woman had
no interest in bones, gems, or archaeological
artifacts. A PhD candidate in environmental
science, she was investigating metal uptake in
local plant life, namely dandelions, and their
proclivity for absorbing soil-borne elements
such as nickel and copper through their root
systems. Her research required a large number
of dandelions from a common ecosystem, and our
facilities team was more than happy for her

assistance with the weeding. Ms. Velasco was
on-site for less than two hours. We did not
expect to hear from her again.

Then last month my boss, Dr. Herman Jacobs,
received an unexpected letter from the
researcher. In addition to sharing a completed
copy of her thesis, in which the Hawthorne was
gratefully acknowledged, the now Dr. Velasco
wished to share one of her more interesting
findings: that the dandelions collected on
museum grounds were found to contain extremely
high concentrations of the metal iridium, an
element not present in samples taken from the
surrounding area.

To Herman, a former biochemist, it was an
interesting and somewhat puzzling discovery; to
a paleontologist like myself, it was potentially
groundbreaking.

A hard silver-white metal from the platinum
group, iridium is exceedingly rare on Earth
but famously common in extraterrestrial rock;
anomalously high concentrations of it in
sediment are often interpreted as evidence of
a past meteoritic strike. The most extensive
and well-known example is what paleontologists
call the Cretaceous-Tertiary boundary. The K-T
boundary was formed 66 million years ago when a
6-mile-wide bolide struck Earth with the force
of more than 4.5 billion atomic bombs, punching
a crater the size of a small country into the
Yucatán Peninsula. The collision sent a blast
of seismic energy and superheated air rocketing
across the planet, resulting in devastating

earthquakes, apocalyptic wildfires, and mile-high tsunamis. The energy of the impact vaporized not only enormous quantities of underlying rock but the bolide itself, hurling the ejecta up into the atmosphere in a vast plume of dust and debris, which, in the hours and days after the impact, began to fall back to Earth.

Evidence of this can be found in rock deposits around the world, in the form of a thin, often blackish sedimentary layer marking the boundary between the end of the Cretaceous Period—the last reign of the dinosaurs—and the beginning of the Tertiary Period. Among the most distinctive features of the K-T boundary is its high concentration of the metal iridium.

It should be clear now why Dr. Velasco's letter set my mind spinning. Her research proves that the earth under the Hawthorne is impregnated with the metal most commonly associated with the dinosaur-killing asteroid. But why? How did it get there? What does its presence tell us about the geological history of our region?

For weeks, these questions spun through my head like a raging tornado. I could think of little else. Sleep became a struggle, productive work a pipe dream. My mind kept returning to Dr. Velasco's thesis, with a vague feeling that its findings concealed a potentially radical secret.

The feeling, I must admit, was strongest when I handled Theo's remains. I sensed somewhere deep within me that he, the dinosaur himself, was urging me down the path of investigation. If that sounds crazy, so be it—it is true! Somehow

he had gotten inside my head, tinkered with the
machinery of my brain and rerouted my priorities
toward this purpose. Why, I could not say. All I
knew was that there was something strange about
the land on which the museum lay. Something I
could not explain, but that Theo desperately
needed me to know.

Then tonight it came to me all at once.

Allow me to set the scene: it was night and
I was leaving work, trekking along the driveway
toward my vehicle as I have thousands of times
before. My mind churned with thoughts of flaming
bolides—specifically, how they often break apart
as they enter Earth's atmosphere, spinning
off smaller meteorites that might crash-land
thousands of miles from the primary site of
impact. As I scaled the shallow incline that
marks the border between Hawthorne Hollow and
the woodland that encircles it, I was so lost in
thought I tripped and fell forward.

I got back to my feet, but as I considered
the slope of the terrain beneath me I paused.

Turning, I cast my gaze over the museum's
acreage. In my head, the hollow had always been
vaguely round. But tonight I observed that,
no, it was *perfectly* round—a wide, circular
indentation in the earth with the museum at its
center, the relatively steep perimeter forming a
raised lip around the grounds.

Like an asteroid from the depths of space,
the realization hit me with a life-altering
impact: Hawthorne Hollow was not a hollow at
all. *It was a crater.*

Like the 110-mile-wide cavity in the Yucatán
discovered by geophysicists Antonio Camargo
and Glen Penfield in 1978—what we now call the
Chicxulub Crater—Hawthorne Hollow stands as
a testament to a prehistoric impact from an
extraterrestrial object, perhaps even a fragment
broken off from the dinosaur-killing bolide as
it screamed through the atmosphere at twelve
miles per second. The impact felt in Cretaceous
Pennsylvania would have been minuscule in
comparison—the object likely no larger than
thirty feet wide—yet with devastating local
consequences, immediately incinerating any
animal within a mile of the blast and sparking
wildfires that would have stretched for many
more, killing thousands.

The implications of this discovery are so
many and far-reaching that I can hardly collect
myself to list them all. Suffice it to say, I may
find my life is about to change (if you'll pardon
the pun) meteorically.

But no matter what plaudits are heaped upon
me or lucrative opportunities laid at my feet,
I shall not abandon my current post until Theo
has been mounted and installed in his new
home. After all, it is thanks partly to his
encouragement that I made the finding at all.

P.S. I dedicate this discovery to my one
and only, the find of my life, the apocalyptic
wildfire of my heart. Oceans could not fill the
impact you have left on my world.

CHAPTER TWENTY-FIVE

THE FALLOUT

Anger obliterated the effects of Simon's sleep aid; as he sat up in bed, it was all he could do not to crush the manuscript into a ball and hurl it across the room.

What absolute nonsense! Not only did Simon feel betrayed, but he was frustrated with himself for having trusted Mueller in the first place. For believing his predecessor had been anything more than the nutcase his superiors had warned him about.

How could a trained paleontologist believe such absurdity? It defied scientific logic on a multitude of levels, most of them geologic. Assuming the museum grounds were loaded with iridium, there was almost no way a Cretaceous bolide could've caused it. Such evidence could only be found in Cretaceous rock, and while many western states such as Montana and Wyoming had been accumulating sediment during that time, much of the American Northeast had been eroding. As a result there was barely any Cretaceous rock left in twenty-first-century Pennsylvania. Most of the state's surviving geological formations predated the dinosaurs by millions of years, which is why no dinosaur bones had ever been found in the state. Any evidence of a Late Cretaceous impact would have long since been wiped clean by the time Isabela Velasco arrived to collect her dandelion specimens.

As for the elevated concentrations of iridium in the soil, how could

Mueller be sure more recent events weren't to blame? Perhaps one of the old factories outside of town had used the metal in their manufacturing process and polluted the region with iridium-rich waste. But then why would the metal be contained only to the grounds surrounding the museum?

Whatever the reason, Mueller's theory was clearly nothing but a wild fantasy, perhaps even early evidence of his mental decline. The way he described Theo's having "gotten inside" his head certainly seemed to indicate a parting with reality. And judging by the following entries, which Simon quickly skimmed before giving up entirely, Mueller's contemporaries were of the same mind as Simon.

To Mueller's apparent indignation, not a single scientific journal had agreed to publish his findings. Some even sent back snide or mocking correspondence, and he learned from a friend that at least one colleague had written the Society of Vertebrate Paleontology requesting Mueller's membership be terminated on the grounds of "abject incompetence [that] threatens to undermine our entire profession." Before long, even those who hadn't known Mueller's name before seemed to have heard about his bizarre theory. Even his oldest friends, all but one Dr. Leonora Brito, had begun to distance themselves from him.

In a matter of months he had become the laughingstock of the international paleontology community, and now, Simon despaired, nothing else Mueller had written could be trusted. Even as bedtime reading his diaries were useless. He couldn't risk being bamboozled again. Better to get them out of his reach.

The next time he was on-site, Simon called Harry to obtain executive approval, marched down to the clammy bowels of the Cave, and, with a feeling of mingled retribution and regret, reinterred the manuscript to its metallic tomb.

CHAPTER TWENTY-SIX

THE PHANTOM REFRAIN

While serviceable in parts of the upper floors, the museum Wi-Fi haunted the basement like a timid ghost. It drifted in and out of Simon's office without warning, sometimes startlingly so. One minute he would be working away in silence, and the next, music would blare from some long-forgotten browser window, his inbox ringing like a wind chime in a storm as three dozen messages populated at once.

That morning the signal was especially fickle, dropping him from the weekly senior staff meeting just as he was about to give his update. As usual, Simon was the only attendee not Zooming in from home.

By the time he reentered the meeting, they had moved on to Fran. She rattled through her updates looking like she had just awoken—clothes wrinkled, thick reading glasses, no makeup. A bed of rumpled yellow linens lay behind her like a slab of scrambled egg.

"The Throw Us a Bone campaign has officially launched. Direct mail appeal should hit mailboxes Friday, and I've got River workin' on a digital follow-up. Evilyn Mitchell's scheduled to come in next week to meet Theo, and we're gonna need the place spotless—lookin' at you, Facilities. Don't want a repeat of the Doyle visit; I'm workin' the old bird for a gift that could pay your salaries for a decade."

Your internet connection is unstable, read a message on Simon's screen.

"After that, we'll be goin' full throttle on HIMA, scheduled for

September fourth. Theme this year is Timeless Treasures. This is gonna be a heavy lift, guys, a real heavy lift, especially now that our event planner's been axed from the budget."

Simon understood that Fran was referring to the Hawthorne's largest annual event, the History in the Making Gala, responsible for approximately half a million dollars of the yearly fundraising budget.

"After last year's virtual gala, we're planning a hybrid event this year. Hopin' to get forty or fifty big donors in the room and simulcast a virtual program. Dinner, music, live auction, and we'll be unveilin' Theo's exhibit at the end of the night. Sponsors are pretty psyched. Already got $145K in the can—"

"Sorry," Simon interrupted, but before he could get his question out the faces of his colleagues froze on-screen.

"Think we lost him," someone was saying as the video unstuck.

"Sorry, having some connection issues here," Simon said. "Just wanted to make sure I heard correctly. Did you say something about unveiling Theo's exhibit?"

"Harry said he talked to you."

"Er," Simon said, but his supervisor jumped in, his video expanding to fill the screen.

"I said I would, I just haven't had a chance yet—"

Craig Rutherford cut across him. "This won't be a problem, will it, Nealy?"

"Well, I'm sorry to say . . ."

The watching faces froze. So did his, stalled in an unflattering open-mouthed, half-lidded expression.

Simon panicked. He waved his cursor desperately. "Come on, come on." He needed to rejoin the meeting, needed to make his case now before the entire senior staff, where his objection could not be so easily brushed off.

Zoom dropped him from the meeting.

Simon cursed.

He tried again to get back in, clicked and clattered, but his efforts were in vain. The Wi-Fi had scudded away, almost sniggering as it went.

~⊶

Several hours later Simon prepared for his next meeting of the day. It was only 1 p.m. but he felt exhausted, his body a dead weight upon his bones and his brain a mushy puddle at the base of his skull. Concerned he was becoming reliant on it, he had attempted to quit the cough syrup cold turkey and barely slept the previous night, lying awake for hours before at last drifting off into semiconsciousness, only to be jolted awake by an appearance from the Bone Man.

He could still smell the creature's fetid breath, could hear the bony jangle of its bag dragging on the ground.

As he waited for his visitor to arrive, Simon perked himself up in the staff lounge with a mug of instant coffee. The meeting was meant to have started already, but his visitor, a representative of Museum Exhibit Solutions, was running late.

A Philadelphia-based firm specializing in the design and construction of complex museum exhibits, MES was one of several companies that had bid to work on Theo's display. Though not the cheapest option, they had impressed the review panel with their slick presentation, 3-D renderings, and ambitious timeline. Simon had some reservations; he'd seen MES's *Liopleurodon* at the Indiana Natural History Museum and been unimpressed. Then again, if he really had only six months to complete the exhibit, he could not afford to be picky.

Shortly before two he received a second email from the rep explaining he was still stuck at home with his young daughter and waiting for his wife to get back, followed by a harried phone call at a quarter to three announcing that he was on his way.

It was nearly four o'clock before there came a knock on the oak front doors. Simon opened them to reveal a sweaty masked man in a wrinkled dress shirt, dark patches of damp blooming under his armpits.

"Hi, Dr. Nealy? Dwight from MES. Great to finally meet you. Sorry again for the delay." He juddered a hand at Simon, then, seeming to remember the pandemic, pulled it back.

"No worries. Thanks for—"

Simon nearly jumped, startled by the appearance of a girl peeking out from behind the man's khakis. She couldn't have been older than five, plump with wide, staring eyes and a dress that appeared to have been pulled from the bottom of a hamper.

"Hope you don't mind," Dwight said. "Wife broke down on the highway. She's still dealing with the car."

A one-armed rag doll drooped from the girl's hand, a beaded eye hanging by a thread.

"No problem at all." Simon smiled at the girl to mask the itchy feeling skittering under his skin, the one that told him this place was not safe for children. "P-please. Come on in."

After twenty minutes of visioning in the Hall of Dinosaurs, they headed down to Simon's office. He worried the child might be scared, but she didn't seem to mind the slow creaky elevator or the moldy darkness of the basement. While the men talked shop at the desk, the girl crouched on the floor, her dress forming a floral-print boulder around her knees as she danced the doll across the carpet in time to a song of her own invention.

"Regarding the *Liopleurodon*, I agree with you," Dwight was saying, his voice raised over the reedy strains of his daughter's singing. "What we originally planned was much more impressive— Ariella, honey," he said, turning in his seat. "Please keep it down. Can you keep it down while Daddy's working?"

"She's quite the singer," Simon said, smiling, as Dwight turned back. "You were saying?"

"Right. Well, I'll just say we faced a diversity of opinions on the client side. They weren't quite sure what they wanted. We'd settle on a design, start constructing, and then they'd change their minds. It was—"

Dwight was inaudible, his words buried under the girl's irrepressible full-throated belting.

His face tensed, a frightening shade of puce. He turned again. "Ariella, why don't you go play in the hallway, sing in the hallway."

Simon experienced a sharp tug behind his sternum, a knee-jerk impulse to snatch her away from the open doorway. "No, don't—"

Dwight's head spun back to face Simon before the rest of him did. His color was fading; suspicion flashed in his eyes. Simon could sense the father's mind working, forming assumptions about why his prospective client was so obsessed with his young daughter.

"Actually, I—I'm sure she'll be fine," Simon stammered out.

Embarrassed, he refused to look at or mention the child again. For the rest of the meeting he remained focused on the task at hand, or tried to at least. Before long the effects of the coffee had diminished appreciably, his mind too sluggish and drippy to process anything but its own exhaustion and his growing need to pee. It was well after five before the meeting sputtered out.

"Well," he said, standing. "Thank you again for coming all the way out here."

"Has this been helpful?"

Simon was relieved to know he hadn't behaved so badly that the salesman no longer wanted his business. "Yes. Yes, I'll be in touch soon."

Inviting his visitors to see themselves out, Simon made a beeline for the facilities.

The restroom was a square, grimly tiled room for one. A trapped moth fluttered darkly in the overhead light. The toilet was stained at the waterline, and when flushed, the cistern shook with a disconcerting rumble.

As Simon washed his hands, he heard a musical sound over the spitting faucet. It sounded like the voice of a girl—singing.

Dwight and Ariella must have gotten lost on their way back to the elevator. Simon cut the water and reached for a handful of paper towel, but as he quickly dried his hands, he heard the singer more clearly, as if she were passing right outside the door.

"Digging for bugs to give them hugs."

A chill danced up his skeleton.

"Under the dirt is where they live."

That song. That voice. It wasn't Ariella's. It was—

But the thought was so wild, so unreal, he couldn't bring himself to finish it.

He emerged into the hallway, looking left and right. No one there. His heart added a steady drumbeat to the melody; although the lyrics had gone, there remained a soft, lilting hum, fading in and out like a radio losing signal.

"Dah dah dah . . . du-dah . . . dah . . ."

The voice was drifting away from him, deeper into the basement. The rational part of his brain told him not to follow, that it couldn't be his sister, but his feet were already moving underneath him and the other half of his brain working to justify what he was hearing.

What was it Evie had said about Morgan's spirit? *That's why you came back, isn't it? Because she's been calling to you?* Was that what she was doing now: trying to get his attention? Wanting him to follow?

"Digging for ants that eat lots of plants." He paused outside Collection Storage. The doors were closed, but he could hear the voice inside. *"Inside their mound is where they're found."*

The door yawned open at the lightest suggestion of his hand. He stepped inside, then jumped at the *SLAM* of the door behind him.

The singing stopped abruptly, like an interrupted record.

Simon reached for the switch on the wall and toggled it on and off. The room stayed dark. Patting his pockets, he realized he'd left his phone. It would have been pitch black if not for the smoke detector blinking out its meager light from the wall, carving hulking shapes out of the blackness in silent, lingering flashes.

Simon raised a hand to his face, confused; a sultry wind seemed to blow across it, tinged with a boggy, feculent smell. Combined with the

sweltering heat that flooded the room and fogged his glasses, it triggered something deep inside him, an animal instinct to run.

He wheeled toward the exit, but the door had disappeared. There
wasn't even a wall. Before him stretched a vast curtain of night, an expanse
of alien wilderness abuzz with the chatter of nocturnal wildlife. His shoes
sank into the sludge of wet earth, a sickening sweat drenching his clothes.

He turned, agape. It made no sense. The other half of Collection Storage was unchanged, mud merging seamlessly into flecked white tile.

Without warning a shape bolted from the undergrowth past Simon's
leg, down an aisle of metal cabinets. As it disappeared into shadow, an
ear-splitting squeal rent the air, ending abruptly in a crunch of bones.
The sloppy, stomach-turning sound of a carcass being thrown back and
swallowed.

Something was down there. He could hear it, jostling the metal cabinetry as it limped down the aisle.

Screeeeap—THUMP.

The smoke detector blinked, revealing thirty bladelike teeth pushing out of the darkness, drenched with blood up to the gums.

Screeeeap—THUMP.

A horn, all the sharper for the chip taken out of it, mounted behind
a scarred and scaly snout.

Screeeeap—THUMP.

A pair of amber eyes with round black pupils, one swollen and leak-
ing pus down the side of the animal's head.

One word repeated in Simon's mind—in recognition, then incredu-
lity, dismissal, and finally fear—as a low breath rumbled through the
room, a rope of bloody saliva stretched from mouth to floor, and the
amber eyes flashed with killer instinct: *THEO. THEO. THEO. THEO.*

The light blinked out, and Simon could sense it even if he could not
see it: the animal pouncing, its sharp-toothed mouth gaping open. He
screamed, stumbled back, and released a grunt as he fell backward into
the hallway, scrambling away from the open door.

He paused as the light poured into Collection Storage. The room
looked empty, yet he could still feel a rumble deep in his bones.

CHAPTER TWENTY-SEVEN

THE CURSE OF
HAWTHORNE HOLLOW

Simon worked from home the rest of the week. He might not have gone back to the museum at all were it not for Evie's scheduled visit; he'd already promised Fran he would be there, and if he should ever manage to talk to Evie on her own, this might be his only chance.

She arrived Monday morning in Fran's Kia, apparently not a moment too soon. Slamming the car door behind her, she hurried up the steps toward a waiting Simon and hooked him in a brief half hug, filling his nostrils with mingled bird smell and powdery perfume. "Never leave me alone with that woman again," she murmured.

"Nice drive, then?"

Fran glowered at them from the driver's seat as her car tore away from the curb.

They waited inside for Fran, Simon anxiously. Now that they were alone, he felt oddly self-conscious, embarrassed to bring up his encounters with Theo and the others. Surely the ghosts she had sensed in the museum were human spirits. She would have no clue what he was talking about, might even think he was crazy. It was a humbling thought.

By the time he worked up the courage to broach the subject, the entrance doors swung open and a red-faced Fran strode in, hands balled into fists.

"I see you two have caught up," she barked. "Perfect!"

Ten minutes later Evie ambled around the Cope Memorial Research Laboratory, surveying the fossils laid out on the tables as Simon described them and pointed out any significant markings.

"The humerus. That forms the upper arm," he said as she paused before a footlong bone in two halves. "We wouldn't usually cut into it like that, but it was necessary to study the microstructure inside. In a female we might expect to find medullary tissue, which can be rapidly dissolved in the bloodstream to produce eggshell during pregnancy. We didn't find any medullary tissue in Theo, which makes it even more likely he was male—"

"And we couldn't be more excited for the world to meet him," Fran interjected in the ebullient personality she put on specifically for Evie. "The exhibit's gonna be incredible, state of the art. The paleontology community's already talking about it, right, Dr. Nealy?"

Simon stared.

"Of course if you decide to fund it we'd love to name the exhibit in your honor," Fran said. "I can't imagine a more fitting testament to your commitment to the Hawthorne and its legacy of—"

"Yes, all right," Evie said, batting her hand. "Where do I sign?"

Fran clapped, her stenciled eyebrows disappearing beneath her bangs. "That's wonderful! Truly, we can't thank you enough. I'll run upstairs and grab a pledge form."

Fran strode stiffly from the room, apparently suppressing the desire to punch the air.

Simon was momentarily speechless. "Evie, that's incredible. I can't even—"

"It's nothing. Only way to get rid of people like that."

Simon stifled a chuckle, but wasn't proud of it. Only in Evie would he overlook such a casual abuse of wealth.

She approached the table at the center of the room. There the surviving pieces of Theo's skull lay scattered and broken, a few still partially coated in matrix, arranged in an approximation of their natural order.

"Didn't I tell you it'd be worth the wait?" she said.

About to ask what she meant, Simon realized she was speaking to Theo—*her* Theo.

"Hasn't stopped chattering since I told him we were coming."

Simon nodded, his smile strained. The clock was ticking. If he was going to ask, he had to do it now.

"Evie," he croaked, and cleared his throat. "The first time we spoke, you said . . ."

She bent down to look closely at Theo's teeth.

"I probably misheard you," Simon said, "but I thought you said there were spirits in the museum."

"That's right. The place is cursed." Once again Evie's tone was so frustratingly mundane that Simon thought for a moment he must have misheard.

"Cursed?"

"The hollow. The land beneath the museum, it's tainted. I sensed it the first time I stepped foot here."

"Sensed what?"

Her hand traced Theo's bones, delicately articulated, like a butterfly on a bed of stones.

"The disaster."

A memory of Mueller's diaries intruded upon Simon's thoughts. "What kind of disaster?"

"All I know is what I see." Evie's gaze had gone slippery, unfocused. Something inside of her seemed to have unlatched, relinquishing its hold on the world before her. "A flash of bright light. A blast stretching miles. Fire falling like rain from the sky."

A meteoritic impact like the one described in Mueller's diaries came to mind. But Simon had already concluded that was impossible. Or at least very, *very* unlikely.

"Thousands lost," Evie intoned through juddering lips. "I can hear them. The screams."

"Screams?"

"Something terrible happened here that day. A breach of the metaphysical order. A thousand spirits released into the atmosphere, trapped by a black cloud of dust bearing down on them. They couldn't break free. The only way out was down through the scar in the earth. Their suffering poisoned the soil, and laid a curse on every spirit whose bones reside in the hollow, in the museum."

"What curse?"

"That their souls should be imprisoned in the hollow like those before them were imprisoned. Lost in the suffering of their dying moments, until their souls at last find peace."

"Peace like . . . ?"

She gave a dreamy kind of shrug. "Every animal's longing is its own."

Every *animal*, she had said.

Simon hated himself for having to ask. He didn't want to believe in ghosts, in curses. He didn't want to be Albert Mueller. "What kind of animals haunt the museum?"

The question was like a hand yanking her from her reverie. The haze cleared from her ice-blue eyes; she almost laughed.

"Don't ask me," Evie said. "You're the dinosaur expert."

CHAPTER TWENTY-EIGHT

AN OPEN QUESTION

"Of course I'm happy to talk taxidermy," Priya trilled through the phone, her helpfulness barely masking the encroaching emotional collapse evident in her tremulous tone.

Simon, who was once again working remotely, could hardly blame the exhibit coordinator. Originally hired to support the director of exhibits—a position created to replace a suite of curatorial staff whose positions had been eliminated, before the director position was also axed—Priya had found herself responsible for an ever-expanding list of operational duties. Chief among them was managing collections, records, and exhibits for the Halls of Man, Gems and Minerals, and Insects and Animalia, making her the only person even remotely qualified to answer Simon's question.

"I just have a few things to get done this afternoon," she said. "Quite a few, actually. I just found out we're reopening Friday, which means I'm—"

"The museum's reopening?" Simon said, inserting a pod into the cof-feemaker and lowering the lid. The executive team must have decided overnight; it hadn't been mentioned at the recent senior staff meeting.

"I was surprised too. It's a good thing, I guess. There's just so much to get done. I'm about to head out to pick up the social-distancing sig-nage—"

"Sorry, I know the timing's awful. It's not important. It's just, some-one from the community asked me and I said I'd get back to them with an answer."

"Of course. No problem. What was their question?"

"It's about our taxidermy collection. Or taxidermy in general, I guess." He pressed a button and coffee dribbled into the mug. "I was— they were wondering, I mean—when the taxidermist stuffs the animal, how much of the original specimen do they keep?"

"You mean like the insides?"

"Specifically the bones."

It was something he'd been thinking about since Evie's visit. He still wasn't convinced a prehistoric curse lay over the hollow. Even if he was willing to suspend his disbelief, it didn't add up. If there was a curse on the animals whose bones were held in the museum, he would have en-countered more than just dinosaurs roaming the halls. He could accept that the arthropods, which had exoskeletons in place of internal bone structures, may not have qualified for reanimation, but what about the modern vertebrates? The mammals, the birds, the reptiles?

"Actually, I was just reading about this for class," Priya said, a spark of genuine interest in her voice. "In a traditional skin mount, like most of our specimens, everything under the skin gets thrown out. They don't even really touch it. They just remove the skin, preserve it by either tanning it or applying chemicals, then stretch it over a kind of internal mount. Some of the bigger ones might be made of wood or polyurethane, but most of the smaller ones are just skin and stuffing."

Simon turned off the coffeemaker. "So it's possible there are no bones in our animal collection at all?"

"We used to keep a few skeletons for research purposes, but we sold them all off a couple of years ago when we started running out of space."

"You don't say."

"Well, if that's all, I really should—"

"Of course." Simon felt awful. "Is there anything I can do? I have a meeting this afternoon, but I can come in tomorrow morning and help you get things ready."

"Would you really? That would be *amazing*. The earlier the better;
I'll probably be here around six."

"Sure thing."

"Thank you so much!" Priya said. "I'll see you tomorrow!"

Call ended, Simon put the phone down and brought the steaming
mug to his lips. Despite the balm of its scent, he remained uneasy. Evie's
curse idea might be ridiculous, but he was quickly running out of evidence against it.

CHAPTER TWENTY-NINE

WITHOUT A TRACE

Simon was halfway up the museum driveway when, with a cold prickle at the back of his neck, he noticed the blood winding out of the grass like a blackish-red serpent. It was semidry, congealed, and laid down in a heavy drip, as if leaked from an open wound. It snaked a path toward the museum, dappling the limestone steps in thick, dark splashes.

Simon's guts were a greasy twist of anxiety. Whose blood was this? How had it gotten here? His mind threw up a gruesome image of Priya, sending a jolt of frigid adrenaline through his veins.

He followed the trail through the open doors and stopped. His stomach lurched, and a hand rose to block the reek of death from his nose.

The floor of the entrance hall was an ocean of blood; scattered body parts and mounds of viscera rose like islands from a dark red sea. The largest of them was the front of the animal, barely hanging together. Simon spotted it with only a modicum of relief: the furry wheat-colored head; the long, ragged trench of a neck; the single shoulder and leg attached by an inch of skin and muscle. A young buck by the looks of it, downy antlers just beginning to sprout from the top of its head. The onyx-colored eyes stared with a peaceful kind of sadness.

The sight was so disturbing that Simon had failed to notice Priya across the room, shouting into a wired phone stretched across the ticket desk, her usual polite demeanor obliterated. "A deer, Harry! A fucking deer! There's blood everywhere, all over the floor. On the ticket booth, the gift shop. Half the merch will need to be replaced."

Simon's fear temporarily yielded to pity. The museum was meant to reopen in two days, and he knew how much help Priya could expect from their mutual supervisor.

"What do you mean I can handle it on my own?" she was shouting.

She noticed Simon, and despite her desperation, smiled quickly and waved.

"I think a bear," she said into the phone. "No, it's gone now. The doors were open when I came in. Must've dragged it in, had its way with it, and gone out again."

But the deer could not have been dragged, Simon thought. Judging by the trail of blood leading from the grass, it had either staggered in or been carried. Were there bears in these woods big enough to carry a deer of this size?

"I don't know," Priya was saying. "Maybe I forgot to lock up last night? It was almost midnight when I left. I was so tired."

Surely such an animal would have left prints, Simon thought. He cast his gaze across the hall, then stopped, squinted, and stepped forward.

Careful not to bloody his shoes, he passed into the shadows collected at the back of the hall and paused before a trail of crusted imprints on the floor. Two sets of them, from the looks of it. Three-toed like a chicken's, but several orders of magnitude bigger. They careened wildly, crossing over each other in great lunging steps. There was no question in his mind: they were dinosaurian. Theropod. The bloody residue of an encounter between carnivores.

Simon's anxiety trickled back, but was overpowered by a flood of curiosity. To which two dinosaurs did the prints belong? The first, smaller set had a sloppy quality to them, a subtle drag that indicated a limp. The owner of the second set was less obvious. Compared to the thicker, rounder profile of Theo's prints, these possessed a more defined V, with longer, slimmer toes ending in lethal claws. And the scale of them—they were nearly twice the size.

Whatever had made these prints was big. *Very* big.

Simon had his phone out and was attempting to snap a quick photo when—

"Dr. Nealy, I'm so sorry," Priya called out, approaching. "What a nightmare."

Simon met her halfway, compelled by a strange urgency to keep her away from the tracks. To spare her from any more upheaval, he told himself.

"Don't apologize. This is—I can't believe it."

"What am I going to do?"

"We'll get through this. I'm here for you. Whatever you need."

She squeezed his arm gratefully. "The Game Commission is on its way. So are the police, and Maurice should be here any minute."

"Police?"

"Harry thinks it may have been a vandal." Priya unlocked her phone. "Sorry, I need to make another call." She headed outside where the signal was stronger.

"I'll join you," Simon said, none too eager to be left on his own.

As he followed her, the larger prints swam behind his eyes. He couldn't help thinking of Maurice's story, and the murderous pink-eyed creature Cordell had spotted in the shadows. At the time Simon had thought the pink-eyed spirit might have been Theo, but as he'd observed in Collection Storage, Theo's eyes were amber.

Maurice was right: something even bigger, something even more terrible, lurked in the darkness of the Hawthorne.

But what?

The official investigation was as inconclusive as Simon's. It came as no surprise to him that the forensics team found no evidence of a human perpetrator. Still he was disappointed when the police concluded in agreement with Priya and a pair of queasy-looking biologists from the Game Commission that the likeliest culprit was a bear.

He wondered what they would have made of the footprints had

they seen them. While Simon was off helping Priya, Maurice took it upon himself to start mopping up the mess in the entrance hall—a most unwelcome sight for the police investigators, who arrived to find their crime scene irretrievably compromised. Simon shared their frustration. He hadn't managed to snap a photo of the tracks. Now he would have only his memory with which to identify them.

Finally the officers departed, and though he now wished he hadn't offered, Simon spent the rest of the day in service to Priya. He helped her load the animal remains in a wheelbarrow and bury them in a ditch Maurice had dug in the woods, post signage and install hand sanitizer dispensers around the museum, cordon off every second urinal and stall in the men's restrooms, call around to a dozen stores in search of commercial-sized boxes of masks, and go around with a rag and bottle of cleaner, trying to magic the place into a state of unearned presentability.

It was nearly five o'clock and they were exhausted, hungry, and covered in deer blood before Harry called an end to their exertions. An emergency board meeting had taken place that afternoon. In light of recent events it was unanimously agreed the reopening be pushed back indefinitely.

It was at once a relief and a biting frustration. "He at least could have told us they were taking a vote," Simon grumbled.

Nevertheless, the trio parted in good spirits.

"I'll lock up," he told the others. "I need to stop by the library before I go."

He hadn't intended to stay more than a few minutes—he had no desire to linger in the museum alone after dark—but it took him ages to find what he was looking for. The library contained no designated paleontology section, the volumes arranged semi-alphabetically across a vast spectrum of subjects on long sagging shelves. Simon walked back and forth along them, holding his neck sideways to read the titles: *Waterfowl Ecology of Eastern Pennsylvania*, by Harold Gardner; *Gems and Minerals of the Middle East*, by Rana Ghazali; *Field Guide to Mesozoic Trace Fossils*, by Elijah Grebek—

A zap of excitement shot through him. Trace fossils, Simon knew, referred to impressions left by prehistoric organisms in rock, often in the form of tracks.

He slid the book off the shelf in a cloud of dust. It was compact but thick, several decades old. The faded goldenrod dust jacket was torn and curling up at the edges, depicting the imprint of an ammonite in a slab of rock.

He carried the book to the table and opened to the table of contents, all thought of spectral dangers forgotten. Simon had been thinking about the footprints between chores and tasks all day.

Based on the shape alone, he had a hunch that they belonged to an *Allosaurus*. Mueller had mentioned in his diaries that they found an *Allosaurus* tooth embedded in Theo's vertebra, which would explain the presence of the spirit of a larger theropod in the museum.

And for a moment the book seemed to validate that theory. Turning to chapter 12, "Morrison Formation," Simon discovered a photograph depicting a trail of *A. fragilis* prints etched into a bed of rock at Comanche National Grassland in Colorado. They looked remarkably like the ones stamped bloodily into Simon's mind. However, an illustration comparing the prints of several theropods, including both *Ceratosaurus* and *Allosaurus*, showed only a small difference in size, whereas the larger prints in the entrance hall were significantly bigger than Theo's. Whatever left them had likely been over forty feet long, closer in size to *T. rex* than *A. fragilis*, the longest known specimen of which measured only thirty-two feet.

Perhaps Mueller had misidentified the tooth. Perhaps it belonged to the larger *Torvosaurus*, which had also shared Theo's habitat. But the *Torvo* prints as depicted here were flared, with pointed-oval toe prints, not a match with the ones in Simon's mind.

Maybe he was misremembering, he thought. If only he had managed to take a photo. He continued to scour the book, but nearly an hour later he still hadn't found a set of prints closer to the image in his head than those of the too-small *A. fragilis*.

Taking the book with him, he boarded the elevator back up to the entrance hall. He wanted it close at hand in case any theories should present themselves in the night.

As the doors gnashed open, he heard something that made him stop: a musical lilt floating across the hall. The familiar tune threw a wave of cold over Simon.

"Dah dah dah, du-dah dah dah."

He stepped into the dark. The entrance hall was airless, poisoned with the smell of the industrial-strength cleaner Maurice had applied to the floors. Simon squinted, molding his vision to the shape of the night.

A wrinkle of movement by the Hall of Insects and Animalia. Simon froze. Listened.

A voice, *her* voice, echoed out of the darkness.

"Digging for bugs to give them hugs."

Simon approached.

But when the voice sang next, it seemed to have moved, now coming from the Hall of Gems and Minerals.

"Under the dirt is where they live."

Not for the first time Simon had the feeling he was being led.

Slowly he followed the voice. The gemological hall reverberated with song as he stepped inside.

"In the grass and in the trees."

He stopped, looking down. He could barely see the floor beneath him, but he had heard it, the faint splash of having stepped in something wet.

As he tilted his gaze back up, a shock wave of cold dread pulsed through him. A dark mass some twenty feet long stretched out across the floor. Whatever it was seemed to be alive—barely. Its breathing was labored, a rumbling moan. A rising swelter enveloped Simon like a summer night.

His first instinct was to turn and run, but the creature didn't move. Couldn't, it seemed. Simon reached his phone and held the flashlight aloft. A glass case of sparkling gems refracted the light and threw it across the animal in a whirl of rainbow color—a horned eye lit up sapphire blue, a crushed rib cage tinted emerald green, a spear of bone jutting out of a broken amethyst leg.

Theo lay on his side, sunk into a sludgy layer of mud stretching between display cases. He didn't seem to register Simon's presence.

Simon's heart thrashed in his chest. What was happening? More than seeing a ghost, he sensed he was glimpsing a scene from another world, a moment from the animal's past brought to life before his eyes. His final moments? There was little chance Theo could have recovered from this; his wounds were too severe.

With enormous effort, the animal lifted its head. Simon jumped back and Theo's deep tremulous cry echoed through the darkness, filling the hall up to the rafters, vibrating down to the core of Simon's soul.

He knew this sound all too well. It nested in the marrow of his bones.

Not a cry of pain, but a wail of mourning.

A keen of depraved eviscerating loss, howling across the emptiness of time as if the animal had been saving it for Simon's ears only.

CHAPTER THIRTY

SOCIAL SERVICES

Simon had often asked himself what he was doing at the Hawthorne, but after the encounter with Theo in the Hall of Gems and Minerals he found himself even less sure.

Morgan, he thought as he lay awake that night, his mind torpid with the effects of cough syrup. *That's why you returned. You felt her calling to you, calling you home.* And for all the good it had done. He'd been back in Wrexham five months and had added little to his knowledge of what had happened to his sister.

In fairness, he'd had quite a lot to distract him—the museum that was liable to go under any day, the pressure of needing to finish Theo's exhibit in time for the fast-approaching gala, the apparitions he couldn't explain except as the vestiges of a prehistoric curse. Then there was the ghostly voice, singing a song to which only he and his sister knew the words.

What did it mean? Did Morgan haunt the Hawthorne? And if so, did that signify her bones lay nearby, perhaps buried in the grounds of the hollow? If she'd summoned him back to solve her disappearance, then why did she keep leading him to Theo, presenting visions of his death rather than her own?

Simon couldn't help but regret moving home. Sometimes when things were slow and the Wi-Fi in his office was working, he would longingly trawl the Field Museum website, hoping to discover his old position had miraculously reopened.

What he found instead was the directory entry for *Kai Liu, PhD, Researcher,* another reminder of a past he'd perhaps been too hasty to leave behind.

One afternoon Simon was meeting virtually with MES to review the first round of designs for Theo's exhibit when his cell phone, connected to Wi-Fi, buzzed with a text.

> Need u help tmrw get me 10am

It was from an unknown number, 610 area code. Local.

Simon ignored it and turned his eyes back to the screen, where Dwight was presenting a 3-D mockup of Theo's mounted skeleton.

"The idea is to capture an authentic moment in time. We know fish factored heavily into *Ceratosaurus*'s diet, so we thought maybe a fishing scene with Theo bent forward over a stream."

"Hm," Simon said.

Dwight paused. "Simon, did you say something?"

"Sorry. I'm just not sure about the pose. Theo was a powerful hunter, athletic. Scary, even. Or so I'd imagine." Simon tittered at his private joke. "Er, this is just a little—I'm not sure."

"You'd like to see something grander. More awe-inspiring maybe."

"Sort of—"

The phone buzzed again.

> This Simon's number yes or no

As Dwight assured Simon the next design was just what he was looking for, Simon quickly tapped out a response: *Who's this?*

A minute later, a reply:

> Evil

Then a correction.

> Evie

He set the phone facedown, feigning attentiveness to Dwight while deciding how to respond. He couldn't imagine Fran being okay with his taking Evie somewhere without her, but nor would she, who treated the donor's every request as a royal decree, approve of his outright declining. Perhaps he should let Fran handle it—but then he'd promised Evie he wouldn't leave her alone with the fundraiser again. She was counting on him.

While Dwight tried to sell Simon on a terrifying design depicting Theo's skeleton leaping through the air, mouth yawning open and claws bared, Simon chanced shooting Evie another quick reply.

> This is Simon. Yes of course I'm happy to help.

Simon texted Evie the following morning to let her know he'd arrived, and got out of his car as she appeared at the door of the building. She was wearing a brightly striped woolen poncho, yoga pants, and her usual bug-eyed sunglasses, toting a plastic Walmart bag Simon did not immediately clock was her purse. She greeted him with a bony, one-armed hug.

"Good to see you, son."

The term of endearment took him aback.

"Er, good morning," he said. "Where are we off to, then?"

"First to pick up my dry cleaning."

"Your dry cleaning. Right."

Evie was already walking around to the front passenger seat.

"Please, let's not dally. I want to be back in time for *Judge Mathis* at three."

Simon frowned at his phone, which read eight minutes past ten.

〜✺〜

The dry cleaners was mayhem. The couple that owned it was down with Covid, leaving the shop under the management of a white-haired fossil of a woman who reminded Simon so much of Kai's late grandmother his heart ached at the sight of her. Worse was that she seemed flustered, and Evie was getting impatient. The shopkeeper couldn't seem to find her ticket and had to track down each item individually, of which Evie claimed there were between twelve and fourteen, or maybe ten, possibly twenty.

"No, sorry. Green," said Simon after the shopkeeper presented the wrong item for the second time. "A green top. *Lùsè chènshān.*"

This time she nodded, murmuring to herself as she walked away, and returned a moment later with Evie's emerald silk blouse.

"You speak Chinese," she said a few minutes later as Simon drove her to their second stop of the morning, an appointment with her financial adviser.

"Just a few words. My ex was Chinese. I only know the word for shirt because his mom's a seamstress."

"You miss him?" Evie said, as if attempting to peer into his mind and finding it clouded.

"Yes," he said. "I think so." Even to him, the answer had the ring of a question.

They arrived at the offices of Larry Ehrenfeld, certified private wealth adviser. While Evie was escorted inside, Simon waited in the lobby, answering emails on his phone. One was from Fran, and he experienced a niggle of guilt. He'd decided it was kindest to all involved not to mention his and Evie's private outing. Still, it felt like a deception.

Not ten minutes later Evie emerged from the office, walked right past Simon, and beckoned him with an impatient wave of her hand.

"Everything okay?" he said, catching up.

"Fine, fine. We have a hundred thousand to work with. It'll have to do."

"Do for what?"

The community center was a rectangular single-story building of no discernible character, the inside pristine but cheerless, its clientele a dreary throng of the poor, strung out, and homeless. With her mismatched outfit and shopping bag purse, Evie almost fit right in.

Simon found himself struggling to remain present. Passing through the doors of the building was like stepping into a dream he barely remembered. The place dredged up memories of similar centers he had been dragged to as a young boy, long before the stability of their home on Granton Avenue, years before Morgan was born. In that moment, he was three years old again, small, helpless, frightened. His hand itched to hold his mother's. Had she ever invited such attachment?

He caught Evie studying him.

"So," he said. "What are we doing here?"

"I'm thinking about giving the center some money. If you like the place."

"Me?"

Simon, who thought he had been summoned merely to play chauffeur, felt oddly touched.

A few moments later they were greeted by a Black woman in unfussy clothes. She introduced herself as Leticia Martin, the center director, and thanked Evie heartily for coming. "So happy to finally meet you in person, you and—"

"My friend," Evie said. "Simon."

A feeling of warmth flooded Simon's chest.

"Wonderful to meet you, Simon. Welcome, both of you. I have someone special I'd like you to meet, but first allow me to show you around."

They followed Leticia on her practiced tour of the facility: the dining room, the fitness center, the TV room, the social worker and nurse case manager's offices. Despite their masks, she appeared to know most of the clients by face if not by name. "Good morning, Jack, Marv," she greeted a pair of unkempt men playing checkers in the games room. "Make it to breakfast this morning?"

"Pancake day," said the younger of the two, advancing his piece in a series of diagonal leaps. "Always make it to pancake day."

The older man cast a suspicious glance at Evie and Simon. "Who're they?"

"These are my special guests, Evilyn Mitchell and her friend Simon. They're here visiting the center today."

The man's eyes lingered on Simon. "You . . ."

"S-sorry?" Simon strained to smile. *He recognizes me.*

"Your mama," said the man, moving his piece. "She used to bring you here."

The assertion caught Simon off guard. He was expecting the man to have recognized him from the news twenty years ago, not as a former client. Is that why this place felt so familiar?

He didn't respond, refusing to acknowledge in front of the others that the man was probably right.

"Before she did it," the man said. "Killed her, I mean."

Leticia interrupted. "All right, Jack, you have a good day now." She ushered Simon and Evie quickly out of the room.

"Sorry about that," she said once out of earshot of the men. "Jack has some mental health challenges. We're getting him help." Simon forced a smile and nodded, trying not to think about whom Jack had meant by *her.*

He felt Evie's hand on his shoulder as they walked on.

At last Leticia led them into her small, cluttered office. Already there was a thin man in his fifties, his long face leathery and prematurely spotted, as if from prolonged exposure to the sun. Simon's impression was of a poor person trying hard to look presentable, his thrift store shirt and slacks clean and pressed, his thinning hair crunchy with gel.

"Evilyn, Simon, I'd like you to meet George." Simon introduced himself without shaking hands; Evie, more circumspect, hung back. "George is a very special client of ours. When he found out you were coming in today, he insisted on meeting you and sharing his story, and I told him you wouldn't mind at all."

Before Evie could correct her, Simon said, "Absolutely. Thank you, George."

They took seats, and Leticia invited George to speak.

He seemed nervous, stammering slightly and losing the thread of the story he had clearly rehearsed. Still, the testimonial hit its mark. Simon felt for him, this unmarried childless man who'd been laid off from his job of twenty years, had a heart attack and a stroke, and, following the foreclosure of his home, ended up on the streets. He'd never struggled with addiction, never "deserved" to become homeless like people believed Simon's mother had—himself included sometimes. "That's when I started coming to the center for lunch," George said. "They tried to get me to talk to Jan, but I didn't want to—"

"Jan is our social worker," Leticia added.

"Yeah, right," George said. "But I was too proud to ask for help. But one of my lunch buddies, he talked to her, said she helped him, and he started pressuring me, 'Talk to her, talk to her,' and I thought, 'Aright, fine,' just to get him off my back. Not like I had anything better to do. And she told me about the transitional housing program . . ."

George described the experience of finally moving into his own studio, of getting dressed in the morning, of sitting down on his bed and putting on his socks.

"That was amazing to me, you know, because I never had that when I lived on the street. When you're homeless, you sit on the sidewalk to put your socks on. And here I had my own bed. I-it made me feel so, I don't know, so normal, like my life finally had some—some—"

Simon, who had been fighting back tears for some time, lost the battle at the moment George himself began to cry.

He had not lived this man's life, but Simon felt he understood him on a psychic level. Understood what it was like to live so long without the meagerest provisions of dignity or hope that he stopped missing them, even hesitated to accept them when they were laid before him like a feast of riches. For Simon, that had meant going to live with Colleen. After he was removed from his mother's so-called care, he hadn't wanted to move in with his aunt. He wished only to be left alone, allowed to get on with life as he knew it. He hadn't realized, until the system forced his hand, how much was missing from his life besides his sister.

In Colleen's home, Simon learned what it meant to be loved and provided for. He learned the meaning of the word *mother*, even if for him it was spelled A-U-N-T. He grew even to find value in and embrace himself: his intelligence, his nerdiness, the bigness of the heart within his small body. For the first time his future lay before him, not as a pre-determined descent into sadness and want, but a runway stretching out toward the limitlessness of the sky. He could do anything, be anything he wanted. Go to college—good ones; pursue his passion; resurrect the dreams of a paleontological career his mother had suffocated with her self-loathing.

It skewered him with pain even as it uplifted him, for it seemed unlikely that Morgan would ever get the same chance, that even if she was out there somewhere, she would never experience *this*. In those first years after she vanished, Simon had wished more than ever that she would return to him, if only so that she too could know what it felt like to live.

Perhaps in some ways he had been privileged. But that wasn't to say his life had been easy even after Colleen. Though he was a man reborn, Simon could never completely shake off the terrors of his past life. They pursued him in his dreams, in his memories, in the face of every little girl he saw on the street, every butterfly and roly-poly. Always Simon was running toward the next achievement, the next degree, the next promotion, as if by reaching the next chapter of his life he could somehow close the book on that nightmarish prologue.

But his relationship with Kai had given him hope. In Kai he had seen the ultimate happily ever after. Marriage, suburbia, domesticity. An extended family so different from his own—literally, so foreign—he could lose himself, and his past, inside it forever.

But just as the degrees and promotions hadn't held the darkness at bay, nor could the illusion of his perfect relationship. Simon had loved Kai, and yet the thought crossed his mind that their affection may not have been the firm foundation on which lives together were meant to be built. A deep respect and friendship mistaken for something more.

Looking back, he wondered if it was Kai he had been in love with, or rather how normal their life together had made him feel.

As George finished his story, Simon returned to the room, joining in with Leticia's generous applause. Evie remained silent.

Leticia let George go, and now that the stage had been set, initiated a frank discussion about the center's financial needs and aspirations. Evie was attentive and engaged, asking shrewd but fair questions. At the end of it she requested a moment to speak privately with Simon.

"Of course, take your time," Leticia said, and left the room.

Evie got up and explored the office, spying the notes on Leticia's corkboard and peeking into desk drawers, as if to ensure they weren't concealing bars of gold. "What do you think?"

"I think you should give them the money," Simon said.

"Yes, I think so too. All of it? She only asked for fifty."

"Evie—"

"Yes, all right. Just making sure."

Her bag rustled noisily as she fished out her checkbook. "Call her in," she said, already writing out a check.

Simon did. A moment later, Evie tore off the check and handed it to Leticia, saying, "It's all I can do at the moment. But let's speak again early next year."

The director's eyes widened at the succession of zeroes scrawled on the paper.

"This is—I'm speechless! Thank you so much, *thank you*. Both of you. I'm going to give you a hug."

She put her arms around Simon and squeezed. "Thank you," she said again.

"No," he said, tears in his eyes. "Thank you."

"A hundred fifty thousand?" Simon said a few moments later as they exited the building and crossed the parking lot. "I thought your adviser said you could only afford a hundred."

"Don't worry. He's used to it by now."

"It's very generous, Evie."

"The rich can't be generous, only guilt ridden."

"Well, the poor can be guilt ridden too."

They reached Simon's car. He stopped at the passenger door and opened it for her. Evie hung back. "You will forgive me for forcing you back there, won't you? If I'd known—"

"It's fine. I'm glad you did."

"And that man who mentioned your mother."

"If I met him before, I don't remember."

"But he was talking about Morgan, wasn't he?"

The man's unsettling words repeated through Simon's mind: *Before she did it. Killed her, I mean.*

"Do you think he might know something?" Evie asked.

"I think if he crossed paths with my mother and saw in the news that her daughter was missing, he'd be crazy not to think she killed her."

Evie gazed at him, doleful.

"Now," Simon said, smiling gently. "I really ought to be getting back."

CHAPTER THIRTY-ONE

MILK AND SUGARBUSH

Following his rumination over George's sad story, Simon found it difficult to shake the thought of Kai from his mind. He returned to the office desiring urgently to call him, to seek reassurance that their love had been more than a projection, a soothing fantasy in which Simon had smugly wasted the best years of his life. He talked himself out of it before the workday was over and worked himself back up on the drive home, finally calling and cutting it off before Kai could answer, Simon cursing himself.

Come lunchtime the following day Kai hadn't replied even with a text. Simon had never felt lonelier, or surer that he would be so forever. He imagined himself as one of those sad older gay men who padded the emptiness of their lives with cats, lingering conversations at the supermarket checkout, and weekly summons to the local college-age handyman to retighten the pipes they had loosened in the week.

Perhaps unfairly, the image brought Zander Steyn to mind. The potter was not very old yet, but the desperation with which he had invited Simon inside for tea gave the impression that he was as starved of company as Simon was.

On a whim of desperation, which he justified as an act of community service, Simon dug Zander's business card out of his wallet and dialed the number.

"Theo, it's so nice to hear your voice!" Zander said. "How are you, my boy?"

"Good, thanks." Simon had to mentally adjust to being addressed as Theo, having forgotten the charade he had previously enacted to evade detection as Morgan Jenks's brother. "I just wanted to check in on you, make sure you've been keeping your chin off the sidewalk."

"Clumsy as ever, I'm afraid."

"Oh, well," Simon said. "Say, if you're not too banged up, maybe I could stop by this weekend."

"Stop by?"

Simon could sense the frown in Zander's voice, the sudden hesitation.

"I mean, if the offer of tea still stands. Maybe something outside. I'm vaccinated."

"Vaccinated. Right."

"Sorry, I just thought—"

"No, no. You're right. It's a wonderful idea. You must come."

"You're sure?"

"I insist on it. Please."

"Say, Saturday, eleven?"

"It's a da—" Zander said, and cleared his throat. "Well, I—I should look forward to seeing you then."

A few days later Simon sat in Zander's chilly backyard as his host prepared refreshments inside. The outdoor area was small and unkempt, a knotty patch of grass butting up against a patio of uneven paving stones. It was barely big enough for the old picnic table at which Simon sat, and the profusion of ceramic flowerpots collected at the edges of the patio.

The back door swung open and Zander emerged, carefully balancing a brilliantly white tea set on a tray. "Here we are," he said, setting it before Simon. His unmasked face, which Simon was seeing for the first time, was pale, slightly saggy, and swathed in fine silver stubble, underneath which Simon detected a hint of rogue handsomeness gone by. "Nice bit of tea to warm your bones, and a slice of cake to thank you."

"Thank me?"

"For helping me before. A-and suggesting you drop by," he stammered with a smile. "Do you take milk and sugar?"

"Both. Two sugars please."

Zander poured. "So, Theo. Tell me about yourself. What is it you do?"

Simon almost answered honestly, but feared mentioning the Hawthorne might spark Zander's memory of the disappearance. Instead he voiced the second thought that came to him. "I'm a detective."

"A detective! Oh, how fascinating. Police?"

"Er, private."

"Like Sherlock Holmes."

"I wouldn't go that far."

"And what sorts of private activities do you detect?" Zander said with an air of theater. "Crime? Murder?"

"Something like that."

"Bound to secrecy. Say no more."

Simon accepted a cup and saucer from his host. Like the rest of the set, they were decorated with a bold pattern of hand-painted flowers he didn't recognize: bulbous and sharp, like pinkish-red artichokes.

"You've noticed my protea," Zander said. "More commonly known as sugarbush. National flower of South Africa."

"That's where you're from. I couldn't place your accent."

"Cape Town, to be exact."

"What brought you to the States?"

"Oh . . ." Zander sighed, as if pondering the great mysteries of life. "Love, I suppose. But it was work that kept me. Nothing as interesting as detective work, I assure you. Then my mother passed, and, well, we were very close, Mum and me. I was an only child, and she was my only family. The only reason I ever had to go back." He smiled sadly. "You're young. One day you might understand."

Simon didn't mention that he already did. "Well, it's a beautiful set."

"Kind of you, very kind of you. Not my best work, I don't think, but it's sentimental."

"You made this?"

"Can't bring myself to sell it. Could make a nice profit too. Bone china."

"Real bone?"

"None realer. Rendered down to ash and mixed with quartz, feldspar, and clay. It's the bone that gives it that lovely translucent white."

"It's stunning, really."

Zander blushed. Simon's smile faltered as something in the upstairs window caught his eye. A gentle twitch of the crochet curtains.

"Do you live around here?" Zander was saying.

"Used to. When I was a kid."

"Did you? I don't suppose you knew the little girl?"

Simon clinked his cup on the saucer, wishing he had lied. "Who? Sorry?"

"The little girl who went missing. Maggie something? Megan? Apparently she lived just over the road. This was years ago, before I moved in. I was renting a place across town then, up by the big Wegmans."

"Mm-mm. No." Simon shook his head.

"Tragic. I still remember it. It was all over the news."

"Really."

"I joined in the search party."

"Did you."

"Oh, I had to. Had to do something."

"And did you find anything?" Simon said, feigning disinterest.

"Nothing at all," said Zander despairingly. "It was terrible. We all wanted to find her so badly. But you know—" He paused midsentence, then looking slightly embarrassed pulled back with a downward shake of his head.

"You were going to say something."

"It's nothing. You'd think it's a bit airy-fairy anyway, a hard-boiled detective like yourself."

"You'd be surprised what I might believe."

Zander seemed to check the area for eavesdroppers, then leaned across the table, half whispering.

"Well, I did have a strange feeling while I was searching the edge of the forest around the museum. I felt I could sense her, the little girl. Or *some* girl."

"Sense her?"

"Her spirit."

Something in Simon's unconscious reaction made Zander pull back and reform his tone. "As I said, it's a bit—"

"No," Simon said. "It's fine."

"It's just that where I come from, believing in spirits isn't some strange thing. It's part of the culture."

"Is it?"

"Oh, yes. Zulu healers—we call them sangomas—commune with the dead to heal illness and strife. We communicate with our ancestors by throwing bones and other items—shells, stones, that sort of thing. The spirits provide answers to our troubles in the pattern."

"Are you Zulu?"

"Not exactly," Zander admitted with a wincing smile. "But I feel a great kinship with them. It's why I'm so fond of my china. It's the closest I'll ever get to throwing bones—literally 'throwing' a pot made from their ash. Working with the materials, I feel I'm something of a sangoma myself."

Simon felt a little uncomfortable at this but struggled to justify the feeling. He couldn't see how Zander's private appropriation of Zulu culture was hurting anyone, or whom it would benefit to call him on it. Besides that, he related warmly to Zander's fondness for bones, a subject most found macabre.

"Say, do you take commissions?" Simon asked.

"I do, of course! Anything you like. What did you have in mind? A raku vase? A bit of crockery? Porcelain, stoneware, bone?"

"Bone. Definitely. I don't mind what, per se."

"Potter's choice. I like it."

"I just wonder, if I were to provide the bone myself . . . some very old bone."

"Animal?"

"Technically, yes."

Zander shrugged. "I don't see why that should be a problem."

A price was agreed for a surprise bone china creation. Zander would get started once Simon had delivered the raw materials. A bag of dinosaur fossil fragments could be ordered online for less than twenty dollars a pound, pieces too small and unremarkable to be of any scientific or exhibition value. Simon was amazed no one had thought of it before.

Three quarters of an hour later he left Zander's house with a warm convivial feeling, each stating truthfully they looked forward to seeing the other again soon. That was *two* friends now, Simon thought. He was becoming something of a social butterfly among the geriatric set.

As he turned off Granton Avenue, however, his spirits moldered. His mind bubbled with a sludge of unpleasant thoughts: of search parties, the woods surrounding Hawthorne Hollow, and the strange feeling the potter had interpreted as Morgan's ghost.

The memory of Theo resurfaced in Simon's mind. Twice Morgan had foisted him on the animal's spectral form, forced him to bear witness to Theo's pain. What had Evie said about the museum's prehistoric specters? *Lost in the suffering of their dying moments, until their souls at last find peace.* Was it peace Morgan wanted for Theo? Release from whatever suffering Simon had witnessed in the Hall of Gems and Minerals?

As he drove he made an unexpected turn, heading north toward the museum. He had a sudden desire to handle Theo's bones, to feel close to the animal that was apparently so important to his sister.

Thanks to Earl and Carol's speedy work, preparation of the skeleton was 90 percent complete—his careful study of them, less so. He shut himself in the lab and made a start: examined every tooth and claw, considered the possible significance of every break and scratch. He even noted with curiosity the conical tooth marks in the bone that Mueller had likened to that of a crocodile.

It was a good observation, one Simon wouldn't have made himself.

Perhaps he'd been rash to banish Mueller's diaries to the Cave. The paleontologist may have gone cuckoo toward the end, but he'd studied Theo's remains for years, including several fossils now lost to damage.

He'd made plenty of good observations, even some credible theories. How many more lay hidden in the entries Simon hadn't read? What secrets was Morgan waiting for him to uncover that Mueller's manuscript might help bring to light?

Simon knew where Maurice kept his spare keys, knew which key unlocked the door to the Cave. Simon was a rule follower, a teacher's pet—a personality trait formed in opposition to his mother's lawlessness and out of a desire to attract, from his teachers, the approval he'd never gotten at home. Still, if he wished to break from that pattern—just this once—no one would stop him. It would be only too easy.

From the Research Diaries
of Dr. Albert Mueller

October 1, 1999

Yahoo! Hoorah! Hip hip hooray!

Today I am celebrating. You may wonder why,
when progress on Theo's preparation has all but
stalled for the last several months. I need
not remind you of the tragedy that occurred at
the Hawthorne this summer, and the resultant
revenue shortage that ended in the unceremonious
disbandment of my team.

I have drenched the pages of these diaries
with my feelings on the latter matter, the
former too painful to address for reasons I
shall not discuss here. In any case, I remain
puzzled as to why my team should have been
slashed from the budget when my department is
more than adequately funded by the Mitchells'
donation! There is a stench of financial
misappropriation in the air, but alas. From five
we have been whittled down to one, and though I
continue—literally—to chip away at the project,
I fear it may now be years before Theo is ready
to exhibit.

And yet today, for the first time in months,
I was given reason to rejoice. Of the many
mysteries that surround Theo's life and death,
at least one has at last been solved.

This morning I had the pleasure of welcoming

to the museum my dear friend and colleague
Professor Leonora Brito of the University of
Cincinnati. Dr. Brito and I met at Harvard in
the sixties and became fast friends, bonding
over our shared fondness for Dusty Springfield
and the programs of Lucille Ball. Today she is
a respected paleontologist specializing in the
Lourinhã Formation of western Portugal, which,
among its many extraordinary qualities, is known
to share many of the same fauna as the Morrison
Formation, including *Supersaurus*, *Allosaurus*,
and even *Ceratosaurus*. Dr. Brito has remained a
loyal friend through the turmoil of recent years,
always seeking to help me back into the fold.

This last week she has been conducting
research at the University of Pennsylvania,
but before she left town, was eager to stop
in to see me—or more realistically, Theo. Dr.
Brito was extremely impressed and made many
useful observations that I will take forward
in my research. I was pleased, for one,
that after looking at the tooth embedded in
Theo's vertebra, she agreed it belonged to an
Allosaurus and that such an animal was likely
responsible for Theo's death. But that is not
why I am celebrating.

You may remember my describing in an earlier
entry a small, slender mystery of a bone
discovered in the matrix with Theo's skeleton.
It clearly did not belong to Theo himself and
appeared to have been scavenged by the same
animal he had. Until today I have struggled to

classify it and far less hazard a guess at its species. But the moment Dr. Brito locked eyes on the fragment, she let out a faint, "My god!"

"You know what it is?"

"I do, of course. Al, look at it. Look!"

"I've been looking."

"Not closely enough. It's the bone of a juvenile. The fibula of a young *Ceratosaurus*."

A young *Ceratosaurus*, found in the same bone bed as Theo? "His offspring?"

"Ah, I don't think so," said Dr. Brito. "The ontogeny of the species is unique. *Ceratosaurus* grew quickly but didn't mature sexually until later in its development. The juvenile couldn't have been older than three years old when it died, likely born before Theo could breed."

"If it's not his offspring, then it must be . . ."

"Go on," Brito said.

"His sibling?" My head swam, the words tripping out of my mouth with abandon. "A sibling dispatched at the same place and time as its brother, perhaps by the same executioner. But how could that be? I thought *Ceratosaurus* was solitary."

"It was. We've found tracks in Lourinhã proving so."

"But this seems to suggest they remained in family groups."

"Ah, but under what circumstances?" Brito said. "Answer that and you've got a real discovery on your hands. Just what you need to be taken seriously again."

"You know the answer already, Leonora. I can
see it in your—"

"I know nothing."

She laid a hand on my shoulder, smiling.

"It's not over for you, Al. Not yet."

CHAPTER THIRTY-TWO

THE MISSING PEACE

As Simon read, his mouth fell open in disbelief.

Mueller's team had unknowingly dug up a second *Ceratosaurus*, potentially a sibling—only part of it, though. Where had the rest gone? Lost to the fickle whims of the fossilization process, or had the siblings been physically separated before death?

Simon recalled the Hall of Gems and Minerals, the prismatic image of a dying Theo wailing in despair. A pain that seemed to go deeper than his physical injuries. Was it the loss of his sibling he had mourned? A sister perhaps, taken by the same animal that left him for dead? Had he died trying to get her back?

Lost in the suffering of their dying moments, until their souls at last find peace.

It all fit: Theo longed for his lost sibling. That longing had followed him into the afterlife, imprisoning him within the boundaries of the hollow.

Like Simon's, Theo's sibling had been taken from him, and he would not rest until they were reunited.

It was clear now what Morgan wanted him to do, and it was not to figure out what had happened to her. She had relinquished that hope already; the mystery was too big, with too little evidence to go on. Whatever he might have told Zander, Simon was no detective; the only clues he knew how to find and interpret were those that lay buried in rock.

She knew this, and for this reason she had called him back. To right not a two-decade-old wrong, but a prehistoric one. To help reunite Theo with his sibling.

It was wild, nearly impossible, and, he allowed, quite possibly an elaborate fiction growing in the fractures of his mind. But regardless of how illogical it seemed, he felt in his bones that he must try—if not for Morgan or Theo, then for himself.

For it seemed likely now that he would never resolve Morgan's disappearance. He would never bring her abductor to justice and absolve himself of the guilt he had lugged around for decades like a ball and chain he refused to acknowledge.

But this. This he could do.

And if he did, perhaps it would almost be enough.

CHAPTER THIRTY-THREE

A BONE TO PICK

Craig Rutherford, who had not stepped foot in the museum in nearly a year, took the meeting from his resplendent home office, his executive office chair framed by built-in bookcases filled with matching sets of untouched leather-bound tomes. By all accounts Simon was lucky he had accepted the meeting at all. There was a slight delay on his end—the Wi-Fi in the basement was as volatile as ever—but judging by the jowly squint frozen on his screen, things didn't appear to be going well.

"The Dolzer what, now?" Rutherford said.

"Dulzura Mesa Canyon," Simon repeated, fingers twitching under the desk with nervous energy. "In southwest Colorado. It's part of the Morrison Formation and has produced some of the most important Jurassic fossils ever discovered—Theo included."

"And you want to go there and what, dig up dinosaur bones?" Rutherford laughed, as if never having heard such a ridiculous request.

"Actually, I believe it could be just what the Hawthorne needs. N-not only would it enrich our fossil collection and create exciting new research opportunities, but it could also add incredible value to Theo's exhibit. Revenue-generating value."

"How's that, now?"

"Well, in the course of my research I've discovered evidence that when Albert Mueller's dig team found Theo they may have left behind a second skeleton, an extremely valuable juvenile *Ceratosaurus* that may well have been—"

"A baby?" Rutherford said, his interest piqued. "You're telling me Theo was a mama?"

"Perhaps."

"Mama and baby *rex*!"

"Er, *Ceratosaurus*," Simon said.

"We'd be the talk of the American Alliance of Museums. We'd have more visitors than we know what to do with, a line clear out to the highway."

"Yes," Simon said. "Yes, I agree!"

"See, Craig?" said Harry, who was also on the call. "I told you you'd wanna hear this. This project's got dollar signs written all over it."

"You bring up a good point," Rutherford said. "Or at least you've reminded me of one—you've never made a good point in your life." He barked out a laugh. Harry laughed too, at first. "Speaking of money, how much is this little field trip gonna cost?"

Simon was prepared for this question.

"The important thing is to consider the net balance," he said. "Conservatively, I project an exhibit of this nature could increase our ticket sales by over a hundred thousand admissions a year, and that's in the first twelve months alone. So from that perspective it won't cost us anything. In fact, it'll generate—"

"How much, Nealy?"

"Well—ideally, I'd like to spend a month in the field. Having done a quick audit of our equipment, I believe we'll need to invest in a few pieces—arm shovels, pickaxes, rock hammers, a few good knives. Then there's labor to consider. A local guide, a couple of experienced paleo people, maybe a few student helpers. Food, a camper van. Travel of course—"

"This doesn't sound good."

"Altogether, no more than thirty-five thousand."

"Thirty-five, you said?" Harry clarified.

"A very reasonable investment, I think."

"Reasonable," said Rutherford. "He thinks it's reasonable. That's great. I'll just tell our exhibit coordinator she's out of a job for a year because our resident dino dork wants to go play in the dirt for a month."

Harry burst with laughter, then, his video blurry, reached out to wipe the spittle off his webcam.

"But," Simon spluttered, desperate to get them back on board, "when you consider the millions the museum stands to earn if we find—"

"'*If* we find.' Now it's an *if.*"

"I mean—you can never be certain. There's so much we can't predict. We won't know for sure if it's out there until we're there."

The only thing Simon was digging now was his grave; he could see it in his bosses' expressions. But it was true: the chances of finding the rest of the juvenile's skeleton, realistically, were slim to none. There was no telling where the remains may have ended up, and that was assuming they had won the geological lottery and fossilized at all.

But Mueller would have tried, would have fought tooth and nail for the dig.

In death there is much that is lost, but never too little to be found.

I say, there is always hope of finding.

"Now, I like you, Nealy," Rutherford said. "I'd love to fund your little science fair project. But I guess you haven't noticed we're in the middle of a pandemic. We haven't sold a ticket in over a year, and I'm not about to shit—forgive my French—but I'm not about to shit thirty-five grand so you can have a monthlong vacation in the Rockies."

"W-what if I found the money?" Simon said. "Got a donor to fund it, say."

"A donor, well, that's a different story."

"I'll speak to Fran. I'm sure she'd be happy to help."

"You know what? I'll do you one better."

Rutherford reached for his cell phone, made the call, and reclined in his chair. Fran answered before the second ring.

"Franny, Craig Rutherford here." He didn't tell her he was putting her on speaker. Fran spoke, obliging to the least extent possible.

"What can I do for you, Craig?"

"Oh, Harry and I are just sitting here with Simon Nealy, who was telling us all about a bright idea he had to lead a monthlong expedition in Colorado to try and dig up Theo's kid's skeleton and we were wondering if you might have any donors who'd want to fund the little shindig. We're looking for thirty-five K. What d'you think?" There was silence; Rutherford smirked. "Franny, you with us?"

Simon felt bad for Fran. Rutherford had done the same to him before: called him out of the blue, unloaded a metric ton of information on him without the relevant context, and got annoyed when he failed to produce an immediate answer.

"Hi, Fran, it's Simon," Simon said. "Not sure if you can hear me. I'm on Zoom."

"What's all this about?"

"Well, as Craig was saying, we have an exciting opportunity to carry out a dig at the site where Theo was excavated, and we think it could be quite lucrative for the museum. The initial costs are around thirty-five thousand. Do you think this is something Evilyn Mitchell would be interested in funding? She's been such a good supporter of the paleontology program, and she and I have—"

"Mitchell? Not a chance in hell."

"You don't think she'd be interested?" Simon pressed.

"I don't care if she's interested or not. She just committed ten times that for Theo's exhibit. I'm not asking her for another penny until it's finished."

"I'm not sure I agree with that," Rutherford said. "We can sidebar on that later. But I agree we don't want to bother Mrs. Mitchell with this. You got anyone else who might be interested?"

"Mitchell's my big dino donor. We could look at foundations, but River's up to her eyeballs in grant deadlines and you wouldn't believe how long these things take to come through. If we get anything, it probably won't be till next year."

"That's what I thought." Rutherford eyed Simon smugly. "Say, Franny, why don't you give me a call this afternoon? I sent your sponsorship packet to a couple of board members and they had some pointers they wanted to share."

"Pointers?"

"Let's talk later." He ended the call and let out a satisfied sigh. "Hate to say I told you so, but—dagnabbit, look at the time. I gotta run, fellas. We're done here, yes?"

"All good," Harry said.

"Actually, I'd really like to—"

"Welp, have a good one."

The meeting ended.

Simon had to stop himself from slamming the laptop shut. He rose and paced, his hands balled into fists. Deciding he needed a better outlet for his rage, he threw open the door and stormed down the hall.

In the length of time it took for the elevator to convey him to the third floor, his anger had hardly dissipated. His ears were crimson and his grin manic as he entered the development office to find Fran on the phone, joined on this occasion by her turquoise-haired development associate, whom Simon knew only by their email signature: *River (She/They)*. They offered Simon a feeble smile, then jumped as Fran slammed down the phone.

"Hey, River," Simon said. "Any chance I could have a moment with Fran?"

"Don't move," Fran barked. "You," she said to Simon, "in the hall."

She pulled the door closed behind her with a slam. "What is it? I need to raise twenty grand before lunch or they're shuttin' the lights off."

"I get it—you're busy," Simon said. "I just wanted to have a word about this dig. I'm not sure it came across in that meeting, but this project is extremely important to the paleontology program, to the Hawthorne as a whole—"

Fran scoffed.

"And I would *really appreciate* your help funding it. I see you have reservations about asking Evie to support—"

"Evie." Fran sneered, still disapproving of the nickname. "Real bosom buddies, aren't ya?"

"No—"

"Oh please. I know all about your little May-December thing. The woman's old enough to be your grandma, but have at it, kid."

"Don't be ridiculous. You know we're just friends. And frankly it's lucky for you that we are, because I'm not sure she'd be supporting the museum otherwise."

"Forget it. She's *my* donor, and it's *my* call."

"But you know she'd fund it in a heartbeat."

"Course she would. That's not the point."

"Then what is the point?"

"Thirty-five grand ain't shit. I'm primin' the pump for a million-dollar planned gift. Seventy-five years old, all those assets, no family? We need to be in that woman's will stat, and I'm not about to let you fuck that up."

"Is that really all you care about?" Simon spat. "Money? I thought we were all here because we care about the museum. Because we're committed to the *mission*—"

"Don't you talk to me about commitment," Fran said, suddenly much closer to Simon's face than the museum's social-distancing policy allowed. "I've been here nineteen years, *nineteen*. While you were sittin' in math class, I was down at the ticket desk shillin' memberships for twenty-nine bucks a pop. When I started, this place was lucky to raise a hundred K a year—now we're doin' two mill in a bad year, double that since Covid. If it weren't for me, this place would've shut down a year ago. While our dufus overlords were sittin' at home scratchin' their scroti and waiting for the apocalypse to blow over, I was here workin' eighty-hour weeks knowin' if I didn't none of us would have a goddamn job in the mornin'. And for what? Senior staff treats me like an asshole—a clown. I know what you call me behind my back."

"I don't—" Simon said, but Fran was on a rampage.

"Nineteen years and I'm the only department head without an executive title. 'Why're you complainin', you're the only female director,' they tell me, like I won it on a fuckin' scratch card. Fourteen years it took me to get to director, *fourteen*, and here you waltz in, résumé shorter than your dick, a director from day one, and, let me guess—I'll bet they're even payin' ya six figures."

Simon faltered, finding himself suddenly without words.

Fran scoffed. "Sixty-two four. That's what they were payin' me before everyone took a twenty-percent cut for Covid, everyone but the leadership and new hires of course. What, ya didn't know? Why would you? You're a man in a woman's world. Three quarters of the nonprofit workforce are women, yet just twenty percent of organizations are run by them. People complain about women making eighty-two cents on the dollar—hell, in our field a gal'd be lucky to get anywhere near that. The nonprofit sector's built on the backs of women. Always has been." She stepped toward Simon, her lip curled menacingly. For a second he feared she might hit him. "So don't talk to me about commitment. Don't you *dare* tell me all I care about is money, 'cause unlike you and your little boys' club, I ain't makin' jack shit. You wanna do your little pet project, dig your little bones? Then why don't you take your big manly salary and make a fuckin' donation."

Simon felt a fleck of moisture land on his face. He stared at the floor. The office door slammed shut.

Alone again, Simon found himself stuck, unable to move, the wheels of his mind gluey and gnashing, as if attempting, for the first time in thirty-plus years, to turn in the opposite direction.

Through the door, he heard River ask something. Fran answered.

"Oh nothin', hon," she said. "Just another goddamn day."

CHAPTER THIRTY-FOUR

FRIGHT OR FLIGHT

Two days later Simon sat typing away in his office. His sympathy for Fran and the female sex in general had shrunk back from the front of his mind, and he had returned to being furious with her. However warranted her grievances, he condemned her refusal to help him as callous, even unprofessional. It wasn't *his* fault the Hawthorne had mistreated her. *He* had no control over the fluctuations of her salary. *He* had been nothing but kind to her, even abstained—in the face of great temptation—to engage in the cruel name-calling in which many of his colleagues had indulged. And she had the nerve to accuse *him* of misogyny?

He wondered if all this inequality discourse—*important as it is*, he hastened to add—had not the ability to reinforce divisions rather than erode them, to make enemies of good men and martyrs of unlikable women. Whatever happened to treating people how you wished to be treated? To good, old-fashioned doing your job?

If Fran wasn't going to help him fund the dig, then Simon would just have to do it himself.

Thus, he had spent the afternoon crafting a proposal to the A. R. Swanson Foundation for Paleontological Research, requesting a grant of thirty-five thousand dollars for his expedition to Dulzura Mesa Canyon. He was just putting the finishing touches on his needs statement when he heard the familiar rumble of spirits. In addition to being afraid, he felt annoyed with himself; he'd been getting better about remembering to leave before dark.

His work saved, he snatched up his things, took the stairs up to the entrance hall, and headed for the exit. His intention to flee quickly was thwarted, however, by the vague sense that something was off. The hall had a strangely airy quality, unburdened in a way he could not put his finger on.

He gazed up to where the trio of pterosaur skeletons had once swirled in a fleshless imitation of flight. Now there were only two of them. In the absence of the third, the *Pteranodon*, he saw only the dark cords that had held it in place. Bolted into the vaulted ceiling, they swished through the air at an unsettling tempo, as if abandoned swiftly only moments before.

Simon listened as a strange murmur echoed through the hall. Not the sound of an animal, but of a person speaking. The voice dribbled through the open doors of the planetarium at the back of the hall.

It grew louder as Simon passed through the doors and followed the carpeted L-shaped hallway into an auditorium of old-fashioned, red velvet seats pointing up toward a multihued cosmos. It churned across a dome-shaped screen, as a British voice—the one Simon had heard from outside—glazed the scene in his velvety narration.

"Traveling across the vast ocean of space at over a billion kilometers per hour, light from the neighboring galaxy will not reach Earth for nearly twenty-five years . . ."

Simon squinted around at the projection booth two-thirds of the way up the auditorium. It was empty but for an ancient and bizarre-looking projector resembling a sphere with two dozen eyes over a metal cage. The contraption whirred and clanked, waving beams of light out of its whirling lenses. Knobs turned and switches flicked unaided, the machine appearing to work of its own volition.

With the deafening strength of a low-flying plane, a terrible, birdlike screech rent the air.

Simon spun around, ducking. Slowly his eyes followed up the screen, his face blanching to bloodless horror.

A giant winged shadow darkened the screen, circling behind it like a vulture with a twenty-two-foot wingspan and a three-foot cranial crest. The animal seemed to register Simon's presence. It beat its wings bracingly and touched down against the domed screen, which buckled under its weight, distorting the flow of stars across it.

CHUNK—a great beak exploded through the screen like a spear. As the animal wrenched its jaws apart, a vertical gash opened in the screen and a second ear-piercing screech drowned out the recorded narration.

The sound brought Simon to his senses with a snap. Stumbling back, he took off through the auditorium, away from the sounds of vicious pursuit, the savaging of the screen, and the swooping of giant membranous wings.

Simon cried out as sharp claws latched on to him, tugging upward, and his feet parted company with the floor. Five, six feet he rose in the air. Then there was a tearing sound and he fell to solid earth, his bloody shoulder exposed where his shirt had torn.

He scrambled to his feet and took off into the carpeted hall, followed by an onslaught of frustrated screams. The pterosaur was too large to pursue him any further. The last thing Simon saw, before he turned the corner, was its gangrenous sharp-toothed beak snapping hungrily through the darkness.

From the Research Diaries
of Dr. Albert Mueller

November 20, 1999

A morass of black unease churns within me. I can
feel it, the angst that has steadily accumulated
under my skin since the day Dr. Brito revealed
the identity of the mystery specimen.

How elated I was to learn the truth, how
alive with the hope of repairing my ruined
reputation . . . yet that glee was nothing
compared to what I feel now in its place, this
dark, brooding turmoil bubbling like a tar pit
risen from the depths of my soul.

I suppose it was inevitable after what
happened this summer. How could anyone experience
what I have—do what I did—and not be haunted by
ghosts of guilt and anxiety? Let it be known, I
never meant it to go that far. Never, *never* under
normal circumstances would I have—

Ah, but there are some forces greater than the
will of man, than the will of any animal, and what is a
man but another beast driven by its basest
impulses? Its hunger. Its thirst. Its animal desire.

Especially the latter. A desire that burns all the
greater when—like mine—it must be suppressed . . .

How unjust it is! What is so wrong with
having a taste for underripe fruit? So rarely
have I indulged in the delicacy—but there is
only so long a beast can hunger.

We all have our weaknesses.

Now I know mine.

But it got out of hand, and for that I have only myself to blame. How I wish I could undo what I did, or at least expunge the vile act from my mind. And yet every time I think of that damnable bone I'm reminded of that moment of weakness, that intrusion of evil into my otherwise clean-handed life.

For the fossil that Dr. Brito identified as that of a juvenile *Ceratosaurus* is proof that Theo lived with a sibling. A female, I am certain. A younger sister he cared for, provided for, protected.

JUST LIKE THE BOY.

I can hardly think of Theo now without being reminded of him. Of *them*—that human sibling pair with whom my life is now forever intertwined.

That poor girl! Even having destroyed the hateful bone and left, for scientific posterity, a pale imitation in its place, no longer can I suppress the guilt and fear of reprisal boiling up inside me.

No longer can I deny what I have done. Or worse, what I have let myself become— a MONSTER.

CHAPTER THIRTY-FIVE

A SKETCHY ACCUSATION

"**A** monster. He called himself a *monster*," Simon said.

"I'm aware, Mr. Nealy. I just don't think it means what you—"

"What else could it mean?"

Simon wrenched the phone away from his face in frustration. Typically Officer Williams's deep voice had a calming influence on his nerves, but the present conversation was proving an exception.

Simon was still groggy after the previous night, his stomach queasy after what he had put it through. In a nervous frenzy after escaping the planetarium, he had barely eaten before downing a third of a bottle of nighttime cough syrup and crawling into bed with Mueller's diaries, not realizing that instead of lulling him to sleep, they would keep him up half the night, attempting to make contact with the detective.

Unable to do so, Simon had driven to the police station first thing that morning only to be met with an abrupt dismissal by the receptionist, who informed him the station was still limiting "nonessential" visits.

You're nonessential, Simon wanted to say, marching back to his car, in which he now sat.

"Didn't you read what I sent you?" he persisted, clamping the phone between his head and shoulder as he flipped through the manuscript in his lap. "It's all here. 'Haunted by ghosts of guilt . . . a taste for underripe fruit.' He was a child predator. 'The boy and his sister,' that has to be us!"

"Mr. Nealy—"

"*Dr.* Nealy."

A glowering silence.

"Please," Simon said, relenting. "Just look at the date on it. November '99. Whatever he feels guilty about doing, he says it happened that summer. *Morgan disappeared that July.*"

"July 14. I'm aware."

"Then you can see it all fits."

"Maybe so," said Williams. "But to do anything we need probable cause that this Mueller guy killed your sister, and this just doesn't measure up."

"What? But—"

"I get why you're disturbed," Williams said. "I am too, believe me. But as a scientist you can appreciate the need for hard evidence."

Little though he wanted to admit it, the detective was right. Simon knew better than to jump to conclusions. In a scientific study, strong conclusions were ones that stood up to a battery of alternative interpretations and possibilities. Mueller's narrative hardly met that standard. How could Simon know he wasn't describing a different sibling pair, a different terrible choice he had made? That it wasn't all some elaborate and tasteless fiction, even that Mueller himself had written it?

Still, a hard knot of obstinacy lodged in Simon's gut; the more he tugged at it, the tighter it grew. There was one part of the diary entry he simply could not dismiss.

"The illustration."

Officer Williams seemed to be expecting this. "You mean the dinosaur eating the leg? I admit, that threw me. It's definitely weird."

"More than weird. Did you notice the pattern on the pants?" Simon waited for Williams to pull up the image.

"Looks like leaves," he observed.

"Look again. They're bugs. The day she disappeared Morgan was wearing white pants patterned with ladybugs, just like the ones in the drawing."

"I don't remember that on the missing persons report," Williams said.

"It wasn't on there. But I was with her that day. I remember." Simon hesitated. Did he remember? Or had Morgan simply worn those pants so often that Simon could hardly imagine her without them? "I'm almost positive."

"Almost?"

"Please," Simon said. "It's Morgan. He knew what she was wearing the day she disappeared, which means he must have taken her."

"Not necessarily. He might've seen her around the museum that day and remembered what she was wearing."

"And hid that information from police?"

"I'd need to dig through the files and check his statement."

Simon suppressed a groan of frustration. Why didn't Williams see it? The "poor girl" Mueller mentioned was Morgan. The object of his guilt, perhaps even—the thought made Simon sick—his "animal desire." Mueller knew what she had on that day because he'd lured her from the Hall of Insects and Animalia. He had taken her and—

What? Fed her to a dinosaur?

His insides froze over, as if caught in an ice age born from his fear.

"The point is," said Williams, "we've got a lot more work to do before we're ready to kick this guy's door down."

"Kick his door down? You mean, he's still alive?" Hadn't Maurice said he was dead, or insinuated as much? *Guess that makes you the new Bert, rest his soul.* Maybe he had misheard. "He must be quite old now."

"In his eighties. Records show he owns a house over in West Chester. Been there over forty years."

"So you can go talk to him."

"If this guy's as nuts as you say he is, I doubt there'd be much point," Williams said. "Give me a few days to look into this, all right? I want to take another look at his statement, see if I can find any holes. Maybe check the handwriting on the document, make sure it's legit. This is going to be an uphill battle and we'll need all the help we can get. If you've got anything more concrete, anything you can find at the museum to suggest Mueller might've—well, I'd be happy to take a look at anything you've got."

"I'll see what I can find."

"Just be careful, Dr. Nealy. Don't go getting yourself"—for a second Simon thought he was about to say *eaten*—"fired."

"Right." He stuttered out a laugh. "That, I think I can manage."

CHAPTER THIRTY-SIX

INITIAL FINDINGS

Before heading into work, Simon stopped at Zander Steyn's house to drop off the box of fossil fragments he had bought online—a mixed bag of mostly low- to mid-quality hadrosaur and ceratopsian bones. The potter answered the door wearing a khaki apron splattered with slip, his hands coated in clay. When he looked down into the box, his smile fell.

"They're quite dark, aren't they," he said. "Could affect the color. Might not get that classic bone china white."

"That's fine. However it comes out is great." Truthfully, Simon had bigger things to worry about.

Zander tucked the box under his arm. "You know, I didn't take you for a dinosaur fan."

Eager to maintain the division between his identity and that of his detective alter ego, Simon replied, "I'm not. But my nephew is. This will be for him. One day."

"Did you hear they're building a new dinosaur exhibit at the Hawthorne—?"

"Sorry, wish I could stay and chat, but I have to get going. Big case."

"I shan't delay you." Simon was already turning to leave when Zander added, "How should I contact you when it's finished?"

"Er—I'll text you. That way you'll have my cell."

"It's been years since a young man gave me his number," Zander said, tittering. "Sorry, shouldn't have said—you're probably not even—"

"I am." Simon wasn't sure why he had said it, why part of him wanted Zander to know. He was fond of Zander, but not in that way.

"Oh." The potter had gone beet red. "Well, that's—"

"Have a good day. I'll see you soon."

"I'd like that. I mean, yes, goodbye!"

Simon arrived at the museum some twenty minutes later and paused midway across the entrance hall, his gaze drawn to the yellow X of caution tape strung across the planetarium doors.

A swell of dread crashed over him as he recalled the nastiness of the previous evening, which had paled in comparison to the implications of Mueller's manuscript. He was reassured, at least, to see the *Pteranodon* reinstated to its overhead display.

He ducked under the barrier and entered the auditorium, pausing at the edge of a puddle of light formed under a giant hole in the ceiling. The planetarium was a scene of destruction. The curved screen hung off the walls like knifed flesh, chunks of old-fashioned projector lay scattered around the room, and Maurice, for once with his mask pulled up over his nose, was on his knees scrubbing a seat encrusted in an off-white substance that reminded Simon unpleasantly of pigeon excrement.

At the sight of him, the custodian nodded and got to his feet. "Hey there, dino boy. I'd stand back if I was you."

Simon did, but his eyes still watered at the smell. "Maurice—"

"What can I say? Demons at it again."

"I'm so sorry." Simon meant it. He couldn't help feeling this was somehow his fault.

"Ain't been too bad except for the last few months. Used to be I just heard 'em, the bangs and the rumbles." Maurice gazed up toward the dome with bloodshot eyes. "They stirred up about something."

"Stirred up?"

"Could be a new demon in town. Or an old one woke up. They do that sometimes—go quiet awhile, then come back. You keep your ears open, dino boy. Something's different. Something ain't right."

Simon thought of the oversized bloody footprints in the entrance hall, and a line of shocking cold trickled from his neck down his back. Looking up, he realized rain was falling through the hole in the ceiling.

"Say, Maurice, I need to grab a few things out of the archives. You mind if I borrow your key?"

"You got an authorization form?"

"Not exactly," Simon said.

"Sorry. Rules are rules." With a sigh, he returned to his knees and continued scouring.

An hour later Simon stood in the earthen-walled depths of the archives riffling through his dozenth drawer of institutional files. Starting in the paleontology section, he had hoped to uncover more of Mueller's personal writings or, better yet, physical evidence connecting him to Morgan. A lock of her reddish-brown hair perhaps, or a scrap of fabric crawling with scarlet printed ladybugs. It chilled Simon to imagine the private thrill Mueller might have derived from inhaling the scent of such an item. But why would he keep it here of all places?

Simon paused as a dull protracted animal sound filled the room, mournful and weird, like the bass note of a dented trombone.

Maurice was right; the sounds were becoming more frequent.

He hoped the custodian wouldn't miss him—or his spare keys.

Simon continued his search and paused as he stumbled upon a large binder, aged and peeling at the edges, wedged in at the bottom of a drawer. None too delicately he yanked it out, causing the cabinet to wobble precariously. He raised the book into the light and smeared the dust from the cover. A plastic window on the spine contained a card bearing a message in Mueller's distinctive scrawl: *READ ME.*

He opened it, revealing the first of many plastic sleeves presenting a time-ordered exhibition of historical documents—news clippings, handwritten correspondence, internal memos. He paged through them with interest. A paper-thin article clipped from the *Wrexham Gazette* reminded him of a prop in a period film, the masthead dated March 6, 1908. DAUGHTER OF POLITICIAN ATTACKED AT HAWTHORNE MUSEUM, MAN ARRESTED, read the headline.

It described an incident in which a nine-year-old Phoenixville girl sustained injuries to her chest, arms, and legs consistent with a knife attack while visiting the Hawthorne with her county commissioner father. The girl was allegedly exploring the Hall of Dinosaurs alone when her scream rang out. Moments later, museum staff found her lying on the floor covered in blood, and the museum's caretaker, Mordecai Jackson, bent over her body.

> Mr. Jackson claimed to have come running at the sound of the girl's cries for help. The child, her mind visibly addled by the attack, was said to have been rambling nonsensically and alleged Mr. Jackson was innocent.
>
> Mr. Jackson was arrested and the child taken to Chester County Hospital, where she is recovering well from her injuries. Commissioner Cromleigh, who was in a meeting with the museum's executive director, Mr. Robert Henry Hawthorne, when the attack occurred, expressed in no uncertain terms his continued support of the museum, which he called "one of the great cultural institutions of our nation."
>
> The museum will remain closed through the end of the week as staff works to bolster security. Police continue to search for a weapon.

Simon turned the page to find a yellowed telegram on Postal Telegraph letterhead, the word CONFIDENTIAL stamped across the upper corner.

```
Wrexham Pa Mar 7-08
Augustus Hawthorne
5th Ave New York Ny


Father,
Received your message this morning. I assure
you situation is under control and no need for
you to question my appointment, which I believe
Ive managed admirably despite the challenges the
satanic museum continues to present. Situation
with girl is being handled. As you know, police
are satisfied that Jackson is to blame, a theory
we support. Girl continues to claim she was at-
tacked by a great flying beast not unlike our new
pterodactyl. We are lucky, even the father is
calling it hysteria. Lets hope that is the last
of this nastiness for a while. RH
```

As he continued to flip through the book, Simon found more evidence of a bloody past long buried. Newspaper clippings dated 1916,
1925, and 1938 described the violent death of a woman in her forties, the
sudden disappearance of an elderly researcher, and the kidnapping of an
infant, whose severed legs were the only parts of her anyone could find.
Simon could draw no connection between the three victims except for
the mysterious nature of the crimes, each one pinned unconvincingly
on the most obvious suspect—the husband with whiskey on his breath,
the disgruntled research assistant, the depressive mother.

At the back of his mind rattled another explanation, one that recalled Mueller's gruesome illustration: that the museum's lost and dead,
like his sister, had been the victims of a rapacious prehistoric appetite.

Awful as it was, he couldn't deny it made a kind of sense. At least
it explained why they had never found Morgan's body. But then what
of the guilt expressed in Mueller's diaries? Had he been the one to
feed her to the carnivore? Or had the attack been unplanned, an un-

expected ambush, leaving Mueller guilt stricken that he had failed to save her?

Whatever the cause of the museum-goers' demise, the local press seemed to have noticed a pattern. According to the author of a piquant editorial entitled MUSEUM OF DEATH: HAWTHORNE BATTLES BLOOD-SOAKED IMAGE: "Naturalist John Burroughs once wrote, 'I seldom go into a natural history museum without feeling as if I were attending a funeral.' However, in the case of Wrexham's Hawthorne Museum, the funerals tend not to occur until after the visitors have left."

By the 1950s, the museum appeared to have gone more than a decade without a death, or at least had become more adept at hiding them. A 1953 letter to Giles Rutherford, then board chair of the Hawthorne, read:

> *Dear Giles,*
>
> *I thank you again for the museum's cooperation in last week's distressing investigation. As I'm sure you'd agree, there could be no matter more serious than the death of an innocent teenage girl, especially in such a gruesome and unaccountable way. The Wrexham police department is determined to bring the culprit to justice by whatever means necessary.*
>
> *Nevertheless, as one of the Hawthorne's most loyal advocates, with many happy memories of hours spent strolling your halls as a boy, and now with my own growing family, I remain committed to the prosperity of your institution and appreciate your note about the delicate nature of this subject and its potential impact on your public affairs. On that basis, I believe it's in the best interest of both the police department and the museum that this crime is treated with the utmost sensitivity.*
>
> *Though they remain understandably devastated, the girl's family has agreed to withhold public comment in aid of our ongoing investigation. Meanwhile, I have taken the liberty of speaking with our mutual friend Gene Withers at the Gazette and am confident that the paper will honor our shared wish for silence until such a time as the museum is ready to release—on an exclusive basis—any and all pertinent details. Once again, Gene sends his sincere thanks for giving him the run of your dinosaur hall for his grandson's fourth birthday, which he tells me has earned him the title of "best pop pop in the world."*

Suffice it to say, we all appreciate our special relationship with the Hawthorne. Equally, I remain indebted to the board, who were so generous in their support of my reelection campaign last year.

I look forward to partnering with you all for a stronger Hawthorne for many years to come.

In ossibus terrae veritas
invenietur,
Don Cranis
Chester County Sheriff

Simon finished feeling deeply uneasy, disturbed by the implications of what he had read. How long had the Hawthorne been leveraging community connections to avoid scrutiny for the deaths and disappearances that occurred on its premises? Simon knew well the power of institutions like the Hawthorne to maintain close friendships. Unlike the corporate world, which worshipped at the altar of profit and would slit any throat to keep shareholders happy, the nonprofit world traded in affinity, devotion. In family legacies that often went back generations. For good and bad, its rivers ran deep.

But how deep? Had this "special relationship" continued as late as the nineties? Had the police intentionally sunk the investigation into Morgan's disappearance?

Simon thought uncomfortably of Williams's refusal to take action against Mueller, and wondered if they were still doing so.

But Morgan's case had been all over the news. The police had been active in bringing the community together to find her. They had even spoken at Morgan's candlelight vigil. The Hawthorne's special privileges had surely lapsed at some point in the past forty-odd years.

If Simon needed more evidence of this, he found it a few pages later in one final clipping from the *Gazette*, this one dated July 15, 1999.

**UNSUPERVISED GIRL, 6, DISAPPEARS DURING VISIT
TO HAWTHORNE MUSEUM**

Simon's throat constricted as his sister's freckled gap-toothed face beamed through the plastic in faded color. It was his first time seeing the article, but he knew this photo. It was her kindergarten school picture, a simple headshot against a basic gray background, the one that came free with the cheapest photo package. Her smile was so exuberant it looked almost devious, her hair a sleek cascade over a nest of inner chaos.

Simon recalled the morning the photo was taken—frantically attempting to tame her tangles with a comb, trying to convince her to wear something other than the ladybug outfit for once, something clean. The portrait was evidence he had failed on both accounts. She was wild and messy, unself-consciously stained. The poster child for parental neglect. A picture of indomitable joy.

When he couldn't take any more, he lowered the binder and closed it. As he went to return it to the drawer, he noticed something slide out and hit the floor. A folded letter, fallen from one of the interior pockets, apparently written by Mueller himself.

To my evil detractors—

I have heard the whispers thronging against me for years, ever since the accusation of one meddlesome VS. You say I am dangerous, that I am insane. You say the ghosts, as I see them, do not exist.

For any who should raid my files seeking evidence against my soundness of mind, I present these documents as proof of what I have known for months to be true—that I am not the only one who has seen them. I am not the only one who knows.

Sincerely,
Dr. Albert J. Mueller

Simon paused, then quickly reread the note, hoping it would make more sense the second time around. *Ever since the accusation of one meddlesome VS.* Was Mueller saying someone with the initials VS had made an accusation against him, an accusation that sparked rumors of his being delusional and unsafe?

Hope fizzed through Simon like a bottle rocket. If the accusation had to do with Morgan, if this accuser had seen something the police didn't know about—but he was getting ahead of himself. He had questions to answer first, starting with the obvious: *Who is VS?*

From the Research Diaries
of Dr. Albert Mueller

August 19, 2000

It is three years to the day since specimen
HMNH 4589 was delivered to the steps of the
Hawthorne. Three long years I have toiled away
at these bones, studied them, hunted for the
truths hidden beneath their stony exterior, not
realizing that all this time I was being studied
too—that I also was being hunted.

How could I have missed the signs! The
looming shadows I dismissed as a trick of the
light, the phantom disturbances I wrote off as
the natural creaks and utterances of an aging
museum! Never did I stop to imagine, *never once*
did the word flutter across my mind—GHOSTS.

It is a matter of consensus among the
metaphysical community that anyplace containing
the bones of the dead is bound to be haunted
to some degree. Being a member of a rather
different community—the scientific one—I never
believed it myself.

Until tonight.

My heart still races with the memory of it.
Woe to anyone who attempts to decipher these
ramblings, for I can hardly keep my hand from
shaking as I write . . . I was working late in
the museum as usual, drafting, by the light
of a dying candle, a strongly worded letter

to the president of the Society of Vertebrate Paleontology. I had recently learned my symposia proposal on the foraging habits of *Brontosaurus excelsus* has been passed over for a third year running—an insult of sauropodian proportions!

My outrage was in full flow when I noticed a change in the temperature of the room . . . It is said that the presence of spirits is wont to turn the atmosphere to ice, but tonight the opposite occurred. Within seconds a sweltering heat had flooded the office, tinged with the swampy odor of sulfur. My forehead unleashed a deluge of sweat and my shirt clung to me like a wet second skin. The candle guttered, as if an invisible presence had moved past it. The hairs on the back of my neck perceived the presence before I did, rising instantly to my defense.

The shadows of my office concealed an unwanted visitor. I could sense it behind me, could hear it—*the darkness was breathing*. Exhaling in short, powerful snorts against my neck. Hot with the stench of blood and rancid meat . . .

As I braced for death, I conceded to the mystics. It is true what they say: we are not alone in this place. A prehistoric creature stalks these halls, a creature I believe to be the reanimated spirit of Theo the *Ceratosaurus*.

I must be going mad!!

The trouble is, I do not feel so. When the sound of heavy footfalls from above sent the animal fleeing from the room, it was not relief I experienced—but disappointment. Despite my fear, a small part of me longs to see him again . . .

September 12, 2000

My wish has been granted! Theo came to me again
tonight and—by the light of the summer moon—I
managed to get a proper look at him. I would be
the envy of every paleontologist the world over
if only they would believe me!

I was leaving the museum at my usual late
hour when it happened. Locking the doors behind
me, I set out across the grounds to my vehicle
when I heard a nasty squelch underfoot—YUCK! I
had stepped in a significant pile of mess, my
pant leg soiled up to the calf. Yet quickly my
disgust turned to curiosity . . .

I stepped back and crouched above the scat.
It was still semisoft, not yet cold, perhaps
an hour old when I flattened it. It emitted
the foul, eggy smell typical of the dung of a
meat eater. Not a bear—the pile was too large
for that, and contained a deer's undigested
rib bone. Even the most robust caniform would
struggle to pass such a snack without grave
internal damage . . .

As I examined the pile, I heard heavy
slouching footsteps in the distance. A chill
raced up the back of my neck.

Turning, I rose slowly to a stand. I remained
calm even as he emerged from around the side of
the museum in measured steps like a lion ambling
across the savanna . . . More than afraid, I was
overcome. My throat gummed with emotion. The
threat of tears prickled behind my eyes—

He was—is—utterly magnificent, even in the

debilitated state in which his soul persists.
In the moonlight his pebbled skin shone ghostly
silver . . . bold vertical markings slashing
down across his body . . . brow horns flushed
with color over golden-orange eyes . . . the
nasal horn just as broken as the one we dug out
of that canyon . . .

   As my mind raced to observe his every feature,

from his horizontal posture to his supine
wrists, he noticed me with apparent surprise. He
stopped abruptly and sounded a warning. Not the
consuming roar of a movie monster, no—this was
more feeling than sound . . . a deep vibration
rattling up my spine without his even needing to
open his mouth.

With that one terrifying note, an ice-blast
of fear froze the blood in my veins. I could
not move, even as the dinosaur began to lumber
toward me . . .

Almost too late, I staggered back and ran—
ran like I had never run in my life. My legs
flew underneath me. A cacophony of discomfort
screamed through my muscles. I was a dead man.
A hole in the grass snatched my foot and tweaked
my ankle with an unexpected jolt of pain—my
ankle was shot! It was all I could do to drag
my foot behind me as I hobbled toward the woods,
the ground shaking beneath me in time with
Theo's slurred gait. Fffft-THUMP. Fffft-THUMP.

At last I crossed the tree line and collapsed
into the undergrowth . . . cowered as Theo reared
his head and his maw of daggerlike teeth bore
down on me . . . But through the gaps in my arms
I witnessed a miracle! The animal's snout seemed
to collide with the air and rebound. He shook his
head, tried again, lunging at me openmouthed—but
the impediment stood! What luck was this! It was
as if an invisible barrier stood between us at
the woods' edge—no part of him could move beyond
the borders of the hollow . . .

I laughed, rejoicing in my bizarre fortune.

Yet when he eventually gave me up and
staggered off, my mood descended into angst and
confusion.

Science alone is insufficient to explain the
dark logic of this place . . . and it is that
which frightens me most of all.

CHAPTER THIRTY-SEVEN

RANK AND FILE

Simon fidgeted in the Hall of Dinosaurs, unable to stop himself checking the time on his phone. Sounds of labor and collaboration echoed through the hall. Men in hard hats and MES shirts bustled before him at different heights, some drilling metal poles into the base of Theo's exhibit, while others, elevated on scaffolding, held the armature straight.

"Ready to go again, Dr. Nealy?" said the videographer from behind her camera. Simon turned to face her and the man with the boom mic.

"Right. Sure." He slid the phone back into his pocket.

It had been decided that before Theo was unveiled at the end of the gala, a short video would play, taking attendees behind the scenes of constructing his exhibit. Simon had been co-opted as star performer, a role for which he felt supremely ill suited.

"Er, what should I . . . ?"

The videographer huffed. "*Again*, take us through what the team's doing here today and the process you took to get here."

"Right. Okay." Simon cleared his throat, straightened up, and fixed a quivering smile on his face. "Today our partners at MES—that's Museum Exhibit Solutions—are here constructing the armature for Theo's exhibit. The armature is the iron framework that will hold the bones in place. It's, er . . . it's incredibly important for keeping the bones in the right position, and making sure that if there's an earthquake or another natural disaster, the skeletal framework holds up. Er, let's see . . ."

"Process—"

"The process, right. Well, for the last couple of months I've been working with the mount makers at MES to design Theo's pose and create detailed drawings showing the position of each bone. Unfortunately some have been lost to time, so we're working with a sculptor to create replicas of the missing—"

"*Fuck!*" erupted a pained voice behind him.

"Cut!" called the videographer through gritted teeth. Simon turned to spot one of the MES guys rushing across the hall, gripping his hand.

"Oh dear. Is he all right?"

"You know what, I think we've got it," said the videographer. "We can always have you record a voiceover in post."

"Oh. Wonderful," Simon said.

He checked the time again. While the video team packed up and the MES team paused to administer first aid to the worker's injured hand, Simon slipped out of the hall and headed for the stairs. Patricia might be back at any moment.

The third floor was as gloomy and quiet as ever. Though many businesses were transitioning back to in-person work, the Hawthorne as usual lagged behind the norm. With the museum opening delayed once again, most administrative staff were in no rush to give up the comfort of their work-from-home lifestyles. Patricia was meant to be an exception, but the seventy-nine-year-old executive assistant worked on-site in only the most theoretical sense, given the regularity with which she was away from the office for personal appointments and errands.

Simon passed her empty desk on his way to the HR office.

That too he expected to be empty. In fact he was counting on it. Though he'd looked on two separate occasions, he'd been unable to locate Mueller's employment records in the Cave. Must be somewhere in HR, and with any luck it contained information related to a complaint made by the enigmatic VS.

Fortunately Mercedes was working from home that day. Thus

Simon did not hesitate to barge into the HR manager's closed office to discover, with a jolt of shock, a college-age woman sitting reclined in Mercedes's seat, an arm buried in a bag of Flamin' Hot Cheetos.

Noticing Simon, she let out a low "Shit" and yanked out her earbuds, which continued to burble with the audio of the Netflix standup special playing on her laptop. She closed it with a *fwap*.

"Sorry," Simon said, scrambling for his mask. "Should've knocked—"

"I was just taking my lunch." The young woman was petite and casually dressed, with a flat voice at odds with her delicate bone structure.

"I'm Dr. Nealy. I work in Paleontology," Simon said.

"McKayleigh. Harry's niece."

Simon reached back into his memory of the senior staff meeting two weeks past, something about a temp being brought in to sort mail and answer telephones while Patricia spent three hours a day at the vet with her diabetic cats.

"Do you need something?" she said.

What Simon needed, he thought, was for her to vacate the office.

"Er, yes actually," he said. "I've been expecting a package and didn't see it by the mailboxes. Mercedes was signing for them, so I just thought I'd pop in and check."

McKayleigh looked around. "Haven't seen anything."

"It's from Paleo Biofacts out of Florida. Should be marked fragile."

She shrugged.

"You want me to go look for it or something?"

"Okay," said Simon brightly.

McKayleigh slumped, pushed back her chair, and bent down for something under the desk. Simon realized she was putting on her shoes.

She disappeared down the hall a moment later and Simon crossed to the metal filing cabinet in the corner of the room. He wrenched open one drawer after another, finding nothing but years' worth of employee handbooks, benefits guides, and museum-branded swag.

He tried the wide cabinet at the back of the room, intrigued to see the upper drawers labeled *A-I*, *J-R*, and *S-Z*. The middle drawer was surprisingly unlocked, and exceptionally organized compared to most

of the museum's records, hundreds of file folders arranged in precise al-
phabetical order. *Leave it to the Hawthorne to still be keeping paper files*, he
thought. It took him only a moment, though he couldn't quite believe
his luck, to locate the file marked *Mueller, A.*, and another to realize
McKayleigh was on her way back down the hall.

Panicking, he shut the drawer and backed away, shoving the folder
down the front of his tucked shirt. It slid coldly down his chest and came
to rest on his waistband.

"Sorry, didn't see anything," McKayleigh said, reappearing in the
doorway.

Simon was already backing out of the room, conscious of her eyes
on his bulging, strangely rectangular midsection.

"No worries. If it comes in, just, er, give me a shout."

His office door shut and locked behind him, Simon bent over his desk
and pored through the documents spread across it.

Mueller's employee file was rather fuller than he had expected, its
varied contents telling the story of a tumultuous and overlong tenure.
Following the strongly worded recommendation letters that accom-
panied the paleontologist's application, and a string of glowing performance evaluations highlighting his numerous research discoveries,
publications, and reputation as an emerging sauropod expert, Simon
sensed a change in the tenor of the documents.

Following the departure of Mueller's biggest supporter, Dr. Glennon
Shiel, the evaluations became progressively mixed. Several supervisors
noted Mueller's irritability, unsociability, and unwillingness to accept
feedback or "align his department's strategy with institutional research
or revenue goals." Wrote one supervisor in 1987:

Though knowledgeable and experienced in his field, Dr. Mueller adheres
stubbornly to dated models and methodologies inconsistent with current
scientific practices, thus producing increasingly outlandish theories. This
may explain why he has not published in years, not counting his unfor-

tunate contribution to the non-peer-reviewed Journal of Exceptional Paleontology *earlier this year, in which he claimed that the swamp-dwelling* Camarasaurus *laid its eggs underwater and its hatchlings were born knowing how to swim as well as modern walrus pups.*

After funding Dr. Mueller's years-long research into sauropod denning habits in good faith, we were dismayed by this embarrassing outcome, which required a further expenditure of funds buying up every copy of the journal to ensure it never saw the light of day.

Executive director Garfield Mitchell, Evie's husband, seemed to despise Mueller especially. Over the course of twelve nonconsecutive years, he had evidently issued Mueller multiple verbal warnings, signed formal reprimands calling Mueller a "crackpot" and "weenie," and been listed in an incident report describing a shouting match between the men that nearly turned physical. As it was Mitchell who had attempted to throw the first punch, before his deputy director leapt forward to restrain him, Mueller escaped punishment. Indeed, Simon wondered if Mueller had been kept on despite his unsatisfactory performance only to prevent him from speaking publicly about the incident.

The file contained no mention of Morgan's disappearance, but, following Mitchell's passing in the first months of the new millennium, Mueller's coworkers began to notice a change in his conduct. Complaints trickled into HR of his dark and furtive behavior. A mother who visited the museum with her young boys almost weekly sent a letter reporting having seen a "small balding man who looked like he had wandered in off the street" walking in circles around the Hall of Dinosaurs, muttering furiously under his breath. She couldn't hear him well but caught snatches of his utterances that made her blood run cold.

"Something about 'the big one needs to feed,' 'the sweeter the blood,' and, 'we're not alone . . . we're not alone in this place.'"

The words had the same effect on Simon as he read; he couldn't separate this image of Mueller from that of Morgan, sprinting through the museum, sobbing in terror, pursued by a shadow of outstretched claws and razor-sharp teeth that momentarily brought the Bone Man to mind.

He skipped quickly through the pages of Mueller's escalating strangeness. After all, that wasn't what he was after. What he needed was a complaint, a lost eyewitness account that implicated Mueller in Morgan's death. But he was beginning to lose hope. All that remained was a photocopy of an email—curiously, much of it redacted—addressed to someone at the museum.

He did a double take at the name of the sender.

Sent: Sat, May 11, 2002 at 1:33 PM
From: Violet Sippel
To: ███████████ ██████████

Dear Mr. ██████████,
    You probably don't know who I am because I doubt my ███████ dated ████████████ was ever shared with you or the rest of the board. My name is Violet Sippel, and from September 1997 to November 1999 I was employed at the Hawthorne as a visitor services associate, selling tickets, memberships, and gift shop goods, before resigning in protest to the Hawthorne's terrible refusal to ████████ ████████████████████████████████.
    I'm writing today to convince you to immediately fire Albert Mueller and launch an investigation into his involvement in the ████████ of ████████████.
    I'm sure you at least know that name. It belongs to the ████████ ████████ who disappeared from the Hawthorne Museum on ████████ ████. What you might not know is that the day after it happened, I sent a letter informing ████████████ that Dr. Mueller ████████████ ██ ██ ██. I had been sent home because I was so upset, but ████████████████ assured me he was investigating what happened that day.
    I now know that this was a lie.
    As far as I could see, no action was being taken. I continued to

follow up with ██████ and my supervisor regularly over the next weeks, but was brushed off with empty answers and threats to my position if I continued to "stir up rumors."

After four months, still nothing had been done. Mueller remained in his role, ██████ remained ██████, and I was beginning to suspect the leadership was purposely ████████████████ ██████████ in order to avoid a big scandal.

This incident has haunted me for the last three years. Many times I've thought about going to the police, but I have reasons why I can't and I'm sure they wouldn't listen to someone like me anyway, not in this town. That's fine. All I want is to see that man removed from the museum before another child is ████.

I beg you to take immediate action. I would be available to address the full board at your next meeting if you would kindly provide the relevant details.

Faithfully,

VS

Simon put down the email, his mind swirling with the potential of what he'd just read. He had found his accusation, but of what? What had Violet Sippel seen or heard to make her so sure that Mueller was guilty? And if the Hawthorne had been investigating him like they had told her, where was the evidence in his file?

As he returned the email to the folder, Simon noticed a backward sentence showing through the top of the paper—the final line of the message, running onto the back side of the page.

Whoever had redacted this document seemed to have missed it too, for they had forgotten to hide one crucial name.

P.S. Once you're done investigating Mueller, you should start on that lying son of a bitch, Garfield Mitchell.

CHAPTER THIRTY-EIGHT

A DREADFUL LIKENESS

Two portraits of Garfield Mitchell hung in the Hawthorne Museum. Both depicted a short, extremely wide-set man with ruddy cheeks, fingers interlaced before him.

Apart from this, the two Mitchells were nearly unrecognizable. The subject of the first portrait, whose plaque bore the dates 1980–89, wore a boxy suit, thick plastic-framed glasses, and a thin blond mustache. A cloud of sandy hair frothed from the back of his dimpled pate, and his smile conveyed a wry grandfatherly warmth.

In the portrait dated 1998–2000, what remained of the executive director's hair was steely gray, like the beard covering his unsmiling face. His wrinkles were deeply inscribed like elephant skin, and the hazel eyes that once sparkled behind his lenses now speared the canvas with quiet despair. He not only appeared far older than the passage of nine years could account for; this man, by Simon's estimation, was utterly haunted.

If Violet Sippel was right, perhaps there was more to the transformation than the loss of the subject's teenage son. The final line of her email seemed to imply that Mitchell had been involved in suppressing investigations against Mueller in order to keep the Hawthorne out of the news. Perhaps by the time the second portrait was painted, the seriousness of his actions was starting to get to him; Simon knew all too well that guilt like that could destroy a man.

And yet it didn't add up. Simon had gleaned from multiple sources that Mitchell despised Mueller. If so, why would he bury an investigation into alleged criminal activity that could be used to justify his dismissal? Simon suspected there was more to the story waiting to be unearthed, but he couldn't think about that. He needed to remain focused on the task at hand, which was uncovering the full details of Sippel's accusation.

After another surreptitious rummage through the Cave, Simon could find no trace of her original complaint. He would write to her at the email address contained in her letter, but he'd need to tread carefully. Invested as she was in Morgan's case, she might recognize his name. He couldn't have her sharing publicly that Morgan Jenks's brother was working for the Hawthorne and attempting to take it down from within. Better she didn't know his identity at all.

Creating a dummy email account for his alter ego, he tapped out a brief message.

Dear Ms. Sippel,

My name is Theo, and I'm a private detective hired to investigate the Hawthorne Museum in Wrexham. It's come to my attention that you previously worked at the museum and may have information related to Albert Mueller and Morgan Jenks, a young girl who went missing there more than two decades ago. It is my hope to speak with you at your earliest convenience. Your testimony would be incredibly helpful in bringing the fate of the girl to light and the person responsible to justice. Would you be available for a call this week?

Theo

Simon hit send, feeling nervous but hopeful.

After a few days he still hadn't received a reply and was more than beginning to fret. Why wasn't she answering? Had she given up on the case after all these years? Had the museum silenced her, paid her off and forced her to sign an NDA?

Later that day Simon was working in his office when Earl stopped by to call him into the lab. "Got something I think you're gonna wanna see," he said with an impish grin.

Following the volunteer, Simon entered the lab to find several new bones laid out on the table, each of them meticulously cleaned and ready for display.

"These look great," Simon said, admiring a humerus inscribed with more of the strange tooth marks that neither he nor Mueller had succeeded in identifying to their satisfaction. "How much longer before you're all finished, you think?"

"Oh, I'd say we're ninety-five percent there. A few weeks maybe?"

"Excellent work, Earl. I can't thank you enough."

"Heck, that's not even what I wanted to show you."

Earl took a slim rectangular box off the counter and presented it to Simon. Through the glass viewing window in the hinged lid, he observed two dozen prehistoric teeth in foam-lined compartments.

"These yours?" Simon said.

"Yes, sir. Thought I'd lost them. Found them in a box in the attic over the weekend. You might wanna grab that one on the bottom row, second to the left."

Simon opened the lid and removed the tooth. He held it in his palm. It was about two centimeters long, conical and curving to a sharp point. "Crocodyliform?"

Earl didn't answer the question. "You might want to take it over to that humerus."

Simon approached the arm bone with its strange indentations.

"Wait," he said, a thought occurring.

Earl smirked.

Simon worked the tooth into his fingers and inserted the point of it into one of the indentations in Theo's bone. A breath caught in his throat. It was a perfect fit.

"Like a cock in a cunt-hole," Earl said. "Or in your case, a—"

"What is this?" Simon cut him off, examining the tooth as he spun it between his thumb and index finger.

"*Eutretauranosuchus*. Late Jurassic species of goniopholidid crocodyliform. This baby was found in Canon City, Colorado."

An ancient relative of the modern crocodile, just like Mueller had guessed.

"Earl, this is incredible!"

"Happy to help. Just wish I had that tooth back in the day. Could've put that question to bed years ago."

Simon's gaze lingered on Earl as the older man returned the tooth to its display box; only now did he remember that this wasn't his preparator's first role at the Hawthorne.

"You worked for Albert Mueller, didn't you?"

"Sure did. Back in, oh, late nineties or so."

The period during which Morgan had disappeared, Simon thought. Had Earl seen something? Heard rumors of Violet Sippel's accusation?

"What was he like, Mueller?" Simon said, turning his attention to the bones on the table.

"Eh. Bit stuffy. Didn't like him much."

"No?"

Earl shrugged, avoiding Simon's eye. "Hard to say, I guess. I didn't stick around long."

"You didn't happen to know someone named Violet Sippel, did you?"

Earl paused. When he answered, the words came out in a tumble. "Sippel, no, doesn't ring a bell."

"Younger girl, I think. Worked at the ticket desk—"

"Well, I better get these packed up." Earl still wasn't looking at Simon. "Got an appointment to get to. Proctologist. I'll spare you the gory details, though maybe you're into that."

"That's fine," Simon said, not completely satisfied he had heard the whole story. "Thanks for everything. And good work with that tooth. Keep this up and we'll have to start paying you again."

With a strained chuckle and a nod, Earl saw Simon out.

A week later Simon still hadn't heard back from Violet Sippel, nor was he any closer to finding the truth about her complaint. He was forced to consider his last remaining option, the one he had been trying to avoid at all costs.

His friendship with Evie Mitchell had continued to blossom. She called him almost weekly these days, and not just to invite him on errands. Increasingly their outings devolved into afternoon coffee or long lunches spent gabbing about the museum, Simon's childhood, the ex he barely even missed anymore. The previous week she had taken him golfing at the country club. At this Simon had proved disastrously bad, and was relieved when they gave up after two holes to motor around the course drinking hard seltzer while Evie provided a running commentary on the color of the passing golfers' auras and who was being hounded by the ghost of their jilted spouse.

Still, he hesitated to broach the subject of Sippel's accusation; there was no delicate way to ask if her dead husband might have suppressed evidence in the case of a missing child. But without a solid lead, Morgan's case would lie cold, no hope of finding out what happened to her.

I say, there is always hope of finding.

Simon had no choice. He texted Evie. She responded after an hour in her usual direct, slightly broken manner.

> Good timing. Cleaning out my storage unit this week end.
> Need u help

Good timing indeed, Simon thought. Even if the unit held nothing of interest, at least they would have a chance to talk.

CHAPTER THIRTY-NINE

MISLAID GEMS

Simon, who wasn't a great lover of heights, large vehicles, or strawberry air freshener, was not at all at home behind the wheel of the U-Haul. He felt minute within it, as if he were commanding not an automobile but a large house or a very small country. Fortunately Evie's storage unit was located at the same complex where he picked up the truck. Evie, when he arrived, was already there in her headband and leg warmers, hauling a rosewood console table out of the open unit and adding it to the apartment's worth of furniture already collected on the pavement.

"What took you?" she said, and disappeared back inside.

"Good morning," said Simon tartly, dribbling down the side of the vehicle like a cowardly child descending a jungle gym.

He touched down on the pavement and walked around to the pile of furniture, shielding his eyes from the sun. "Where's all this going?"

Evie was a shadow moving in the darkness of the unit. "Fifth and Main. I've decided to open an antiques shop."

"Right. Of course."

"Are you helping or not?"

Simon stepped inside. The unit was chockablock with furniture, paintings, bubble-wrapped objets d'art, all of it expensive looking but ill cared for, accessible only by the narrowest of paths. "You can start moving that pile into the truck," Evie said.

After barely an hour of manual labor Simon was fighting the temptation to feign an injury to get away. The heat was punishing and the truck slow to fill; the big pieces were too heavy for him, and Evie kept changing her mind about the small things, dispatching items into the truck only to send him back in to fetch them again. He was exhausted, thirsty, soaked through with sweat.

"You didn't want to hire people?" he asked.

"Strangers? Goodness no. You never know what kind of energy you'll attract. The last thing I need is a malevolent spirit sneaking into my Tiffany mirrors."

Evie explained she'd been renting the unit for the past five years, since downsizing from the eight-bedroom colonial mansion where she and Garfield had raised Theo. "I always planned to open a shop, and Garf's been on me to do it while rents are down."

It took Simon a moment to understand her meaning.

"He ran the Hawthorne, didn't he?" he said, taking a pair of nesting tables from Evie and moving them into the truck.

"More like it ran him. Now, where's that vanity?" she murmured, casting her eyes around.

"What was he like?"

"Garf? He was a good old boy. Family man. Loved his gems and minerals, his food. Between him and Theo, they could eat for an army."

"He was in charge when Morgan went missing, wasn't he?"

"Terrible time." Evie inspected a vase, which Simon recognized as one of Zander Steyn's. It reminded him of the potter's recent text informing him his commission was ready to pick up. Simon hadn't yet responded. "It was all anyone was talking about. The board was in a panic. They were saying it might be the end of the Hawthorne. It consumed him, all those late nights and emergency board meetings. I feared for his health. I could see it was wearing him down, he was at a breaking point. I begged him to retire before the job killed him."

"But he didn't?"

"He said he had a plan. Promised it would all be over soon." Her eyes were unfocused, the vase forgotten in her hand. "Then a week later, he died."

"I'm sorry," Simon said.

"Heart attack. I was asleep when it happened. Found him the next morning in his study." Through her sadness emerged an effortful smile. "But he's still with me."

She looked around, apparently distracted by an unspoken thought. She handed Simon the vase and drifted toward a dusty curio cabinet half hidden behind boxes. He could just make out through the glass a robust assortment of gem and mineral specimens mounted on marble bases.

"Those were his?" Simon said, approaching the cabinet.

"Thinking about donating them to the museum."

"I'm sure Priya would be delighted."

"Yes," said Evie. "Yes, I think I will. Move those boxes aside so I can look at them."

Simon set the vase down and cleared a path. The boxes were cardboard and heavy. "What's in here?" he groaned as he shifted the pile.

"Oh, just recycling. Papers from Garf's office."

Simon hefted one box after another, including one that felt overloaded, badly taped. Too late, he attempted to secure the bottom; with a tearing sound the bottom split and the contents exploded against the floor.

"Just leave it," Evie said, but Simon was already bent over, scraping up the assorted files as he apologized. They were work documents, from the looks of them: business plans and reports, meeting agendas with notes scrawled in the margins, what appeared to be a blueprint, or a copy of one, on which had been drawn a number of meandering arrows and circled plot points. One circle, he noticed, contained the letters *VS*. A scribbled note read, *Girl taken out side entrance??*

The blueprint seemed to transform before Simon's eyes, taking shape as the ground floor of the Hawthorne.

He crouched, his brow furrowed. "What is all this stuff?"

"I told you, Garf's office things. Just leave them."

As he realized what he might be looking at, a grim resignation came over Simon; he could not delay the conversation any longer.

"Evie," he said as she whisked a bedsheet off a Victorian writing slope, murmuring appraisingly to herself. "Did Garf ever mention he was dealing with a complaint at work, an issue between staff?"

"He never talked to me about museum business. Said he was preserving my rose-tinted view of it. We had so many happy memories there, with Theo."

"Then I'm guessing he never mentioned the name Violet Sippel."

"I told you, we didn't—" Her eyes found Simon, quizzical. "What's this about?"

His crouched stance becoming uncomfortable, Simon sat back on the concrete floor and sighed.

"Violet Sippel was an employee at the museum when my sister disappeared," he said. "I found an old email saying she shared sensitive information with your husband, information related to Albert Mueller and my sister that she seemed to think Garf had ignored, or—well—"

"Don't be ridiculous," Evie said, batting a hand. "Garf would never. If he knew anything about what happened to your sister, nothing would have stopped him from launching a full investigation. *Especially* against Albert Mueller."

"All those late nights, emergency board meetings," Simon said. "I wonder if that's exactly what he was doing. Investigating Violet's accusation."

Evie froze, then swiftly turned away, engaging in a private whisper. Simon couldn't make it out.

"Evie?"

When her eyes returned to him, she looked stricken.

"He says it's true."

Simon took in the tumult of paper at his feet. "And all this?"

"He doesn't want me to look," she said. "But he says you must."

Evie busied herself at the other side of the unit as Simon checked one paper after the other. Though Violet Sippel's accusation remained elusive, it didn't take long for Simon to realize he'd been right. Investigative documents relating to Morgan's disappearance filled several boxes, many of them bearing notes in small, cramped writing that Evie confirmed was Garfield's.

The documentation was varied and exhaustive, from photocopied time cards and volunteer schedules to increasingly frustrated entreaties from the board to "address the rumors going around" and "follow up with updates on the investigation." From what Simon could tell, Mitchell had been putting them off, feeding them only bits and pieces of what he knew, repeating the same request for more time.

Among the files Simon discovered an audiocassette, like something out of a nineties voice recorder. The label penned in Garfield's writing read RUTHERFORD 3-11-00.

"Evie," Simon called across the storage unit.

She appeared, looking anemic. "You found something?"

"I'm not sure yet. You wouldn't happen to have a cassette player, would you?"

Her expression clouded. She wandered out of sight. From the depths of the unit came the sound of rummaging and a disjointed series of mumbles. "Thought he had . . . where did I put . . ."

Simon clambered to his feet and found Evie digging through a box of old electronics.

"Ah, here it is."

With a great upward tug she produced what he recognized as a boom box. Large, rectangular, and dirty silver, it came equipped with twin woofers, tweeters, radio tuners, telescopic antennae, and a central cassette player, giving it the appearance of a friendly 1980s sitcom robot.

"We need an outlet," Simon said, power cord in hand. "Or D batteries. Looks like it takes both."

There didn't appear to be any of either in the unit.

"Get those files in the truck," Evie said. "We'll come back for the rest."

❧

Thirty minutes later they pulled up outside the site of Evie's new business, an empty shopfront still advertising the name of the previous tenant. Simon parked, and a bell above the door tinkled as they entered.

The inside of the shop was bare walled and warm, in need of fresh paint. Having carried the boom box to the nearest outlet and plugged it in, Simon silenced the blare of radio static that issued forth and inserted the cassette.

His finger hovered over the play button as he looked up at Evie. "You're sure you want to hear this?" he said.

She nodded stiffly.

He pressed play, then stood beside her.

There was a momentary crackle before a man's voice spoke, ringing, good-natured. "Sorry about that. You were saying?"

"That's Garf," Evie said.

"I was just thanking you for your impassioned presentation to the board of directors this evening," said a new voice, also male. "Not to mention your diligent attention to this serious matter. As you said yourself, the safety of our visitors is of the utmost importance; our first priority must be the safety of every man, woman, and child who steps through our doors."

The voice was older, more refined. "Is that—?" Simon said.

"Eberhard Rutherford," Evie answered.

"Craig Rutherford's uncle, right? Wasn't he executive director at one point too?"

"He took over after Garf left, but decided he liked it better on the board."

Simon knelt and rewound the tape. "Sorry, just wanna hear this bit." He let it play.

"As a follow-up to tonight's meeting," Rutherford was saying, "I'm calling to let you know the board has carefully considered both your findings against Albert Mueller, and your proposal to terminate him and inform the police of Miss Sippel's testimony."

"And your decision?"

"I'm sorry to say, we've determined by unanimous vote that this course of action doesn't support the museum's strategic focus at this time."

"Strategic focus—?" Garf said. Rutherford abruptly cut him off.

"I trust I don't need to explain to you that like many of our country's finest institutions, we rely on the support of the public to fulfill our vital mission. And while we take great pride in our illustrious history, it is, like the history of our great nation as a whole, not invulnerable to challenge."

"What do you—?"

"For decades," Rutherford proceeded with the heedless determination of a charging rhinoceros, "the board has worked hard to ensure a pristine public image befitting an institution of our prestige, this in order to ensure the Hawthorne's financial solvency through this period of time in which museums across the nation—not just ours—face unprecedented economic challenges—".

Garf attempted to cut in. "I understand that, but—"

"I am speaking," Rutherford interjected.

There was silence.

Rutherford continued. "As I'm sure you're aware, recent events have blighted that pristine image, and not just the disappearance of the Jenks girl. There was also the embarrassing dismissal of that archaeologist fellow for stealing valuable human remains. Though I know you had reservations about it, we hope our promotion of Amir Saad to chief anthropology curator will ensure things in that department do not get any worse.

"Of course the board doesn't blame you for any of this, Garfield, despite both events' taking place on your watch."

"I appreciate that," Garfield muttered sourly.

"Still, we find ourselves in a precarious position. According to your most recent quarterly report, admissions are down more than fifty percent, memberships are nearly as bad, and some of our most loyal donors—friends of mine, even—are downgrading their annual support, if not withdrawing it altogether. The finance committee has looked closely at the numbers and tells me that if the Hawthorne continues down this path, it won't survive another five years. One more major scandal, and the museum may well fold before Christmas."

"With all due respect, Eberhard," Garfield said, the directness of his tone a welcome reprieve from Rutherford's blustering, "you're not telling me anything I don't know, or indeed, anything I haven't already reported to the board."

"I'm simply providing context for our assessment on this matter."

"Which is?"

"That in light of the museum's present instability, we feel Miss Sippel's testimony alone doesn't justify the dramatic action you've proposed. First, we're unsure if the girl can be trusted. You're aware that she was having an affair with that married preparator fellow, the one who resigned in shame last April. How can we be sure she isn't simply helping him get back at Mueller for catching them at it?"

"Earl would never—"

"Second," Rutherford continued, "we feel that firing Mueller would only reinforce the narrative that the Hawthorne's payroll is filled with criminals and pedophiles, not to mention give him reason to speak out about your previous scuffle. It was you who threw the first punch, wasn't it, Garf? The executive committee seems to think Mueller may have grounds for a lawsuit should he choose to pursue one, a financial burden we simply can't bear. For that reason, the Hawthorne shall take no immediate action and leave the case in the capable hands of the authorities."

"You can't be serious. You're suggesting I sit on my hands, pretend Violet Sippel never said a word?"

"As far as the police are concerned, she hasn't," said Rutherford. "I spoke with the chief this morning—he says they haven't heard from her at all. Don't you think if she were telling the truth, she would have made an official report by now?"

"Would it make any difference if she did?" said Mitchell scathingly.

"We understand this decision is likely frustrating to you."

"*Frust—?*"

"*Nevertheless.* Speaking not only as board chair but as a direct descendant of Augustus Hawthorne himself, I wonder if I might offer a few words of reassurance."

"I don't know if those words exist," Garfield said.

"Then humor me."

From here Rutherford's speech was measured, carefully enunciated, as if the slip of a single syllable could be grounds for misinterpretation.

"There is nothing more important, nor more noble, than preserving for future generations the venerable institutions from which we ourselves have gained, institutions not just of brick and mortar but of flesh and blood. Institutions born of the great families—the great men—who built this nation through sheer force of will. As you're not a member of The Family, I don't expect you to understand this. But I—we all—expect you to respect it, and to prepare to face the consequences should you fail to do so.

"Good night, Garfield."

There followed several seconds of static before the recording ended with a click.

Simon and Evie did not speak, yet their minds seemed to be working on the same frequency. They now knew that, unbeknown to Violet Sippel, Garfield had followed the lead she had given him about Mueller. His investigation had found Mueller guilty. But the board had blocked him from taking action.

At last Simon spoke. "At the storage unit you said Garf had a plan. That he told you all his troubles would be over soon."

"Yes. Yes, that's what he said."

"Maybe he was planning to defy the board. Fire Mueller and go public with the accusation anyway."

For the second time Evie turned away and summoned the spirit of her late husband with just the sound of her voice. When she returned to Simon a moment later, she looked, to his surprise, a little annoyed.

"He won't say."

Crouching before the boom box, Simon rewound to the final seconds of the call and let it play.

"I don't expect you to understand this. But I—we all—expect you to respect it, and to prepare to face the consequences should you fail to do so."

He sighed and removed the tape from its cartridge.

"Those numbers," said Evie, peering over his shoulder. "On the label. What are they?"

He held it up to her: *3-11-00*. "Looks like a date. March 11, 2000."

Evie's face drained of color.

"What is it? What's March 11?"

"Three days before I found Garf in his study."

CHAPTER FORTY

BROKEN BONES

During the past hour Evie seemed to have cooled to the idea of an antiques shop. Simon drove her back to the storage unit, replaced the few items they had taken away, and returned the truck to the rental office, but not before moving five boxes of Garfield Mitchell's investigative files into his car.

"What will you do now?" Evie said as he loaded them into the trunk.

"I need to take a closer look at everything, see if I can find anything about Sippel's accusation. I still don't know what she saw."

"And if it's not safe?" Evie asked, voicing a thought that until then had remained unspoken between them.

Simon closed the trunk. "I have to try. My whole life I've felt like I could have done more. Now, maybe I can."

He worked from home the following morning despite having good reason to be on-site. MES had recently completed the armature for Theo's exhibit and was beginning to construct the skeleton, a process he ought to be monitoring closely. But the dinosaur, and even Theo's sibling, were far from Simon's priority now.

Standing over a box on the table, he methodically sifted through each of Garfield Mitchell's documents—an incident report, a few newspaper clippings, a performance evaluation for Violet Sippel. Simon wasn't sure whether to be reassured or troubled that the author had described her as "bright, resourceful, but at times nosy and unwilling to consider she may not have the full picture of things."

He exhausted the box and started on the next. By lunchtime, he was three and a half boxes down and beginning to sweat. Sippel hadn't acknowledged his email or either of his increasingly desperate follow-ups; he wasn't even sure she was still monitoring that account. If there was nothing in these boxes, he had no other avenue to explore.

He glanced at his phone and noticed a text from Zander.

> Terribly sorry to keep pestering you, I can only imagine how busy you must be. Was just hoping to clear out some space in the studio. Happy to drop your commission by if you don't have time to pick up, just let me know best address!!!

Damn. Simon had been meaning to get back to Zander all week. He picked up his phone and responded.

> Sorry, yes, very busy week. I can stop by today!

Zander replied at once.

> Free now 😌

It was just as well. Simon could use a break—anything to delay the inevitable disappointment of his search.

He threw on some clothes and drove to Granton Avenue. As he raised his thumb to the doorbell, he heard Zander talking to himself within, his voice despairing. Simon rang and footsteps approached. The door flew open to reveal Zander in a state, tears streaming down his splotchy cheeks. "Oh, I am such an idiot," he moaned.

"What's wrong?"

He retreated from the door. Simon followed him inside, and Zander indicated the flimsy shelving unit against the wall.

"I only wanted to give it a polish before you arrived, but you know how clumsy I am. My hand slipped and it fell and, well, the damn thing's so fragile—"

Simon observed, stashed on a low shelf, three broken chunks of figural china—beige, with hand-painted details in shades of brown and gray. A long sweeping tail, a scaly two-legged body, a large head with sharp teeth protruding from a lipless mouth.

"A dinosaur?" Simon said. An attempt at one, at least. A generalized sort of theropod reminiscent of *T. rex.*

"I thought it fit, given the raw material, and the color."

"It's beautiful."

"It was." Zander's eyes filled back with tears, and he collapsed into a chair. "What a *domkop,*" he said, softly sobbing. "I'll refund you of course, every penny."

"Forget the money. That's not important." Simon's heart ached for the blubbering potter. He squeezed his shoulder, consoling.

Zander reached up and lay his large, calloused hand on Simon's, his reddened eyes turned upward with a yearning sparkle.

Simon drew his hand back, not too quickly. "Well. I should probably be—"

"Please don't go. Please—" Zander dropped his head and gripped it. "Why must I always ruin everything?"

"It's fine. I just have some work to do. Meeting an informant in twenty. But I'll see you again soon." Simon backed up toward the door, Zander gazing at him dejectedly. "I'll see you soon," he promised, and left.

Simon wiped the tears from his eyes as he parked. He never meant to hurt Zander, but there was no question he had. The question now was whether he really *would* see him again. Perhaps it was time for "Theo" to slip quietly into obscurity. It might be the kindest thing, if he could manage it in a town the size of Wrexham.

The first thing he saw, as he opened the door to the apartment, were the cardboard boxes piled on and around the kitchen table. With a sigh he closed the door and resumed his former spot. Might as well get it over with.

He continued to search through the jumbled documents. A few minutes later he paused at a number ten envelope addressed to Garfield Mitchell. The envelope was torn open at the top, and inside was a folded letter, typewritten on the same old stationery as the sinister correspondence Simon had been receiving in his mailbox at work.

He glanced at the bottom of the page, noting Violet Sippel's sign-off with a surge of adrenaline.

It couldn't be—but it was: the original letter she had written to Mitchell. Simon's eyes jumped back to the top of the page and skimmed down over the brief introductions and formalities to read:

Yesterday, July 14, I arrived at the museum around 8:35 a.m. before my 9:00 a.m. shift. I often get in a little early because I take the bus and it sometimes runs late. Since I had extra time yesterday morning, I went downstairs for a cup of coffee in the staff lounge where I ran into Albert Mueller. He looked no different than usual, disheveled and a little awkward but friendly enough. He's always been pleasant, but they say many psychopaths are. He said hello and we chatted a bit. Then he told me to have a good day and took his coffee back to his office while I stayed in the lounge until it was time to clock in.

At five minutes to 9:00, I headed to the first floor to begin my shift. I have to pass by Dr. Mueller's office to get to the elevator. This morning the door was slightly open. I could see him pacing back and forth inside. He saw me looking and called me in.

Although only fifteen minutes had gone by, he was not the same man I had seen in the lounge. He looked extremely agitated, very jittery. I thought perhaps he had drunk his coffee too quickly.

He asked if I could do him a favor. He described two children, a boy of about ten and a younger girl, who would soon be visiting the museum. He wasn't sure what time exactly, just that they'd have prepurchased tickets. He asked if, when they got here, I would give him a call.

Thinking nothing of it, I said, "Of course," and asked if they were family. At first he said no. Then yes. "Well, something like that," he said. He smiled, but he seemed nervous. I should have known then he had a guilty conscience.

I started my shift. It was a normal Wednesday morning, not too busy. We had one large group of senior citizens on a bus tour. Shortly before 10:30, two children, a white boy and girl about the ages Mueller described, came in. There was no adult with them, which was unusual, but my understanding was that Mueller would be joining them. I took their tickets, but before I could even ask them to wait, the little girl ran off in excitement. The boy chased after her. When I got Dr. Mueller on the phone, he thanked me and said, "I'll be right up."

After that, everything was normal until about an hour later. I was back in the lounge having my lunch when I heard the police were there and why. A little girl missing? The same girl in ladybug pants I had served at the ticket desk? I suddenly felt dizzy. My throat was closing up and I could hardly breathe. I'm prone to panic attacks under stress, especially when it comes to anything that involves the police.

My dad was called to pick me up. I didn't want to go, but my coworkers insisted. They didn't understand why I was so upset. They practically dragged me to the elevator from the lounge. I looked into Mueller's office as I passed. The door was open. He still wasn't back. Where he was and what he was doing with the girl, I don't want to think about. I got into my dad's work van and we left.

I understand that the police interviewed some of the staff after I went home. My family has a bad history with the police in this town, especially on my mom's side. I'm sure you know who LaDarius Turner is, the off-duty officer who was shot dead by police for intervening in an attack. LaDarius was my mom's brother. So you can understand why I have issues with Wrexham Police, especially being half Black, and I prefer not to interact with them if I don't have to. That's why I am coming directly to you.

Needless to say, I believe Albert Mueller may be responsible for taking the little girl from the museum. It brings me no pleasure in making this accusation, but I feel I have no choice based on what I witnessed yesterday.

I of course shared all of this with my supervisor once I calmed down yes-
terday afternoon, but I wanted to make sure you were aware so you could
lodge an urgent investigation. I only hope there's still time for the girl to be
safely returned to her family.

I'm using sick time for the rest of the week to deal with the shock, but I
would be happy to address any questions you have by phone. Please call me
at my parents' home number below.

Sincerely,
Violet Sippel

A number followed. Simon would try it later and find it disconnected, once he no longer felt as if he'd been walloped by the clubbed
tail of an ankylosaurid.

Mueller had been expecting them at the museum that day. But how
had he known they would be coming? Had he been there when Joelle
bought the tickets?

At least, Simon *assumed* she'd bought them. Was it possible she had
procured them by other means? Stolen them, even?

Or had someone gifted them to her, eager to get the children inside
the museum on their own?

CHAPTER FORTY-ONE

LIFE AND DEATH

Upon reaching Officer Williams's voicemail, Simon left a message requesting a prompt callback, then fretted for three days as the detective failed to get in touch. By day two he was starting to fear he hadn't adequately conveyed the significance of Sippel's letter, a scanned copy of which he had sent to Williams's email. He went on to leave two follow-up voicemails before at last his phone buzzed, displaying Williams's name.

"Sorry, I was out a few days," Williams said. "My wife had a baby last Saturday."

"Oh goodness." Simon felt embarrassed. "Didn't realize you were expecting. I hope everything went well?"

"We're the proud parents of a beautiful baby girl."

"Wonderful. Congratulations."

"Very kind of you," Williams said. "So about this letter."

"Yes. Right. Did you have a chance to read it?"

"I did."

"It proves Mueller was waiting for Morgan and me to show up, that he had plans for us."

"It's certainly suspicious," Williams said. "But I'm afraid there's a problem."

"What problem?"

"I spent some time last week reviewing the evidence collected back in ninety-nine, the statements they took from the folks working at the museum that day—including Mueller."

"Yes?"

"There's a reason they never went after him in the first place: he had an alibi."

"What alibi?" Simon said.

"Apparently he never even left the basement. He was down in the research lab all morning."

"Witnesses?"

"One of the curators. Doesn't work at the museum anymore, but I gave him a call. His story was consistent with his written statement. Says Mueller was already in the lab when he went in there a little after 10 a.m. Neither of them left except for a bathroom break or two—nothing more than a couple of minutes. Says Mueller was still in there when he left around one in the afternoon, hours after Morgan disappeared. Mueller's statement lines up."

"But that can't be right. Violet Sippel said she called Mueller after Morgan and I got to the museum, that they spoke just before 10:30." Simon had read her letter so many times by this point he practically had it memorized. "If he was in his office, he couldn't have been working in the lab when the curator said."

"Sippel didn't say where she called, did she? Maybe she reached him in the lab."

"Or maybe Mueller was lying." Something about this unnamed curator didn't sit right with Simon. "This curator, he's not named Amir Saad, is he?"

"They asked to remain anonymous. But off the record, no."

"And you believe them? I mean, one witness. If there'd been two or three—"

"I hear you. But let me put it this way: there's one witness that puts Mueller in the lab when Morgan went missing, and none that put him in the Hall of Animals where she was taken."

Simon recalled the elderly visitor who claimed to have seen Morgan leaving the hall with a boy with brown hair. Could it have been Mueller she saw that day, mistaking his small stature for that of a child? It happened to Simon all the time.

Williams didn't think much of the theory.

"Whether Mueller was down in the lab or not," he said, "the fact remains—the statute of limitations on kidnapping ran out after five years. To arrest him after this long, we need probable cause of murder, and I'm not sure we're there yet."

"Surely that's for the courts to decide."

"Believe me, I've been pushing for it."

"And?"

"Chief says we don't have enough evidence to go to the judge. Won't even let me try."

Simon let out a scoff worthy of Fran Boney. "Corruption!" he said. "Pure corruption. The police have been helping cover the Hawthorne's tracks for decades and they're still—"

"Still what?" Williams said, an audible edge in his voice. "Still crooked? Are you accusing *me* of being crooked, Dr. Nealy?"

"No, of course not—"

"'Cause to tell you the truth," Williams said, "I don't need to be doing this right now. I got more than enough to keep me busy. Homicide rates in this county have jumped thirty percent since Covid started. I got more cases than I know what to do with, *current* cases, not to mention a wife who just gave birth who needs my help and a baby daughter who needs her daddy. I was supposed to be off this week, but I came back early to help my community, to help *you*. So I'll ask you not to question my integrity or the integrity of my colleagues. A lot of us have been working for years to root out the kind of bullshit you're talking about, and allegations like that don't help."

"Sorry," Simon said, cowed. "I didn't mean to—I just don't know what I'm supposed to—"

"I get it. You're just trying to get some closure. But we don't play like that anymore."

"And you've been great," Simon said. "Really. I appreciate your help."

"All right," said Williams, apparently placated.

"I just think it's worth tracking down Violet Sippel, seeing if she'll talk to you. There may be something else she remembers."

"I wish that was possible," Williams said.

"You wish?"

"I looked her up this morning. According to our records, Violet Sippel went missing in 2002. We still don't know where she is."

From the Research Diaries
of Dr. Albert Mueller

May 25, 2001

Since my lucky escape from Theo, I have
encountered several more prehistoric spirits—
not all by accident . . . Where before I used to
dismiss them, more and more I find myself seeking
them out . . . The first bump or scrape and I
am out of my seat, reaching for my sketchbook
on my way to go find them . . . Its pages are
filled with them, too many to name . . . the
Triceratops with the broken horn (can often find
her grazing in the African diorama—careful,
she spooks easily) . . . Beth, my beloved
Bronto (just the thought of her ravaged beauty
brings tears to my eyes) . . . the dome-headed
Pachycephalosaurus with the crushed-in skull
(nasty temper) . . . I could go on!!

But there is one spirit I dare not approach,
the big one the others run from . . .

Like many in my profession, I bridle at the
lazy representation of prehistoric species as
mindless, terrifying monsters. They are *animals*
for goodness' sake, the most <u>incredible</u> and
<u>beautiful</u> to ever walk this Earth . . . Yet—I am
ashamed to say it—just the thought of Pink-Eye
fills me with dread.

I could barely sleep following our meeting
last night. I was taking my evening stroll

through the Hall of Dinosaurs when I heard it,
or rather felt it—a low, rumbling call, shaking
the museum from above like an upside-down
earthquake. It was like nothing I had
heard before . . . So intrigued was I that
I did not even waste time grabbing my sketchpad.
I followed the rumble to the third floor, deep
into the shadows of the executive suite . . .
and what should I find staring back at me but
a pair of BURNING PINK EYES, the vertical
pupils as red as the ropes of bloody saliva
stretching from the horrible mouth to the floor.
The thing was twelve feet tall if it was a
foot!!!

A ghostly white hand swung out of the
darkness and knocked me clear against the
wall—OH, THE PAIN! It was like a searing blade
against my skin, blood oozing from a trio of
wide slashes in my chest—

I did what any sensible prey would do—I fled!
Scrambled up the window behind me and wrenched
up the sash. The animal lunged out of the
shadows—I swung my leg over, was halfway out,
when suddenly the lights blazed on and rough
hands pulled me back.

It was the cockeyed caretaker—he was shouting
hysterically. THE DOLT THOUGHT I WAS TRYING TO
LEAP TO MY DEATH!!!

I tumbled back onto the floor and he held me
down, though I fought. He did not realize the
danger we were in, deaf to the warnings buried
under my screams—

Screams that tore like blades through my

memory—screams like the girl's. She who went
into the museum and never came out . . .

I never wanted her to die—whoever is reading
this, you MUST understand this! I did not realize
what I was doing when I found her and brought
her down to the basement . . . I was ignorant, a
fool—a slave to my basest needs. How could I know
then that such a monster lived in the museum?

How could I know—as I know now—I had
delivered her straight into the jaws of death???

CHAPTER FORTY-TWO

DANGEROUS TERRITORY

Simon shoved the manuscript into his nightstand drawer and slammed it shut, wishing he could lock it away. Shaking, he climbed out of bed, went into the kitchen, and turned on the coffeemaker, his mind a black, smoking crater.

Mueller's words had confirmed the worst: his alibi was a lie. On the morning of July 14 he hadn't been working in the research lab. He had been upstairs, looking for Morgan. He had found her, perhaps missing Simon, perhaps glad the boy was out of the way. In any case, he lured Morgan down to the basement, probably with the promise of more insects to look at—thousands of them in Collection Storage. What happened when they got there, Simon could only speculate.

He pictured Mueller pulling Morgan toward a dark corner—somewhere her pleading would go unheard—when there came a deep rumble from the shadows. A sound he didn't understand at first, even wrote off, as Simon had, as the tired groaning of an angry boiler.

But eventually Mueller realized it wasn't mechanical; whatever was making that sound, it was *alive*. A pair of bloody-pink eyes emblazoned the darkness. Something moved in the shadows. In his terror Mueller turned tail and fled, leaving Morgan to fend for herself—no, thrust her toward the creature, offering up a tasty distraction so that he could get away.

One way or the other, he ran. And the last thing he saw as he looked back was a giant reptilian mouth emerging from the shadows, gobbling up a leg clad in ladybug pants—an image he would later commit to drawing paper.

In some ways it made so much sense. But in other ways, less so. Such a killing, for example, would have left gruesome evidence—body parts, viscera, at the very least blood. How had Mueller managed to hide the evidence before the police searched the building? What had occurred between the time Violet Sippel saw him in the lounge and the time he called her into his office to make him appear so agitated? And perhaps the most unanswerable question of all: How had Mueller known to expect Simon and Morgan at the museum in the first place?

His mind whirred as coffee trickled into his favorite Field Museum mug, already half forgotten. Within moments, Simon found himself sobbing, great wet tears thudding the countertop as his head collapsed against his chest, burdened by the horror he now knew his sister had endured. He couldn't stop imagining her final moments, the sound of her screams, the lightning strike of fear that flashed through her as she realized it was already too late. How much of it had she felt? How long had the pain lasted before the darkness closed over her honey-green eyes?

As a paleontologist, Simon tended to think of predation in scientific terms—as the functioning of the food chain in a given ecosystem, as a tug-of-war between opposing adaptations. Forced to envisage Morgan as prey, he wasn't sure he'd ever see it the same way again.

His gaze burned fiercely through his tears. He was angry now, furious, pulsing with a bloody desire for revenge. But this new information had changed everything. All this time he'd been operating under the assumption that Mueller killed Morgan; now it seemed he hadn't, at least not personally. Her killer had been something far stranger, far harder to explain—the ghost of a species he couldn't even identify. Not just harder to get back at, but the thought of trying left him cold with fear.

Mueller had taken her, though. Had taken her and inadvertently led her straight to the animal.

He had been the cause of her death, if not the direct purveyor of it.

That was a crime Simon knew how to punish. An easy target for the vengeance building pressure inside him. A handy distraction from his never-ending guilt.

Simon would turn the entry over to Williams first thing in the morning and secure Mueller's arrest. He deserved whatever was coming to him. How satisfying it would feel when it finally happened.

But wait, Simon thought, *what about the alibi?* His experience with Wrexham Police told him it would be held against this evidence, used to write off Mueller's words as the ravings of a known lunatic. Before he did anything else, Simon needed to prove that Mueller was lying.

And the curator too. How do they fit into all of this?

Simon was frustrated. The answer to everything seemed to lay just out of reach. But there was only so much he could dig out of the Cave, only so much he could find without the cooperation of the museum's administrative gatekeepers. In order to see that Mueller was punished, Simon would need support at the highest level.

The thought of going straight to Craig Rutherford made him uneasy. Rutherford was—how had Eberhard phrased it?—"in The Family." Was he aware his own uncle had conspired to block Garfield from taking action? Would he seek to protect his uncle when he found out, following in the footsteps of so many executives before him?

Perhaps, Simon thought, he ought to speak with Harry, feel him out for a potential alliance. Even if he and Craig did go way back, Harry was a father of daughters, one of them about Morgan's age. He might have a heart for Simon's plight.

He texted Harry the following morning requesting a check-in call.

Good idea, Harry wrote back. *Have a few questions 4 u.*

This surprised and unsettled Simon. Questions were one thing Harry never had, not as far as Simon's work was concerned.

Come that afternoon, he learned they pertained to Theo's exhibit.

"How much longer's it gonna take to finish?" Harry said with a note of hostility Simon hadn't heard from the VP before. "The gala's less than a month out and Craig's breathing down my neck."

Simon couldn't help but enjoy hearing Harry like this, finally experiencing a taste of the work-related pressure his direct reports had been under for months.

Although Simon was out of the loop on the status of the exhibit, he allayed Harry's concerns with a volley of made-up excuses and empty promises. "It'll be done in plenty of time, I assure you."

He left his play for the end. Just as they seemed to be wrapping up, Simon tossed off casually, "Just one thing quickly before we finish."

"Sure," Harry muttered. "What is it?"

"It's just, I was looking through some of Albert Mueller's old files the other day and I saw something kind of strange."

"Yeah, I'll bet. Guy was a nutcase."

"It's just—you probably know about the girl who went missing here back in the nineties. Morgan something?"

Simon expected Harry to pretend he had even if it wasn't true, but an unexpected silence followed. It bore down on Simon as if possessing a physical weight. Something wasn't right.

"Harry?"

"What about the girl?" He sounded odd, frightened almost.

"You know what, I'm sure it's nothing—"

"No. No, I think we ought to take this up with Craig. ASAP."

"Really? It's probably just—"

A double beep told him Harry had ended the call.

Simon knew he had messed up, but his anxiety became exponentially worse when, less than ten minutes later, Patricia added a new meeting to his calendar. Thirty minutes with Harry and Craig Rutherford. The invite was titled *Theo Progress Update*, but that did nothing to quell the dread squeezing Simon's chest like a vise.

He had gone too far. Made it obvious that he was researching Mueller's ties to Morgan. They might even have clocked that she was his sister by now.

Simon had never been more certain he was about to be fired, but a voice at the back of his mind told him that was the least of his worries.

Remember what happened to Garfield Mitchell.

And Violet Sippel.

He had no evidence the Hawthorne had done anything to harm either of them. Still, knowing the museum's culture of suppression at any cost, he couldn't rule it out, either.

He had to do something. Had to change the narrative, make the leadership see him—and the case against Mueller—as something other than a threat.

Simon joined the call early, but both Harry and Rutherford were already on. He caught the words "Have you been documenting—?" before Simon's video appeared on-screen.

"Dr. Nealy," said Rutherford. "Working from home, I see." His tone was friendly, but there was something missing from his patter—the jollity he usually faked so well, the twinkle in the baby-blue eyes.

"Wi-Fi's been on the blink in the basement, so I just thought—"

"I hear you've hardly been on-site in weeks. What's wrong? Something got you spooked?"

"Spooked?" Simon felt his smile waver. "No, sir."

"That's good. 'Cause whatever you might've seen—whatever you *think* you know about Albert Mueller—*drop it.*"

Simon's stomach lurched.

A corner of Rutherford's mouth twisted up, as if to dispel the dark atmosphere his words had cast.

"Believe me, you wanna stay focused on that dinosaur. Make sure it's up in time for the gala. That's what you're here for. In fact, were it not for that, I'm not sure we'd still need you at all."

Simon perceived a threat in the statement.

"I understand."

"Good," said Rutherford. "I like to be understood."

"It's just—"

The other men's expressions reacted in unison. Simon felt queasy, but he had no choice; their cooperation was his only hope of taking Mueller down.

"I know it's an uncomfortable and, er, delicate matter. The girl."

Harry paled.

"But perhaps it could be a positive story for us," Simon said. "I mean, if Mueller *is* responsible, and he was caught as the result of an internal investigation."

"What investigation?"

"The one the museum's been carrying out in secret for years. The one spearheaded by Eberhard Rutherford, carried on by his nephew, both of them descendants of Augustus Hawthorne himself. A family legacy of honor and justice, passed down from one generation to the next. The press attention could be helpful right as we're about to re-open."

Simon noted the flicker of Rutherford's brow at the mention of the word *family*.

"Pretty clever little spin, Nealy. But I'll ask you to leave the PR strategy to our marketing team. We don't pay you for that—or to go digging up dirt on feebleminded former employees. Your job is to put up a new dinosaur exhibit—at least until the gala's over."

"But—"

"I think we're done here," Rutherford said. "Oh, and Harry, tell Facilities to change the locks on the door to the Cave. If I find out our little friend's weaseled his way down there again, you're both extinct."

CHAPTER FORTY-THREE

MUELLER'S FINAL WORD

At the senior staff meeting the following Monday, Maurice's firing was announced alongside an update about the museum's ongoing toilet paper shortage and justified as a security issue. "I was informed of a serious breach of protocol that put the institution's most sensitive data at risk," said Clayton, the twenty-nine-year-old facilities director who looked like his hands had never touched the handle of a broom in his life. Simon could not remember having once seen him in the building.

Though he had never exactly warmed to Clayton, Simon had given him a pass for being the most attractive member of staff by a mile. That pardon had ended earlier that morning, when Simon arrived at work to find Maurice hanging up his keys on the rusty nail in the basement storage closet, his faded blue coveralls folded on the shelf, missing his name for the first time in nearly two decades.

The custodian had blamed the wetness of his eyes on the dust.

"Maurice, I don't know what to say," Simon had said, close to tears himself. "This is all my fault." He had admitted to having taken the keys and accessed the Cave without permission. "If they're going to fire anyone, they should fire me. They probably will anyway, once Theo's exhibit is done."

There had been a flicker of anger in Maurice's expression, but it quickly faded.

"Don't worry. God's got a plan for all of us."

Before leaving, he had clapped a hand on Simon's shoulder. "See you around, dino boy. Don't let 'em get you." Simon had questioned whether he meant the demons in the museum or the ones terrorizing it from the comfort of their home offices.

"I've spoken with operations," Clayton was saying, "and until we're able to fill the position, we've agreed to push back reopening. With one less person to clean, prep, and set up on the day, it also means the gala's going to need to go virtual again this year."

It was evident by the thumbnail of her flaming puce countenance that Fran was hearing this for the first time. Simon sympathized, but for his part he approved of the change; if there were no guests, there was no need for Theo's exhibit to be finished by September 4.

Or so he thought. He was informed by Fran late the following night, via the longest email he had received in his life, that the unveiling of Theo's exhibit would remain the grand finale of the program. Simon's speech before an audience of 350 would now be delivered via livestream from the Hall of Dinosaurs. A brief video of Theo's construction would follow, then back to him for the live reveal.

In addition to the revised run of show, Fran had provided a detailed outline of the script, including Simon's speech, which mostly entailed lauding the attendees for their "outstanding generosity" and "heartfelt commitment to science and education."

"In a museum known around the world for its bones," it concluded, "you are its beating heart."

If only that were true. Simon had seen the heart of the Hawthorne, and it was monstrous.

How could they continue to turn a blind eye to Morgan's disappearance? How could a family legacy, already sullied, be used to justify the protection of a suspected child killer?

All Simon thought about anymore was Mueller and the evidence that was needed to secure his arrest. Unwilling to risk another visit to the Cave, he devoted himself to the one piece of evidence they could not take away from him: Mueller's manuscript. His unease deepened with

every page, each entry more bizarre and demented than the last, illus-
trating the slow, fabled deterioration of sanity that Simon's coworkers
had whispered to him like a ghost story around the campfire. A descent
into black anarchic madness, down to the last dreadful page.

January 17, 2002

   i have been seeing less and less of Theo he
has become quite reclusive i cannot help but
observe a deep sadness to him a DEPRESSION as
potent as my own . . . So many of the spirits are
suffering it seems (HOW COULD I) the *Ankylosaurus*
with ragged bleeding stumps for back legs the
emaciated mother *Chasmosaurus* who would starve
to death and may have done so before abandon her
nest of stillborn eggs (WHAT HAVE I DONE) the
others too Beth and Theo and all of them their
howls fill the museum like a miserable chorus i
feel their despair as if it were my own—
   which it is.
   for despite the gulf of time that once
divided us are we not connected by the universal
agonies of existence?
   our pain.
   our fear.
   our loss.   our love.
                    (RETURN TO ME MY LOVE)
                    (MY HEART IT BLEEDS)
in the blackness of night their wails seem to
stagger from my own throat i cannot be certain
whether it is their misery i am hearing or my
own . . .

                              or is it the misery—
                              of the little girl—
                              who haunts my subconscious
                              and these halls—

                                        (say her name)
        MORGAN JENKS

     i've seen her too lurking in the shadows she
runs from me hides . . . who could blame her
for being scared? (HOW COULD I) does her pain
speak through me blended with my own? or perhaps
the brother too all three of us together, so
vicious the howls of our unholy trinity that
blood should stream from my ears and beckon the
spirits with its scent to sate their hunger on
my suffering

                        (KILL ME)

     if only i could take it back the pain unfasten
it like a noose from around our necks, the
animals' and mine and hers (BONES) (SO MUCH BLOOD)
     the pain, it makes me

                        want to die
                        (I WANT TO DIE)

                but I'm also scared

                    for what if

                    my soul
                                      too
        should remain?

CHAPTER FORTY-FOUR

AN ACCELERATING DESCENT TOWARD TOTAL CHAOS

In the weeks leading up to the gala, the people closest to Simon seemed to think he was not his usual self. Dr. Romina Godoy wrote asking if everything was okay after he failed to respond to her email about Ibrahim et al.'s controversial new paper on the aquatic hunting adaptations of *Spinosaurus aegyptiacus*. Evie Mitchell claimed she perceived a taint in Simon's aura after he missed their scheduled champagne brunch. Earl was so frustrated that his boss had stopped laughing at his jokes that he resigned. Zander, who'd not heard a word from young Theo since the crying incident, wrote a lengthy text blaming his behavior on loneliness and entreating Simon to visit again. Dwight from MES left voicemails requesting the paleontology director's presence in the Hall of Dinosaurs to answer several questions that needed to be addressed if the work was to be completed by September 4. Even Philomena appeared to have noted the increasing inconsistency with which her owner remembered to feed her, an oversight she settled by filling the apartment with dead mice.

Indeed, it seemed the only person who failed to fully appreciate the change in Simon was himself, so obsessed was he with Albert Mueller. For weeks he neglected all obligations in pursuit of his crusade against the paleontologist—namely, the task of negating his alibi.

Simon was kept busy, for a few hours at least, by the boxes of Mueller's old things he had hauled out of storage. He pulled them apart in search of undiscovered journals, finding only the detritus of Mueller's thirty-year career—internal memos, unpublished papers, photographs of Mueller working in the lab and at community events. One, taken at a long-ago History in the Making gala, depicted Mueller in his late fifties, posing with a crowd that included Garfield and Evie Mitchell and a handsome thirtysomething Simon registered only dimly as someone he knew. More curious was a private handwritten letter—drafted by Mueller but apparently never sent—expressing his incandescent desire for an unnamed love.

"Since the moment I laid eyes on you, my heart has burned for you, my loins throbbed with aching desire. I cannot survive in this state of agony a moment longer, cannot live another day without knowing the mysteries of your body, knowing the slippery warmth of your mouth around my turgid c—"

Simon tore the letter to pieces without reading another word, suppressing the revolting thought that it might have been penned with a child in mind.

Still he kept searching, never wavering in his belief that the evidence he sought was in the next box, the next cabinet, the next room.

There is always hope of finding. There is always hope of finding.

The words became a mantra in his head, filling the space left by his slipping rationality—for little did Simon realize the signs of his encroaching madness had already begun to show. Come the week of the gala, he had detached himself fully from the mundanities of housekeeping and personal hygiene. He lost touch with the boundaries of professional decorum by which he had loyally abided, missing meetings, dressing strangely, even snapping at Fran when she called to harass him about his speech. There too were the reports of Simon digging holes in various corners of the museum grounds, as if attempting to uncover a body, and of his audible mutterings about spirits around the museum. Rarely was Simon spotted not in conversation with himself, and those close enough to eavesdrop on these utterances were often disturbed by what they heard. In a frightened letter to their landlord, Simon's elderly neighbor claimed to have caught him in the hallway saying to no one in particular, "Ripe fruit is the sweetest, but the big one will take what it can get."

Though he couldn't remember doing it, Simon even left several messages on Kai's voicemail late one night, which he only realized the following morning when he received an angry, sobbing message back asking Simon not to contact him again.

"You're sick, Si," Kai said. "You need help. You're so s-sick."

Simon didn't believe it, of course. He believed he was seeing clearly for the first time in years. He had changed, sure, but how could he not when he was one shred of evidence away from avenging his sister? How could he not go a little mad when for years he had tried to protect Morgan from harm, only to learn that in a single moment of selfishness, he had delivered her into its waiting arms?

Simon did not just want Mueller to be guilty. Simon *needed* him to be guilty, so that he didn't have to be. He *needed* Mueller to be convicted, to absolve himself of the crimes for which he himself had never been tried.

But as the days ticked by, Simon's redemption seemed only to pull further away from his grasp, and he, away from reality. He was falling fast, as if through a gaping hole in the earth. There was nothing to hold on to. Nothing to slow his catastrophic descent into an abyss from which, he sensed deep in his bones, there would be no return.

Simon awoke on September 4 with only the vaguest sense that the gala was just hours away. Like the rest of the senior staff, his inbox ran over with screaming emails from Fran about last-minute program changes, appropriate video backgrounds and attire, and the staff's role in filling the chat box with "oohs" and "aahs" as the live auction items were being presented. Simon had seen none of this, not answered a single call or email, not even Harry's increasingly desperate attempts to confirm that Theo's exhibit was ready and Simon's presentation would go off without a hitch.

He was at home in the dark, gibbering by the light of a single bulb (for such conditions had become second nature to him now) as he re-read Mueller's diaries for the umpteenth time, determined to wring one final, crucial piece of information from them.

His phone rang. Simon was not in the mood for calls. But as he went to silence it, he noticed the location on the screen read *Allentown, PA,* and it triggered something urgent in his subconscious.

"What is it?" he answered brusquely.

"Er—hello, am I speaking to Simon Nealy?"

"Simon, I'm Simon. Who's calling, I'm very busy."

"Mr. Nealy, my name is Jennifer Green. I'm a nurse practitioner at the Lehigh State Psychiatric Annex. I'm calling with some unfortunate news regarding your mother, Joelle Viccio."

The black fog in which Simon had existed for weeks seemed suddenly to clear.

"My mother?" he said. "What's wrong? Is she okay?"

"I'm sorry to say she's not well at all. We've had an outbreak of Covid at the annex, and she's tested positive. We've had to move her to Cedar Crest, the main hospital in town."

"Oh goodness."

"I'm not sure how much—" The nurse faltered, distressed. "If you'd like to try and see her, I recommend you not wait."

CHAPTER FORTY-FIVE

MAIASAURA

Simon remembered little of the weeks after Morgan disappeared, but he would never forget the night of July 14.

It lingered in his mind as he flew down the 78 toward the hospital. The sky that night had been a smear of twilight blue, reaching toward inky purple, and the police had just dropped him and Joelle home from the station. Simon had barely eaten, just a Snickers bar an officer had brought him while his mother was being questioned for a third consecutive hour. It seemed the police had doubts that even a mother as clearly deficient as Joelle would send her children to a museum alone while she was picking up trash on the side of the road, that she had no idea where her daughter was.

Once the police car had driven away from the house Joelle went out again, slamming the door behind her. Simon knew innately she was going to get drugs. He could always sense when a relapse was coming, like an animal attuned to the coming of a storm.

He climbed the stairs weakly, a staggering void, empty skin. Nothing about that day had felt real. Even then part of him expected to open the door at the top of the stairs and find his sister laid out on the floor, legs kicking behind her head, a barrel of rubber insects spread before her on the rug.

But the room was dark. Hollow.

The emptiness hit him like a screaming train. An unforeseen obliteration.

He crawled into bed, the top bunk—her bunk. He sobbed and breathed in the lingering scent of her on the sheets, as if, like oxygen, he needed it to survive.

Eventually he slept. Sometime later he awoke to a bellowing scream. A hand pulled his ankle and his body slammed against the floor.

"Not her bed! Not you!"

Simon cried out as the rug skinned his belly. Joelle was dragging him across the floor.

"STOP! STOP—"

"I told you to watch her! I told you!"

Simon fought as she dragged him toward the stairs. "I'M SORRY, PLEASE—!"

"YOU PROMISED!"

She shoved him viciously, and he pitched backward. The stairs bashed and battered his body as he tumbled down them, then spat him out across the floor.

He lay punch-drunk, his head spinning when he tried to lift it. Somewhere above, a door slammed shut.

Tears of hatred cut like fire down Simon's cheek as he drove. He dragged his sleeve across them.

And yet, for a reason he didn't fully understand, his foot leaned harder on the gas.

The hospital staff stopped him at the reception desk. "Sorry, no visitors for anyone over the age of eighteen—"

"My mom's sick. She's going to die."

"I'm sorry, but for your own safety and the safety of others—"

Simon wasn't listening. "My aunt, she died of—they wouldn't let me in to see her either—" His voice cracked. He was holding back tears. Why? Colleen he could understand, but why cry for Joelle?

The expression of the receptionist wilted behind her N95.

"Do you have a tablet? We can bring it to her so you can video chat."

"Not with me."

"We might have one you can borrow. But you'll need to go back to your vehicle."

The receptionist took Simon's phone number and he returned to the parking garage. He waited in his car for more than half an hour, his heart pounding. He feared what his mother might look like, whether she'd be able to speak, that she might already be dead.

Finally the video call came through, and a face appeared on the screen of his phone—a woman's, most likely. It was hard to tell through the layers of PPE covering the face and head. "Are you Simon?" she said.

"Yeah."

"I'm going to set you up here to talk to your mom, okay?"

"Okay."

The camera lurched across a sterile room of beeping equipment and bustling nurses, and settled at a lower angle on Joelle. She lay half awake in bed, somehow more pallid and withered than when he had visited her at the Annex. She didn't yet require the use of a respirator, but a thick plastic tube and cannula attached by a head strap pumped oxygen into her nostrils.

"Joelle, it's your son," said the nurse in the background. "It's Simon. He's called to check in on you." Joelle stirred, her eyes searching hazily around the room.

"Simon?"

"Hi, Mom."

Her eyes found the camera. Simon braced himself for the flash of hate, but it didn't come. She inhaled a ragged breath. A gentle smile filled the hollows of her face.

"Simon." Slow. Dreamy. "All grown up."

She turned her head away and hacked three times, her cough congested with sputum. But when she eased back to him, her smile remained.

"So handsome."

Simon grimaced, struggling to process this version of her. He was used to seeing her drug addled and delirious, but never like this. Her coffee-brown eyes sparkled with a softness he hadn't seen in them before, or had forcibly ejected from his memory to more easily reconcile her cruelty and neglect.

"Mom, how are you?" he said as she coughed.

Her gaze ran adrift around the room. "Where . . ."

"You're in the hospital. You're sick. But the nurses are taking care of you."

"Sick . . ." She coughed, nodding slowly, as if possessed of a grave understanding. "Yes . . ."

The nurse's voice intruded. "Are you tired, Joelle? Do you need to rest?"

"Wait," Simon said. "Please. Just a couple of minutes."

He had only planned to say goodbye, but that had changed. *She* had changed. He had questions he needed to ask while he still had the chance.

"Mom, I need to ask you about Morgan."

She let out a sound halfway between a cry and a cough.

"I know it's hard, but this is important. Albert Mueller. Do you know who that is?"

She shook her head, still convulsing with coughs.

"Joelle, are you—" began the nurse.

"Please, can we have a minute alone?"

The nurse made an affronted noise, but seemed to grant the request. Simon had lost Joelle again, her eyes tremulous and faraway. "Mom, are you listening?"

She came back to him, anxious.

"The night before Morgan was taken. Do you remember that night?"

"'You'll look after her, won't ya?'" She was repeating the words she had spoken to him that night. "You said . . ."

He suppressed a swell of anger; on some level, she still blamed him for what happened. "You came home with tickets to the museum."

"Museum . . . Simon's favorite . . ."

"Y-yes," he said.

"Si and his dinosaurs . . ." A smile flickered on her lips and melted instantly to sorrow. Her body shook, not with coughs but sobs.

Simon's heart clenched. He couldn't help it; she looked so depleted, so vulnerable. He was reminded of the night she'd pushed him down the stairs, how when he finally limped back up to his bedroom hours later, he found her asleep on the upper bunk. How she crushed Morgan's pillow to her body, breathing in the lingering smell of her like she couldn't survive without it.

Simon wanted to cry.

No. Remember, it's her fault that Morgan's gone.

"The tickets. Where did you get them?"

"Tickets . . . ?"

"To the museum. Did you buy them?"

"Museum . . ." He was losing her again. "Shouldn't let you . . . not alone . . ." A tear trickled down her face. "My," she sobbed between coughs. "My Morgan . . ."

Simon's throat constricted. He felt his defenses weakening against her pain, a pain likely to surpass his own. To lose a child she had grown inside her, given life to, nurtured—however imperfectly—for six years, that was pain only a mother could understand. Pain on a level his male psyche was not hardwired to comprehend.

Yet it was perhaps *because* she was a mother—a woman—that Simon had found it so easy to blame her. To condemn her as a "bad mom," the worst kind of woman it seemed possible to be. To hold her to the highest standard of perfection with no allowance for her vulnerability, her struggle, her debility, her humanity. A standard of perfection to which, for all his shame and regret, Simon could not truthfully say he held himself.

"M-mom," he stammered. "Please, the tickets. Where did you get the tickets?"

"Man . . ." She could hardly seem to breathe, coughing between each word. "Gave . . ."

"A man? What man?"

"Museum . . ."

Simon faltered. "A man from the museum gave you the tickets? Someone you know?"

"The B—" A sudden attack of coughing.

The nurse returned. "Okay, that's enough now." The camera lurched as she took the tablet away.

"No, wait!" Simon shouted.

The camera jerked suddenly back down, close to Joelle's face. She had hold of the device, refusing to let go until she told him everything. Perhaps on some level she had wanted to do this for years.

"You said a man from the museum gave you the tickets," Simon said. "Who?"

"The B—" she wheezed out, coughing. "The Bone Man."

CHAPTER FORTY-SIX

HISTORY IN THE MAKING

Simon called Officer Williams as he drove back toward Wrexham, desperate to tell him what he had just learned: that Mueller—the Bone Man—had contrived to get him and Morgan to the museum by giving Joelle free tickets. It had to count for something, and if Williams needed a witness statement from Joelle he didn't have much time to take it.

The call rang through to voicemail. Simon tried again without success.

"Oh, for shitting sake!"

He was on his fourth attempt when he received a call of his own, from what he recognized as the Hawthorne's general number. He put it on speaker.

"Hello, this is—"

"*Where the hell have you been? I've been trying to reach you for days!*"

"Fran. Sorry, I—"

"*Sorry? The biggest event of the year is tonight and you're nowhere to be found!*" The gala. Simon had completely forgotten. He was meant to be presenting live from the museum in just a few hours. "*Where are you now?*"

"Just driving back from Allentown—"

"*Allentown?*"

"Family emergency. My mom's in the hospital with Covid."

"*You better*—oh. Sorry to hear that," Fran said. "Just get to the museum ASAP! I'm leavin' for the hairdresser's, but Priya's here. Her and River are runnin' the broadcast from the Hall of Dinosaurs. Marketing was supposed to do it, but Dave shit the bed big time. *Big time.*"

"Oh no," said Simon guiltily. He hadn't exactly done his part either; the script Fran had written for him lay all but unread in his inbox, and he hadn't laid eyes on Theo's exhibit in weeks. "I know how hard you and River have been working on this."

"You don't have to tell me," she said. "Just get here as fast as you can."

Simon stopped at home before heading to the museum, inadequately prepared—though he lived there—for the neglected condition in which he would find it. There was no time. Leaving the mess to deal with later, he mollified a yowling Philomena with food, showered, and threw on his least-wrinkled pants, shirt, and jacket before heading out.

He arrived at the museum a few minutes after five. The entrance hall was abuzz with activity. In one corner a five-piece band warmed up for their live-streamed set. In another, River was adjusting a digital camera on a tripod, while her subject—a glamorous stranger in a tuxedo—posed before a step-and-repeat banner, complaining the lighting would wash out his tan.

Priya, in an elegant dark green gown, monitored the shot from her control station of multiple laptops. "A little higher, River, and move the camera forward a bit."

Simon stopped by her table to check in. "I'm here. I just need to run upstairs—"

"You're fine," Priya said, eyes glued to her screen. "The virtual reception just started. You can join from your office computer. Just make sure you're in the Hall of Dinosaurs by six thirty to film your segment."

"Will do."

Simon took the stairs up to the second floor. Inside the east wing of the Hall of Dinosaurs, Dwight from MES stood answering emails on his phone as his colleagues took down ladders and pulled up tarps.

"Dr. Nealy!" he exclaimed, catching sight of Simon. "Perfect timing. We've just finished. Guys have been working around the clock for days. Well, what do you think? He's something, isn't he?"

Simon barely registered the salesman's patter. Suddenly he was standing in a swampy coniferous forest of Late Jurassic Colorado, gazing awestruck at a *Ceratosaurus* in his prime, tromping through the trees in search of a meal to scavenge, his nose upturned and sniffing.

"We're thrilled with how he's turned out," Dwight was saying. "Great suggestion on your part, setting him in a scientifically accurate environment—those ferns and cycads look awesome." He paused, seeming to read into Simon's silence. "A-as you'll notice, we had to change the pose slightly to accommodate for the unexpected weight of the skull— the armature couldn't handle it. We sent you the revised designs for approval but we never heard—"

"He's wonderful," Simon said. "Truly. Great work, Dwight."

"*Phew.* That's a relief. Er—if you'd like to take a closer look, I'd just like to point out a few things."

Dwight walked him around the exhibit, highlighting the points of interest: easy-to-miss details, areas of special challenge and achievement. In the wake of his first boyish flush of awe, Simon's enthusiasm became more complicated. He couldn't help noticing slight deviations from the original design—the height of the right leg, the exaggerated curve of the tail. Scientific inaccuracies most people would never notice, but that would needle Simon each time he looked at the exhibit. Ultimately these mistakes were his responsibility; he berated himself for not correcting them when he still had the chance.

"I took the liberty of submitting the final invoice to your finance team. I wasn't sure if you were, er—anyway, they said there was a check waiting upstairs. Any chance you could—?"

"Right. Of course. I'll grab it now."

Simon left the hall, barely able to tear his eyes from Theo, in adoration and judgment both.

Up on the third floor, Simon found the check waiting on the CFO's desk. On his way back toward the elevator, he happened to glance into the mailroom. There was a letter in his box. He stepped inside, his curiosity curdling to fear when he withdrew the envelope and found it bore no return address.

It was postmarked a week before from Chadds Ford. Why was that town familiar to him?

He didn't want to open it, considered simply throwing it out, but something stayed his hand—a tainted curiosity. Turning the envelope upside-down and digging his nails under the flap, he tore it back until the paper shell fell away and he was left holding a musty sheet of Hawthorne letterhead, almost—but not exactly—like the two that had come before. Instead of newspaper clippings, the message appeared to have been pressed by hand, each letter the black imprint of a different rubber stamp.

IF U WANT WHATS LEFT OF UR SISTER
MEET ME OUTSIDE MUSEUM
SEP 4TH 11PM
—THE BONE MAN

Simon convulsed. Bile burned like acid at the back of his throat. *What's left of your sister.* But how could there be anything left? If Morgan had been devoured by a prehistoric spirit, what part of her could remain, and how could Mueller still have it?

It had to be Mueller who had sent the letter, didn't it? Who else could the Bone Man be? He'd been harassing Simon since his arrival, taunting him with clues about his sister's death. At the same time, Simon couldn't help but think with horror of the creature from his recurring nightmare. The rattling of its breath, the jangle of its bag of bones—Morgan's bones, the meat-scraped core of what was left of her. It was like the creature and Mueller had merged to form the same loathsome monster. And it was coming for him.

He looked again at the proposed meeting date. *September fourth.*

That was today. Mueller would be there in just a few hours. Why did he want to speak with Simon? It felt like a trap. And yet it might be his only chance to confront Mueller, to get him to confess. Simon didn't know what he would do, but he still had time to think about it, and the gala to get through.

After delivering Dwight's check, he retreated to his office and sifted through hundreds of unopened emails to find the one with the link to the gala's live broadcast. The program had just begun. The tuxedoed man, apparently the emcee, mugged for the camera, his image freezing and stuttering as he spoke.

"But tonight—all about Timeless Treasures, and no, I'm not talking—the Hawthorne's board of directors." The presenter filled the void of laughter with his own. "No, I'm talking about the timeless treasures that fill—museum's halls, and our imaginations, with wonder and excitement every time—through these doors."

At the start of the board chair's prerecorded remarks, Simon clicked over to email, and after several attempts, managed to print out the speech Fran had prepared for him. It was several pages long. There was no way he'd be able to memorize it all, but he read through it, practicing his cadence, watching the clock with deepening anxiety.

The program flew by. Craig Rutherford presented a local insurance company with the Philanthropist of the Year Award. Then the band performed, the failing audio exploding the chat box with comments of "Can't hear anything!!!" and "HOW U TURN ON THE SOUND?" The emcee facilitated the live auction, valiantly hawking collections of random donated goods as if they were luxury packages. A massage voucher, a ten-karat gold necklace, and a finger painting of a tree comprised a TREEt Yourself Spa Package. An overnight stay in a board member's vacation home and a twenty-five-dollar gift card to Mel's Cheesesteak Hut performed the role of the Romantic Couple's Retreat on the Allegheny River.

Before Simon knew it, it was nearly 6:30. He closed his laptop with a shaking hand and pushed back from his desk.

River was in the Hall of Dinosaurs when Simon entered, their aquamarine hair as depleted and washed out as they looked. "Hi, Dr. Nealy," they trilled, standing before a digital camera on a tripod. They looked panicked, unequal to the responsibility laid on their shoulders. "If I could just get you—"

The lights flickered overhead. Simon stopped, eyes flashing with concern. After a moment the lights steadied and the pair exchanged a look.

"T-they've been doing that all week," River said with feeble optimism. "I'm sure it'll be fine. Would you mind standing on the X for me? Going live in just a few minutes."

Simon's mark was just beside Theo's exhibit, allowing River to pan over for the reveal once Simon finished his spiel. He felt sick and overheated as he ran through the speech under his breath, cursing as he repeatedly forgot what was next and had to check the printout quivering in his hands.

"Your notes are in the shot. Can you go without them?" River said. Embarrassed to admit he couldn't, Simon folded them up and tossed them aside. "Great. Okay, one minute left."

Simon pawed the sweat from his forehead. He wrote off the deep rumble in his abdomen as nerves.

As River counted down from ten, Simon's blood thrummed in his veins. He felt as if they were counting down to his execution. They indicated the last few seconds on their fingers. *Three. Two. One.*

The silence in the hall was absolute.

Simon stared into the gaping black eye of the camera. There were no words left in his head, only the heartbeat walloping his eardrums like muted cymbals. *Thud-thump, thud-thump, thud-thump.* River's wide-eyed face appeared from behind the camera. Their hands juddered spasmodically.

"Er—er—good evening," Simon spluttered. "I'm—my name is Dr. Simon Nealy, and I'm the curator of, er—no, the director of paleontology and curator of Dinosauria here at the Hawthorne Museum." The vibrations through his abdomen strengthened, and sweat was dripping down his temples in rivulets; the hall was suddenly unbearably humid.

"In my role as director of—already said that. My—my role is to oversee the museum's renowned collection of prehistoric fossils—"

The lights slammed off, plunging the hall into instant darkness. "No, *no*," River whimpered.

"What—are we still—?"

"I don't know, I—I need Priya!" River's phone screen was a beacon of light on their frantic face. "No service!"

Simon's horror was interrupted by another; he noticed a swampy stench in the air, like rotten eggs.

"Wait here," River squeaked.

"Wait!" Simon called out as their dark outline scurried from the hall.

And yet Simon sensed he wasn't alone. It was an instinct more than an observation, a conclusion drawn from the abrupt agitation of his senses, the hair needling out of the back of his neck.

Then he heard it. Something moving in the dark.

He could feel it too, its closed-mouth cry vibrating through every inch of his body.

The forward-facing eyes of a theropod shone like pink rubies in the darkness.

A thunderous footstep, and a gigantic snout emerged into a shaft of moonlight. The skin was rough and white as snow. *White skin and reddish-pink eyes*—a gasp caught in Simon's throat. Paleontologists had suspected a few dinosaurs might have experienced albinism, but with pigmentation so rarely preserved in fossils, it was impossible to—

A three-fingered hand exploded out of the shadows. Simon leapt back against the exhibit. It juddered, not against Simon's weight but something far larger. A dark shape leapt clear off the platform, flying over Simon's head and landing heavily between him and Pink-Eye.

Theo. Simon could tell by the ghostly shape of him: a fraction of Pink-Eye's size, badly wounded, but with fight still left in him, crouched before Simon in a stance of fierce defense. As in the Hall of Gems and Minerals, Simon sensed he was witnessing a moment snatched from Theo's prehistoric past. He rumbled out a warning to come no closer. Pink-Eye returned a terrible, blood-curdling snarl.

Theo charged. A pair of great white jaws clamped down on his neck, wrestling him to the floor with a ground-shaking slam.

Simon stood back, gaping in terror. A disembodied voice screamed, from both within and without him: *Ruuuuuuuun!*

He slid away and sprinted toward the exit. The sound of heavy foot-falls pounded behind him, gaining on him, galvanizing his fear. He screamed and was hoisted up into the air, an excruciating pain impaling his shin and calf. The marble floor lurched underneath him, a clawed alabaster foot swinging in and out of sight.

Without warning, the vise on his leg released him and Simon col-lapsed onto the floor. It walloped the wind from his lungs. He was breath-less, woozy. The doors of the hall waved and danced in the distance.

As he crawled toward them, dragging his bleeding leg behind him, a shadow moved over him, slow as a storm cloud. Footsteps like tiny earthquakes. He could feel Pink-Eye's foul heat behind him, smell the pestilence oozing from its scarred and weeping skin. Inch by inch, Simon turned his head to look. He let out a loose, garbled cry at the sight of the dinosaur towering over him, its giant head cloaked in darkness. Simon couldn't see its face—only its pink eyes, framed by the lacrimal horns of a white-skinned devil, its mouthful of daggerlike teeth dripping blood onto the floor in heavy splashes.

The jaws parted with a monstrous resonance, and suddenly the giant maw plunged. He contracted into a ball, screaming—and he kept on screaming. He screamed and he screamed and he did not stop.

Not when the lights staggered on, vanishing the spirits from the hall.

Not when he heard Priya and River racing over to him, calling his name.

Certainly not as the camera, knocked over and lying sideways on the floor, broadcast his terror to an audience of 350.

Even when the chat box filled with messages of "Why's that child crying?!?" and "GOOD GOD HE'S GONE MAD!" Simon was helpless to hold back the torrent of his fear.

CHAPTER FORTY-SEVEN

THE TWO OFFICERS

Simon lay in bed at Wrexham Hospital, his leg elevated in a sling and tightly bandaged. The pain had diminished a great deal since they'd put in the stitches. The doctor, describing the wound as the weirdest dog bite he'd ever seen, had been generous with the painkillers. Still, Simon struggled to sleep, the image of Pink-Eye's gaping maw too fresh in his mind.

With his phone to distract him, he unlocked it to find a voicemail from Harry informing him in a tone of clumsy formality that he, Simon, had been fired from the museum and banned from the premises forthwith.

Though it stung, Simon couldn't say he was surprised; he'd been expecting it for weeks. If anything, his episode in the Hall of Dinosaurs merely gave them a convenient cover by which to get rid of him before he could dredge up any more institutional secrets. No doubt they would present a more sympathetic face to the press.

The Hawthorne Museum and Dr. Nealy mutually agree this separation is the best course of action as the former paleontology director seeks treatment for his personal mental health challenges. Nevertheless, he remains a valued member of the Hawthorne Museum family, and we will do everything in our power to get him the help he needs.

They could say what they wanted. Simon's priority continued to be the Bone Man.

It was after midnight, more than an hour after they were meant to have met. Mueller would be gone by now, and Simon had no way to contact him.

Only Williams did. He had access to Mueller's personal address. He knew where Simon could find him.

The hospital released him early the next morning. Unable to drive and without a vehicle anyway—his sedan still waiting for him outside the museum—he called a car to transport him and his medical crutch to the police station. The sour-faced receptionist who had turned him away before was no more welcoming today, but this time Simon refused to take no for an answer.

"I don't care what your policy says! I'm not leaving until I speak with Officer Williams."

"Officer Williams is off today."

And yet no sooner had the words been spoken than the detective came through the station door, a messenger bag slung over the shoulder of his wrinkled T-shirt, dark pillows under his eyes. At the sight of Simon at the counter, he sighed.

"Williams," the receptionist said in surprise.

"I was just picking up some files. I'll take care of Dr. Nealy."

"It's against protocol—"

"Thanks, Lorraine. I'll make this quick."

Williams didn't regard or speak to Simon until they came to a small interview room. "Take a seat," he said, and closed the door. Simon hesitated. The room wasn't unlike the one to which his mother had been confined for hours after Morgan disappeared. He felt suddenly claustrophobic.

"I'll stand, if that's okay."

Williams sat on the edge of a table. He didn't ask about Simon's leg. "You wanted to see me?"

"I've been trying to reach you for weeks," Simon said, and launched into an update on all that had come to light since last they spoke: Mueller's final diary entries, the video call with Joelle, how she had received the museum tickets from "the Bone Man," someone connected to the Hawthorne.

When Simon finished speaking Williams simply stared.

"What?" Simon demanded. "Why are you looking at me like that? I'm trying to tell you—".

"I heard you, Dr. Nealy. You're saying Albert Mueller lured you and your sister to the museum."

"Yes. He did—"

"And his alibi, the alibi I verified myself, that's false. When no one was looking, he hightailed it upstairs and grabbed your sister."

"Yes. Yes, he needs to be placed under—"

"Then what did he do with her?" Williams said.

"What?"

"After he took her. What did he do with her next?"

Simon stammered. "I—I—well, I'm not sure—"

"Not sure? Really. 'Cause I hear you've got a theory. I hear you've been shuffling around the museum, muttering a story about Mueller feeding your sister to a dinosaur."

Simon reddened. "Who told you that?"

"The chief has friends on the board. He's been keeping me apprised for weeks. Thought I ought to know what I was dealing with."

"Don't you see? They're trying to turn you against me. Our organizations have been working together for decades—"

"Working to get you fired for losing your shit live on camera? You going to blame that on corruption too?"

Simon's embarrassment grew.

The detective exhaled, looking compassionate. "I'm sorry, Dr. Nealy. I'm sorry if by trying to help you, I made this whole thing worse for you. If letting you in on all the details of the case brought something out in you I didn't expect."

"It didn't bring—"

"I feel for you. You and your mom. Joelle, right? After everything you've both been through, who could blame you? But I say this as a friend, Dr. Nealy—Simon. What you need isn't answers. What you need is help."

Williams was starting to sound just like Kai. "You don't under-stand—"

Williams moved closer. "I can get you the care you need—"

"No!" Simon wobbled back, unsteady on his injured leg. "I'm not crazy! I'm not crazy and neither is my mother!"

He threw open the door and hobbled out into the hall, hurrying back toward the street.

"I'm not crazy," he muttered to himself. And for perhaps the first time in months, he believed it without question.

There was a woman outside Simon's apartment when the car pulled up to the curb. She was hammering the door and shouting, something about "I know you're up there!" Simon would have recognized her Delco accent and orange hair a mile away.

"What are you doing here?" he said, swinging the car door open.

Fran turned, her face contracting in rage. She stormed down the stoop toward him, fists swinging at her sides. *"You son of a bitch—"*

Simon retreated into the safety of the car.

"Don't even think about it! Get outta there!" She yanked him by his shirt out of the car and slammed the car door shut. Simon's crutch clattered to the ground. The driver wasted no time in zooming away.

"You ruined my event!" Fran snarled, the lapels of Simon's jacket bunched in her fists. *"Months of work! Three hundred fifty of our biggest do-nors! Now the sponsors are demandin' their money back—we might even* lose *money!"*

"I'm sorry," Simon cried.

"You oughta be fired!"

"I—I was!"

Fran unhanded him in shock. "Say what?" Simon wobbled back to-ward the road. Fran grabbed his crutch off the ground and thrust it at him.

"Last night," he said, steadying himself. "They fired me."

"Well—good," she said, though she sounded a little less sure. Her eyes flicked to Simon's bandage. "What happened to you, anyway? River said you were torn to pieces when she found ya, but you wouldn't stop screamin' long enough to tell her why."

"It was nothing. It doesn't matter." Simon wobbled and leaned on a tree trunk for support.

"Oh, get upstairs. Come on." She reached out a hand.

Warily Simon accepted her help inside, up to the second floor, and finally into his apartment. As her foot met unintentionally with a polystyrene takeout container, Fran gazed around with unvarnished disgust. "Jesus, Nealy. Your place!"

"I've been busy," he panted, exhausted from the climb.

"Doing what? Making crack?"

Simon limped across the room and collapsed on the couch.

"Well, thanks for the visit. This has been fun."

But Fran didn't leave. Something on the dining table seemed to catch her attention. "What—?" She approached the table. "Is that—?"

Simon couldn't see what she was looking at. Had he left something incriminating lying out, something he wasn't supposed to have?

"What's this about, Nealy?" The front page of an old *Gazette* dangled from her hand. Morgan's face smiled out at him, beatific.

He sighed.

"It's nothing. Just go."

Underneath Morgan's photo was a smaller image, of an undernourished dark-haired boy of ten. Fran noticed.

"Is that *you*, Nealy? You're the brother?"

Simon flinched, the words an unexpected trigger.

"Half brother, technically."

"You never said."

"I didn't want anyone to know. It's why I took the job. Part of the reason, anyway. I've been trying to find out what happened to her."

He half expected Fran to keep pestering him, but she looked wan.

"I remember when it happened," she said, gazing at the clipping.

"Before I started at the museum—I was workin' for a children's charity then. But I saw it on the news. My daughter was about the same age as your sister. Cried my eyes out. Prayed for her every day. Prayed that whoever took her got what was comin' to him," she said, her voice a growl. "I helped plan a candlelight vigil for her at the museum."

"You did?" A memory flooded back to Simon, of a frizzy-haired woman racing to Joelle's side as she lay thrashing in the grass, fighting off invisible monsters. "I think I remember you. You were there with your daughter."

Fran scoffed, for once in disbelief rather than disdain. "You and I go way back. Who knew."

Her gaze fell to Morgan's photo. She seemed to repress a swell of molten fire.

"Well, lemme know when ya find the sick fuck that did it. I'll help ya cut his dick off and feed it to him for breakfast."

"I have," Simon said.

"What?"

"Albert Mueller. He was expecting us that day. Me and Morgan. He had it all planned out."

Fran had questions. Simon directed her to the pages of Mueller's diaries, and told her what his mother had said about the Bone Man giving her the tickets. He was relieved when Fran reacted like Williams had not, and openly denounced the police's inaction.

"Fuckin' pigs. But what do ya expect? Wrexham P.D. have had their hands down the Hawthorne family boxers for years."

"If I could just get to him," Simon said. "Mueller. If I could just—" He couldn't finish the thought. What *would* he do if given the chance? Confront him? Attempt to extract a confession? Put his hands around his throat?

There was something Simon wanted even more than all that, an idea the Bone Man's recent letter had put in his head. *What's left of your sister.* What he wanted more than anything was to recover her remains—whatever was left of her, anyway. In a way, it was what he had always wanted: to bring her back home.

"Have you checked his house?" Fran said.

Simon looked at her. "His house?"

"In West Chester. Dean Street, right? The brown monstrosity with the shingles?"

"You know where he lives?"

"Could probably find it. We held an event there once."

Refuse crunched under Simon's feet as he pushed himself up and staggered toward her, his heart pitter-pattering in his chest.

"Take me there."

CHAPTER FORTY-EIGHT

A FLASH OF BLINDING LIGHT

The house, with its dark shingle siding, flaking green shutters, and general aura of disrepair, was a scowl among a street of redbrick smiles. "Looks about right," Simon said as they pulled up.

"Looks better than I remember," said Fran.

They parked and got out. Fran stood behind Simon as he clomped up the steps to the door, ready to catch him should he fall. He paused on the welcome mat, a rope of anxiety tying his insides. After working toward this moment for months, it had come too soon—he wasn't prepared. What would he say when he saw him, the man who had all but murdered his sister?

There was movement inside, voices, which surprised and disconcerted him.

"Well, are ya gonna ring the bell?" Fran said.

Simon did.

More voices. A muffled "I'll get it." It didn't sound like a man of Mueller's age.

The door swung open. The man in the doorway was not yet forty, average looking but athletic. Tattoos flourished down his biceps, which stretched the armholes of his fitted tee. "Can I help you?"

Simon and Fran exchanged a glance. "Er—good afternoon," Simon said. "We're looking for Albert Mueller. I believe this is his address?"

"Nope."

"Oh." Simon caught Fran's eye; she shrugged. "Er, any chance you might know where we could find him?"

"No idea who you're talking about, pal."

A woman appeared behind him, inquisitive, balancing a small boy on her hip. He was waving a toy dinosaur in the air.

"Can we help you?" she said.

"We're looking for Albert Mueller," Simon said. "I believe he used to live here."

"He did."

"He did?" the father said.

"We're renting the place from him," said his partner. "Through a property manager. He's a bit frail, I think. They said he was going into assisted living or something. You might want to—actually, hold on."

She handed the child to the man and disappeared inside.

The boy dropped his dinosaur with a little "Oh," and Simon bent down to pick it up. The boy grabbed it back.

"*T. wex.*"

Simon was in the process of correcting that assumption when the mother returned.

"Not sure if this helps," she said. She held out a folded document to Simon.

He took it and opened it. It was the rental agreement for Mueller's house. Simon's eyes paused at the section where it listed the parties involved. Under *Tenant(s)*: the names of the couple and their former address. Under *Landlord*:

Elite Property Managers on behalf of Albert Mueller, with a mailing address of—

The paper shook in Simon's hand. His knees threatened to buckle. *No*, he thought. *No. It can't be—*

"Hey," Fran said, catching him as he began to stagger. "What's up?"

"N-nothing. I'm fine." He smiled for the benefit of the parents, who looked uneasy, and handed back their agreement. "Thank—thanks for your help. We'll be going."

Simon wheeled around. Fran helped him down the stairs, refusing to let it go. "What the hell's up, Nealy? What'd that paper say?"

"It doesn't make sense," he murmured.

"Should I drop you home?"

"Exactly," he said. "That's exactly where you should take me."

CHAPTER FORTY-NINE

HOUSE OF BONES

They turned onto Granton Avenue and parked in front of the two-story townhouse in which Simon had been raised. The vibrations of the rumbling engine sent a sense memory of Pink-Eye's growl through his body, ratcheting his nerves so taut they strummed.

Fran reached for the ignition. "Keep it running," Simon said. "You should stay here in case something happens."

"Somethin' happens? He's eighty fuckin' years old, Nealy. What do you think—?" Her cell phone bleated. "I need to get this, it's my title sponsor." She answered, "Bev! Perfect timing. I was just about to call you back." She frowned as Simon, refusing to wait, swung open the door and slid out. "Avoiding you? Why would I be—?"

The door swung shut. Simon turned and looked up at the house named on the paper. His mind swam with memories, which were poisoned by the knowledge of who now lived there. How long had he been here? How close had Simon been to finding out, all those times he had visited this street?

He thumbed the doorbell and heard the buzz inside. Nothing. He made several attempts to extort a response by knocking. No one came.

His hand grabbed the knob and turned. Locked. There was no key under the welcome mat, either. But in the soil of a plant pot he noticed a strange-looking rock. It was made of plastic, and when he shook it, it rattled. Simon pried open the bottom and found a key.

He glanced back at the car. Fran was still on the phone. He caught her eye and pointed at the door to indicate his intentions. She shook her head in confusion, then waved him off.

Simon closed the front door behind him as he stepped inside. Darkness veiled the finer details of the room, but what he could see of it was almost exactly as he remembered—cramped, untidy, an affront to the senses. No one seemed to be here. He started across the living room and paused. He heard something upstairs. It sounded like a cough.

The carpeted stairs dampened the sound of his hobbling with one hand gripping the banister and the other hoisting his crutch. It was warmer up here, intensifying the greasy odor that clung to the walls. He reached the landing. Doors onto the larger bedroom and the only bathroom hung open. The third and final door remained shut.

Simon listened, hearing nothing. With a few deep breaths he slowed the vicious pounding of his heart.

His hand found the doorknob, paused, and with a sudden twist he thrust open the door.

From where he stood, the room looked hardly large enough to be a bedroom at all, but clearly it was; a slant of light through the crochet curtains cast a glow over the twin-size bed. Simon stepped inside. The smell hit him like a sack of shit in the face, so rank and powerful that for a second he feared the shape under the comforter was a decaying body.

Then it stirred, drawing in a wheezing breath.

"Hello?" Simon said.

"There you are." The voice was high-pitched and reedy, like a creak in the dark. An arm resembling a bone draped in wrinkled skin slid out from under the covers, a skeletal hand fumbling across the nightstand.

"Who are you?" Simon said.

The hand reached toward a bedpan, just out of reach at the edge of the table. "Please . . ."

"Are you . . . Albert Mueller?"

The arm withdrew. The bedsprings whined; the person under the covers was sitting slowly upright.

Simon fought the urge to scream as the cadaverous face crept into the light—Albert Mueller's face, or a ghostly vision of it. Emaciated, cheeks dripping like melted ice cream, skin as crinkled and translucent as tissue paper. A nimbus of white hair danced upon the age-spotted head. His eyes bulged like cloudy marbles from the deep hollows of their sockets, then squinted.

"Who is it? Who's there?"

Simon's fingers trembled with fear and adrenaline, his heart like a jackhammer in his chest. "I—m-my name is Simon—Simon Nealy. I work at the Hawthorne Museum of Natural History—"

Mueller whimpered, apparently in reaction to the institution's name.

"M-my sister was Morgan Jenks," Simon said. "You . . . you're the reason she's dead."

"Y-yes," Mueller breathed. Then, shaking his head, "No . . ."

"Don't lie, Dr. Mueller," Simon said. Surprise flashed in Mueller's eyes like faraway lightning. "That's right, I know who you are. I read your research diaries. I know what you did. You took my sister from the Hall of Insects."

"Yes . . ."

"You took her down to the basement."

Mueller's face twisted as if tasting something sour. His chin drooped against his bare chest, and his knobbly shoulders began to shake; he was sobbing.

"Don't do that," said Simon. "You don't deserve to—"

"P-p-promised . . ."

"What?" Simon lumbered closer to the bed, his head jerking back from the smell. Judging by the stained floorboards, he guessed Mueller's bedpan had recently taken a tumble.

"P-p-promised," Mueller wheezed, "w-wouldn't hurt her . . . H-how could I know?"

"What are you saying? You're saying there was someone else?"

"My truest," squeaked Mueller. "The love of my heart . . ."

Simon remembered the sordid letter he had found among Mueller's things. But for whom had he written it? One woman sprang instantly to mind. The thought sent a shudder through Simon's body, but it fit.

She had taken the tickets. She had allowed him and Morgan to visit the museum unsupervised. Had she been in on it the whole time? Offered them up like animals for slaughter?

"My mother?"

"No. No, no," Mueller said. "*The Bone Man.*"

"But *you're* the Bone Man."

Mueller opened his mouth to speak and broke off with a little whimper, then stared into his lap. His cheeks colored. He had soiled himself.

Simon grimaced, torn between sympathy and revulsion.

Then an icy prickle danced up the back of his neck as a person he hadn't realized was there spoke behind him.

"I'm afraid you're wrong, Dr. Nealy."

Even before Simon turned to face him, Simon knew who was standing behind him, even what they would say next; on some level Simon had known since being handed that rental agreement and reading the potter's address after Albert Mueller's name.

"The Bone Man," Zander Steyn said, "is me."

"You? But that's not possib—" He trailed off, his fierce expression slowly fading. "You called me Dr. Nealy."

"Oh dear." Steyn chuckled good-humoredly. "You'll have to forgive an old man his forgetfulness. Theo, I meant to say. A very fine alias—though between you and Albert's old specimen, things at the museum are in danger of getting confusing."

"You know who I am?" The realization struck Simon like a fist: "You're the one who's been writing to me."

But how? Why? It didn't make sense.

None of this makes sense.

"You're confused. Frustrated, even. Don't worry, son. It's all right. If you'd join me downstairs for a cup of tea, I'd be more than happy to tell you everything."

CHAPTER FIFTY

THE BONE MAN'S TALE

Steyn stepped aside so Simon could pass.

He hesitated. Tempted to hear what Steyn had to say, he nevertheless had the feeling he was being lured into a trap, that he ought to get out now while he still had a chance. Steyn was dangerous, after all. A killer.

Maybe. Simon still wasn't clear on the potter's involvement in Morgan's death, or how it happened. Even *if* it happened. Nothing seemed certain anymore. And Simon *needed* to be certain. It was why he had come here: to learn the truth, for his own sanity. Even if it drove him mad.

He nodded and limped out onto the landing, relieved to escape the eye-watering stench of Mueller's sickroom. Simon made his way downstairs and Steyn lagged behind, giving his guest a moment alone below. Simon crossed to the window and looked out onto the street, disconcerted to find Fran's car was gone.

"Expecting someone?"

Simon jumped. He hadn't heard Steyn descending the stairs. "No." He retreated from the window. "I was just looking at my old house."

"Ah, yes. Chez Nealy-Jenks-Viccio," Steyn said sardonically. "Come through to the kitchen now." He wasn't asking anymore.

Silencing the warning bells of his unease, Simon obliged. He noticed

the repaired china theropod on a table as he passed, the faint seams de-
marcating where the pieces had been rejoined.

He sat at the kitchen table while Steyn filled an enamel kettle and
put it on the stove to boil, then laid a tray with the same hand-painted
floral tea set from which he'd served Simon before.

Simon peered around the dated kitchen. The ceramic crockery inside the glass cabinets looked homemade. A few framed pictures hung
on the wall. One showed a much younger Steyn at an event at the Hawthorne, a brother of the photo Simon had found among Mueller's old
things.

"It was you in the photo," he said. "You used to work there, didn't
you?"

Steyn turned, confused until his eyes found the picture. "Oh, the
museum. Yes, yes. In a past life." He returned to his work, dropping a
teabag into the spouted pot, and adding something to the milk jug that
Simon didn't see.

"That's why you came from Cape Town? To work at the Hawthorne?"

"Goodness, no," Steyn said. "I chased an old flame to New York.
Ended up at the American Museum of Natural History. The relationship
fizzled, but I was settled by that point."

"What did you do at the museum?"

"I was an anthropology specialist. It was fine for a few years, but
eventually I decided I needed a change, a step up. A friend told me about
the Hawthorne job. I wasn't sure I was very interested, to be honest
with you. Wrexham seemed so small, so provincial, compared to what I
was used to. Then my mother . . ."

Steyn faltered.

"She was hit by a car back home, crossing the road." There was a
tremor in Steyn's voice. "She passed very quickly. Not even time to say
goodbye."

"I'm sorry," Simon said.

"Very kind of you." Steyn turned his head around to smile. "Anyway, I knew then I couldn't go home. I would only be reminded of her.
I took the job."

"You were a curator, weren't you? Of archaeology?"

"Assistant curator. I oversaw the Hall of Man and the museum's collection of ancient artifacts and human remains. That's how I acquired the nickname the Bone Man. This was back before people started calling us grave robbers, crying 'appropriation' over every last specimen. 'No, you *mustn't* remove an artifact from its country of origin. If a person wants to emigrate, that's fine, but god forbid a skeleton or a pot—'"

The kettle let out a stuttering whistle. Simon too was boiling. "You're the one who said Mueller was in the lab all morning."

Steyn emptied the steaming kettle into the teapot. "We had to tell the police something."

He carried the tray to the table, pulled out a chair, and sat. "Just give that a moment, shall we?"

"I don't understand."

"It needs to steep—"

"*I mean Morgan.*" Simon thrust the words through gritted teeth. Fury and adrenaline chomped at his self-restraint. "Tell me everything. From the beginning."

"Of course," Steyn said, almost kindly. "Of course I shall.

"I suppose it all started when I moved from New York. It wasn't easy, if I'm honest with you. In time I would come to love this town, but in those early days—well, I was a young man. Not much younger than you, in fact. It was quite the culture shock coming from the hustle and bustle of the city, and though I enjoyed my new position at the museum, getting to curate my own collection and such, outside of work I was dreadfully lonely and bored.

"A friend back in New York suggested I take up a hobby. In the Hall of Man we had these wonderful paleolithic clay pots, perhaps you've seen them. I'd never thought of myself as a very creative person, but I enjoyed working with my hands, and these pots were fairly rudimentary. I was inspired to try my hand, as it were, and enrolled in a beginner pottery course at the community arts center. That's where I learned to throw. Just simple things at first, wobbly bowls and mugs. A bit of fun."

"What does this have to do with Morgan?" Simon said.

"I was getting to that. Milk and two sugars, isn't it?" Steyn poured Simon a cup of tea from the pot, added the sugar and a generous portion of milk, and set the saucer before him. He took his own with a squeeze of lemon. "Where was I? Ah, yes. Well, I had just started potting when a young woman moved in across the street with her young son. Petite, dark hair, quite beautiful in those days. Your mother. I went over to introduce myself and we got talking. I could tell she wanted me—I was rather more handsome back then, and more inclined toward the female sex. We started seeing each other. Before I knew it we were meeting for intercourse three, four times a week. Gave my nickname a whole new meaning, she said. It became our dirty joke."

"You said you weren't living here when Morgan—" Simon said before Zander interrupted.

"You will forgive an old man a white lie, won't you? I've already forgiven yours."

Simon was angry with himself. How had he not seen it before? "That's why you took her from the museum—because if she disappeared from the neighborhood the police would come knocking on your door. *You* gave my mom the tickets—"

"You're jumping ahead. Please, indulge me." Steyn raised his cup to his lips and blew. "Your tea's getting cold."

"What happened next?" Simon said.

Steyn paused and lowered his cup. "Well, it didn't last long. You know better than anyone, she had problems. Her substance abuse got out of hand. It was rather unattractive. I tried to help her, but some people just don't want to get better. So we parted ways amicably—on my side, at least—and eventually she got pregnant from that red-haired creature. He left, didn't he, after she had your sister?"

Simon glowered.

"Anyway, I was getting better at pottery. Rather good, in fact. I started experimenting with more advanced techniques and materials, and developed a particular affinity for bone china. I told you before about the significance of bone in Zulu culture, how sangomas throw them along with shells and stones to call upon their ancestral spirits. I thought that if I did the same with pottery, I might summon my own departed spirit. I might be able to speak with my mother.

"At first it was a sort of fantasy, but the more I thought about it, the more plausible it seemed, and the more determined I was to try it. Still, traditional bone ash would never do. Most of the stuff you get off the internet is made from low-quality livestock, goats and cows. But a sangoma, he must choose his bones carefully, must know where the animals came from and how they lived. I would need to make my own."

Steyn sipped his tea.

"One day I was leaving the hollow when an animal shot out across the road. I would avoid it normally, but something came over me. I kept driving, felt a bump. I pulled over and saw it was a badger, dead but intact. I checked its bones through its fur and they weren't too badly broken.

"I brought it home and then stared at it for days, mostly trying to work up the nerve. I'd never dressed an animal before. Mum would have been ashamed of my cowardice. I took a knife and carved it into pieces, pulled away the meat and skin, retching all the way. But a few hours on the boil took the flesh right off. Once the bones were dry, I took them down to the arts center and bisque fired them in the community kiln. Ground them with mortar and pestle, down to a fine ash. Barely enough to make a thimble, and not great quality, but I was on to something.

"I continued to experiment over the next months. A fox that wandered into the yard. A family of kittens left in a box on the corner. The pit bull that lived at the end of the road."

"Bruiser?" Simon said, incredulous.

"No one missed him, believe me. But the owner of the arts center, my old pottery teacher, caught me taking the bones out of the kiln. I still remember the look on her face. I told her it was my friend's border collie, which I was fashioning into a memorial vase. Well, that changed her tune. She thought it was wonderful, even seemed to think there was money in it. On her advice I set up a little side business turning people's dead pets into custom ceramics. Suddenly I had access to all sorts of different bone types to play with. If my customers got a pot made with cow bones, they never knew the difference.

"But I still wasn't happy with the result, even began to despair of animal bones altogether. On an online web forum I met a new age sangoma out of Ohio, named Travis Anderson, who advocated passionately for the throwing of nontraditional bones, to strengthen one's connection to the dead."

"Nontraditional?" said Simon, already dreading the answer.

"Human. Well, naturally I was curious. And it would be only too easy; who should know if I pilfered a few of the museum's human remains? Nothing of great scientific significance, of course—I'm not a monster. Just a few little bones. And then a few more. To my surprise, the quality of the glaze it produced was remarkable. I had finally achieved the brilliant translucent white that bone china is known for. But as vessels by which to speak to the dead, they were useless.

"Travis said it was because my ash was only partly human—I was having to mix it with animal bone to get the quantity I needed. He suggested I buy a full human skeleton—there are places you can get them if you know where to look. But as a Zulu, I knew better. I knew that a sangoma never acquires his bones in such a manner—no, he obtains them through careful selection followed by ritual sacrifice. To get through to my mother, I needed to do more than make beautiful pots." Steyn raised his cup for another sip. "I needed to kill."

"But why?" Simon demanded. "A little girl who did nothing to you. Why Morgan? *Why not me?*"

"If it makes you feel better, it almost was."

"W-what?" Simon felt strange, his skin prickling as his righteous fury mutated to fear.

"Of course an adult would have given me more to work with," Steyn said. "But I thought a child would be easier to overpower, to make disappear. I had my eyes on you for quite a while. A boy so meek, so solitary, no friends but his younger sister. No one but his drug-addict mother to make a fuss if one day he went astray on his walk home from school.

But you were only a tiny thing, scrawny. I'd hardly get a saltshaker out of you. I needed her bones too. Your sister's."

"Tell me what happened that day," Simon said. "At the museum."

"You're sure you want to know?"

Simon hesitated. "Of course."

"If you say so," Steyn obliged. "You've probably already worked out that I knew you'd be coming. The tickets I gave your mother were only good for the fourteenth. I thought it wise to keep my head down; if someone saw me with you and Morgan, they might suspect. So I went to see Albert in his office first thing that morning. Told him my neighbor's children would be arriving soon, that I wanted to surprise them with a private tour of Collection Storage and needed his help."

"And he agreed?"

"The old queer had held a flame for me since I arrived at the museum. For months he'd been begging after my body. Cornering me after meetings, leaving me dirty little letters. He said he loved me, that he would die if I didn't give him what he needed. He said he would do anything for me. Private tours were strictly forbidden for anyone but the most generous donors—he could be fired if anyone found out—but he was true to his word. On my orders he spoke with the girl at the front desk—"

"Violet Sippel," Simon said.

"Nosy bitch. Fortunately she bought the story too. When she called to tell Albert you and your sister had arrived I instructed him to get you. Bring you down to the basement and make sure no one saw."

"But he only took Morgan."

"He couldn't find you. You weren't where your sister said you'd be."

Simon must have left the Hall of Dinosaurs by then. "We probably just missed each other."

"He assumed you'd already made your way down to the basement. He brought Morgan to me in the lab and was surprised when you weren't with me."

"How was she?"

"Starting to become a problem, in fact. Getting fussy, nervous. She began to cry."

"Cry?"

"For you."

The words impaled Simon's heart like the tail spike of a *Kentrosaurus*. For the first time he questioned whether he really wanted to hear this.

"You haven't touched your tea."

"Just get on with it," Simon spat, not meeting Steyn's eye. "Please."

Steyn sighed, displeased. "Well. With the state she was in I didn't have much time. Someone might hear. One child would have to do. I put a rag of chloroform over her mouth. As you can imagine, Albert was horrified. Seemed to think I'd done it by accident, the *domkop*. He was down on the floor, trying to help her while I opened the chamber."

"The chamber?" Simon said.

"The lab contains a hidden room behind the bookshelf—"

"I know. That's where I found Theo's bones."

Steyn looked a little put out. "Well, at the time only I knew it was there. I'd seen it in old blueprints while conducting research for a centenary exhibit. I'd been working on the room in secret for weeks, preparing it."

Simon suppressed a shiver. "Preparing it?"

"For you and your sister. I had it fully equipped. Tarps, tools, the sacrificial dagger. And my spiritual accouterments, of course. A Zulu *ibheshu* and skins. A beaded headdress ordered direct from KwaZulu-Natal."

"And Mueller just went along with it?" Simon said, still struggling to believe it.

"Went along with it, no, not once he realized what was happening. He went to pieces, threatened to involve the police, the whole lot. But I told him I would testify that he was in on it from the start—or alternatively, if he helped, I'd give him everything he wanted."

"He believed you?"

Steyn looked contemplative, as if mulling over a crossword. "You know, I think on some level he might have liked it. Not the murder part, but that it would be ours to share. A secret tying us together forever. Still, it was lucky the room was soundproof. It was Albert's screams I had to worry about. In the end your sister was no different than the badger."

Simon tasted bile. He reached for his cup and swallowed two gulps of cold tea.

"Well, not entirely like the badger," Steyn mused. "She was too big to boil. Actually, it was Morgan's love of insects that gave me the idea. Your mother complained about it once. Said it was unnatural for a girl to like such things."

"No." Simon's breakfast flickered at the base of his esophagus. "Please tell me you didn't—"

"I never realized how efficient the little *goggas* are. What are they called, the flesh eaters? Dermestid beetles? Thought they'd be at it for months. But they cleared the carcass in less than a week."

Simon slammed the table and jumped to his feet. Nausea and dizziness hit him like a one-two punch. Despite his crutch, he wobbled and grasped for the table.

"Of course the police were long gone by then. They'd searched the lab with the rest of the museum, but they didn't know about the hidden room. The smell wasn't bad, not compared to the chemical stench of the lab. Albert was so nervous I thought he'd be the death of us, but in the end he pulled it together. Managed to convince the police we'd been in the lab all morning. The old detective was sure the kidnapper had taken your sister in a van. He didn't waste more than two minutes on us."

Simon melted back into his seat, the room beginning to spin. He reached again for his tea.

"After a few weeks your sister's bones were ready for firing, but I didn't want her in the house. I was afraid the police could change their minds any minute and kick the door in, so I hid them at the museum, taking only as much as I needed for my make. It was important that it was something special, something Mum would like. She was rarely without a cup of rooibos in her hand, and I thought, *Of course—how about a tea set?* Something beautiful and hand-painted. Sugarbush always were her favorite."

Simon's teacup hit the floor with a sound of breaking china.

"It was the perfect thing," Steyn said. "And Morgan . . . *she* was perfect. She brought Mum back to me. I could feel her in the clay running over my hands as I threw it. Could hear her voice in my head, singing 'Thula Baba' like when I was a boy."

Simon's eyelids began to droop. Steyn had spiked his tea. In his infirm state he failed to register that Steyn was choking up.

"Then j-just like that, she was gone. I couldn't get her back. I've tried for decades, but no one's bones have worked like Morgan's. Not even Violet Sippel's, much as I enjoyed punishing her meddling."

He dried his eyes on his shirtsleeve, cleared his throat.

"These last few years," he continued, "I've begun to wonder if there wasn't something different about Morgan. Something special. If perhaps it wasn't a family trait."

A blunt spear of understanding penetrated the fog of Simon's mind. He was in danger. He staggered from his seat, but his legs folded underneath him; he fell to the floor with a clatter of his crutch and a stab of pain through the sutures in his leg.

"I did some digging on your strange little family. Unfortunately, your mother was under lock and key of the government by then—I couldn't get to her if I tried. But I thought, *What about the brother?*"

Simon dragged himself across the kitchen floor, his vision blurring in and out.

"Then what should I find a few days later but an article in the *Gazette* announcing your appointment to the Hawthorne Museum. It was destiny," Steyn said, a bit of his old fervor returning. "The ancestors had delivered you to me. 'But you mustn't,' I said to myself. After Violet Sippel I had promised my bone-harvesting days were over. I'd managed to avoid suspicion for more than two decades. If I took one more, I'd be risking everything."

Simon collapsed on the linoleum, staring, unable to move.

"So instead I sent letters to the museum, watched you from out on the grounds. Childish, I admit. A cheap attempt to rattle you. Like a child tapping at the terrarium, trying to make the spider move. I was desperate to take you, but I couldn't. I mustn't. So instead I took pleasure in watching you squirm from behind the glass.

"Then one day a miracle occurred: you showed up on my street. I was astonished—perhaps you could tell. Here was my opportunity. I would get you inside, incapacitate you, boil you down to bones. But you were cautious, even gave a false name. You refused to stay. I took it as a sign from my ancestors, from Mum. It wasn't meant to be.

"Then you rang up and invited yourself to tea. What was I to do then? I should refuse you and avoid temptation, but I couldn't help myself. I wanted more of you. If not your bones, then your company would have to do. I agreed, and stayed on my best behavior. It would have been easy though, just as easy as it was today—a few drops of Rohypnol in your tea and you'd be out like a light in twenty minutes. But I was good. I let you go.

"And every day since then I've regretted it. It's been forty years since Mum died and I think about her every day. Her voice. Her laugh. The little humming sound she made with each sip of tea. I realized nothing else mattered. Not even being arrested. Even when the police called, asking questions about the day we took your sister, and I knew that I'd be risking it all if I took you now, it didn't matter. My mind was already made up. I would rather spend the rest of my life in prison having spoken with her one last time, than as a free man who never tried."

"Morgan," Simon murmured.

"When you came back to collect your commission—I fixed it by the way, did you see?—I thought it would be easy. Turn on the waterworks, force you into a false sense of sympathy for the sad, lonely old potter. I only needed you to stay for a cup of tea. But I misjudged it. Took things too far. You were gone in a flash, likely never to return. And so it was decided: I would have to take you from the museum. Lure you out to the grounds, catch you unawares, and incapacitate you with chloroform. I sent a letter. I was ready for you. But you didn't show."

Simon's perception was slipping. He began to lose grasp of where he was, what was happening. All he knew for sure was that someone was in the room with him, a man. He stood. Feet crossed to the counter. A drawer opened and closed.

"But now you're here," the man was saying. "The ancestors have delivered you to me once again. And this time I won't refuse their gift."

He was approaching Simon now, an advancing blur. Something long and metallic flashed in his hand.

Darkness pressed in on Simon's peripheral vision. "Morgan," he murmured again. A tear of despair tickled his cheek. He sensed it was his own.

"Don't fret, my son," said the man's voice as the world contracted down to the tiniest pinprick of light. "Rest your eyes. Sleep. You'll be with her soon."

CHAPTER FIFTY-ONE

NO CLOWNING AROUND

Simon awoke, barely. Pried apart his crusted-together lids, and could scarcely see through the clouds in his eyes. His mouth tasted of stale vomit, and a gaping ache throbbed in his skull, as if a great mouth had taken a bite out of his head.

He blinked. His vision cleared slowly, like morning fog, and the ceiling of a room came into focus. Simon was undressed down to his boxer shorts. As he attempted to sit up, his head sloshed and wailed, and fell back with a *flump* of plush pillows.

Still, he managed to take in the bedroom. The egg-yellow bed linens, the whitewashed furniture, the desk against the opposite wall, buried under a jumble of papers and news clippings. He managed to retrieve his phone from the nightstand. The time read 7:29 a.m.—Monday. He'd been out for more than twelve hours. But how—

The clock ticked over, and the phone blared out its preprogrammed alarm. Simon recoiled from the assault of sound, dropping the phone. The door swung open and Fran came in.

"You're up."

She walked over, bent down for the phone, and silenced it. Simon collapsed back in relief, panting. "Good mornin', sunshine. How do you feel?"

"Not bad for carrion. Where am I?"

"My house. Couldn't take you back to your shithole of an apartment. No offense."

Simon didn't have the strength to riposte.

"You want something to eat? Coffee?"

"Coffee, please."

Fran left and returned a minute later with a farmhouse mug and a long-sleeve shirt. "My husband's. Your stuff's in the wash."

"What happened?" Simon pulled on the shirt. He drew back the overlong sleeves and accepted the mug with thanks. "I thought Steyn was going to kill me."

"He was."

"But I thought you left. Your car wasn't there when I looked out."

"We can get into all that later. You need to rest."

"No," Simon said. "Please."

Fran sighed. Looked around, pulled up a cushioned wicker chair, and sat.

"All right. Where do I start?"

"What happened after I went inside? You were on the phone with your sponsor."

"Right. Well, they were bein' assholes. *Fuckin'* assholes. Tryin' to renege on their twenty-five-thousand-dollar pledge after the livestream heard round the world. I managed to talk them out of it. Convinced them to roll the funds over to next year's event in exchange for a few extra splashes of public recognition. That's *if* the Hawthorne makes it another year—a *big* goddamn if, if ya ask me."

"But what about—"

"Yeah, yeah. So my contact says she's got a check for me if I can come pick it up right away. You're still inside, but she's only ten minutes away—I figure I'll be back before you notice I'm gone. By the time I've got the check I'm starvin'—haven't eaten all day—so I stop at a drive-through for a shitty chicken salad before I head back and park up in front of that house you went into. Well, shit, now the lights are on inside. Did you turn them on, I think, or has the owner come home?

"I get out and walk up to the house to check things out. Take a peek through the curtains. I can see through the living room into the kitchen. There's a light on, a man at the counter—I don't know him."

"Steyn," Simon said. "He used to work at the museum. He killed my sister."

"Him? You said Mueller—"

"I'll explain. Just keep going."

Fran harrumphs. "So I see this Steyn guy, right, and either he's talking to himself like a lunatic or to someone I can't see. I've got a feeling you're in there with him. Maybe it's all right, maybe he's a friend of yours. Then I see a flash of metal. The son of a bitch is holdin' a knife. Somethin' doesn't feel right. But before I can do anything, someone's potterin' down the stairs. I squint through the window and wouldn't you believe—"

"Mueller."

"Ancient as the Earth itself, and his bathrobe's hangin' open. I can see everything: full bush, sack swingin' like a pair of marbles in a stocking covered in cat hair."

"I get the picture," Simon said, unable to erase the image bleached into his brain.

"Well, Steyn sees Mueller come down. I get away from the window so he doesn't see me too. Then Steyn starts shoutin'. 'Don't come in here, Albert. Go back upstairs.' I peek through the curtains and Mueller's not backin' down. He staggers toward the kitchen, and he seems to be shoutin', tellin' Steyn off, and now Steyn's mad. Screamin' at Albert to fuck off, get back upstairs. You're screamin' too—or someone is. I can hear it."

"I was awake?"

"You tell me. Anyway, Steyn goes after you and Albert goes nuts. He charges at Steyn, knockin' the knife out of his hand, but Steyn's stronger. He grabs Mueller's robe and shoves him against the wall. That's when I come to my senses. I haul ass up the stairs and bust into the house. Steyn's got Mueller on the floor now, stranglin' the little fucker.

"I reach for the first thing I see—some ugly dinosaur statue on a table—and break it over Steyn's head. He falls sideways, out like a light. I kneel down over Mueller, but he's white as a sheet. Broken as a bag of snapped twigs. And I hate him for what you told me he did to your sister, but he looks so small and scared, and I'm losin' him, I can tell. So I talk to him. 'You're okay, Mueller,' I tell him. 'Everything's gonna be okay—'"

Fran broke off, a wedge of emotion stuck in her throat.

Simon sensed there was more she wanted to say, but she simply shook her head and sucked in through her nose. "Anyway, he croaked. In my arms."

"I'm sorry," Simon said. "That must've been awful."

She shrugged.

"Fran, I can't thank you enough. You saved my life. You both did, I guess."

She nodded. A smile.

"So what happened next?"

She cleared the phlegm from her throat and continued. "Next I went lookin' for you. Find you lyin' in the kitchen. You're passed out again, but you look okay. I think about callin' the police then and there, but Mueller's dead, you're knocked out, and I just coldcocked a stranger with a fuckin' dinosaur. I panicked.

"You wake up as I'm draggin' you out to the car. I just about manage to get you in the backseat before you blow chunks all over the place."

"I thought I might have," Simon said, still tasting it. "Sorry. I don't remember any of that. Must've been the Rohypnol."

"He roofied you? That'll do it."

"So then—"

"So then I run back into the house, use Steyn's landline to call the police, and get us the hell out of there before they show up. Now it's all over the news."

Instantly Simon reached for his phone. He ran a search and pulled up a local news article reporting that Albert Mueller, eighty-two, long-serving former paleontology curator at the Hawthorne Museum of Natural History, was found dead in his home, and his caretaker, Zander Steyn, had been taken into custody. Police concluded that there had been a scuffle, and Mueller had somehow landed the blow that knocked Steyn out before his injuries caught up with him. The mystery caller had not been mentioned.

"Good," Simon said.

"All right, I told you my side. Now you tell me yours."

True to his word, Simon recounted everything that had happened between the time he entered Steyn's house and the time he blacked out on the kitchen floor, including the potter's grisly confession to having lured to the museum, abducted, and murdered Morgan in an appropriated ritual of animal sacrifice.

Fran's face was a splotchy mixture of nausea and rage. She was shaking, building up pressure inside, like something that was about to explode. Simon felt momentarily frightened, then weirdly inferior, guilty that he hadn't reacted the same way.

Fran was out of her seat now, pacing. "I'm gonna kill him. I *shoulda* killed him. Well, aren't you gonna call the police?" she snapped. "Aren't you gonna tell them what he did to your sister?"

"They think I'm crazy, remember? They won't believe a word I say."

"But you've got proof. That tea set. If it's got your sister's bones in it, it'll have her DNA—"

"It won't," said Simon despondently. "Not after being fired at nearly two thousand degrees Fahrenheit. According to a study by Karni et al., DNA degrades completely at around three hundred seventy-five degrees."

Fran rolled her eyes.

"Well, fuck," she said, dropping down into the chair. "So you're not gonna do anything? You're just gonna let Steyn get away?"

"Don't say it like that, please. You know I don't want to."

"Well then—"

"There's only one piece of evidence that'll change their minds about me now," Simon said. "Her body."

Fran went white. Her eyes darted away, running across the floor like mice.

"What is it?" Simon asked.

"There was somethin' I didn't mention before," she murmured. "But it's probably nothin'. Seemed like Mueller was off his rocker."

"He said something?"

Fran didn't answer.

"Fran. What did he say?"

She was on her feet again, restless.

"Right before he died, Mueller grabbed my wrist to pull himself up. He was wheezin', tryin' to get his last words out. Desperate, kinda. I couldn't understand. 'What is it?' I said. 'Come on, Mueller.' His teeth were all black. Breath like he'd been eatin' dog shit.

"'*The girl*,' he said."

"What girl? Morgan?"

"'*The girl*,' he said. '*She's in the museum.*'"

CHAPTER FIFTY-TWO

SKYFUL OF ASH

No one had expected such a turnout. More than fifty came in their mourning clothes and stood around the hole in the earth, the churn of dark cloud above like the ejecta from an apocalyptic impact. Academics, museum colleagues, donors, former students. Many of them silver haired now, professors and researchers themselves. Their heads hung in respectful silence, their fingers loosely braided before them. A few words were spoken by a few people—"brilliant," "eccentric," "mulish," "a man of great passion and deep *compassion*"—and the casket was delivered finally into the ground.

Fran's phone buzzed as she stood beside him in a knee-length frock. She muttered a curse and grudgingly silenced it.

Simon's thoughts returned to the man in the casket, who once had reminded him so much of himself. A man Simon had pardoned as eccentric and misunderstood, had later condemned as a murderer. A man who had done a terrible thing for love, and gave his life trying to stop it from happening again.

Simon remembered Mueller's dying words, and the theory that had occurred to Simon the first time he heard them.

But how could it be? How did nobody spot it?

The service concluded with an invitation to throw soil on the casket. Simon joined the line while Fran stalked off in the opposite direction, lifting her black veil to answer an incoming call. "Frank, thanks for callin' back. How are things at the *Inquirer*? No, I'm not asking for more money. I got somethin' for you I think you're gonna like."

A hulking figure entered Simon's periphery. He experienced a moment of dissonance as he turned to find Craig Rutherford beside him; the ED was far taller than Simon had guessed by his virtual presence.

"Smaller than you look on Zoom," Rutherford remarked, apparently of a similar mind about Simon. "Gotta say, I'm surprised you're here. Didn't get the impression you liked Mueller much."

"I'm not sure I do."

Simon waited for two men to pass, clapping the dirt off their hands. One of them was Maurice, who started to walk over, then stopped when he noticed it was Rutherford that Simon was talking to. The friends regarded each other with nods, and Maurice walked on.

"He didn't kill Morgan, though," Simon said. "Mueller."

"That so."

"If you don't believe me, ask your uncle. He was board chair when Steyn was caught taking human bones from the museum, didn't you know? They fired him—quietly, of course—and rewarded his boss for the oversight with a significant promotion. A bit odd, don't you think? Unless Amir Saad, being an expert in evolutionary anthropology, had spotted that the bones in question weren't ancient remains at all, and the board promoted him to keep him quiet about it."

"Where's the proof, Nealy? You're gonna need a lot of it to sway our friends at Wrexham P.D."

"Don't worry. Evidence is on the way as we speak."

Rutherford shot him a scowling look.

They stepped forward in line.

"It's like we say at the museum," Simon said.

"What's that, now?"

The sky swirled darkly overhead, as if preparing to unleash a rain of fire.

"In the bones of the Earth shall the truth be found."

A few hours later Simon approached the arrivals area at Philadelphia International Airport in the car Fran had helped him retrieve from the museum grounds. Through the throng of vehicles attempting to pull up to or escape the curb, he spotted a small, thin Chinese American man of thirty-three, a rolling suitcase at his side.

Simon smiled and so, seeing him, did Kai.

His happiness was evidently genuine, belying no hint of fear or withholding. Simon's heart swelled with gratitude.

At last he parked and got out. The men embraced. A comforting warmth flooded Simon's body, bearing not a trace of romantic feeling. "How are you?" Kai said, and pulled back.

"Glad you're here. Thanks for coming."

Kai nodded.

"We better go," Simon said, and took the carry-on to the trunk. "Priya's waiting at the museum."

It was a fifty-minute drive to Hawthorne Hollow. Simon parked his car in the dirt shoulder and texted Priya as they approached the building on foot. She greeted them from the door.

"You must be Dr. Liu," she said, excited but hushed.

Simon introduced them. "Kai's a researcher in biological anthropology at the Field Museum."

"So good to meet you. We'll need to be quick. Cleaners have been in and out all day."

She stood back so they could enter. Simon's mouth fell open as he stepped inside the entrance hall; it was spotless.

"We're unveiling Theo to the public on Monday. Big press event. Rutherford thinks a big splash will make people forget what happened at the gala."

Guilt formed like a gastrolith in the pit of Simon's stomach.

"Don't worry," Priya said. "Fran told me everything. About your sister. I'm so sorry, Simon. I can't even imagine." She touched his arm and smiled, her kindness going some way toward dissolving his guilt. "This way."

She led them into the Hall of Man and locked the doors behind them. "We should be safe to talk in here." Simon turned to Kai, but he had wandered off. His dark triangular eyes devoured the room, a smirk flickering on his face at the outdated exhibits.

"Kai."

He turned at the sound of Simon's voice. His gaze shifted from Simon to the glass case at his side.

Kai's expression turned serious. "Is that it?"

Simon nodded.

Kai approached. Simon and Priya stood behind him as he appraised the case, surveying the bones laid out in the shape of a skeleton: a small broken skull, a few vertebrae and ribs. The red velvet lining cast a gentle blush on his cheeks, which otherwise had drained of color.

"Oh my god."

Simon and Priya exchanged a tense glance.

Kai gaped at the descriptive label.

Homo neanderthalensis child, c. 38,000 BC

"These bones." He crouched at the side of the case to view the skull in profile. "They're *homo sapiens*."

"Child? Adult?"

He did not speak.

"Kai."

He kept his eyes on the specimen and wet his lips, like he always did when he was nervous.

"Child," he said. "Five to seven years old."

Simon's mouth went dry.

"It is, isn't it?" he said.

Kai regarded him, wan, his eyes brimming.

"It's her."

CHAPTER FIFTY-THREE

THE LONG DARK AFTER

Kai and Priya filed the report together, making no mention of Simon, who sat waiting in the car outside the station. He wanted to give Williams no reason to dismiss their claims.

Loath though the detective was to pursue any case involving the Hawthorne, having noticed how closely the police chief guarded its interests, Williams didn't feel he had a choice. According to Dr. Liu, an expert in human remains, a display case in Hawthorne's Hall of Man contained the skeleton of a child approximately five to seven years of age, a skeleton for which, when the exhibit coordinator went digging, no record of acquisition, accession, or provenance was found.

A skeleton that seemed to have materialized silently, and without notice, some twenty years prior, following the disappearance of a six-year-old girl.

The police chief, a cock-nosed golf swell named McGinty, didn't take kindly to Williams's investigation, but there was little he could do to stop it. Although the *Gazette* remained suspiciously quiet on the subject, the *Philadelphia Inquirer*—thanks to Fran's philanthropic relationship with the managing editor—ran a splashy story on Kai's discovery the day after he and Priya filed their report. Wrexham Police was forced to act, and the Hawthorne to once again delay Theo's unveiling. In the official press release Rutherford was quoted as saying, "We are confident the police will find no evidence of wrongdoing on the part of the museum or its staff, past or present. However, we take the community's concern very seriously and are cooperating fully in the police investigation."

From what Fran and Priya said, the reality within the institution was very different. Rutherford was irate. Marshaling all of his resources, both financial and social, he fought tooth and nail to delay the seizure, perhaps to give the museum time to comb through the archives and eliminate the evidence, but not even a descendant of Augustus Hawthorne had the might to overrule a warrant signed by a judge. Forcing entry to the museum, the police confiscated the remains along with more than four thousand historical records from the Cave.

After a few days and a sad goodbye, promising the visit would not be his last, Kai returned to Chicago, and Simon, left to the darkness of his thoughts, fell into a deep depression. He understood this was counter-intuitive. There had never been more cause for optimism. But having learned to live without hope for so many years, he couldn't bring himself to trust it now; somehow or other, justice would elude him again.

Five days after the remains were seized from the museum, Simon, unable to get out of bed for the third day in a row, woke to the ringing of his phone. He answered it, blearily.

"Good afternoon, Dr. Nealy," said the voice on the line.

"Williams?" Simon sat up.

"I understand if you've got nothing to say to me, but I wanted you to be the first to hear. We just got the results back on the bones we took from the museum. Carbon dating, DNA, dental records. The works."

"And?"

"They're a match," Williams said. "It's your sister."

Simon collapsed back against the headboard, numb.

"We've been going through the records and found some things, but it's not adding up right. I don't think it was Mueller. Not just him, anyway." Williams paused. "You already know that, don't you?"

"Y—" Simon croaked, cleared his throat. "I do."

"How about you come down to the station, tell us what you know," Williams said. "If you're willing to talk, we're ready to listen."

~~❧~~

Following his arrest for Mueller's death, Zander Steyn had managed to escape prosecution after claiming his mentally debilitated ward had come at him with a knife, forcing him to fight back in self-defense. An investigation had been dashed off, and Steyn released without charge.

The second time the police came to arrest him, kicking down the door of his townhouse, the former assistant curator wasn't there. Steyn had seen the writing on the wall the moment the *Inquirer* reported on the mystery skeleton in the Hall of Man. His car was found abandoned in the long-term parking lot at Newark Liberty Airport, where he had boarded a plane to Addis Ababa before catching a connection to Johannesburg. Simon was assured an extradition was forthcoming, but it was a weak salve on the sting of Steyn's escape.

Simon blamed himself. He should have told Williams about Steyn sooner. Gone straight to the police, like Fran had said. But would they have believed it? Was there anything he could have done to persuade them? Or, Simon wondered, was it just the way of things that only the innocent should ever be punished.

On a more satisfying note, the discovery of Morgan's remains had brought ruin to the name of Hawthorne. Armed with the letters and emails Simon handed over to them, the *Inquirer* published a punishing exposé on "The Family" and its decades-long conspiracy to suppress evidence in the disappearance of Morgan Jenks.

It had been a scheme of willful ignorance more than outright subterfuge. Documents recovered from the archives suggested extremely few members of the leadership had direct knowledge of Steyn's actions, perhaps none other than his direct supervisor, Amir Saad, and Eberhard Rutherford. While some believed Mueller was the culprit, others maintained the girl had been spirited away by a stranger with a van.

Crucially, the leadership welcomed this lack of clarity. They were in agreement that given the museum's blood-splattered history, any finding that associated the institution with death or violence was a potential threat; better not to pursue it at all. Let it, they thought hopefully, die a quiet death.

Ultimately, this obfuscation was the institution's undoing; without investigating Morgan's abduction, they could not know which institutional records were most worthy of destruction—even less, where to find them in the frenzied disorder of the Cave. Instead, they protected their secrets with locks, authorization forms, and top-down approvals, none of which came to much use when the police came beating down their doors.

Due to the state's five-year statute of limitations, the time for criminal proceedings had passed, but, as the ruling member of The Family, Craig Rutherford was forced to resign in shame along with half the board of directors. If his LinkedIn profile was to be believed, he would remain out of work for more than a year before embarking on his new career as a two-bit leadership consultant, registering an LLC under the name Craig Rutherford Advising Partners, and launching a fittingly named new website for his business, crapconsulting.com.

Rutherford's departure left the Hawthorne in need of new leadership. Simon had expected one of the Davids would take the helm, but there were rumblings that the remaining board members—a younger and more progressive group on the whole—had a different vision for the future of the institution, or, as it was now to be referred as, the *organization*, the first of many steps to dismantle the Hawthorne's unearned elitism and renew its focus on community service. Less than a day after Rutherford resigned, the board appointed Fran Boney as the museum's first ever female executive director, albeit interim, in recognition of her demonstrated leadership and commitment.

As her first order of business, Fran offered Simon his job back—and her second, third, fourth, and fifth, trying to convince him to accept it. Grateful though he was, Simon couldn't stomach the thought of returning to work in the same basement where his sister had been murdered in cold blood, visions of which had replaced the Bone Man as the focus of his night terrors. But Fran offered up her old office on the third floor, promised he would never have to set foot in the basement again, and, when neither of those worked, reminded him that were it not for her, he would have been living out the remainder of his life as a sixteen-piece dinnerware set.

In the end, Simon agreed on three conditions: (1) that Maurice be rehired with back pay for the weeks he was out of work, and issued a formal apology on behalf of the museum; (2) that Priya Chandra be promoted at once, even if Simon had to take a pay cut to make it happen; and (3) that neither of them knew he had anything to do with it.

Simon had been thinking a lot about privilege, a conversation with himself that was still ongoing. He couldn't say for sure whether he had earned his title and salary through his own hard work and excellence, if his future success had been foretold the moment he had been rescued from poverty and delivered into Colleen's middle-class care, or if his hiring was simply the lucky result of the museum's culturally embedded preference for white men of a certain pedigree. He guessed it had probably been a combination of all three. But, however he had gotten where he had, he was at last ready to fulfill the biggest responsibility of his position, which was to use what little power he had for the betterment of those who deserved it.

Fran concurred, and the following week, Simon resumed his old post, not with lofty ambitions of research excellence, but with a humble promise to finish what he had started. He felt he owed Theo that much, at least.

In the first week of November 2021, the Hawthorne ended its twenty-month closure with the grand unveiling of THEO THE CERATOSAURUS PRESENTED BY THE MITCHELL FAMILY. The event was attended by more than one hundred special guests, including the naming donor herself.

Simon was relieved Evie had shown up. She had kept her distance from the museum ever since the *Inquirer* had reported on the suspicious circumstances of Garfield Mitchell's untimely death, with "some speculating the Hawthorne had Mitchell assassinated to stop him going public with his investigation." In the absence of any real evidence, the general consensus was that his death had been coincidental, but Evie, who claimed her husband was still "hiding something" from her, was less convinced.

The unveiling was her first visit to the museum in months. As Fran led the crowd in a countdown from ten, Evie squeezed Simon's hand.

He could feel the electric current of her anticipation through her skin. She had been waiting years for this, decades. The whole family had, according to her.

But as the curtain came down, her smile slouched. A crease formed in her brow. Not disappointment exactly, but a kind of surprise. All Simon could get out of her was a cryptic "He seems sad."

Simon had not yet decided whether he believed in Evie's powers of clairvoyance, but for weeks he too had sensed a deep dejection in the dinosaur. Though the museum was all but silent during the day, at night Theo's desperate moans still rumbled through the building like a tremor in the foundations of the earth.

It was a misery in stark contrast to the dinosaur's reception. In the days that followed the unveiling, Theo would be met with a fanfare like the Hawthorne hadn't seen in half a century. The *Gazette* proclaimed him "the fearsome pride of Wrexham," the exhibit was featured in a spread in *Museum* magazine, and the local community was wild for him, with paid admissions skyrocketing more than 800 percent. Yet despite the exaltation he brought to many, the sounds he sang from the darkness were heavy with mourning, with a despair that no amount of accomplishment and esteem could make right.

Simon understood the feeling all too well. The unveiling was one of the crowning achievements of his career. He should have been basking in the glow of saving the museum from financial and reputational collapse. But like Theo, he was bereft.

"He wants his sibling," he explained to Evie one morning over brunch, making up for the one he had missed weeks earlier. "That's all he's ever wanted, to be reunited with her."

For the first time Simon told Evie about the bone Mueller had excavated with Theo's skeleton and later destroyed, and his own theory that if they dug at the site where Theo was found, they might uncover enough of the juvenile to raise her spirit inside the museum and finally lay Theo's soul to rest.

"You must go," Evie said.

"I wish I could. The problem is, the museum's still recovering financially. There's just no budget for fieldwork, and the dig would be expensive."

"How much?"

Simon could hear Fran's voice in his head, a repeat of their recent coaching session in the art of major gift fundraising. *Just tell her the amount, clear and simple. You don't need to beg or grovel, and for Christ sake don't apologize for askin'. Just put it out there and see if she bites.*

And if she doesn't? Simon had asked, sweat beading on his forehead as he scribbled notes in his pad.

Keep calm and ask her for half.

"Thirty-five thousand dollars," Simon said.

Evie riffled through her tote bag—whether searching for her checkbook or something to throw at him, he was not sure. At last she produced a pack of gum. "Juicy Fruit?" she said.

"No, thanks."

She dropped the bag to her feet, put a stick of gum into her mouth, and smacked.

"So what do you think?" Simon said.

"Mm? Oh, that should be fine. I'll write the check today. When do we leave?"

"Oh," Simon said, a smile breaking out across his face. "Well—"

"One other thing," she said. "Can I bring Arthur?"

CHAPTER FIFTY-FOUR

WHEN THE DUST (UN)SETTLES

On day three of the dig they found the *Stegosaurus*. A subadult, fragmentary but nicely preserved. Not the young *Ceratosaurus* they were looking for, but Simon was thrilled, experiencing a euphoric blood rush of excitement like only discovering a new dinosaur specimen could give him. Over the course of a few days he and his team—three students and two faculty members from the University of Pennsylvania paleobiology department—cleared the site to expose the skeleton, mapped it using smartphone photos composited with basic photogrammetry software, treated the cracked and unstable bones with consolidant, and dug the herbivore out in small- to medium-sized blocks of matrix, light enough to be transported to the field truck by hand or on wheels.

Before they were sealed in paper and plaster and left to dry, Simon was pleased to observe, on one of the dermal plates, an elliptical gap nearly identical in shape and size to Theo's bite. Three sets of tooth marks were later found on the rib and leg bones. One had been left by a medium-sized theropod, another much smaller, and one larger than the first two combined. The image of Pink-Eye's plunging maw flashed through Simon's mind.

He could be sure of nothing until he had a closer look in the lab, but it seemed they were on the right track.

Unfortunately it was the only promising sign they would have for weeks. After that first burst of good fortune, their prospecting turned up little but the kind of teeth and tiny fragments suitable only as gift shop fodder. The brutality of the elements didn't help morale. The canyon was like a clay oven, roasting the team at temperatures above one hundred degrees Fahrenheit. The only person who seemed to be enjoying herself was Evie, who spent her days laid out in front of her luxury sleeper trailer in a two-piece bathing suit and sunglasses, Arthur perched on the back of her sun lounger.

The students battled on, but the experienced paleontologists complained incessantly, not seeming to mind if their expedition leader heard. Nealy had brought them on a wild goose chase. Nealy had no idea what he was doing. It riled him in part because it was true. The juvenile's bones, if they were out there, would likely be in the vicinity of where Theo was found, but Mueller's diaries gave them only a few scant details to go on. Their guess was about as good as Simon's.

Time tumbled away. More than halfway through the month, there was still no sign of the juvenile. In the third week, Simon was buoyed by the arrival of Romina Godoy, who had just finished a long-delayed research trip to the Houston Museum of Natural Science and driven up to join them in the field. At least Simon would have a friend to comfort him when the trip ended in ruin.

With Romina at his side he led the team farther into the canyon. Just over a mile southeast of the trail they came upon a short, rugged orange brown cliff formed by lateral accretion—sediment deposited on an incline rather than in horizontal strata, often formed at the bank of a river or stream. It looked promising even before he noticed the trunk gnarling out of the rock. Bells of recognition rang in his head.

Didn't Mueller say something about a tree?

He reached around for his pack, dug out his copy of the August '97 entry, and skimmed quickly through the text, speaking under his breath.

"'A leafless tree growing diagonally out of the rock like a great twisted hand beckoning us forth.'"

His eyes rose from the paper. The trunk was badly weathered, but he could see how it might once have resembled a hand.

"What is it?" Romina panted, stopping beside him, her T-shirt darkened with sweat at the bra line.

"I think this is it. This is where he found Theo."

"How do you know?"

He pointed out the similarity to Mueller's description.

"If she's anywhere, she's here."

It turned out the cliff was chockablock with fossils, an intriguing mix of terrestrial and marine. Simon surmised the area had been covered in floodplains, the perfect environment for a carcass to wash into a river or stream and quickly become buried under sediment. A week ticked by, each day bringing new discoveries, fresh gasps of excitement and opportunities for instruction. Simon stopped to assist a pair of students, who were debating whether they were looking at fossilized bone or regular rock.

"There's an easy way to tell," he said, teaching them a trick he'd picked up as an undergraduate on his first dig at Hell Creek. "Just lick it." The students exchanged smirking glances. "No, really," he said. "As the animal's organic material breaks down after it dies, it leaves behind a porous internal bone structure of inorganic minerals, minerals with their own distinct taste that stick to the tongue. Try it, you'll see."

The braver of the students bent down and touched her tongue to the rock. "It stuck," she said. "It's bone!"

The students were delighted.

Pleased though he was to see his team enjoying themselves again, Simon was growing increasingly concerned. They only had a few days left in the field and hadn't found a trace of the juvenile. He feared the whole trip would be a failure, an abuse of an old woman's generosity, though Evie didn't seem to mind. Her only concern was for Theo, as Simon learned two nights before decampment, when he knocked on the door of the trailer where Evie and Arthur slept.

She answered wearing a bathrobe and a sheet mask. "Mind if I borrow the bathroom?" Simon said, waving his toothbrush. While the faculty shared the small camper van, Simon had been roughing it with the students in sleeping bags and tents.

Evie let him in without speaking. When he was done with his nighttime ablutions, he came out to find her seated on the banquette, her face bare, shiny, and pensive. Arthur snoozed in his cage.

"Well, good night." Simon made to leave, pausing as Evie spoke.

"He needs his sister."

She wasn't looking at him, her gaze adrift. He didn't need to ask whom she meant.

"I don't know if she's out there," Simon said. "It was always a long shot. I'm sorry, I should've told you before. This whole trip was a waste of time."

"No." A cloudy certainty settled in Evie's features. "She's here."

"You sense her?"

"Since the moment we arrived. She's waiting for you."

"What if I can't find her?" Simon said.

"You will. The same way you found Morgan."

"Morgan came to me."

Her head tilted toward the window, as if hearing something on the wind outside.

"Because you were listening for her."

Simon returned to his tent a few minutes later and lay awake for hours, tossing and turning in his sleeping bag. Despite their friendship and his growing open-mindedness to the metaphysical, he remained ambivalent about Evie's clairvoyance. At times he had no question of it, and at others, like tonight, he couldn't help but suspect her of the same grief-induced lunacy he'd witnessed in his mother, and at one time feared had been passed on to him.

Perhaps they were both unhinged, and simply so attuned to each other's madness they had grown to manifest not just their own delusions but each other's as well.

Something rustled outside the tent. Simon lifted his head to look. The canyon was full of wildlife—rabbits, hoofstock, coyotes. He laid his head back on the pillow, wishing he hadn't forgotten to replenish his stores of nighttime cough medicine during their recent supply run.

The rustling came again, an insistent *scritch scritch*. Simon jerked his head around and stared.

A shadow engulfed the side of his tent. The peculiar shape of it was hard to rationalize as anything one might find in the area—perhaps a golden eagle, with its two birdy legs, if not for the four-fingered hand, the bony bumps along its neck, back, and tail, and the slender face with gentle nubs over the eyes and near the end of the snout. Without opening its mouth the animal was making a noise halfway between a chirrup and a purr.

When Simon unzipped his tent there was nothing there. At least nothing he could see. Beyond the borders of their campsite was a dark curtain of wilderness, untamed masses of Gambel oak and twisted trunks of mountain mahogany. A gibbous moon glowed silver-bright against an ocean of stars.

The sound of a snapping branch drew Simon's gaze. His heartbeat quickened. He retreated inside to pull on his shoes and grab a flashlight, and he emerged waving it over the darkness.

Something darted across the beam of light, three feet tall and spry as a deer, then disappeared into a thicket of brush.

Slowly Simon crunched toward it. He sensed a twitch of nervousness within the brush.

The glare of his flashlight revealed a gold, black-pupiled eye. A lithe smooth body glistening with blood, which dribbled out of the stump of its missing arm.

The animal took off again.

It went on like this for nearly half an hour, the animal scampering off and Simon clipping along in its wake. They left the campsite, following a similar path to the one the team took to and from the dig site each morning. It was leading him toward the cliff where Theo was found. Toward it, but not there exactly. The gnarled tree trunk had just come into view when Simon's guide, having briefly vanished, rematerialized up a hill crowded with large flat rocks.

Simon groaned. Forced beyond the shallow limits of his athleticism, he started up after it, hopping between rocks, thrusting through a coppice of buckthorn that bit at his bare skin and left his legs dripping blood. He fell behind, losing sight of it as it clambered ahead.

"Wait," he panted, his leg muscles burning. He scaled a small boulder. "Hold on—!"

The boulder shifted underneath him, forcing him to leap onto the ground below. He pitched forward and fell onto hard earth with a grunt of pain.

Grimacing, he pushed himself up with the hand not holding the flashlight, whose light shone askance over the rock beneath him. The same sandstone, at almost the exact elevation, as the rock in which they'd been digging for a week.

He spotted a protrusion, slightly darker than the surrounding rock, but he couldn't immediately tell if it was bone. It was too firmly embedded to pull out. After brushing it clear of dirt, he angled his body down and pressed the tip of his tongue to the rock.

It stuck.

Adrenaline surged through his body. Reaching for the sharpened end of a broken branch, for he hadn't brought his field kit, he carefully dug away at the rock surrounding the fossil. The sandstone was soft and came away easily, revealing more and more of the bone fragment. At last it popped free.

The jagged lump in Simon's hand appeared unremarkable, but he knew better. After all, he had handled more than a dozen such bones belonging to Theo, though none as small as this.

There was only one species in Late Jurassic Colorado known to have osteoderms like this, and this one clearly belonged to a juvenile.

Could it be her?

A coo drew Simon's eyes upward. The ghostly dinosaur stood perched on a boulder above him, silhouetted against the whiteness of the moon.

For a moment she watched him, and he her, drinking in the tiny wonders of her aliveness. The gentle swing of her tail. The way her chest rose and fell as she breathed. The celebratory arch of her neck toward the sky, as if knowing what awaited her on the other side of night.

EPILOGUE

DAWN OF A NEW ERA

"In paleontology, they say the chance of a dinosaur skeleton becoming fossilized is one in a million. But what about the chance of two skeletons—say, a brother and sister?"

Simon's voice shook as he addressed the crowd, a far larger one than at the last unveiling. More than three hundred board members, donors, staff, and press crowded the Hall of Dinosaurs for the big event. He tried not to look at the news camera glaring at him from the side of the room, and gripped the podium to steady his trembling hands.

"When we set out to the Morrison Formation last summer, we could only hope to be so lucky. But thanks to my dear friend Evie Mitchell, whose generous gift made the dig possible . . ." Simon smiled at Evie in the front row, who waved off the obliging applause from behind her sunglasses. ". . . our amazing team of students and faculty from the University of Pennsylvania . . ." A whoop geysered at the back of the hall. ". . . and the enthusiastic support of our then-interim executive director, Fran Boney, that's exactly what we found.

"For the last year, my team and I have been working tirelessly to prepare, study, and conjure up the story of these bones into a new, scientifically accurate update to our beloved 'Theo the Ceratosaurus' exhibit, in honor of the close family bond we now believe these two animals shared. On behalf of the Hawthorne Museum of Natural History, I'm excited to unveil the exhibit to be known henceforth as 'Cerato Siblings Presented by the Mitchell Family.'"

The sheet suspended behind the podium fell, eliciting a wave of gasps. Applause erupted through the hall.

Simon's lips twitched into a smile as he glanced proudly at the exhibit over his shoulder.

The multispecies tableaux was twice the size of the original, encompassing the entire southeast wing of the museum's second floor. Theo's posture had also changed, giving the team a chance to fix the inaccuracies that had niggled Simon before. Where previously Theo tromped through the artificial landscape, sniffing the air for food, now he stood back in a protective pose, guarding a newly added specimen: the reconstructed skeleton of a juvenile *Ceratosaurus*. The same one the team had excavated in the final hours of the dig after Simon led them straight to it, claiming to have stumbled upon the spot during a sleepless hike the night before.

"By studying these fossils," he continued, "all excavated within a square mile of each other at the Dulzura Mesa Canyon, we're finally able to form a picture of what happened the day Theo died, the events of which have confounded the museum for the better part of three decades.

"It's a story unlike any other in paleontological history: a story with exciting scientific implications and, more important still, of fierce love and brotherly sacrifice. I'm honored to be able to share this story with you today."

Simon faltered; a lump had formed in his throat. He panicked, but Evie, removing her glasses, held him in the slender-armed hug of her ice-blue eyes. Simon breathed out, and smiled.

"Theo's story starts 150 million years ago, in the Late Jurassic. A time of rising temperatures, emerging life-forms, and some of the largest dinosaurs that ever lived. In what is now the American West, gargantuan long-necked sauropods such as *Diplodocus* and *Supersaurus* dominated the landscape and decimated lush coniferous forests with their unwieldy appetites, while apex predators such as *Allosaurus* and *Torvosaurus* were among the most lethal hunters of the Mesozoic.

"The horn-faced theropods exhibited before you were members of a smaller and scrappier genus named *Ceratosaurus*. It was long thought that *Ceratosaurus* was a solitary animal, but thanks to our discovery at Dulzura Mesa Canyon, we have good reason to believe that in times of stress, they remained in family groups for extended periods.

"How do we know this? For one, although we can't know for certain, we can speculate that Theo and the juvenile were together the day they died. In addition, both skeletons exhibit a peculiar indentation in the lacrimal horns not observed in other specimens of this species. Putting two and two together, I conclude in agreement with Dr. Leonora Brito of the University of Cincinnati that these animals were closely related, likely siblings, as Theo was not sexually mature enough for the juvenile to have been his offspring.

"It's not clear what circumstances had led up to this moment. Perhaps the pair had become separated from the rest of their family by death or natural disaster. Perhaps they had been abandoned. Whatever the case, all they had now was each other. The youngster depended on her older brother for food, warmth, protection from predators—and perhaps in a way we don't yet understand, his survival depended on her just as much."

Simon cleared his throat.

"We believe that on the day they died, the siblings were searching for food along one of the many rivers and tributaries that crisscrossed the fluvial landscape. Their scaly feet squelched in the mud. Large opal-winged dragonflies buzzed around them. The ceratosaurs were well adapted for catching aquatic prey, but the fossil record shows fish populations dwindled around this time. Their primary food source was scarce. The pair would have been hungry, perhaps starving.

"But just when all hope seemed lost, Theo spotted along the bank of the tributary a herd of *Stegosaurus* sating their thirst. Lethal prey, perhaps bigger than he would typically take on, but it was do or die. If they didn't eat soon, his sibling—for the purpose of this story, let's call her female—would perish.

"And so Theo set his sights on the easiest target, an adolescent at the fringes of the group, and charged. Before the herbivore knew what was happening, Theo had leapt on its back. His tiny arms were ill-adapted for gripping—he only managed to hold on by biting down on one of its bony plates, stripping flesh from its sides as his feet struggled for purchase.

"But even as the rest of its herd scattered, the *Stegosaurus* was by no means defenseless. Wielding its superior heft, it threw Theo to the ground like a ragdoll and brandished a tail like a seven-foot medieval weapon, barbed with a quartet of lethal spikes. Before he eventually overtook it, it impaled his right leg—a crippling blow.

"Nevertheless the job was done. The elder sibling probably filled his belly first. Then the juvenile stepped forward, as illustrated behind me."

Audience members craned their necks for a better look at the third specimen on exhibit, the partial *Stegosaurus* the team had brought back from Colorado, its missing pieces filled in with sculpted replicas, lying prone at end of the platform as the skeleton of the juvenile stepped forward to feed.

"But in the Jurassic period, big kills often drew big scavengers, and the siblings were about to face one of the biggest yet—a forty-foot predator known as *Saurophaganax maximus*, the largest terrestrial carnivore for hundreds of miles. Imagine an *Allosaurus* the size of a full-grown *T. rex*, with a mouthful of serrated teeth, long arms ending in protracted claws, and sharp bony notches above its eyes like devil horns."

Simon didn't mention the burning pink eyes or snow-white skin, being unable to verify Pink-Eye's albinism in the fossil record.

It had been thanks to Romina that Simon finally identified the larger theropod's species. The tooth Mueller had found lodged in Theo's vertebra, presumed to be that of an *Allosaurus*, hadn't matched with the size of the bloody footprints in the entrance hall. Simon had mentioned the quandary to his theropod-expert colleague over a dinner of baked beans and sausages at the campsite (holding back a few unnecessary details), and it was she who suggested the culprit may have been *Saurophaganax*.

Simon had smacked his forehead. "Of course!" It was obvious now that she said it; *Saurophaganax* was so morphologically similar to *Allosaurus* that some contested it was just a supersized subspecies of that genus. If anything, he was a little embarrassed the thought hadn't occurred to him before.

"Unwilling to abandon his hard-won kill or his sister, who would soon die if she did not eat, Theo jumped forward to challenge the intruder," Simon continued. "Backing up to the apparent safety of the water's edge, the juvenile chirped and growled as they fought to the death—what would almost certainly be her brother's.

"Even in top condition, Theo would have been no match for such a fearsome and outsized opponent. Before the end of the clash, his tail was crushed, his ribs were shattered, and he limped around on his injured leg, barely able to walk. But still he did not back down. Not while his sister was counting on him.

"Mustering every last ounce of fight left in him, he made one last run against his foe . . . And then, in an instant, his sister was gone."

There was silence in the hall, the audience thinking.

"Snatched," Simon explained. "Snatched from the bank of the tributary by a *Eutretauranosuchus*, a ten-foot-long semiaquatic reptile that wouldn't have looked very different from a modern crocodile. One second the juvenile was there, the next, a dark shape disappearing under the water with hardly a splash.

"Realizing what had happened, Theo charged in after her, and instantly he sank into the mire. He managed to scare off the crocodyliform, but the end had come swiftly for his sister—he was too late to rescue her, and too weak to save himself.

"In the stream where his sister died, he also laid himself to rest. If you look closely you'll see some of his bones, like the juvenile's, are covered in small conical indentations—the bite marks of the silent killer.

"Very soon after, maybe only hours, heavy storms rolled in and the plain flooded. The *Stegosaurus* washed into the river, and all three of their bodies were buried in sediment, the first step of the fossilization process. The first of many steps that led them here, reunited for the first time in millions of years.

"To teach us," Simon said. "To inspire us. To remind us what it means to be alive."

Fran closed out the program with a champagne toast and the crowd dispersed with their glasses to mingle, nibble hors d'oeuvres, and admire the exhibit's rich detail up close. Simon spotted Evie at the exhibit guardrail and started toward her before Fran's voice rent the air.

"Nealy," she barked, stepping down from the podium, glass in hand. She looked remarkably sophisticated in a velvet cocktail dress, her unruly hair pinned back with a beaded tyrannosaur. Her appointment to the role of president and CEO—an elevated rebranding of the executive director title, which, it was uniformly agreed, was cursed—had done wonders for her wardrobe and the museum's coffers. Nothing could be done to smooth out Fran's rough edges, but Simon had come to appreciate them as part of her uniqueness, like an imperfection in a prized fossil.

"Christ, Nealy. That speech was somethin'." She clinked his glass with her own.

He thanked her.

"I need you to tell that story at our campaign event next week. The donors'll eat that shit up. If we can get the right people in the room, it might even push us over the ten-million mark."

At the start of that year, in honor of the museum's 125th anniversary, the Hawthorne had embarked on a four-year capital campaign entitled *Hawthorne Evolved* to transform the museum inside and out. The $30 million renovation would see the exhibits rearranged and updated; the research facilities moved, modernized, and expanded; the entry reimagined, with the addition of a new gift shop and café; the facade returned to pristine condition; and a parking lot installed. Though it hadn't yet been publicly announced, even the name and mission statement of the organization would be transformed—a move to distance it from the taint of its founding family.

Though the scientist in Simon was excited for the planned improvements, the child in him resisted. He had emotional ties to the Hawthorne name and the building as he remembered it from his youth.

Despite the despair it had wrought on his life, some part of him felt compelled to safeguard it, in repayment for the small amount of good it had done him. He supposed that was how toxic institutions always managed to survive. But nothing could escape the evolutionary imperative. Everything must adapt or perish—even Simon himself.

"Happy to help," he said.

As he began to head off, Fran put a hand on his shoulder. "Nealy— you doin' okay?"

It wasn't the first time she had asked. The ordeal they had shared at Steyn's house, and the nurturing care Fran had provided afterward, had bonded them in a way Simon couldn't quite put into words. Fran seemed able to sense when something was troubling him, when a wound had opened somewhere deep inside him, often before he realized it himself.

"Surviving," he said.

She squeezed, smiling. "Glad to hear it." Then she left him, stopping to throw her hands in the air at the sight of a woman in a spangled gown. "Trish! My god, you're practically a skeleton! Lose any more weight and we'll have to put you on display."

Simon headed off and was stopped again, this time by Priya, whose name badge displayed her associate director title.

"Amazing speech!" He thanked her, and they chatted for a moment about the doctoral program Priya had recently started. Simon had offered his feedback on her research proposal, but though she graciously accepted, she hadn't needed any help. No one in the organization had any doubt that she would make a fine director, VP, and ultimately CEO one day.

"By the way," she added, "congrats on your paper in *Modern Paleontology*. I didn't understand all of it, but it seemed really good!"

"Thanks," Simon said. "Glad someone liked it."

The publication of his research on *Ceratosaurus* family dynamics had sparked a passionate debate on paleo Twitter. Some had called Simon's credibility into question, even cruelly so. But he knew the truth about Theo and his sibling, had seen it with his own eyes. Even without sufficient proof to meet the rigorous standards of peer review, he believed firmly in his responsibility to publish.

"I noticed you dedicated the discovery," Priya said.

"I did, yes."

"I was surprised."

"That's fair," said Simon, who had not fully worked through his feelings on the matter himself. "But whatever else he might have been, he did save my life. And if it weren't for his research diaries, we wouldn't know half as much as we do about Theo. It was as much Mueller's discovery as mine."

The reverence in her expression made Simon blush.

There was a tap on his shoulder, and he turned to find Maurice, sharply dressed in a three-piece suit and tie. Priya excused herself, and Maurice gave him a fist bump.

"That was one mighty fine speech, dino boy."

"Thanks. Snazzy suit, Maurice. Is it new?"

"Thanks to you."

That week was Maurice's first as facilities and maintenance manager, a revamped position replacing the director role from which Clayton had recently been fired.

"I told you, I had nothing to do with it," said Simon unconvincingly.

They parted in nods and smiles and Simon cast his gaze around, relieved to find Evie still standing before the exhibit.

He stepped up beside her.

"What do you think?"

She turned, her expression opaque, as if he had caught her between dimensions. She stroked his arm by way of hello.

"Does your Theo approve?" he asked.

"Oh yes." To Simon's surprise, she grabbed his hand and squeezed, swinging it slightly. A bracelet jangled on her wrist like a tambourine of gems. "Yes, I think so."

There was a sadness in Evie's expression that made Simon wonder if her son's spirit was no longer with them.

He changed the subject. "Have you picked a name yet?"

"I have. I think."

"Oh yeah?"

"I was thinking," she said, "Morgan."

Simon was taken aback.

"Just an idea," she said.

Simon thought for a moment, gazing up at the siblings.

"It's perfect." But now he found he was a little sad himself.

It had been more than a year since the police had returned Morgan's remains to him, both the partial skeleton from the Hall of Man and, at his request, the tea set recovered from Steyn's kitchen. The latter Simon kept behind glass in the entryway of his apartment. Fran and Kai said it was morbid, but the paleontologist, whose everyday work concerned the handling and keeping of bones, didn't see it that way. To him it was no different from an urn on a mantelpiece, or a specimen in a museum: a vessel by which to remember and learn from her.

The rest of her remains had been laid to rest at the cemetery, in the empty grave marked with her name, though Simon had replaced the original headstone with a more elaborate one adorned with a kaleidoscope of hand-carved butterflies. With special permission from the Annex, his mother had been allowed to attend. It had been the two of them, the undertaker, and a hospital aide. Joelle sat heavily sedated in her wheelchair, her expression loose and vacant. Simon worried she wouldn't realize what was happening, but as the casket was lowered into the ground, a tear sparkled down her wizened cheek, and Simon knew that, at least for that moment, she was with him.

Life was better now, on the whole. He was back to sleeping without pharmaceutical aid (his addiction was now for dietary melatonin supplements and app-based sleep stories). No longer did he wake screaming in the night (now he endured his lingering nightmares in silence like the people he thought of as normal). Still, things were not perfect. His trauma and guilt—the core of his suffering—remained entombed under compacted strata of abuse and self-loathing, but Amira was helping him chip away at them one layer at a time. Though the excavation was slow going, it helped knowing the truth of what happened the day Morgan disappeared—that there had been real monsters to blame, and so little a boy of ten could have done to defeat them even if he tried.

It helped too knowing he had helped bring closure not just to his own family but to another as well; since the day the juvenile's bones were delivered to the hollow, Simon had not seen or heard from her or Theo again.

He wondered if Morgan knew. If wherever she was, she was proud of him.

"It's strange, isn't it?" he said.

"Hm?" Evie said. "What's that?"

"How one act of violence can impact so many. One moment of evil, or desperation. How even the simplest, most innocent act of survival—to eat, or defend oneself, or soothe one's pain—makes waves. Ripples across the planet, and millions of years."

"Like a pebble dropped in a pond," Evie agreed.

"Or an asteroid smashing into the Yucatán Peninsula."

"That's the cruelty of life. But also its mercy," she said. "It's the waves that wash back on us that steady our rocking."

She squeezed his hand. He squeezed back. He did not ever want to let go.

But he did, instinctively, as a sound filled the room. A sound, judging by the nonreaction of the other guests, that only he, Evie, and Maurice could hear.

The deep, sonorous bellow of ghosts.

Simon's heart ached. Though Theo was at peace, the others still appeared to him from time to time, in the emptiness of the museum, or out on the grounds, howling at the silvery glow of the moon. He no longer feared them, perceiving these calls for the cries of help they were. Wails of lament. Sounds of everlasting anguish, like the ones that still reverberated through the tender chambers of his own haggard heart.

He would never be able to help them all.

But he would try.

He had decided months ago. Ultimately, it was why he had agreed to come back to the museum. One by one he would unravel their stories, unearth the sources of their sorrow, right the wrongs that tormented them even in death. And when his work was done here, he would move on to the next museum, the next prehistoric mystery in need of a detective, the next broken family begging to be mended.

Already he could hear them calling to him, pleading, their sadness and loss echoing across the chasm of time. Just as his would, forever and ever, until the day not very far from that one—a blink of an eye in geologic terms—his pain too would be laid to rest, and his body, like all things, reduced to memory and bone.

ACKNOWLEDGMENTS

Though at times it may read like a nightmare, this book has been a dream come true on so many levels. I'm thrilled to acknowledge the individuals whose brilliant contributions have been instrumental in bringing it to fruition.

To my agent, Maria Whelan, and my editor, Loan Le, thank you for indulging this boyhood fantasy of a novel with more enthusiasm than I could have hoped for, and for giving it the home I didn't realize it needed. Shortly after Atria bought *The Paleontologist*, I was going through my old dinosaur books for research and inspiration when I found my beat-up copy of one of my all-time favorites as a kid: the 1992 edition of *Simon & Schuster Children's Guide to Dinosaurs and Other Prehistoric Animals*, by Philip Whitfield. Only then did it hit me that my supernatural thriller about prehistoric ghosts was being released by the same publisher that had produced one of the defining books of my dinosaur-obsessed childhood. I could not be more grateful to you both for making such a special moment possible.

Thanks also to the team at Atria/Simon & Schuster for helping to hatch this little monster of a book onto an unsuspecting public: Libby McGuire, Lindsay Sagnette, Dana Trocker, Nicole Bond, David Brown,

Karlyn Hixon, Morgan Hoit, Dayna Johnson, Gena Lanzi, Paige Lytle, Shelby Pumphrey, Kathleen Rizzo, Faren Bachelis, and Elizabeth Hitti. Special thanks to designer Claire Sullivan and art director James Iacobelli for the marvelously bone-chilling cover.

From the very beginning, I knew this story would not be complete without the help of a uniquely talented illustrator able to blend scientifically accurate paleoart into nightmarish horror. I could not be luckier to have come across Armando Sánchez Rodríguez's work on Instagram and convinced him to take a chance on me, an unknown author whose debut hadn't even been published yet. Armando, thank you for your incredible work and creative partnership. *The Paleontologist* would not be the book it is without you.

Thank you to Chris DeLorey, owner of Educational Biofacts and Dino Depot and former education director at Brevard Zoo, for welcoming me into your fossil preparation laboratory and your Florida community of dinosaur-loving paleontology geeks. Your expert guidance on the excavation, preparation, and conservation of fossils, and your excitement for this book, have meant more than you realize.

Claire Duleba, Maya Lim, and Melissa Wells, thank you for your support and energizing feedback on early chapters and drafts of this book. Thank you to Anna Akers-Pecht, William Chyr, and Maya Lim for your translation assistance. Shout-out to Kimberly Jenks for unknowingly lending Morgan your last name, and Keith Winsten, for permitting Craig Rutherford temporary use of your eyebrows. I assure you the resemblance stops there.

I would be remiss not to acknowledge the authors whose works of nonfiction made the research process for *The Paleontologist* a genuine pleasure: Dr. Michael J. Benton, author of *Dinosaurs Rediscovered*; Riley Black, of *The Last Days of the Dinosaurs*; Dr. Steve Brusatte, whose *The Rise and Fall of the Dinosaurs* is an all-time favorite; and Dr. Lance Grande, whose book *Curators: Behind the Scenes of Natural History Museums* proved to be an essential resource and informed the voice of Albert Mueller's research diaries.

I'm equally grateful to the storytellers whose works of fiction, on both page and screen, blazed the trail for this story and inspired a love of dinosaurs in so many, myself included: Arthur Conan Doyle, Michael Crichton, and the creators of the *Jurassic* film franchise. And although somehow I didn't discover *Relic* until after this book was written, there's no denying that Lincoln Child and Douglas Preston beat me to the monster-in-a-natural-history-museum genre by decades, and in such fabulously entertaining style.

I thank my parents, Mary and Bryan, for their support, and the museums that helped shape my imagination and this book.

Finally, thank you to Adam, my first reader, best friend, and loving husband. Writing books on top of a full-time career is no small commitment of time. Thank you for understanding, for never feeling neglected, and for all the little things you do to allow me to take on a second job that I love. To borrow a few words from Albert Mueller: oceans could not fill the impact you have left on my world.

ABOUT THE AUTHOR

LUKE DUMAS is the Pushcart-nominated author of two novels, including the critically acclaimed *A History of Fear*. He received his master's degree in creative writing from the University of Edinburgh and is a graduate of the University of Chicago. Born and raised in San Diego, California, he has worked in nonprofit philanthropy for more than a decade with organizations such as San Diego Zoo Wildlife Alliance and the American Red Cross.